W9-AAW-342

COLD TIMES

ELIZABETH JORDAN MOORE

SUMMIT BOOKS
NEW YORK LONDON TORONTO
SYDNEY TOKYO SINGAPORE

SUMMIT BOOKS
Simon & Schuster Building
Rockefeller Center
1230 Avenue of the Americas
New York, New York 10020

Designed by Nina D'Amario
Manufactured in the United States of America

10 9 8 7 6 5 4 3 2 1

Library of Congress Cataloging in Publication Data

Moore, Elizabeth Jordan.
Cold times / Elizabeth Jordan Moore.
p. cm.
I. Title.
PS3563.06158C65 1992
813'.54—dc20 91-32750
CIP

ISBN 0-671-63860-2

ACKNOWLEDGMENTS

My abiding gratitude belongs to my teacher, Madison Smartt Bell, and my appreciation to the University of Southern Maine and Ken Rosen, who, in establishing the Stonecoast Writers' Conference, provided stimulating shelter to isolated beginning writers. I am grateful to my editors at Summit Books and to canny Jane Gelfman. I want to thank the courteous staff in the research room of the Portland Public Library, who enthusiastically respond to telephone queries regarding the most diverse matters. The existence of this willing band of erudite and generous individuals seems a small miracle to me.

Geoffrey B. Moore
1938–1974

PROLOGUE

THE CHICKENS

Cornish, Maine, June 1958

The dawn had not yet begun. High and distant where the world is thin and grey there were a few stars, paling memories of light spinning farther and farther apart; near to the earth a waning moon, strangely oval and draped in a misty ring, traveled upward in the charcoal sky as if led to morning by the very bright star that rushed before; where it lifted from the landline, drawn by a stretch of pines solid as a wall, the sky was pale purple. There was stillness, except for the sound of frogs' voices: resonant, weary, and infrequent.

A narrow road ran in front of the pines, silvery against their blackness, and from the road rose a cleared field, pale green as moss on granite. A shadowy path made by tire tracks led from the road to a shack which sat like a boulder in the middle of the field. The truck, parked nearby, stood out hard and metallic, the moonlight swimming in its bumpers and the long mirrors attached to its doors. Behind the shack was a bare earth yard and then the land rose to where the wellhouse hunched and the long barn stood, its ridgepole lost in the drooping, wet-leafed woods.

Kendrick Rudge slept in the woods. He was curled under spruce boughs like a fox, berry netting covering his face and his small, square hands; dreams like young horses gamboling turned him on his fragrant bed.

Within the barn the fire began. Slowly at first; then it shot through old hay quick as spring grass, caught ivy-like around timbers darkened by time and palms, knocked at the shingles like roots pushing through earth. The chickens burned like feathery torches.

Black smoke rose to stain the lightening sky, now empty of stars, of moon. Many died before the flames or even the smoke could reach them, because, in the way of chickens, they scrabbled and scratched with their ancient feet upon each other's faces, and in tall piles in the tall narrow barn, they died.

Tunneling out of his sweet bed, Kendrick ran, white berry netting drifting behind him like a cocoon. The tall barn whistled and stomped as he flew by, calling for his father. When he burst through the door and landed by their bed, the netting fell from his shoulders and slipped about the floor dreamy as fog.

Jarvis Rudge ran from the shack in his underwear, his legs and feet white as milk. Howling, he stood before the noisy barn, his thick fists raised into the air, the fire sounding like a roaring train about to sweep over him. Viola ran to the pipe that stuck up from the dirt and turned the spigot to fill her bucket. She wore one of his undershirts and her fine black hair flopped in one braid between her shoulder blades; the red glow of the fire danced on her skin. She couldn't believe the sound of it; it was like a living thing prancing on arched, quick feet. Beneath it her husband's bellow was the squeak of a tiny creature.

Kendrick tugged on her arm: "Mum!"

But she turned toward the flames. "Kendrick, go!" she yelled, shaking him off. "To Poulin's. Tell them to call the fire barn!" For a moment she watched him start across the field, his shirt flapping from his square body, then she ran.

The fire worked steadily while pale streaks like a dropping net surrounded thin clouds in the east. Viola threw water as high up the grey boards as she could, fearful of the leaping sparks and the air-devouring heat. Jarvis stumbled toward her.

"Jarvis!" she cried. "Get the other bucket!"

He laughed in a high-pitched, toneless way. "You might as well piss on it, Viola!" he screamed.

But she ran back to the spigot; there was nothing else she could do.

The barn burned flat to the ground and smoldered most of the afternoon. The stench of meat and dung and old melted shingles filled the air like light. The men stayed on to spray water over the long, charred rectangle. When sunset came Jarvis told Viola, "I've waited long enough. He shows up, you tell him I had to go do something."

"What? Where are you going?" she asked, but he got in the blue truck and slammed the door.

She stood and watched him ride over the grass to the empty road. The sun was falling behind the thick wall of second-growth pines and it splintered through them and sent long points of light across the greening field. The blue truck went along by the encroaching juniper and past the line of maple trees and was gone. When she turned she saw Kendrick. He was standing on the small rise beyond the barn site. As she watched he disappeared into the trees, the white berry netting trailing from his shoulder.

Viola went inside. She made corn bread. She stirred the gritty mixture with her back to the low window above the sink, and the two younger children sat at the table and watched her. Krista was six, thin and small with the sharp little face of bird. She was like her mother—the hazel coloring, the deep eyes, the stark bones. Flynn, a year younger, was like his mother also. Viola put down her bowl and got a match out of the box. She ran it along the side of the stove, then opened the oven door and held it to the pilot light. "Set the table, Krista," she said, as she straightened.

Krista slid off a little stool and pushed aside the blue curtain that hung over some shelves. She reached into the shoebox for silverware. "Everyone?" she asked.

"Just us three," Viola told her, and picked up her knife. She started to cut the potatoes, working in hard, jerky motions because she was angry and worried. She cut her finger and blood sprang from it like a sudden blooming. "Damn!" she said, and looked for a cloth to tie around it. Krista stopped, one hand lifted to the table, and watched her. Blood dropped down Viola's wrist. Flynn started to cry. He backed from his mother and sat hunkered under the table, his head held in his hands. There he wailed and rocked, getting louder and louder. Viola pressed her finger against her skirt and knelt, reaching for him with her other hand. But he screamed louder and jerked away, his small fist flailing at her until she left him and went outside. She stood in the dooryard. The air smelled like singed hair, the falling light shimmered through it, the field in front of her was in shadow and the pines beyond the road were dark. Viola lifted the hem of her skirt and wrapped it around her finger. Then she leaned back against the side of the shack and watched the changing sky.

Krista squatted beside the table. She held a clothespin doll in her hand, and humming "The Farmer in the Dell" over and over, she danced the little doll back and forth on its wooden legs. Flynn paused and watched her dancing, then lifting his face, wailed with his eyes tightly closed. But he peeked again and again at the little figure and his voice grew softer and then he was silent. He looked at his sister. "Hab-it," he said.

"Flynn come get her," Krista coaxed. Backing with the doll in her outstretched hand, she drew him from under the table.

He sat in the corner with the doll and she dipped a cloth in the bucket and washed off his streaked face. "Hab-it," he said, pulling back from the cloth, patting the doll's yellow yarn hair.

Viola woke when the blue truck roared up over the field and crashed into the front of the shack. The building heaved and shuddered, her frying pan banged onto the floor, the oven door fell open; Viola got up from the mattress, pulling herself from her dreaming; the front window spat glass from its unpainted mullions. Bits of it were tinkling onto the floor when she staggered across it and pulled open the door. She stepped out into the moonlight while behind her Flynn started wailing. She turned back: "Krista," she called, "stay in the bed with him. There's glass all over the floor." She pitched her voice higher, trying to get it above Flynn's. "You hear me, Krista?"

"Yes, Mum!"

Viola could hear tears in her voice. "It's okay," she yelled. "You'll be all right you stay there." She stepped forward and jerked open the passenger door. "What are you trying to do, Jarvis, kill us!" she cried.

"Goddamnit," he muttered, heaving his shoulder against the door. He fell backward out of the cab and Viola heard his boots thud against the running board. She hurried around behind the truck.

He was sprawled mostly on his back with one foot still on the running board. When she put her hands under his armpits and hauled, the smell of beer rose from him like dust. He struggled for a moment when his foot hit the ground, then went limp, heavy as water-soaked wood. She dragged him a few feet and let him down, then went back to the truck and climbed into the cab.

Viola laughed thinly when it started—she wasn't expecting one thing to be that easy. The wall creaked as the truck jerked backward, shooting the beam of one headlight through the empty window. She parked it beside the shack and went inside, where it was quiet except for the sound of Krista humming. Patting her hands along the table, she found the lamp and lifted the chimney. She lit the wick and carefully lowered the chimney over it again. Her broom was in the corner and she swept up as much of the glass as she could see in the thick burnished light, then tacked a grain bag over the shattered window. Rummaging in a cardboard box under the counter, she found the old crib sheet she'd had back in Dixfield.

Jarvis lay in front of the shack with his legs bent under him like somebody who'd been shot. His head was twisted toward the road and his mouth was open. Viola pulled his legs out straight. She worked his boots off and set them up beside his feet. "Damn you," she said, but she covered his face with the crib sheet so the insects that would come with the morning couldn't feed on it.

The second time she woke, the birds were loud. Sunlight was coming through the narrow window above the sink and warming a rectangular place on the floor beside her. Viola set her hand into the warmth and lay still, with her eyes closed. She could hear Flynn; the sound of him snoring came from the lean-to tacked onto the side of the shack, where the two little ones had their mattress. He was making small, neat noises like a piglet. Viola opened her eyes.

She took up some clothes and the bucket and a bar of soap and went out into the day. The sky was pale blue, the pines across the road shook with crows. Jarvis lay on his back asleep, one knee drawn up and the crib sheet pushed off his face. It sat near his mouth looking like a small dirty parachute. She went around back to the spigot and let the water run over her sore, blackened feet. While the bucket filled she raised her face and made herself look at where the barn had been. The smell was as terrible as on the first day. Beyond the charred area the woods seemed closer, thicker. Viola stripped off the shirt she slept in, splashed herself with water and rubbed soap into her shivering skin. Then she dumped the bucket over herself to rinse and bent under the flow to shampoo her hair.

Her temples ached from the cold; she felt dizzy as she straightened and began to dry herself. Her limbs were all gooseflesh and her hip-bones jutted out from her meager body like an old cow's. Viola laughed at herself and stood taller in the sun. She pulled a jersey over her head, put on her underwear, buttoned the skirt. She was toweling her hair when she saw Kendrick come out of the woods and cross the field to her left. He was moving slowly, head down, feet held wide apart. Tears made her eyes ache. She pulled the towel from her head, lay it across her shoulders, and stood waiting.

Kendrick, at nine, had his father's square face and sturdy limbs, the same thick brown hair. His eyes were green and long like her husband's. As she watched he went on to the front of the shack before turning back to come to her. She reached her hand out and rubbed up and down his arm. "You okay?" she asked him.

He nodded, not looking quite at her, and when he nodded, she squeezed his arm. "What happened?" he asked.

"You mean besides eight hundred chickens burning up?" The tears started down her face and she grinned and, dropping her hand from him, wiped the back of her arm across her eyes.

"The window's gone," he said flatly. "Dad's sleeping outdoors."

"Drank too much beer," she said after a moment. "Crashed that damn truck right into the house." She licked her lips. "We're all okay though." She smiled at him and touched his arm again. "You sleep in your special place?" she asked.

He nodded, then raised his eyes to look beyond where the barn had been to the tall birches shimmering gently in a breeze that didn't reach them.

Viola smiled. She could smell the sweet spruce on him. "You must be real hungry," she said.

"What we gonna do now?"

"I'll make you some breakfast," she told him. She bent to pick up the bucket.

"What we gonna do now, Mum?"

She stopped and ran her tongue around her lips again. "Your dad'll think of something." She lifted the bucket toward him. "You get me some water and I'll get you some breakfast. We got no chickens but we do have some eggs left yet."

* * *

They ate lunch late, and Viola had filled the sink and was doing dishes when Mr. Leavitt arrived in a red pickup that said "Leavitt's Poultry" in thick gold letters across the doors. He got down heavily from his truck, a man of fifty, dressed in khaki pants and shirt. His head was long and oval like a melon, his faded yellow hair was shaved high up the back of his neck. The baseball hat perched squarely said "Red Sox." Another man, wearing a gray suit and hatless, got out of the cab. Viola pushed the grain bag aside so she could see them, and when they moved out back she went to the narrow window above the sink and watched.

"This is a real mess, Rudge, a real mess," Mr. Leavitt said as they walked up and down the perimeter of the barn. He took off his hat and wiped at the sweat on his forehead with the back of his arm, leaving damp little spots on the sleeve. "Goddamn," he said sorrowfully.

"We did what we could, Mr. Leavitt," Jarvis told him. He spoke slowly and indistinctly and he walked with his arms folded across his body. The man with Mr. Leavitt followed just behind them, busy at intervals with the small notebook and short gold pen he held in his hands. "Fire chief thinks old hay rottin' underneath started it," Jarvis offered.

Mr. Leavitt nodded deeply, stopped and spoke over his shoulder. "Rudge says moldy hay started it," he said. "Damn!" He looked at Jarvis and raised his pale eyebrows. "That's a lot of chickens to lose," he said.

Jarvis nodded and tossed the butt of his cigarette into the ruins. "You figure it'll take long to get set up again?" he asked.

Mr. Leavitt turned and started back toward his truck. "Bound to," he said, "after a loss like this! Have to get Mr. Chamberlain's report"—he gestured in back of him with his shoulder—"see how that settles out. Ain't going to be nothin' happening fast."

Jarvis walked beside him. At the corner of the shack he paused. "How long, you think?"

Mr. Leavitt stopped. He watched the ground, his lips working against each other. Then he shrugged, lifting his shoulders stiffly as if they hurt him. "Can't give you a date, Rudge," he said, "but it's going to be a while. Year anyway 'fore I could even start thinking 'bout building again."

"A year." Jarvis pulled a Camel from his shirt pocket and stuck it in his mouth. He looked out across the field. "You got anything for me till then?"

Mr. Leavitt turned partway toward him. "Wish I did," he said. "You got my number. You call me in a couple of months." He straightened. "But you and your family can stay on here till you find something for the meanwhile."

Jarvis ground his lips against the unlit cigarette. The tip of his tongue spat tobacco out past it. Mr. Leavitt was staring at the shack. "Looks like something happened to that window," he said.

Jarvis twisted to take in the window, then looked at Mr. Leavitt. "Fire truck backed into it," he told him. "Didn't have much room to turn around."

"Careless buggers," Mr. Leavitt said. He opened the door and swung up on the running board, settled himself on the seat. He shut the door softly and spoke through the open window. "I'll give you a good word any time you ask for it," he told Jarvis, and started the truck.

Jarvis didn't say anything. He was working some matches out of the back pocket of his pants. Mr. Chamberlain climbed into the cab, said something to Mr. Leavitt, and got out again. He crossed to the blue truck and opened the door. "Keys in it?" Mr. Leavitt called.

Jarvis didn't answer. He drew in hard on his cigarette and tipped his head back to blow the smoke out of his nose. His eyes shifted as the motor turned over. Mr. Leavitt waved once and started toward the road. The blue truck backed the length of the shack and then followed him. Jarvis stood in the exhaust and smoked his cigarette. Behind him Viola and Kendrick were hunched at either end of the window, their two hands lifted to hold back an edge of the grain bag. Krista stood behind her mother, her bare toes curled into the floor. Flynn was playing with small stones under the table. Viola and Kendrick watched through the empty window. Looking beyond Jarvis, who stood with his feet apart and his head drawn down into his shoulders, they saw the red and then the blue truck turn right onto the road and go on past the high-growing juniper and the line of maples. Jarvis shifted and drew his arms in closer to his body, the muscles in his back jabbing at the faded blue shirt like rocks rising out of an ocean.

"Kendrick!" Viola said urgently, but he had pulled the door open and rushed outside. She followed and reached to catch hold of his arm, but he went and stood where his father would have to look at him.

"Dad, where's he taking our truck?" he asked.

Jarvis looked stiffly down into the child's face. "Our truck!" he spat. "Our truck." He laughed hoarsely, and Viola reached toward Kendrick again. "That son of a bitch will take 'our truck' any goddamn place he wants to," Jarvis hissed. "Because he owns that goddamn truck." He leaned back from the boy's face and his mouth tensed into a smile. "He owns the dirt you're standing on, and the air above it." He looked up into the sky as he spoke and raised his hands toward it, the cigarette pointing from the ends of his fingers. But Kendrick had folded his arms across his body and was looking at the ground. His throat felt as if his father had jammed his fist down it. "He owns the goddamn ashes!" Jarvis screamed above him.

When Kendrick lifted his face his father was staring off into the pine trees. He spoke almost softly. "Viola," he said without turning. "You pack anything you got that you want to keep. We're leaving for Portland."

She stepped toward him. "Portland!" she said. "It's too late. It's almost suppertime. We'll go in the morning then. Stay the night and go in the morning."

He turned around hard and leaned his face into hers. His eyes were bloodshot and he smelled like the fire. "That goddamn shack is going up in five minutes, so if you want anything out of it, including your children, you better move!"

Viola turned and ran inside. "Krista, get your things!" she called.

The child dropped the corner of the grain bag and got down off the stool. "Mum?" she said, and stared around the room.

Viola gripped her by the arms. "Put your clothes in a pillowcase. Get Flynn's, too; bring your doll, anything else you want." She shook her. "We got to leave *now!*" Viola turned her head. "Kendrick!" she called. He pushed the door open. "Help me," she said.

They stood down by the road. They had packed everything they could in Kendrick's old American Flyer wagon. Viola had put her pans and her dishes and the shoebox of silverware in a crate that egg cartons had come in. On top were foodstuffs; half a loaf of bread, the round tube of Quaker oatmeal, four cans of Campbell soup, and a jar of mustard. She'd dumped their clothes in on top and they spilled over like pale ribbons. Kendrick held his father's toolbox. It hung silvery from his hand. They were wearing their shoes. They waited.

The sun was behind them, beginning to fall rapidly now toward the pine trees. It flickered across the bumpy, pale tar of the road and shot up the tire tracks and through the new grass of the narrow field. Jarvis backed out the door, pulled it shut, and, still moving backward, started toward them. After half a dozen steps he turned and ran.

"Let's go," he said as he bent and lifted Flynn carefully and set him on his shoulders. They started down the road, which still held the heat of the midday sun, Viola hurrying on the sides of her shoes. They had passed into the shade of the maples when there was a loud explosion behind them. They couldn't see for the trees, but it stirred a wind up and the wide, fluted leaves trembled; blackbirds burst from their coolness and struck for the sky, Flynn's long, high wail rising with them as his fists knocked on his father's head.

But Jarvis was laughing. Laughing, he trotted down the middle of the road with the screaming, flailing child, and he spun and trotted backward, calling to his wife, "I left the goddamn gas on, Viola! There'll be nothing there but one Christly great hole in the ground!" He turned and faced down the road, eastward toward the city, rushing on with the frantic child, Kendrick hurrying just behind them with the toolbox thumping against his leg, Viola drawing the wagon, which rattled like a stone in a can, Krista running with her, steadying the load with one hand and holding her brightly dressed clothespin doll with the other.

PART ONE

THE FROGS

Dunham, Maine, June 1958

1

Logan Pembroke was standing to his knees in earth-colored water. Up the hill from him stretched pasture, June-high grass, which ran for a mile before meeting fence. The small pond was in the low corner of the field, and it was made of melting snow, of spring rain. When autumn came it was gone to smooth clay holding sleeping frogs, holding the roots of cat-o'-nine-tails—reeds growing taller than this boy, which flared as the maple leaves were falling, and shed their soft seeds to stand dried and delicate as snakeskin while the pond filled with snow. The frogs that emerged in the spring drummed louder and louder as the mud warmed and the evenings lingered into soft hours. Their frog songs were roaring and sweet.

Logan Pembroke was ten years old and he hunted the frogs. He was a round-faced boy with a bony nose like a beak. He wore brown shorts and his back was bare. His eyes were squinted up against the long light which dove through the grass, floated on the water in sharp patches, danced on his skin like pale fire. The reaching light billowed about his soft body as he stood with a stillness and grace unexpected in a boy so clumsy-looking. In one hand he held a net made from shiny black cord. His shadow fell across the pond as unmoving as a log beneath the water. When he struck with the net, the flesh on his torso jiggled in a way that was almost tender.

The frog's legs stuck through the net but its body was caught. Logan gripped firmly, crimping the net above its head, while the long, pale feet paddled in the air. He waded to shore where a stone wall separated the pasture from the road, and he set the net upon a flat rock. The round, flecked eyes stared unblinking past the boy.

The velvety skin of the throat pulsed in and out. Logan smashed its head with a sharp, rectangular rock. He hit it many times and a greenness seeped from it. One eye remained intact and continued to stare. The boy hunkered over it and watched very closely as he brought the rock down. At length he waded back into the pond and rinsed the net, delicately, as ladies do with hand laundry. Then he stood again, still as a dead tree, his shadow striking farther across the water, his round, heavy face quiet and watchful.

Across the road, under the pendant limbs of a pine tree, stood the smaller boy, Ronnie. His weight was more on one foot than the other, his arms were folded across his pale belly. Curious and a little frightened, he watched his brother's square, still back.

The boys slept in the narrow attic. It was reached by a drop ladder that folded down into the living room and could be raised during the day. Their beds were under the open window at the gable end and separated by the milk crate that held the lamp. The window at the far gable was open also and the night air streamed through, smelling of pines. Greyish moonlight fell over the lamp and the bare floor, and over Ronnie's arm and part of his face. He was snoring, open-mouthed, and he moved and mumbled as he slept. Logan leaned on one elbow and peered at his brother's face, watching how it was vacant, then tensed, and was vacant again. He looked like a baby that wasn't born yet. Logan had seen pictures of those babies at the fair—unfinished, ancient-looking, floating around in water like frogs. The noise downstairs grew louder, his father and Thumper Smeaton drinking beer in the kitchen. A fist coming down on the table, laughter; then his father's voice resumed, louder, up and over Thumper's. Thumper's shrill giggle climbed with it. Logan didn't like Thumper; he thought he was stupid. Ronnie feared him. Thumper was a little man with bowed legs. He never shaved but his beard wouldn't grow out. He always wore a dark, stained hat that was stuck on—high wind couldn't shift it. He helped their father slaughter the pigs. Logan straightened and flung himself onto his back. He lifted the arm he'd been leaning on and shook it to get the tingles out. Below, again the banging on the table and the sound of the voices beating up the ladder to the attic like the voices of trolls or goblins or the unpredictable gods in stories.

* * *

The year moved from the summer and the nights began to cool. The four of them were sitting at the table in the narrow kitchen. The clock on the stove whined softly like a machine worn out to its last thread. Silverware clacked on dishes. The small window above the sink was north-facing and overlooked the sloping backyard and the hog runs. The dark pine woods hung over the last weathered enclosure where the grey sow stood, her hornlike nose thrust between two boards, her nostrils beating slowly in and out. The sky beyond was the color of wet slate. The harvest moon had not yet risen. Across the road the soft wind shook silklike seed from the cat-o'-nine-tails. The clock on the stove whined on; a bone clunked on Gage Pembroke's plate. "You got any more potato?" he wanted to know.

Linette Pembroke got up, her hand out for the plate. She had red hands, Logan's mother, and the rest of her skin was very pale. The veins showing at her temples and on the insides of her wrists and elbows were fine, like the veins in a leaf and iodine blue. She wasn't much over thirty but her youth was long dead in her. Logan was his father's child, Ronnie her dear own, and she held him close, like a life ring, like a lover, as if he were still in her and she were in him. She stood at the stove and spooned potato onto her husband's plate. "More peas?" she asked without turning.

"Woulda said so," he told her, tapping his knife on the tabletop. He was watching Ronnie, the way the spoon went deep into his mouth. "'You swallow that thing you'll wish you hadn't," he said, and he chuckled a little, making a sound as if he were clearing his throat.

Ronnie snatched the spoon out of his mouth and set it on the plate. It sounded like tin, vibrating there for a moment before it was still. Ronnie leaned forward, his chin almost in the food, and watched it.

Linette stood at the edge of the table between the two of them, Gage's plate in her hand. "There's another chop," she said, her voice pale like her skin.

"Get it," he told her, his eyes on the top of the boy's head, "and quit interfering."

Linette made as much noise as an earthworm recrossing the kitchen. "You're just like her," Gage said, his heavy face twisting slowly. His nose was long and pointed and his nostrils taut. Ronnie raised his hand and stuck a finger in his ear. He carefully worked it back and forth.

"Ma, I want more potato," Logan said. His voice was loud. Ronnie made a quick sound like an air pump as he sucked up some spittle that was running down the side of his mouth. She reached her arm and took Logan's plate. "More peas, too," he said when she was almost to the stove. "More meat." Ronnie sucked up spit.

"Meat's gone," she said quietly as she brought the plate to him.

"Aw, Ma," he complained, and put his hand out for the salt shaker.

Gage cut the chop with short flicks of his knife. It rapped on the plate. The clock on the stove whined. Linette sat down in her chair. Her hands were in her lap and she squeezed a balled-up rag first in one fist and then in the other. She watched Ronnie from the side of her face, her pale lids lowered. She could hear them both chewing and Ronnie's openmouthed breathing. She concentrated on that damp, slightly abrasive sound. Gage sucked on the bone.

"You better finish your supper," he said, dropping the bone onto his plate and shoving it from him with the side of his hand. "You get any punier you might just turn into a girl."

Ronnie looked up at him quickly, his face showing alarm. Then it softened into curiosity and he picked up his fork. Logan hooted and pointed at him; then he looked at his mother. "What's for dessert?" he asked, pushing his empty plate toward the center of the table with the side of his hand.

Outside, beyond the hog runs, the hot yellow moon began to climb in its shocking beauty from the trees.

Ronnie followed him along the slope of the yard, Logan's square back sturdy in the dark jacket, the collar pulled up so he looked almost neckless. Ronnie took little steps, his face turned slightly to the right. It was a Saturday late in March and the yard was hard ruts, frozen footprints. The grey sow had farrowed in the night. Thumper had brought them word of it at breakfast.

Ronnie climbed up beside his brother on the fence and looked into the dark shed. She lay flat, her short legs straight out and limp in the matted hay. She grunted steadily and softly as all along her belly, pink as the inside of his own mouth, Ronnie saw them wiggling and squirming, not one as big as her ear. Ronnie's mouth was open; he breathed through it, his eyelids drooping as he watched. He blinked and straightened when one fell from the middle of the line and, squeaking frantically, struggled to regain its place. Ronnie stared, his face tensed, as its limbs flailed against its brethren. When the little creature managed to climb higher and almost disappeared in the soft swell of the sow and only its short tail flicked, Ronnie's own arms went slack and he slumped against the wooden fence.

"Ten," Logan said above him. "She done good this time."

Ronnie looked along the line, his lips moving as he said the numbers silently, got confused, and started again. He was at six when Thumper stepped out from the darkness in the corner of the shed, the hat jammed over his short forehead. "Was 'leven," he said, and flung something that flopped against Ronnie's face and fell into the dirty straw. Ronnie blinked as one foot slipped off the bottom rail and swung in the air. Thumper's face bobbed before him and choking, wet sounds came out of it that were laughter. "She rolled on this one," Thumper said, stooping to pick it up. "Too little to suck on a tit anyway." He held it out flat on his gray palm. It looked perfect, just tiny and thin and the eye was closed.

Ronnie started to cry, a high, mewling sound. He turned to look behind him, then slipped off the rail. Landing on the hard ground jarred him and he stood with his knees slightly bent and cried, his shoulders lifted and his thin hands crossed.

Logan got down and stood beside him. "Why don't you eat it for breakfast," he told Thumper. "Raw." He glared at his face and at the thing in his hand. Ronnie snuffled and wheezed and watched him.

Thumper giggled and leaned over the fence, brandishing his palm at them. "You better watch out or I'll throw you in the pigpen. Mumma pig eat you up, spit out the pieces for her baby pigs." Thumper had no teeth and his threats came out like something chanted and powerful.

Ronnie wailed and backed up, his fists shoved against his eyes. "Don't let him, Logan!" he screamed. Thumper laughed as Ronnie half turned toward the house. "Ma," he whimpered, "Ma."

Logan reached out and shoved him with his stiffened arm. "You're a snot-nosed baby!" he said, despising his tears. But Ronnie cried harder and Logan twisted from him and faced Thumper. "You jerk!" he spat. "You old stupid jerk!" He picked up a hoe handle that was leaning against the wall of the pigpen. He held it by the splintered end and swung it over his head so it made a sound like a hissing snake. "You try it!" he cried. "You try it! You and that old pig, too!"

Thumper retreated to the doorway of the shed and Logan brought the handle down hard on the gate so it stung his palms and the sharp end of the broken wood stabbed him. He looked surprised and brought it down again and harder. Beyond Thumper the sow's grunts grew loud and uneven, Ronnie was crying and scrambling up the hill toward the house. Thumper giggled and retreated farther into the darkness of the shed, his gray fingers closing around the dead piglet on his palm.

Logan built the lean-to from boards that had fallen off the hog runs. It was out back to the left of the house on a small rise of land, hidden by thick old pines and two spindly chokecherry trees. He was hunkered down under his roof and he could hear Ronnie coming through the low branches. Twigs snapped, scuffling, and then his pale pointy face peering between two crooked boards. "You can come in," Logan whispered through the cracks. "You can come."

More scrabbling, and then Ronnie stood in the doorway. "Whatcha doin'?" he asked softly, looking around the small hut. He had on the new blue sneakers that his mother had given him; his feet looked large and expensive. His fly was undone. The brown jacket that had been Logan's two years ago drooped from his shoulders, billowed out from his narrow hips. The pockets were ripped and a blue gum wrapper was hanging from one of them. It slowly fluttered down and landed in front of his sneaker. Logan's eyes dropped with it. "You wanna come huntin' with me?" he asked.

"S-sure," Ronnie answered, stepping a little closer so that his new sneaker came down on the wrapper. "Huntin' what?" he asked in a loud whisper.

Logan raised his eyes slowly up Ronnie's body. "We'll have to see what's out there," he told him, shifting his gaze until he was looking out through the door. "You got any more gum?"

Ronnie opened his mouth wide. A small black wad sat on his tongue. He closed his lips quickly over it. "Last piece. Honest," he said and blinked several times.

Logan stepped toward him and Ronnie backed out of the lean-to, almost tripping on the thick, white heels of his new sneakers. Logan kept coming and as he stepped around him he knocked against his shoulder and went on into the woods. It was almost May but the air had a raw feeling to it. Logan turned. "Ain't you coming?" he coaxed.

Ronnie nodded and began to run clumsily through the naked raspberry briers and the stiff patches of juniper, his new sneakers heavy and precious on his feet. Soon they were trekking through the pine forest, which was smooth underfoot, cold in the shadows. Ronnie scuttled along with his shoulders drawn up; Logan never looked back. He moved with something close to grace, his thick body seeming to stretch and grow more supple. After they had gone quite a distance, moving gradually but steadily downhill, Logan stopped and held his finger to his lips. Ronnie half crouched and watched him, his mouth hanging open, the white tips of his new sneakers pointing toward each other. He slowly became aware of a throbbing sound, and as he became aware of it, it grew louder and louder, a clamor rhythmic and high-pitched. "Ducks!" Ronnie said in a loud gasp. "Millions of 'em!"

Logan didn't speak. He changed direction slightly and started off again. Ronnie followed, his sneakers slipping on the damp, pine needle-covered earth. As they went on, the noise grew in volume and intensity and the ground under them became damper, moss-covered, thick-smelling. Logan drew up behind the tall trunk of an elm tree. Ronnie came along, head down, arms out to help his balance. He almost walked into his brother, recoiled and stood blinking at him. "You ain't got your gun," he whispered eagerly.

"It's frogs," Logan told him, "hatched-out frogs."

"You ain't got your net," Ronnie said.

Logan raised his hands. He turned them to look at them front and back. He peered around the tree, then glanced at Ronnie. Gesturing with his head, he went down the small slope and started across a flat area that was covered with humps of grasses and from which rose a sparse grove of alders. With his first step the noise had ceased utterly in the midst of a downbeat. But Logan smiled and kept going.

"Logan, it's wet!" Ronnie's high voice called behind him.

Logan whipped around and jammed his finger against his mouth. "Sssssshh," he hissed. Then he started off again, fast, his feet, clad in Gage's old black boots, slapping against water.

"Logan!" Ronnie squealed. He stepped after him but what looked like new grass was wet underneath. The dark pines rose up behind him and a wind was shaking in their tops with a low whistling sound. "Logan!" he called again.

Logan had passed the second group of alders. His dark jacket flashed between the new-leaved, narrow trees.

Ronnie teetered for a moment and then launched himself toward a hummock. He managed to stop with both feet on it, his arms flailing. The silvery leaves of the alders vibrated gently in the wind that came from the pines, and the sunlight danced on them as if they were water. Blue jays swooped and cried out. "Logaannn, Logannnnnn!" Ronnie called, and the jays shrieked louder at him.

Logan was far away now but he looked back. "I'm hunting!" he yelled. "You said you wanted to come and now all you do is whine like a damn baby!"

Ronnie sobbed and called again, his brother's name turning into a yelp as he lost his balance and slipped off the hummock. Whimpering, he started leaping across the soggy earth, the coat rocking sluggishly on his narrow shoulders. Each time he reached a firm spot he paused there, his darkened pants plastered against his shins. Logan went farther and farther from him—Ronnie could barely hear the splashing of his boots.

The sun had climbed higher. It glittered on the bright leaves and the pools of water. Ronnie's feet stung with cold. His new sneakers were as heavy as stones. Logan was a dark shape moving at the edge of the flooded area where the ground abruptly ascended. Ronnie closed his eyes and started hopping after him.

"My sneaker! My new sneaker!"

Logan was partway up the hill. He turned at Ronnie's shrieking voice. He was small down there, perched on one foot, humped up like an injured bird. "What!" Logan yelled down the hill at him. The alders rippled, the jays cried. "What?"

"My new sneaker!" Ronnie sobbed. "It came off. It's gone!"

Logan felt a little thrill jump in his gut. He straightened and drew the clean air into his lungs. "Put your hand in and fish it out!" he bellowed, and as his words echoed in the woods and across the flat, flooded area he turned and kept climbing, cursing when Gage's old boots shifted around his feet and he lost his balance on the brown pine needles and had to fling his hands into the damp earth to help himself.

Ronnie didn't reach home until after lunchtime. He was shivering and his nose was clogged so he was breathing through his mouth. Linette wrapped his legs in a towel she had hanging by the cookstove. She hung a second towel to be warming and made him soup and sat with him while he drank it. Logan was sitting in the living room listening, his boots muddy and rank on the braided rug. She was hovering around Ronnie's head making soothing sounds, and then she knelt and wrapped the second towel around his thin knees.

Later, when Ronnie was warmed, Linette followed him into the woods. He stood on the slope and pointed while she waded barelegged and with an old wooden rake hunted for his lost sneaker until it was late and she had to go home and make supper. They hurried back through the woods, her hand on Ronnie's shoulder, and she was promising him new sneakers, not knowing where she'd get the money this time, she couldn't ask the minister twice.

MONEY

2 When the Rudge family arrived in Portland late that June night, they made their way to the Salvation Army, where they were taken in, and stayed there for several weeks before an apartment was found. Their new home was down on India Street, on the second floor of a narrow house that was dim and damp-smelling. The rooms opened into one another and there were windows only in the gable ends. There were front stairs, and a door from the kitchen opened to a dark hall leading to the outside staircase that hung from the back of the building. The gas heater occupied half the living room and when the winter set in it cost more than they could afford and it sent most of its heat straight up and out through the roof. They had been given a bed and three cots, a kitchen table and chairs, blankets and towels with old twisted monograms, sheets the soft yellow of faded newspapers, a few cooking pans. They were like refugees anywhere.

Every day of that summer Jarvis Rudge rose early and walked downtown to the ManPower office, a dingy, nearly empty storefront on Longfellow Square. The men were mostly thin-looking with gray skin and shaking hands; the Power part was Mr. Nappi, who was tall and thin with a potbelly poking at his cowboy shirt and frizzled yellow hair that bulged from his narrow skull. Mr. Nappi had a loud, scraping voice. His office smelled like dirty clothes; there was the jangling sound of Mr. Nappi's phone, the screeching sound of Mr. Nappi's voice, the greedy jingle of coins rolling in the dry pits of his palms. Jarvis often got a full day's work from Mr. Nappi. He moved furniture and washed floors, he scraped paint off buildings and repainted them. He cleaned fish. A good week's pay, after Nappi's cut, was twenty-five dollars. Some weeks he brought home twelve. He spoke to no one except what was necessary, ate his lunch in the emptiest shade he could find and smoked until it was time to go back to work.

The two younger Rudge children spent the hot days of summer playing in the backyard, which was about thirty feet deep and bordered by a high cement wall rising to meet the small back porches of buildings on the next street. Krista dug in the Mitchell twins' sandbox. They were two blond girls who lived downstairs with their mother and were always inside watching their television set. Its strange noises came out the window while Krista built houses and Flynn hunted small stones which he put carefully into his Maxwell House coffee can. He rustled in the sticky weeds; he searched slowly along the high cement wall. Viola could see her children from the screenless window in her kitchen: the tops of their heads shone like feathers as they bent over their work. When she was done cleaning her house she went out to be with them and walked about in that airless yard where nothing grew but stinkweeds and stones. Kendrick roamed the city: he followed his father to ManPower, he found the park and the library and the waterfront; he went anywhere they were digging up streets, pulling down buildings, laying iron girders. When autumn came he and Krista went to the big stone school by the cemetery; Flynn stayed to home with his mother.

Shortly before Christmas Jarvis found a job working as a cutter in a printing company. He was responsible for his machine, he turned out his own work, he began to get back some of the pride that had been burned from him by working for Nappi. Although the pay wasn't steady—they got sent home when work was slow, they stayed long hours overtime for a rush job—it was much better wages than ManPower. By the spring he had bought a Ford convertible, used but clean, red with a black top, and they were thinking about putting children's beds on the layaway.

Behind Jarvis's cutter was the three-color press, long as several pool tables, clacking and thumping all day like a train. Jarvis liked the sound of it—it was soothing, it gave him almost a sense of privacy as he worked carefully at his own machine, his cigarette resting neatly in a quahog shell. The shop manager was Mr. James Burke. He was almost as small as a child and his hair, which he kept very short, sprang up off his skull, stretching to make Mr. Burke look taller. On a Friday in June he hurried over to Jarvis, his thin tie fluttering over his shoulder. "Got that Armstrong job ready?" he yelled above the press noise.

"Right here," Jarvis said, and lightly tapped the box he'd just finished packing.

"Great! Great!" Mr. Burke cried, seizing it in both hands and hefting it up to his chest. "Can you help collate this afternoon?" he asked. "This can wait"—he reached with the toe of his shoe to nudge a pallet of manila paper destined to back receipt books—"but Maine Indemnity is screaming for their new forms."

"All right," Jarvis told him. "I'll go back there soon's I have my lunch."

Mr. Burke licked his lips quickly as if they tasted bitter. "Yes," he said, "just as soon, just as soon as you can." He hurried away, his spine curving backward to balance the box in his arms.

After lunch Jarvis set the cover precisely over his machine and went out back where the collating operation was. Molly Baldridge ran it; he'd worked with her a couple of times on rush jobs. She was a middle-aged woman with dark, ear-length hair that was swept back so it always looked as if she were in a gale. Molly wore sneakers all through winter and baggy dungarees and plaid shirts that hung out over them. There was always a Pall Mall in her mouth.

Her voice was hoarse, her eyes were watery, there were little gray-rimmed holes in the fronts of her shirts.

"Hey!" she greeted Jarvis, and when he told her why he was there, "That stupid son of a bitch, he's always in a hurry for something and half the time he don't know what it is." The Pall Mall jumped and jerked in the corner of Molly's mouth as she spoke. She twitched her face and let out a stream of smoke. "Well, you can sit right there," she told him, pointing to a stool at the end of the long, pitted counter. "You want to work the stapler for us, okay?"

He nodded and sat down, but Molly didn't seem to feel too urgent. She leaned against the counter and addressed the two women who were seated at a card table finishing their lunch. "Ladies," she began, and flipped open her Zippo, "we got 'mergency help here in the person of Jarvis. Seems Maine Indemnity stuck a stick of dynamite up Burke's ass and they're threatening his fuse with a blowtorch." They giggled and she nodded with mock seriousness and spun the wheel on her Zippo so the flame reached up to the cigarette. "Now, when you ladies have finished your lunch we'll get on to it, Mr. Rudge's presence making our load a little lighter."

They giggled again and got up from the table, crumpling their paper bags and tossing them toward the wastebasket.

They sat in a line at the counter and put together a fifteen-page booklet. Molly started, Marilyn and Sarah each added five more pages, and Jarvis thomped the stapler through them at the end of the line. When they'd got it going smoothly they took up the conversation they'd been having before Jarvis arrived. Sarah asked, "Now Molly, how many husbands is it you said you've had?"

"I get mixed up," Molly said. "I married Chet twice, you know." She passed five sheets to Marilyn and opened her Zippo. Gathering up five more, she blasted out smoke and said, "Only three. But Chet being twice makes it four sets of wedding vows."

"Well my Lord!" Sarah giggled. "That's a whole lot!"

Molly shrugged and made a sound at the back of her throat. Jarvis whomped the stapler. "Guess I was lookin' for something," Molly said. "I'm still lookin'." She paused, frowning while her fingers worked like little pieces of machinery. "I tell you though," she said, "if I coulda just collated 'em I woulda had one fine husband!"

Jarvis brought the stapler down, the women roared with laughter, ashes fell on Molly's pages. "I'm serious. I mean it!" she said, and they laughed harder.

It was after seven when they finished. "Goddamn," Molly said, getting wearily off her stool. "We must of made one of them for every man, woman, and dog in the state of Maine."

"Oh no, Molly," Mr. Burke said. He'd come in behind them. He wore rubber-soled shoes and was quiet as gas. "These forms go out all over the country!" he told her.

"Well by God!" Molly took her cigarette out of her mouth. "I never knew we was doing such important work!"

"Oh yes," he said reverently. "Oh yes. It's a big job," he told them, and rocked back on his heels.

The women got their purses and Jarvis picked up his lunch box and followed them out the door. They went through the darkened shop toward the exit. "Oh, Jarvis," Mr. Burke called, pattering up behind him. "Can I talk to you for a minute?"

Jarvis stopped and turned. "My wife's holding supper," he said.

"Won't take long, not long."

Jarvis nodded and Mr. Burke hustled ahead of him and opened the door of his office. He shot in and sat behind the desk, very upright, with his hands reaching to hold a piece of paper. "Well, I don't want to waste your time," he told Jarvis, "so I'll be quick. The boy who had the job before you is coming back from the army. We had to promise he could have the job again if he wanted it." He smiled a tight little smile and half lifted the paper in his hands.

Jarvis was tired. He'd already figured what the overtime would bring this week's pay to. It took him a moment to understand what Burke was saying to him. It was like a mallet on the top of his head. "You never told me that when you hired me on," he said slowly.

Mr. Burke lifted his shoulders slightly and rustled his paper. "We didn't expect he'd be coming back, to tell you the truth. Figured he'd get some kind of training in the army." He looked up at Jarvis. "I got a letter here saying you've done a good job for us." He held it out. "And here's your pay." He picked up the brown envelope with his other hand and set it on the edge of his desk. "We'll take you on again when there's an opening," he added quickly, "but right now we can't do anything."

"You little son of a bitch," Jarvis said. His face had gone pale and was now reddening.

Mr. Burke pushed the letter at him but it fluttered off the desk onto the floor.

"You little bastard," Jarvis said in a louder voice. He bent and scooped the letter up and crushed it in his fist. Then he leaned over the desk and thrust it at Burke's face. "Why don't you shove this up your ass!" he told him.

Mr. Burke flung himself backward and his chair banged into the wall. "Don't take that tone with me!" he said.

"Don't take that tone with me," Jarvis mimicked in a high voice. He rested the knuckles of his left hand on the desk so he could reach farther with his right. He crackled the mauled paper under Burke's nose. "You're a regular little son of a bitch, ain't you," he said softly.

"Ease up!" Mr. Burke told him, making his voice go as deep as he could and pushing the small brown envelope toward Jarvis. "Now take your money and get out of here."

Jarvis lifted his fist, turned it, and dropped the paper on the desk.

"You go," Mr. Burke said. "You get out of here." He looked at his phone and at the distance between them. "Take him out of here!" he demanded in a high voice.

Jarvis swung around, his hand still in a fist. Molly was standing in the doorway. "Take him out of here," Mr. Burke said again.

Molly looked flat at him. She took her cigarette out of her mouth with one hand while she touched Jarvis's arm lightly with the other. It felt like a stone and Molly shook it gently. "Let's get out of this place," she told him, her eyes still on Burke. "He ain't very good company to spend Friday night with."

Turning, Jarvis knocked her hard with his shoulder. He went out the door and slammed it. Black lines like a spiderweb appeared in the glass. "Jesus!" Mr. Burke said, his face twisting in pain.

Molly stepped forward and picked up the pay envelope. She pointed her cigarette at Burke. "You got a nephew can't find a job?" she asked him. "You give Jarvis that army boy line?"

"Good night, Molly," he said, looking right at her.

"That man's got a family." She tucked the envelope carefully into her pocket. "But you ain't exactly burdened with a sense of shame, are you, Burke," she said, and put her cigarette in her mouth. She left and hurried down the dark hall and out into the evening.

It was twilight. The air was hot and dusty. Jarvis was backing the red car out of its parking spot. The top was down, so she could see him clearly, and the way he was pitched forward in the car made it look as if he were going to pull the steering wheel out of it. Molly ran but he stepped on the gas and the car shot ahead. She hollered out his name. At the street he slammed on the brakes, and she caught up and leaned into the open car. "Why don't you buy me a beer," she said. "Then I'll buy you one." She kept her voice even. It hurt her to look at his face. She drew on her cigarette and turned her head to stare out over the street. "Then you be kind enough to drop me off at fifty-two Oxford Street so you can go on home."

He stared straight ahead over the wheel. Only the muscles in the side of his face moved, rippling like a snake under sand. She opened the door and slid into the car.

"Dad must be working overtime," Viola said again. "We better eat 'stead of waiting any longer." She opened the oven door and took out the meatloaf, the potatoes that had been in there too long and were shrunk in their dark skins. Flynn watched her. "Da." He frowned. She called the other children. "Da," he said again.

After supper she ran the bathwater. Flynn stood beside the tub and slowly worked at the buttons on his shirt. When the tub was full and he was naked he peered over the edge. "Cowd," he said gravely.

"No, Flynn, it's lovely and warm," she told him, swishing her hand back and forth. She helped him climb in. As she soaped his back he sat very still with his eyes half closed, his little body rocking gently under her hands.

Viola wrapped him in a towel and brought him into the living room, where the older children were playing cards. She set him on Kendrick's cot and went through to the front room and looked out the window. It was dusk and the street was quiet. Then a boy came around the corner and clattered over the uneven bricks on his bicycle. "Is he here yet?" Kendrick called.

Viola didn't answer. She was watching up the street, where a drunk man was coming along, his arm linked with a brightly dressed woman who was moving gracefully despite her high heels and the burden on her elbow. The man was singing. He was singing "Roll Me Over in the Clover." The woman had a hat on as yellow as a daffodil and wide around as a manhole cover.

The humming ceiling light cast a small greenish glow over her. Viola sat at the table with a mug in front of her. The sodden tea bag rested on the spoon beside it. She could hear Flynn snoring in the next room. Above her rain was falling steadily, rapping on the shingles. In the living room Kendrick made a soft grating sound turning on the canvas cot. She knew he wasn't sleeping. Later, when she went through the room, he whispered loudly, "Mum!"

"You still awake?"

"Yup."

"You should be asleep." She reached out in the dark to stroke his forehead. Her fingers traced his eyebrows, one and then the other, back and forth, one and then the other. He settled slowly on the pillow; his skin and the bones under it were the most treasured thing in her world.

"You think something happened to Dad?" he whispered.

"No, I don't. I think he went out for beer. It's too bad he don't trouble himself to get home at a decent hour." She straightened up and went on toward the front room. "You get to sleep," she said.

The children poured cereal into their bowls. Viola had her back turned to them. She was waiting for the toaster to pop. She drank from her coffee mug. Drumming her fingers on the counter, she waited, and when it finally did pop up it made her jump. She cut the crust off it and brought it to Flynn. He leaned back from it and looked at her. " 'Am!" he said loudly. " 'Am!"

She whirled and went to the refrigerator. She yanked the door open, grabbed the jar from the shelf and brought it to the table, bent to spoon it over his toast. The other two ate their cereal. When they knew she wasn't looking they watched her.

Sunlight came thinly through the back window; they began to hear noises from the apartment downstairs. Viola poured herself another mug of coffee and nearly dropped it when a horn sounded outside in the street.

"Mo' ju!" Flynn cried, holding his glass up. "Mo' ju, mo' ju," he chanted, but Viola was through the curtain and hurrying to the front room. Behind her he started wailing.

She looked out. Mrs. Mitchell was coming down the front stoop. She stuck her head into the window of a station wagon that had pulled up at the curb. Mrs. Mitchell was wearing her shiny blue bathrobe. Her ass, which was full as a kettle drum, slowly rocked back and forth. A man got out of the car, came around to the curb, and followed her up the steps and into the house.

After Viola did the dishes she lay down on her bed. "Take the kids outside," she told Kendrick when he came and stood on the threshold watching her. "Make sure Flynn wears his hat."

"It's hot out."

"His visor hat," she said.

She could hear them going down the front stairs: Kendrick first, then Krista's light foot, and Flynn pausing between each step and dragging something. The street door banged. It was quiet.

Viola lay flat, her dented loafers sticking up at the ends of her feet like driven stakes. She felt quite sure there had been no accident. This address where they were living was on his license, and no policeman had come in the night to knock at her door. She kept seeing him when she closed her eyes: his head was turned from her, he was wearing that dark green jacket, half of the collar turned up; he was hurrying away.

Krista touched her gently and she opened her eyes and then sat straight up. "What is it?" she asked.

"There's a lady here."

Viola's heart lunged in her chest like a fish trying to get off a hook. "What does she want?" she asked, and quickly stood on the floor.

"She wants Dad," Krista said, backing up.

"What did you tell her?"

"I told her no, he wasn't here. So she said could she see you."

"Where is she?"

"In the kitchen."

Viola could smell smoke before she went through the bedspread she'd hung as a curtain over the doorway. She was standing there in front of the sink, a skinny, dark-haired woman in baggy clothes. Krista peered around her mother to see the lady: she was tapping a very long ash into her palm. "I was hoping to see Jarvis Rudge," she said, "but your girl told me he wasn't to home."

"That's right," Viola said, stepping farther into the room, "he's not home just now." She stopped so the table was between them. "I'm his wife," she said.

"Molly Baldridge, from down to Delmar's." She nodded and puffed out smoke. "I got his pay envelope and I wanted to give it to him." She pulled the narrow envelope out of her back pocket and set it on the table.

Viola looked at it for only a moment. "Jarvis forgot his pay?" she asked.

"No, I was just hanging on to it for him."

Krista was staring at the lady, the way her cigarette moved when she talked. "Go get Mrs. Baldridge an ashtray," Viola said. "And then go outside with your brothers." Krista went into the living room and came back with her father's round blue ashtray. The lady was still standing in front of the sink with her hand cupped. "You go outside with Flynn," her mother told her, taking the ashtray and setting it on the table near the lady. "You stay there till I call you." Krista went slowly toward the door. She turned to watch the lady snap open her lighter. The flame she made was tall. "Hurry up," Viola scolded. She went through the door as slowly as she could and out onto the staircase.

"Little girl looks just like you," Molly said.

Viola nodded. "Would you like a cup of coffee? Or some tea?" she asked.

"Hate tea," Molly told her, "and I don't really have time for coffee. Got laundry in the machines up the street," she said, gesturing behind her with the hand that held the cigarette.

"Well, I thank you for bringing this envelope." Viola looked at it and frowned. "I don't remember him telling me he was leaving early," she said.

"Shit no. He worked late. We all worked late, collating forms. He come in and helped us all afternoon. Then that asshole Burke called him in. When the work was all finished, wouldn't you know. Wasn't Jarvis's fault. Burke's done it before. One of his nephews or some other half-assed relation needs a job he don't hesitate." She drew on her cigarette and frowned. Viola watched her. She didn't understand exactly what Molly was talking about but she sensed what was coming and it was making her feel sick. Her face grew darker and more closed. "I wonder does the little bastard charge 'em a sort of tax every week for stealing 'em the job in the first place," Molly was saying.

"He took away Jarvis's job?"

"Gave it to some pimply cousin or something."

"But he got the six-month raise," she whispered harshly.

"He earned the damn raise. He done a real good job, but that Burke's a shithead. He don't have any respect." She squashed out her Pall Mall butt in the ashtray.

Viola was staring at the tabletop where the envelope was.

"He left in a hurry, so I grabbed up the envelope," Molly said. "This morning I remembered I had it and I knew you lived down here on India Street near the station."

"Thank you for bringing it."

"He wasn't looking for it, was he?"

"He didn't mention it. He had to go out early," Viola told her.

Molly nodded. "Well, I'm going to miss him. He's a good man to work with."

"My husband always works hard." Viola sounded fierce and angry. "Thank you for bringing it," she said again, stepping back from the table.

That night Flynn wouldn't stay in his own bed. He lay next to Viola, diagonally across her bed, so he took up more room than her husband. He was a restless sleeper and made little sounds like a pony snorting. Viola lay flat on the edge of the mattress, his head against her shoulder. She had fifty-three dollars and forty cents. The rent was due on Monday. She was almost out of groceries. Maybe she could pay the landlord one week at a time, stretch it out until he came back. She knew he'd be back. She didn't want to think about what if he didn't come back. Maybe he was hurt and someone stole his wallet and there was no way they could identify him. She would call the police. She would say a missing person. Like her cousin Ailene back in Rumford. He never did come home, Ailene's husband, just sent the kids birthday cards two months late from his new address in Concord, and no matter what they said everybody thought Ailene was a fool and a failure. Flynn stretched and pushed his head into her shoulder. Viola pulled away from him and got out of the bed. She went across the linoleum to the window. Below her the street was shadowy; pale warmth from the yellow streetlights fell in small oval areas on the gray brick. The space before their own building was empty, but farther up and down, and all across the street, cars were parked. She watched as a thin grey cat ran out of an alley and under one of the cars. The wind knocked at the window glass and it shifted in the worn frame. When part of a newspaper skidded under the car the cat shot into the street and ran, his tail held low to the bricks. Viola closed her eyes and pressed her cheek against the cool glass. Behind her Flynn groaned in his sleep.

"You make the kids breakfast, okay?" she asked Kendrick. He was standing beside her bed. It was raining and it pattered against the glass of Viola's window like fingers.

"You sick?" He was pale and his hair stuck up straight from his forehead.

"No," she said. "I didn't get much sleep is all and I wanted to stay in bed a bit."

"Does your back still hurt?" he demanded. He was standing with his feet apart and his hands on his hips.

"Just a little." She smiled at him. "I'll get up soon. I was just hoping you'd help me out this morning."

"What should I make them?"

She smiled. "Cereal, toast," she said softly. "I got the juice ready last night."

He stepped closer. "Krista says she ain't going to school. Says she's sick."

"Is she?"

He shrugged.

"Well, maybe she'll get up when she hears you making breakfast."

He turned and went out of the room. She closed her eyes. She could hear him moving around in the kitchen, she could hear Flynn talking. The refrigerator opened and then someone shut a door hard. "I don't hafta!" she heard Krista screech.

"You do too!" he yelled.

Viola sat up against the pillow. Her back was aching the way it used to when she was pregnant. "Krista!" she called.

"Now you got Mum upset," Kendrick said loudly.

Krista came to the doorway. She'd been crying and her pajama top was stained. "I don't feel good," she said.

Viola beckoned.

Krista came to her slowly. Viola put her palm against the child's forehead. "You're cool as a cucumber," she pronounced.

"My stomach hurts," Krista said.

"Mou! Mou! Mou!" Flynn cried from the kitchen.

"Krista, you get dressed and eat your breakfast. Then we'll see how you feel."

"Mou!" he screamed.

"Krista, go get dressed!"

She turned and ran crying from the room. Viola heard her bare feet slapping across the living room floor.

"Mou! Mou! Mou!"

"It's Cheerios, Flynn," Kendrick coaxed.

It was Tuesday night. Flynn slept across her bed like a stretching cat. Viola lay on her side in the space that was left. She could feel his breath steady as a clock against the back of her neck. The shade was not drawn and pale white light drifted in patches on the floor like thin smoke. She lay as rigid and alert as a person awaiting bad news in a doctor's office. It was quiet in the apartment and the smell of burned butter hung over the rooms. She got up, moving carefully, and set the covers back over Flynn. She walked across the cool floor into the living room. Krista's narrow arm hung out of Kendrick's bed, her hand almost touching the rectangle of thin moonlight that trembled on the floor. Kendrick was facing the wall, one arm flung over his head. Viola went on through the curtain to the kitchen. She heated water for tea. While she waited she took the brown envelope out from under the silverware tray and counted the money again. She had six dollars and some pennies: she counted it twice and put it back. The kettle started whistling and she grabbed it quick before it woke the children. Farming work was all she knew. Taking care of chickens, growing tomatoes. She didn't know where to call Mr. Leavitt, ask him did he have any work. Maybe the landlord would know something. She would ask the police tomorrow, did they have a missing man, but she didn't want to tell anybody her husband had gone away and left her.

She sat there long after the tea was drunk. In the silence she could hear her children breathing. How loud they were! As she concentrated on the sound it seemed to grow. How was it they didn't wake themselves? She got up from the table and opened the door to the hall, went through it and out onto the stairway. Down in the yard Mrs. Mitchell's pale blue sheets filled the clotheslines; above the cement wall a door slammed, an angry voice cursed in one of the apartments, a light came on and soon went off again. Viola leaned heavily on the rail to take the weight off her back. The night air was warm and gentle.

When she heard the car she didn't believe it could be the right one; she'd been waiting too long. As she went back through the apartment she moved more quickly until, by the time she reached the threshold of their bedroom, she was running.

And then she was looking down onto the top of his head, and his arm reaching to close the car door. If she'd had a rock in her hand she would have dropped it on him. She hugged herself and swung slightly forward and back and she started crying. He dug into his pockets, one and then the other. Didn't he know the door was open? She watched to see that he was not coming up the front stoop and then she turned and ran back through the apartment. By the time she reached the stairway Kendrick was behind her. She could hear him breathing quickly through his mouth. They didn't speak.

Moonlight was spilling all over the yard. Mrs. Mitchell's sheets shone like water. They heard his feet on the bottom stairs. And then he turned the corner and was on the landing. They were here, anchored in this building, and he was free, coming and going. The top of his head and his shoulders were rising toward them and moonlight was sliding over him like silk.

"Jarvis!" she cried.

He paused and looked toward them. "You're still up," he said, almost annoyed.

"Where were you?" she called down on top of him.

"We're moving to the country," he told them, still climbing. "Back to the country, Viola."

"Where were you!"

"Met a man. Got a little mill makes lobster traps." The higher he climbed the more fully the moonlight fell on him; even his feet shone white now.

"Traps?" She leaned off the top step toward him. "You shouldn't have done that! I thought you weren't coming home. Ever!" She was crouching, her hand reaching out in a fist.

He pulled her up, holding that fist, and put his other hand on her face. "Sweet Christ, Viola. What are you talking about?" he said, his voice harsh. "I got us a house in the country. Say you're glad!" he demanded, shaking her arm.

"Where, Dad?" Kendrick pulled at his sleeve. "When we goin'?"

But Jarvis shook her again. "Say you're glad, Viola. Ain't it what you been wanting?"

She stared into his face and brought her fist up and bored the knuckles of it hard into his chest.

"I thought you'd be glad," he said, and she pushed harder, but he still didn't seem to feel it, just dropped his hand from her shoulder to grip tightly the small bones in her elbow.

She made a strange little sound in her throat and her fist unfolded and she pressed her palm flat against him so she could feel his heart beating.

"Where we goin' to now, Dad?"

LINETTE LEAVING

3 The summer that Logan Pembroke was eleven his mother ran away. Logan was making himself breakfast when she came out of the bedroom and walked through to the kitchen with a suitcase held in her two hands and lifted high against her chest. She was wearing a yellow sleeveless dress. There was a faint stain on the front of it. Ronnie was following her, breathing quick, shallow little breaths high in his chest.

Logan didn't say anything. He was frying eggs. Linette peered out the window at the thermometer. "Seventy-two degrees," she told Ronnie.

"Seventy-two degrees," he said.

She looked at Logan, at his back, which was broad already, at his thick neck; his arm moved and he flipped an egg. "We're going now," she said. "I expect you want to stay here."

Logan took his pan off the heat and turned to her. "Where?" he asked. She didn't look good, her face was very pale and stained under the eyes with dark circles; he'd heard her crying in the night again. No, he did not want to go anywhere with her, her of the tears and the sadness that were an invitation to his father's bullying, and seemed to Logan a kind of disease he sure didn't want to catch. She moved her head and some hair slipped from the barrette that held it on the back of her neck. She had curly black hair with red light in it; it glowed like something alien and exotic above her dull face. She took one hand from her suitcase and brushed at it, trying to twist it back into the barrette. As she was fumbling, Logan stepped forward and took the suitcase from her. He held it as she raised both arms above her head and refastened the clasp. The sun, coming through the glass in the back door, caught in her beautiful hair, danced along the luminous white insides of her lifted arms and in the hair that curled where they met her body. In that moment she was so alive. He stared at her, at her beauty and her mystery; he did not want her to leave. But she lowered her arms and turned to Ronnie. "We better hurry," she told him. "I don't know when he's comin' back."

They went out the door and Logan followed with her suitcase. The morning was very bright and clear. Logan was barefoot; they were wearing sneakers. They went down the driveway past the unmown lawn. There were crows calling loudly somewhere up back in the pine trees. At the road Linette hesitated. Then she took the suitcase from Logan. He was careful that her hand shouldn't touch his. "We'll go this way," she said to Ronnie, and they started off.

He stood and watched. The tar was hot under his feet. Something was moving in his chest and climbing up behind his eyes and Logan did not like it. He glared down the road at them. They looked like children, like two stupid children, and he hated them. Then he remembered his eggs, sitting now greasy in the pan, and he started back up the driveway, hunger turning in his belly like a malady.

It took Linette and Ronnie about two hours to get to the center of Dunham where the minister's house stood next to the wide white church. Mrs. Littlefield had flowers growing along the front; the long screened windows were open. Mrs. Littlefield was out in her garden behind the ell hoeing young tomato plants when Linette and Ronnie came to her door. Her baby was out there with her and the little boy was on the swing.

Ronnie stopped by the door but Linette came on to the garden. "I was hoping to see the reverend," she said to Carole Littlefield.

"How are you, Linette?" Carole pushed her sunhat up off her forehead, looked at Linette and her suitcase, and then pulled it down again.

Linette nodded. "I was just hoping to see the reverend," she said.

"Conrad's away but he'll be back later this afternoon." Carole looked past Linette at Ronnie standing by the door and then down the empty driveway. "Did somebody drop you off?" she asked.

"We walked."

"All the way from your house?"

Linette shrugged.

"Is everything all right at home?" The baby was pulling on her, and Carole bent and took her up.

"Will he be back soon?" Linette asked softly.

"Why don't you come in the house and wait; you look done in."

They sat almost motionless at Carole Littlefield's kitchen table. It was quiet and smelled of the bread she had made that morning. She gave them cool juice to drink. She excused herself to put the children down for their naps but they barely noticed. When she came back into the kitchen Ronnie was asleep with his cheek flattened on her table and Linette was sitting in the chair, her eyes almost closed. Carole came and touched her shoulder. Linette looked up. "It's so quiet here," she said.

When Conrad got home around four-thirty they were asleep in the guest room, their sneakers on the floor, their still bodies flat under the twin spreads. He stood on the threshold of the darkened room and watched them, their vacant faces, the little points their feet made.

"What does she want?" he asked again when they'd retreated to the hall.

"Well, I'm not sure," Carole said. "She wants to see you. But I expect there's something wrong at home. You know what they say about her husband." She shook her head. "They're exhausted. I just think we should let them sleep and you can ask her when they wake up."

It was evening before Gage got home. He parked the truck and came in. He was hungry. He'd had a good day, arranged some deals, done some drinking with the men over at the Curtis farm in Gray. There was a pot of stew on the stove. He got himself a big bowl and sat down with it and the loaf of bread. When he was done he left the table and went into the living room. He sat down in his purple chair and put the radio on. When Logan came in later his father was asleep, slumped in the chair with his mouth hanging open. Logan turned down the radio and climbed the ladder to his bed.

In the morning Gage asked vaguely, "Where the hell is she?" Logan was making himself a cup of coffee. "She went away," he told his father. "On a visit, I think."

"You're shitting me!" Gage accused.

Logan shrugged.

"Who in the hell would she visit?"

He shrugged again, poured canned milk into his coffee.

"Her own people don't want her."

Logan sat down with his mug.

Gage was in the doorway, his face humped up in a frown. "When's she coming back?"

"Don't think she is," Logan told him.

"The hell you say!" Gage banged a chair out from the table and sat down. He glared suspiciously at Logan. "She take that boy with her?"

Logan nodded.

"Goddamn fool," Gage said, sitting back.

Peter Horton was a deacon's son and in Logan's class at school. He came with his father that following Monday. Logan stood behind a pine tree and watched. Their car was a small green sedan that looked almost new. Mr. Horton went up to the house. He was wearing canvas shoes and brown pants with a belt. Logan was surprised when Gage let him through the door. Peter stayed in the car, reading a comic book and chewing gum. Logan came up the drive, not looking at him, and climbed the steps. They were in the kitchen.

Gage was drinking a beer and Mr. Horton had a cup of coffee in front of him. Gage was at that point where he felt content; Logan could read it in his face. "I ain't going to lie to you," he was telling Mr. Horton. His voice was pleasant. "This ain't an easy life. That woman, God bless her"—he made a half-Catholic gesture with his hand—"she works awful hard and she got tired. She needed a vacation. That's what it is, you know. Most people get vacations. Now I'll bet you get a vacation." He smiled at Mr. Horton and leaned back in his chair, waiting for him to answer.

"Well yes, I do," he said after a moment.

Gage smiled benevolently and nodded. "You own the hardware. Don't you?"

Mr. Horton said, "Yes, I do."

"I been there," Gage assured him. "Lots of times. I've bought from you. You got just about everything." He hesitated and then frowned. " 'Cept that one time I needed a big I-bolt and I had to go—"

Mr. Horton straightened in the seat as if he'd been jabbed: "We have a large selection—"

"Where *do* you take your vacation?" Gage interrupted. He glanced up at Logan. "You want to sit down with us, son?" he asked. "This fellow's come here to talk about your mother." He smiled again. "He was about to tell us where he takes his vacation."

"Hello, Logan," Mr. Horton said, turning in the chair to look at him.

"Where?" Gage asked, a little impatience coming into his voice now.

"Well, we go to a lake over by New Hampshire," the deacon said. "My wife's family owns a couple of cottages there."

"A couple," Gage said, pulling his shoulders up high. "That's real nice for you. Ain't that nice?" he said to Logan.

Logan didn't answer. He was still standing almost directly behind Mr. Horton.

"I wish I could take my wife to a lake," Gage said, "but who'd feed the pigs? She done the next best thing. Took herself off to visit with the minister." He beamed, raising his eyebrows and nodding at Mr. Horton. "She's a real religious woman. She knows what the open arms of Jesus mean." He sighed. "I'm just thanking God she's getting such a good rest." He lunged across the table toward Mr. Horton. He was frowning. "I don't begrudge her one second of it. You don't believe I do, do you?" he demanded.

"Well, no. No," Mr. Horton said. He was getting up to leave.

"We miss her! We miss her, the boy and me," Gage insisted. He had gotten up too. He was still leaning over the table and he gestured toward Logan as he spoke. "Ain't easy with her gone. But we want her to have her vacation, so we ain't begrudging her one minute of it!" Mr. Horton was backing toward the door.

Gage stood on the top step and waved him on his way. "Stupid son of a bitch!" he told Logan, his lips twisting over each other to wrap the words in loathing.

Logan went there on his bike. He stopped at the crest of the hill and waited until he saw Reverend Littlefield drive off; then he went down fast and turned into their driveway, his fenderless back wheel kicking up stones. He left the bike in the corner where the ell met the house, and he knocked on the back door.

Carole Littlefield didn't know who it was on the other side of her screen, so he told her. "Oh," she said, and opened it.

She led him into her front room, where his mother was sitting in a small rocking chair by a window. Ronnie was on the floor building blocks with Jimmy Littlefield. When Linette saw Logan she smiled at him as if he were a stranger. She rocked a little. She looked very tired but immensely calm. Ronnie got onto his feet and moved closer to his mother. "Hi, Logan," he said carefully.

Logan could feel Mrs. Littlefield behind him. He twisted his shoulders a bit, and Carole called Jimmy to her and they left the room. "I've come to take you home, Ma," he said, stepping close to her and keeping his voice low. She was still wearing that yellow dress, but Mrs. Littlefield must have got the stain out. Her hair was as dull as if it had been dyed.

She looked at him and her face became sad and then fearful and then pouty like a child's. "You can ride my bike," he told Ronnie without looking at him, "and I'll walk her."

"It's too big," Ronnie protested.

"You don't got to sit down," Logan said. He was watching Linette. She raised her face and looked at him, her eyes pleading.

"It's quiet here," she said. "I'm helping out. I ain't a burden."

He wanted to punch her face and break her arms. How could she sit there like that and let them shame her, shame her! It was as if she were in the center of a crowd: they with their laughing, jeering faces, spittle on their lips; she some kind of naked joke thinking she was dressed pretty. And he had to wade through them, pushing their backs apart, through the combined stench of their contempt and his shame, to take her away from their eyes. He stepped forward and grabbed a hold of her wrist and jerked her to her feet so that the chair was left rocking by itself. "You'll be all right," he told her, his voice raw with hatred and pity. He pulled her to the door and nodded that she was to go on ahead of him. He didn't even look at Ronnie.

He carried her suitcase for her. The day was hot. Ronnie pushed the bicycle, and every time he complained Logan rushed forward and landed the suitcase hard between his shoulder blades. It was midafternoon when they reached home. Logan left them without even going in the house first. He went off into the overgrown field beyond the driveway. He walked until he was tired and his throat burned with thirst, but he went in large circles so he could see, peering through leaves and raspberry briers, if she should take up her suitcase and start off down the driveway again.

THE STATE BOYS

4

Where the Rudge family went to was North Royal. They rented there from a dairy farmer named Gordon Cord, who ran the place with his wife, Marvina. The tenant house was down the hill from the farm, separated from it by a neglected orchard. When they arrived in June the apple blossoms had fallen and the earth under the twisted old trees was covered in the glossy petals. Their little house was close to the road and a chest blocked the front door. The inaccessible screened-in porch hung crookedly from the face of the building, the planks were stove in and mingling with the clay beneath. There were two rooms. An enclosed stairway led to narrow bedrooms under the eaves, where the children slept. The back porch was open and overlooked the shed and the outhouse, the rising fields, and the woods. Viola walked out after supper, past the orchard, past the white farmhouse whose long ell ran to the barn, past Marvina Cord's garden. She walked slowly under the old trees that lined the road; she went in the falling light, which, reaching through maple leaves, fanned between the knobbly trunks and lay like silk upon the boggy area stretching toward pines on the far side of the road. The light touching there on the reeds and the thick, flat grasses haloed the rounded hummocks, blazed on the purple water. Viola stopped on her way to gather flowers and they rose about her throat, small white bells and spiky lavender stalks, yellow weeds graceful as lilies. She came back through the orchard, through the heavy smell of the trees, their new fruit tight buds. She climbed the steps holding her flowers and the night fell down gently, as it does when the summer is new.

The Cords had two state boys named Hewitt. They were nine and seven, their names were Frederick and Daniel. They worked on the farm, they slept upstairs in the attic. Whenever the Rudge children approached them they ran away, then stood at a distance and watched, their faces as impassive as the faces of soldiers in ancient statuary.

"They're out there again tonight," Krista complained one hot evening early in July. "They're always sneaking around." She spooned mustard onto her hot dog. Kendrick stretched up high in his chair and looked through the window. He saw them standing like shadows in the dreamy light of evening, the older one in front and his brother an indistinct shape just behind him.

"Go ask them to come in," Jarvis told him.

But Viola reached out and touched his arm. "Wait until we've finished eating, son," she said.

"Well, invite 'em for dessert," Jarvis insisted.

Kendrick finished his plate and hurried outdoors. "They won't come in," Krista called after him, twisting around in her chair. "You can ask 'em but they won't ever come in."

"He works them kids like animals," Jarvis said.

Viola was cutting Flynn's hot dog into small bites. "That ain't right but it's none of our business," she told him. Jarvis looked over her head and out the window, where he could see Kendrick hurrying up the hill into the orchard. One boy stood up straighter as he approached; the little one shifted close until he vanished behind his brother. Then Kendrick turned and they were following him down through the orchard while behind them the cows were moving the other way, through the high grass toward the barn, their big bodies almost disappearing as they passed from where the sunset caught them into the shadow cast by the barn. "Here they come!" Jarvis said to Krista.

"This is Freddie and Daniel," Kendrick explained as they crowded into the room behind him.

"Come and sit." Viola lifted her hand from Flynn's shoulder and gestured toward the table. "Kendrick, bring the stool from the porch."

They moved forward in a kind of lurching motion and the taller one sat down. The little one leaned against him, half perched on the edge of the seat. "We're glad to be finally meeting you boys," Jarvis told them.

Kendrick put the stool down next to them. "You want this?" he asked Daniel. Daniel's chin was pointing at his chest. He shook his head slowly, as if it weighed a lot, and so Kendrick climbed up on the stool.

"We got cobbler," Viola said, putting her blue dish on the table. They watched it. Their heads were shaved down to nearly nothing, a dark shadow with the skin showing through and a few scabs where the razor got them. She set glasses of milk before them and then cut the cobbler. When she handed them the plates their glasses were empty. White curving marks like school paste stood above their narrow lips. Jarvis refilled their glasses while she served the family.

"You boys lived here long?" he asked.

Freddie hesitated with the fork almost to his mouth. Then he nodded. "Two years," he said. "We're going home though. Sometime. Pretty soon," he said, and ate. They had on gray overalls, and the metal adjustments were pulled up so far they shone dully on their backs. The lamplight glowed in the hollows between their quill-like collarbones.

"Well," Jarvis told them, "we were real pleased to see kids living here when we moved in. It's good to have neighbors."

Freddie looked at him; then he bent and scraped up the remains of the cobbler with his fork. "We got more pie?" Jarvis asked Viola, but she shook her head. The boys watched the empty dish.

"Sorry I can't offer you seconds," Viola said. Freddie looked at her. There were purple stains on his lips. His tongue went out, touching them, as he studied her face, the way her hair fell along the side of her neck. Her voice was slow and reminded him of music.

"It was good," he told her softly.

Daniel was watching him. Then he twisted his neck, and his head shot forward and he threw up everything back into his plate. He barely made a noise except a final, retching sound at the end.

"Oooop!" Flynn gasped. Krista cried out and clapped her hand over her mouth. Jarvis rose from the table, holding his plate high.

Viola reached her cloth from the sink. "No harm done, it was an accident," she said, but they were gone, quick as light and as silent.

"It's okay," Jarvis called. "Come back!" The screen door made a soft tap as it swung back and closed. He looked out the window to see them disappearing into the orchard. "Jesus," he said, and looked at his wife.

"He just ate too fast," she told him.

"Those kids act like they're starving!"

Viola started working the pump to wash Daniel's mess down the sink. Kendrick brought their glasses to her. "I'm sorry, Mum," he said.

"It's no one's fault. Poor little boy," she said, and smiled at Kendrick.

When they'd cleaned up, Kendrick followed her out onto the back porch. They stood with their elbows leaning on the railing and looked. The broad field rolled slowly toward the woodland. The dips were black but the tops of the hills caught the final glimmering as silveriness weaving among the grasses. There were a few very small stars close to the dark trees as if emerging from them. They looked cool and sharply cut, traveling above the almost solid shape of the woods. Viola sighed and breathed in the sweet odors of the evening: grass and the orchard trees, the smell of water in the small stream that flowed past the shed, cows and turned earth. Fireflies began flashing in the field, their light of the same shape and beauty as the light in the stars that fled from the woods. And they heard little frogs, and cow voices from behind the Cords' barn where they waited, the night mist beginning to shift about their black-and-white bodies.

* * *

Krista left Flynn sitting on the back porch taking his stones from one can and putting them into another. When she went he looked up. He was holding a smooth green stone in his palm. Krista hurried. The boys were crossing the road and going into the bog, entering it opposite the farmhouse where it was shallowest. Kendrick had the rope. They followed close behind, Freddie and then Daniel. They were carrying old boards they had taken from the tumbledown shed beyond the Cords' barn. Krista slipped among the tall shiny grasses. She was trying to stay on hummocks. Red-winged blackbirds perching on the tallest reeds trilled like insects. The boys went on steadily, sloshing through dark water. Krista, waving her arm to shoo bugs, fell off a hummock, her foot sinking into black, oozy mud. She shrieked and hopped to the next grassy mound. It was just past noon and the sun was hot. She turned once to look toward home. In the long field the cows stood with their faces in the grass and their cordlike tails flipping to slap against their ribs. When she looked back, Daniel was entering the piny woods that rose above the bog.

It was hot in the woods and still. The light where it streamed among the boughs was yellow. It smelled dry and the only sounds were creatures: the voices of birds, the sharp tapping of a woodpecker, insects buzzing. Krista went up through the small pines and on to where they grew tall, their long bodies straight, their limbs beginning high above the forest floor and stretching out against the sky. She continued to climb and then she was in maples and then a few birches shimmered higher and higher. The long, slender trunks rippled like the bodies of piebald ponies; the leaves, flickering in the light, were bright green. When Krista stopped to rest she heard a voice: Kendrick giving orders. She went on quickly, climbing higher, treading on old birch leaves.

The oak was on a flat table of ground at the crest of the hill. It was a tall tree, thick-trunked, the bark ribbed like an old hide. The branches went out parallel with the earth and then curved upward to hold the thick, shiny leaves into the light. Krista stood behind a spruce and watched.

They were building a tree hut, passing those old shed boards up to Kendrick, who sat astride one of the branches and hauled them with his rope. "Gimme another one!" he called. Daniel stood back, watching as Freddie tied the next board on and lifted. When Krista stepped out from behind the spruce he reached and tugged on Freddie's overalls.

"Hi, Krista," Freddie said when he turned and saw her.

"What you doing?"

"We're making a tree hut." Daniel looked at the ground and kicked leaves. Kendrick leaned down over his branch, his face red.

"What do you want, Krista!"

"I can help," she said loudly. She started swinging her arms.

"We don't need you." He dropped the rope. "Tie another one on, Freddie," he said.

The board started up. Krista jumped forward and lifted it with Freddie, standing on tiptoe to reach. Daniel settled onto his haunches and picked up a small branch. He threw it at her and it bounced off her knee.

"You quit it, Daniel!" she said, turning on him, her finger pointing.

Daniel looked at the ground.

"Don't holler at him," Freddie said. He'd stepped closer to Daniel.

"Then you tell him to quit throwing things at me." She backed up and started swinging her arms again.

"He didn't mean no harm."

"Krista, go home," Kendrick demanded, leaning out of the tree. He looked big hanging into space like that. "You're causing trouble. Go home!"

Krista looked at the ground. Then she turned and started down the slope. She could hear their hammers banging as she passed under the maple trees.

She didn't return until the light was coming in wide bands that swarmed under the limbs of trees and plunged sideways through the grass. She trotted across the road and moved steadily through the bog, some of the hummocks familiar to her now. Frogs jumping into the water scared her and she gave out little shrieks as she went. There were blue-headed dragonflies coursing low over the purplish water, there were brown butterflies in the small pines where it was hot. The tall trees dropped long shadows, a small breeze was shifting their feathery limbs. The birches leaned like resting horses, their leaves glowing in the long light. In the maples the voices of birds were loud. She went up, up, toward the spruce grove and she could hear the boys laughing.

"I'm the furthest!" Kendrick shouted.

She stepped out from the fringes of the spruces and came to stand where the longest reaches of the oak's limbs fluttered above her head.

They stood on their platform about eight feet above the ground. The slanting light swam through the leaves and patted on Kendrick's brown chest and the round little shoulders of the state boys where they stood—in profile to her, with their toes hooked over the edge—and peed in long curving arcs onto dry oak leaves. Their water made quick pattering sounds like mice feet. The little one, holding himself and peeing onto the forest floor, laughed as loudly as the big boys. Krista put her hand on her hips. She tipped forward on her toes and watched them.

"You!" she yelled, and they wheeled toward her.

"You!" and their hands flashed across the front of their pants. "You . . . you *boys!*"

They jumped up and down on their platform and whooped at her like Tarzan, then scooped up acorns collected in a pile at their feet and threw them. They fell like pebbles on the dry leaves; as Krista turned to run, two caught her between the shoulder blades.

She sped through the spruce trees and down the hill and into the birches. On through the maple trees and down until she came to the tall pines that grew with green moss like a fallen veil around their roots. There she stopped and looked behind her defiantly, waiting for the sound of their feet. She stood there trying to catch her breath and the wind sang through the tall trees, and long shafts from the descending sun reached onto the mossy floor and all the golden light shimmered. As her heart began to slow down she heard birds. She saw them. Two birds, large as robins and dull red in color. They swooped through the trees calling in soft, quick voices. They rose and fell, one chasing the other. They flew in a wider and wider pattern until they disappeared in the long light and were gone.

In the quiet they left behind them she went on. She was tired and home was far away. She wished she hadn't come out at all but stayed there with Flynn moving stones. But as she was leaving the tall trees one of the birds flashed in front of her and began to climb. Krista was in motion, and the motion carried her beyond the last tree just as the pursuing bird swept past. The tip of its wing, or maybe only the small storm of air its wing set up, brushed her cheek. It was a touch of such delicacy and power that Krista stopped still. The bird soared after its mate; higher they went, and higher, into the feathery trees.

When she came up the back steps she could hear her mother in the kitchen, water flowing, dishes tapping against each other. She opened the door and slipped in. "Star!" Flynn called. He was sitting in his father's big chair holding two cans full of stones.

Viola looked up. She was stirring batter for muffins. The long silver tin was on the table beside her. "I was starting to worry about you," she said.

Krista stepped closer to the table. Viola swept the spoon around the bowl. It made a soft scraping sound. "Something happened, Mum," Krista said.

"What?" Viola's spoon went round and round.

"Guess!" Krista said. She put one arm behind her back and rocked slowly on the balls of her feet.

"I can't guess," Viola said. "You tell me."

Krista smiled and stretched up high on her toes. "A bird patted me," she told her mother.

The next week Krista went to lunch at the farmhouse. "You sure she asked you?" Viola checked again.

Krista nodded. "Freddie said."

Viola watched as she started up through the orchard; then she turned back to the stove. Flynn had a summer cold and she was making him soup. She didn't like the way he was coughing.

Krista entered the kitchen behind the boys. She looked around. There was a big yellow clock with red hands hanging on the wall above the broad table. There was a salt and pepper set like a hen and rooster. There was chewed-up red linoleum that caught at her toes as she went forward. The stove was huge and gleamed like teeth. The air smelled like bacon. Mrs. Cord came through the door from the next room. She was huge—bigger than the principal at the school in Portland, bigger than Mrs. Mitchell. She had on a flowered housedress that was longer in back and her feet bulged over her sneakers. She looked down at Krista. "You're the tenant's daughter, ain't you?" she said. Her voice was high and loud.

Krista looked at her feet.

"She is," Freddie told her.

Marvina went to her stove. The flesh on her arm shook as she stirred something in a pot there. Freddie opened a can of tomato soup and dumped it in a pan and added water and stirred. He put it on the stove. Krista and Daniel stood near the table and watched him. Freddie moved quietly around Mrs. Cord's back. She kept on stirring. Her hair was as dark as water in a well; it was pulled back tight and wound in a bun. Freddie got out white bowls and filled them with soup. He brought them to the table and they sat down. Marvina crossed from the stove to the cupboard near the door to get a box of salt. The floor shook as she passed. Daniel carried the crackers to Krista. Then he walked around the table and got back on his chair. Krista's neck was on a level with the tabletop. She spooned her soup carefully, her elbow cocked up in the air so she could get at it. She rustled in the wax paper and pulled out a saltine. Mrs. Cord crossed the room again. Everything shook. She got somewhere behind Krista and started chopping.

"Can I have the crackers?" Freddie said, and Krista pushed the package toward him. He knelt up in his chair to reach. Then he crushed some in his hands and sifted them into his bowl. He gave the box to Daniel, who crushed three of his own. Krista watched the boys as she spooned up more soup. Somewhere behind her the knife was working hard. Freddie got the saltines and put more of them into his soup. And more of them. A pile began to rise up in his bowl. Then the floor was shaking beneath Krista's chair, and she turned her head. Mrs. Cord was at the sink. The water came on hard and then was shut off abruptly. Krista stared at the bun on the back of Mrs. Cord's neck. It looked like a curled-up hose that had been driven in there with a nail. Mrs. Cord's big arm rose. She took down a red fly swatter that was hanging from a cup hook on the windowsill. She slapped three times and the flesh on her arm jiggled. When Krista looked in front of her Daniel had a big mound of saltine flakes in his bowl. The floor shook and there was the Whomp! Whomp! Whomp! of the knife again. Krista ate more soup, and then heard Daniel giggling softly. He was watching his brother. Freddie had his mouth wide open and his tongue was out. There was a big blob of pinkish saltines on it. Daniel giggled louder. He spooned up from his own bowl until he had a mouthful like Freddie's. They both started laughing, making funny muffled sounds. Daniel spit everything back into his bowl and they laughed harder. Their shoulders jerked up and down, their laughter came out squeaky.

SMACK! Krista jumped as Marvina Cord brought the fly swatter down hard on the table next to Freddie. She raised it and battered at his head. He lifted his arms around his skull and closed his eyes tight. Marvina Cord hit him harder. She lashed at his shoulders and the back of his neck and his head, which he was covering with his raised arms. There was on her face a look as steady and interested as any marksman's. She lunged along the table and started in on Daniel. She hit his head and his bent back and she flung her arm out straight and hit Freddie across his face. Her raised black eyebrows curved across her red forehead. She slapped Daniel again, quick as a striking snake, and one cry came from him. "Mr. Cord hears 'bout you wasting food like this, playing around like idiots, you'll be sorry you ever thought of it," she told them in a loud, slow voice. She stood still with her arm lifted and her eyebrows settling slowly in one straight line. She looked from one of them to the other, just shifting her eyes to do so. They sat still with their heads hanging down. Krista bent her own head. Then the floor shook and the knife started up, WHOMP! WHOMP! WHOMP!

It fell in even strokes. The boys grinned in front of them and raised their spoons. Krista watched them as they ate more; they ate quickly. Freddie's cheek had an imprint like webbing on it. A red line oozed on his top lip. "Do you want more crackers, Krista?" he asked her in a high, clear voice, struggling to push the few that were left toward her. Daniel sat with his face hanging over the bowl, his hand moving the spoon, his nose and his eyes running. There was a dent in his cheek. Freddie knelt in his chair to push the crackers until they touched Krista's bowl.

"Thanks, Freddie," she whispered. She looked into her bowl. It was half empty. She tried another spoonful. She swallowed and set the spoon in the bowl without letting it make any noise. "I better go home now," she said softly. "My mother wants me." She rose carefully. They watched her. She worked to push her chair in. They watched her while she backed up. She turned toward the windows, away from the center of the room. She could hear the knife coming down hard as she got through the door.

* * *

The children came along the field from Creeley's stepping high through the grass, berry boxes in their red-stained fingers. Daniel's was nearly empty. He was chewing as he followed Freddie.

"My mother will make shortcake," Kendrick said.

"With whipped cream," Krista told them.

They waded across the stream that bounded the pasture from the yard and came up the slope toward the house, carrying their baskets carefully. Jarvis stood watching them. He'd taken off his shirt and was mopping his face with it.

"Mrs. Creeley let us pick, Dad," Kendrick called.

"Raspberries!" Krista cried.

He waited until they were closer. He looked at Kendrick. "You take my hammer?"

Kendrick stopped and the other children crowded behind him.

"DID YOU take my hammer?"

"I put it back. A couple of weeks ago."

"Ain't here." Jarvis stepped closer. "Ain't where it's s'posed to be." He took another step so that his toe was touching Kendrick's. Freddie backed up until he was walking on Daniel. "I told you not to take my stuff. Ever! You lost my goddamn hammer!"

"I didn't!"

"You lost that goddamn hammer! I got to fix that step so somebody don't get killed"—he jerked his arm out, gesturing toward the porch—"and YOU lost my goddamn hammer!"

Kendrick backed away from him. "I didn't," he said, but softly. Freddie started to detour around the outhouse, Daniel following him. They stopped and looked back. Daniel crowded against Freddie and put a berry in his mouth.

"You're a goddamn careless kid. Stay the hell out of my tools!" Jarvis told him before he twisted around and made for the house.

Kendrick thrust the box of berries at Krista and ran. He ran straight out over the lawn and across the road and into the bog. His feet made small sucking sounds in the mud. He was crying.

Jarvis stomped up over the broken step. Viola was standing at the door watching him. "He's got to learn, Viola!" Jarvis said loudly through the screen. "He better stay the hell out of my stuff!"

Flynn was pressing against her. She was peeling a banana for him.

"You could break your leg on that step. How the hell am I going to fix it now!"

Viola patted Flynn's shoulder and broke off some of the banana and fed it to him.

Jarvis mopped at his face and his armpits with his rolled-up shirt. "I'll have to ask that bastard Cord to let me borrow his hammer."

Viola turned and went back into the kitchen with Flynn. Jarvis glared at the empty screen before stomping down one step and sitting with his legs hanging over the broken one. He kicked at it and stove it in some more, then lit a cigarette and looked out across the field.

The sun pressed against the earth like a paw on a bird; the cows were bunched under the elm trees. Viola sent Krista to him with a glass of beer. She came quietly and set it down near him, then retreated. Jarvis nearly knocked it over with his elbow when he turned and it was there. He drank it, got to his feet, and went up through the orchard.

Viola kept a big piece of shortcake for Kendrick. The moon was rising when he came home, the hammer was hanging from his hand. He put it on the table and sat down. Jarvis came in from the front room. "It's a good thing you found it," he said.

Kendrick didn't speak. He broke off a piece of shortcake with his fork and put it in his mouth. Jarvis was standing back, almost in the doorway. "You ask me you want something," he said. "You can use my stuff but you ask me first."

Kendrick was watching his plate. He nodded.

Jarvis stepped forward and picked up the hammer. He looked at it. "How big's your tree house?" he asked.

Kendrick shrugged. "Not too big."

"You got a roof on it?"

He nodded.

Jarvis watched him but Kendrick was still looking at his plate. He broke off another piece of shortcake and put it in his mouth. Jarvis turned and went from them into the front room. "You want your supper now?" Viola asked. "I gave you the dessert first, sweeten you up," she teased, stroking the back of his head.

"He was right," Kendrick said. "I did leave his hammer out there."

* * *

In the farmhouse, in the unfinished attic, hot in the summer like a breathless pit, the state boys slept. They lay together in an old iron bed, on their backs, their arms flung out. The light from the late-rising moon fell upon the stained mattress and quivered about their narrow feet. Beyond the window a little blur glowing at the end of the orchard was Viola's lamp.

Marvina Cord sat downstairs in her living room with her thick feet up on an old upholstered hassock and a magazine open on her thighs. Her hand rustled in a box of chocolates, and insects threw themselves against her screens. Sucking on a hazelnut, she lifted the magazine and held it closer to her face to read about an operation to separate Siamese twins. Gordon Cord lay on the couch with the toes of his sweat-stained socks pointing at the ceiling. His jaw hung open on his neck, which was like turtle skin; his snoring sounded damaging to the inside of his head. Marvina glanced at him, then studied her magazine. She frowned. It was hard to believe there were so many feet of guts in a baby. In each one of 'em. She touched her own belly with the flat of her hand. She slowly rubbed.

Gordon raked air across the back of his throat, half gagged, and sat up. He pivoted on the sofa until his feet hit the floor, and he glared at Marvina. "You got dessert or what?" he said. His voice was quick and querulous. He had a long face, pale around the mouth and red where his cheekbones pulled the skin taut.

"I got raspberries with cream." She was still reading. "Tells here 'bout babies born stuck together," she said, making a small gesture with the magazine. She looked at the space in front of her. "Sharing their guts," she said meditatively.

"Huh?" he grunted. He stared at the floor between his feet and breathed loudly through his open mouth.

Marvina brought in the tray and set it on the table. She stirred sugar and canned milk into his coffee. He frowned at the big dish of berries. "You want sugar, bowl's right there," she told him. He plunged with the spoon. They ate fast and without talking. The insects flapped like bats against the screens. Above them Daniel shifted on the mattress and his thumb slipped from his mouth. He pressed his sweaty head into his brother's shoulder.

DANIEL

5 The summer ended quickly: nights cooling by the third week of August; day colors deepened; winds drew billowing clouds white as souls. At night the sky was sharp with stars and among their number sped the dying, as swift in their fall as hawks. September came: leaves turning, crickets throbbing; blackbirds flocked; tomato plants shoulder-high turned charred and limp, collapsed on themselves, their fruit gone pulpy—all in the quickness of one cold night. The children waited in front of the farmhouse for the school bus, their jackets zipped, warm hats flattening their hair. By noon recess they ran bare-armed and sweaty, sand tightening the fit of their shoes. Kendrick was in fifth grade; Freddie, who'd stayed back, was in third. Krista entered Mrs. Pollard's second grade holding on to Daniel's damp hand.

In Mrs. Pollard's room was a bulletin board covered with pictures of old-time New England autumnal scenes; there was the smell of chalk, the waxy odor of crayons; there was Mrs. Pollard's firm voice and the high, busy voices of the children. Viola kept Flynn home with her. He watched out the window as the yellow bus went by and then he came into the kitchen. "Mou, allgaw," he said. With a pencil he drew little stones on the papers that Krista brought home and he kept them under his bed in neat rows.

Daniel didn't speak to anyone and he couldn't do what the teacher told him, just sat there with his head down. But that wasn't the worst trouble for Daniel. On the day Krista brought her doll Rebecca Jane to school it happened for the first time. Krista was worrying about her, how she was leaning on a shelf above the coat hooks where Mrs. Pollard said she had to stay until recess. Her neck was bent and every time Krista looked at her it seemed Rebecca Jane was about to fall off that shelf. Mrs. Pollard got cross. "Do your work, Krista," she said, "or from now on your doll will have to stay at home." Krista hunched over her paper, holding her pencil tightly.

When she looked up again from her math sheet it was because the room was dead quiet: None of the children was erasing, or sighing, or shifting in his seat. They were looking at Daniel. Krista couldn't see anything but the back of his head. It was tipped forward. His shoulders looked real stiff. She waited. Mrs. Pollard was helping somebody across the room and the light from the windows settled around her like a thin dress. She straightened slowly, her eyes on Amy Morin's paper. "Daniel!" the children were gasping. "Daniel!" They got louder. "Mrs. Pollard, *Daniel!*" they called in exaggerated whispers. Mrs. Pollard crossed in front of the room and came down the aisle. When she stopped beside his desk Daniel didn't raise his head. His shoulders tightened further. "Daniel, come with me," she said. Her voice was low: Krista had to lean forward to hear her. He didn't move. Mrs. Pollard reached down and shook his shoulder gently. "Daniel," she said, "I'll help you."

He worked his way slowly out of the chair. They went down the aisle and the only sound in the room was Mrs. Pollard's skirt rustling like wrapping paper around her legs. Her hand was cupping the back of Daniel's head, carefully, as if it were an egg. He was twisting his shoulder, in toward his body, away from her, but her fingertips stayed there, on his hair, lightly. "I have to step out," Mrs. Pollard told them as she turned in the doorway, her eyes going up and down the rows, her hand spread over Daniel. His chin was pulled into his chest, his eyes were closed, he was turned toward her now so if he opened them all he would see was her blue skirt. "These problems should be done by the time I get back," Mrs. Pollard instructed them. Then their feet went down the hall—an even, soft slap-slap of her shoes and the slow scuffing of Daniel's. Children got out of their seats and crowded around to look at the puddle under Daniel's chair.

It didn't happen every day, but often, and he'd leave with Mrs. Pollard and come back wearing different pants culled from the Lost and Found, rolled up at the bottom or riding above his socks. The children stopped talking about it. They barely looked when Mrs. Pollard and Daniel left the room together, her hand a gentleness on his shoulder.

They made masks for Halloween. Krista was gluing ears on hers. She had squeezed out too much Elmer's and they kept sliding around. She bit down on her lip and tried to press an ear back in place but when she took her hand away the ear came up stuck onto her fingers. "If you have more glue than you want, come get a Kleenex and wipe away the extra," Mrs. Pollard called. Krista got out of her seat and went to her.

Mrs. Pollard smiled and held out the box. Krista was turning with three Kleenexes in her fist, when there was a terrible sound at the back of the room and the door burst open.

"Here you are!" a voice bawled: "D-rrry pants! You ask for it you get it!"

Krista pulled her arms against her sides and watched as Mrs. Cord stomped down the aisle toward Mrs. Pollard's desk. She was waving a paper bag in her hand; children ducked under its sweep. Pushed low onto her forehead by the black bun of her hair was a red painter's hat. She wore a thick gray dress and a long, dark blue cardigan sweater. "Diapers!" she screeched. "Rubber pants!"

She pulled up in front of Mrs. Pollard's desk, reared back on her heels, and swept the bag through the air in one final arc. Krista retreated until the chalk tray was pressing against her neck.

"In school he's your problem!" Mrs. Cord hollered, leaning over the books on the front of the desk, her eyebrows drawn together like a streak of black paint under the visor of her hat. "I don't wanna hear about it!" She snatched items out of the bag and slapped them down on the desk. "You can't handle it, you shouldn't be here!" she told Mrs. Pollard.

The back of Mrs. Pollard's neck was red. She stood partway out of her chair as Mrs. Cord peered into the bag to be sure it was empty and then flung it into the air. It swerved by the desk and descended, making a soft scratching sound as it skidded on the floor near Krista's shoes. Lurching around sharply, she stomped back down the aisle. Her pink sneakers smacked over the linoleum and sounded like flat tires rolling on. No child lifted his face until she was beyond him. At the door she stopped and twisted around. "No more phone calls!" she bellowed before she stalked out into the hall.

Mrs. Pollard reached to pick the bag up off the floor. It crackled stiffly as she opened it. She put the things into it and placed it under her desk. Then she came around in front of the class. "Children," she said, her hand patting at the front of her blouse, "I'm very sorry that happened to interrupt our day." Her voice was shaking. Krista stepped toward her. Mrs. Pollard was white except for high on her cheeks where the color burned. "Sometimes," she said, speaking faster, "sometimes people don't behave very well. Even grown-up people." She looked around the room, her eyes skimming over the tops of their heads. "Now let's finish our masks; we have some time before the bus." She cleared her throat. "Who needs help? Raise your hand."

Krista walked slowly back to her seat, the Kleenex rolled up tight in her fist. Daniel's arms were wrapped around his stomach and each hand held an elbow. He was rocking, his folded arms brushing against the edge of the desktop, his eyes almost closed, a funny smile on his face. His chair was squeaking softly, like the metal hasp of a clothesline twitching on a gusty day.

The year drew on; the afternoons were darkening when they climbed down off the bus. Freddie and Daniel went to their chores, trotting hurriedly up the driveway, their clothes shuffling around their narrow bodies. Marvina stood, eager to tell them what to do, her arms folded on her chest, her breath moistening the glass of the shed door. Kendrick and Krista came down through the orchard, where the trees stood cramped and bent waiting for the winter. The sky beyond the little house, rising from the field and the wood line, was grey and still. Then the snow came and softened the world, tree shadows lying across it like strokes from a fine-tipped brush.

"Mum, can Freddie and Daniel come and see the tree?" Krista asked.

Viola was stamping out shapes with a cookie cutter. Flynn stood on the chair beside her trying to get his finger into the bowl. "When did you want them to come?" she asked.

"Now," Krista said.

"What about tomorrow afternoon?"

Gordon Cord stomped between the orchard trees. His dark winter coat was falling loose from his high shoulders, his long bare head was held a little to one side. His fingers, hanging below the coat cuffs, were red. The snowfall was not yet deep, the sky was silver-colored, the sun was setting behind the farm. Marvina was coming too. She moved more slowly. There was a dark kerchief tied around her hair. The boys were following behind them, making a different way through the trees, and as they got nearer they began to run. Krista turned from the window. "Mum, the Cords is bringing them," she said, almost whispering.

Viola looked up quickly. "What are you talking about!" she said, and hurried to the window. "Oh my God! What did you tell them?"

"I didn't . . ." But Viola was turning to reach for her coffeepot.

Freddie pressed close to her as he came in. She smelled like warm food and soap. She looked into his face. "We've been watching for you," she told him. He lingered, pressing close; her voice was joyful-sounding, her words were praise. But Daniel was bumping against his back. Freddie moved into the house and then he could smell the tree.

"Come see the tree!" Krista cried, pointing to the front room. "Come on, Daniel!"

"Yil, come. Yil!" Flynn urged, taking his hand.

Viola was unzipping Daniel's jacket, rubbing his cold cheek. "Wait just a minute, Flynn," she said. Daniel was staring up at her, watching her mouth move. He twitched as Gordon and Marvina stomped into the house. "Merry Christmas," Viola said. "I'll have coffee in a minute. Come sit down. There's cookies."

"Can't stay long," Gordon chafed. "Chores, chores to do." He looked sharply around the kitchen, motioned at Marvina, and lunged for the table.

"Jarvis will be home soon," Viola said, setting mugs down in front of them. She was relieved to hear the percolator start tapping. "I'll be right back," she said, and went into the front room with a plate of cookies for the children.

"Dee." Flynn was pulling him to his crèche, which was his dearest possession. He touched Daniel's face. "Yil," he almost whispered, and carefully lifted up a tiny ox to show them.

"I'm hoping for a sled," Kendrick told them.

"That's nice, Flynn." Freddie touched the ox's horn. Daniel didn't notice. He was watching Viola coming toward them with a plate of cookies.

"Here you are," she said, setting it on the little table. "Now come in the kitchen and get your eggnog."

They followed her and took the glasses, returning slowly to the tree in a line, Daniel last and pausing to sip from his glass.

"It's ready," Viola said, taking the coffee from the stove. "What do you take in it?"

"Cream-sugar, cream-sugar," Gordon said.

"But canned milk'll do," Marvina told her.

Viola sat down with the Cords, who were hunched over her table in their dark clothes. There were cookie crumbs around their elbows, their lips had bits stuck on. They drank the hot coffee as if they were hungry for it. "Children sure love Christmas," she said.

"Every day's the same on a farm." Gordon drank noisily and snapped at a cookie in quick little bites.

"I s'pose so. Well, I bet you've got a big tree up there with all the room you have," Viola suggested.

"You wanna look at trees go out and stand in the woods." Gordon laughed with a clotted, wet sound and nodded his head at Marvina.

"Needles make a mess everywhere," she said as her hand went out for another cookie. "Started a lot of fires, trees in houses. Burned up old Mrs. Holland last year." And she nodded, pursing her lips so a little crumb fell off. She skewered it with her fingertip and put it on her tongue. "Didn't even get out the bed, fire caught her so quick," she said.

"The poor soul!" Viola gasped.

"I told her." Gordon's voice was deep, accusatory.

"His aunt," Marvina explained, nodding and gesturing toward him with her thumb. "Weren't she?"

"No sense a-tall," he said loudly. He stood up, hunching his shoulders to settle the coat on them. His hand went forward and hung over the plate, then traveled to his coat pocket. "Come on," he told Marvina. He turned toward the front room. "Time to go," he announced loudly.

The boys came to the doorway and looked for Viola. "I'm sorry you have to leave so quick," she said. "But you come again." She gathered their jackets and helped Daniel with his. Then she gave him a box. "You share these with Freddie," she told him. He held it against himself and stared up at her.

"Can't they stay, Mum?" Krista begged, pulling on Viola's fingers.

"They have to go," she said. "You get their presents, quick now."

Gordon was stomping down the steps. Marvina, the box of cookies Viola had given Daniel under her arm, thumped after him.

"Merry Christmas," Viola told the boys as they went through the door.

The big dark figures and the little boys struggling up the hill after them merged in the spidery shades of the orchard. The sun was gone, there was no color left in the sky. Viola hugged Flynn against her. Then she turned to Kendrick. "You're right!" she said, laughing. "Those people are awful!"

Beyond the glass it was night. The window was rattling in its casing. Freddie Hewitt woke up. Spring was coming but the attic was horribly cold yet and he didn't want to leave the bed. He postponed, half dozing, and then finally he rose. Daniel followed him. Down the steep dark stairs they went to the narrow front hall, Freddie holding his arms out so Daniel wouldn't tumble past him. They went through the living room, past the red glow of the stove, on through the dining room to the kitchen. Marvina wouldn't let them keep a bucket upstairs to pee in—she said boys were nasty enough as it was. Freddie hurried; his bladder was like a sharp stone in him. But Daniel didn't get past the kitchen.

He pulled a chair out, quick as an elf or a burglar.

"Come with me," Freddie whispered, turning at the threshold. "Stay out of her stuff. Come with me!"

But Daniel was climbing up.

"Come with me!" He had to go; he was starting to pee right there. He shuffled down the long dark corridor of the ell toward the privy.

Daniel reached for the latch on Marvina Cord's cupboard. The glow in the glass door of the kitchen stove lit his work. His hand sought the tin. He had it. He brought it down onto the counter and pried open the little round top with a spoon end. It pinged on the counter and then he was diving in with the spoon itself. He chewed and sucked on it with his eyes almost closed.

Marvina was in the doorway. She was watching him. She waited until he dipped again with the spoon. Then she leapt across the floor with fierce agility, her big feet bare and a crocheted afghan flung over her nightgown. Her hair was undone and lying on the wool squares like sleeping snakes.

"What the hell do you think you're doing!" she asked him, her voice raised high in triumph.

He fell into space at the sound of her voice, her naked soles slapping on the linoleum; the tin falling with him left chocolate like a sooty pile on the floor. She got him by the arm and dragged him to where she could turn on her overhead light.

"Stealing food! Making messes!" she yelled. And she shook him until his teeth were rattling like dice and his limbs were flapping as if they'd been rived from the bones that gave them shape.

Freddie came running down the dank corridor and into the kitchen. "Daniel! Leave go of him!" he cried.

"You get to bed!" Marvina bellowed, shaking Daniel harder.

Daniel was making funny high-pitched noises, not loud; on his mouth chocolate glistened like new-turned earth.

"You're hurting him! Daniel!" Freddie wailed, and he got hold of one of Marvina's hands and tried to twist her fingers out of his brother's flesh.

Marvina lifted Daniel high into the air. He hung from her hand, which was like a meat hook; he was making a high tittering laughing sound. Freddie butted her with his head, he bit her too, but all he could get was afghan, nightgown, something rubbery.

Gordon was there then. The long underwear he slept in was dirty like ashes from a fire. He picked up Freddie and threw him into the dining room. Glaring at Daniel, who still hung from Marvina's fist, he asked her, "What's he done?" Then he raised his long arm and pointed at Freddie: "You get upstairs now unless you want to make it harder on him," and he folded his hand into a fist and stuck it in Daniel's face. From the floor where he'd landed, Freddie watched that fist.

"Now!" Gordon bellowed, and Freddie got up and went from the dining room toward the front of the house. His stomach was twisting up in little knots and his eyes blinked rapidly as he listened for the sound of his brother's voice, for the din of what they were doing to Daniel.

Daniel was still hanging. "What's he done this time?" Gordon asked again.

"Stole food. He come down here in the night and stole food."

"Sneaky thieving boy, ain't he," Gordon said, taking him from her. "What did you do? What did you do?" he demanded, shaking him.

Daniel giggled. Chocolate stains ran down his chin.

Freddie waited on the stairway to the attic. There were thin, rubber, chewed-looking treads and he was sitting on one of them, shivering. He couldn't hear much, just the tone and noise of Gordon's voice, the sound he hated most in the world and the one he strained now to hear. It was cold and he waited. Outside snow started falling and the wind ran through the trees like a black hound.

This boy wouldn't answer him so Gordon shook him harder. Didn't he know Gordon meant it? But the boy just giggled with his pale, dirty face hanging before his own like an insult.

"What did you do?" Gordon shouted into that dirty face. "What did you do?"

Stuff came out of the face, spattering bits of chocolate, and some of it hit Gordon.

Gordon brought his hand down in a rabbit punch and it broke Daniel's neck the way such a blow is intended to do. Gordon let him fall. He lay on the floor. "Well, you see what you made me do," Gordon told him.

"A bad boy," Marvina said, looking down where he was, small and dirty, on her linoleum. She turned from him and stirred up the fire in the stove and they sat down at the table and waited.

Freddie waited too, on the stairs, hunched on the chewed-looking tread holding his arms, the blanket from the bed pulled around his shoulders. After a time he came down the stairs, cautiously, ready to retreat, listening. He stepped down the last step into the hall. He couldn't hear anything. As he went forward to the threshold of the living room Marvina appeared before him suddenly, looming up still and massive like a dead tree.

"What do you want?" she said.

"Daniel. I'm waiting for Daniel."

"You go to bed. He ain't feeling good. That chocolate stuff he ate made him sick."

"Daniel's sick?" He tried to see past her into the room but she was darkness and around her was darkness.

"I'm keeping him down here where he can puke."

"He's throwing up?"

She shrugged slightly. "Maybe he's done with it now but I'm keeping him down here just in case. You go to bed." She stepped toward him. Freddie could smell her sweat and the soap she washed her face with. He backed up. He was still trying to look past her.

"You get to bed," she said again. "He don't get better by morning you'll have to do his chores and yours, too." She stepped again. Freddie retreated. She stood and watched him start up the stairs. "Quit dragging that blanket on the floor," she told him. He climbed slowly and when he knew she was gone he sat on the stairs again and waited.

Marvina went back to the kitchen. Gordon had dressed himself: pulled his pants on over his long johns, put on his tall rubber boots and his coat. "Where's my lamp?" he asked her, and she got it for him. He picked up the child's body and Marvina put on her coat and followed him.

"It's snowing out!" she said, pausing on the threshold, stunned. It drove down into her face, the dooryard was already covered, the wind was sending a hollow, moaning sound from the woods. "It's s'posed to be spring!" she protested to his back, which was disappearing into the whiteness. He kept on toward the barn. She turned around and went back in the house to get her boots.

She found Gordon in the old tack room. He was wrapping a stiff harness around Daniel like a shroud. The bits and the buckles made a soft clanging sound. Gordon hooked on an old flatiron and two doorstops he found under the bench. Then he carried the child from the barn—heavier he was now and held taut in the coiling leather—and Marvina followed with the lamp. They went along close to the house. Freddie had climbed to his room but when he looked out the gable window they had already gone by and were crossing the front lawn to the road. The heavy snowfall came down on them with a hissing sound. The wind shook the trees and caught at Marvina's hair and her nightgown. Gordon stumbled where the shoulder rose from the road. He cursed and went up over it and down the other side into the bog. Marvina hiked up her nightgown with the hand that wasn't holding the lamp and she followed him.

Snow was still falling when the morning came. Wind peeled it off the driveway and flung it in great piles against the side of the house. The limbs of the pines were pulled earthward while the maple trunks rose white as bones into the ashy dawn. Krista shoved open the back door and came down the steps with the bucket in her hand. She wore her brown coat and the hood was up. Her unbuckled boots flopped about her legs. Three robins crouched in the snow near the bottom step barely moved as she passed by. Squinting through spinning snow toward the outhouse, she made her way slowly down the incline.

Ice snapped from the hinges. She lifted the bucket and stepped up, reaching to pull the door closed behind her. Turning, she started and nearly dropped the bucket. "Freddie!" she cried.

He was sitting on the bench to the left of the hole, his knees drawn up to his chest, his arms locked around them, hands stuffed up opposite sleeves. The black woolen hat they had given him for Christmas was pulled down to his eyes. He frowned at her, then slowly unfolded his arms. "They done something to Daniel," he told her.

Krista stepped forward and picked up his hands. "What are you doing here?" she asked.

"I can't find him."

"Daniel's lost?" She tugged on him. "You come in the house and tell Mum." She pushed the bucket into the corner with her foot. "Come on," she urged.

The wind plunged with long, hollow wails beyond the walls, and the small building wavered. When Krista lifted the latch the wind caught the door and smacked it wide open. The diamond-shaped window cracked. Krista jumped outside and tried to get the door. "Help me, Freddie!" she called.

He slowly lowered one leg and then the other. He climbed down stiffly into the snow and hobbled toward her as the wind swirled up high in a gust and slammed the door against the corner of the outhouse. Together they pushed it and he leaned hard while Krista settled the latch. Then they started for the house.

"Mum!" Krista called as she stamped her boots on the porch.

"Freddie!" she cried as she opened the door. "He was waiting in the outhouse, Mum. He's all cold."

Viola came from the front room, wearing one of Jarvis's flannel shirts over her nightgown. "Freddie!" Krista cried again.

He stood, a little more on one foot than the other, holding himself with his arms. Viola came toward him, her hair falling down one side of her neck. "Freddie?" she said. She reached to touch his face. "Freddie, you're frozen! What have you been doing? You come in here, I just opened up the fire."

She sat him in the little wicker rocking chair next to the stove in the front room, bent to open the door and reached in with the poker to stir the wood. She leaned forward and breathed into it and the flame stretched like a heart beating faster. His shoulders kept twitching, his teeth were chattering. "I'm going to get you something hot to drink," she said. "Don't you get out of that chair."

The couch, opened up into a bed, nearly filled the room behind the little rocker. When Viola came back with cocoa Jarvis sat up and turned toward them. "What's going on?" he asked.

Viola set the mug in Freddie's hands and guided it toward his mouth. "Freddie was waiting in the outhouse," she explained. "He's real cold. Krista brought him in to sit by the fire."

Jarvis swung his feet onto the floor. "What happened? The Cords go out and lock the door on you?"

Freddie's hands wouldn't work yet, so Viola held the mug until he finished. "I'm going to get you more, and a hot breakfast to go with it," she told him. "Do you feel *any* warmer now?"

He looked up at her and nodded. He watched her go back in the kitchen with his mug.

Behind him Jarvis was stepping into his pants. He got a shirt from the narrow bureau. Scratching an opening in the frost, he peered out the glass in the front door. The snow had sifted through onto the porch, breaking one of the screens loose from its frame. It shuddered, making a wavering shadow. Frowning at the strange sound behind him, Jarvis turned back into the room. It *was* the boy's teeth. "Jesus, you are cold!" he said. "You come get in the bed. It's all warm for you. You come on now." He reached forward and rocked the chair impatiently. "In the bed. Take off that coat. And your shoes."

Freddie plucked at the loops holding the wooden buttons on his coat. Jarvis pulled the child to him and undid them. He pushed Freddie toward the bed and when he sat there Jarvis knelt and untied his shoes, which were unyielding as nails and heelless. Freddie lay down in slow jerky motions like an old person. Jarvis pulled the covers up and folded them tightly around him. "Mrs. Rudge is fixing you something hot to eat," he said. He stopped on his way out of the room to open the door of the stove and jab at the wood with a poker. He straightened and almost glared at Freddie. "What the hell did they go and lock you out for? Are they crazy?" he demanded before he turned and went into the kitchen.

"That kid is froze!" he said to Viola. "What the Christ is the matter with those people!"

She shook her head. She was bringing a mug of coffee to the table for him. "Krista, come and eat," she called.

"Freddie said they done something to Daniel." Krista got slowly into her chair, watching her father's face. "Freddie said Daniel's lost."

"Is that why Freddie came down here?"

She shrugged. Then she nodded.

Viola looked at Jarvis; then she brought Freddie's cereal to him. He ate slowly and she supported the bowl and stroked his hair back from his brow with her other hand. He'd been red but now he was pale, like old paper. "Daniel," he said softly. "I can't find him."

"Eat," she said. "Where could he be, Freddie?"

"He's gone."

"Where would he go?"

"I can't find him." He watched her face.

"We'll find out where he is. You finish this cereal and then you rest. We'll find out where he is." She fed him the rest of it, then pulled the quilt up until just his eyes showed. Half closed, they watched her. "Don't you worry anymore," she told him.

When she returned to the kitchen Jarvis was stomping through the back door. The cold air shot in ahead of him. "Bad storm," he said, pulling off his gloves, "but the wind's mostly blown the snow off the driveway. I'll be able to get out."

"Jarvis, stop on your way and tell them Freddie's down here. Ask them where Daniel is. Freddie's all upset, Jarvis. He says he couldn't find Daniel."

"He's lost," Krista said.

Jarvis nodded. "I'll ask 'em. They're crazy people, letting that kid out in this kind of weather." He took up his lunch box and went through the door.

Viola hurried after him. "Come back here and tell me what they say." He nodded and she watched him go down the steps. The robins were still huddled beside the porch, drawn down so their red breasts were barely visible. The wind was twisting their feathers. They didn't move as Jarvis went by them and started up the rise.

Jarvis drove the short distance and turned into the Cords' driveway. It was empty and the wide truck tracks had been buried. The snow had stopped falling but wind blew it sideways off roofs and trees and lifted it from the backs of the hills. Jarvis got out of the truck and slammed the door. He narrowed his eyes against the blowing snow and could see the hind legs of cows shifting beyond the partially opened door of the barn. Gusts of wind kept sending snow like little points of ice against his face. He started forward as a large figure emerged from the barn. The weight of a bucket tipped her only slightly. She wore a kerchief, and her long dark coat swung about the tops of her unlaced boots as she moved toward him over the white dooryard.

"Mean storm," he said, planting his feet firmly.

"Can't never count on Easter." She shifted the bucket to her other hand.

"Your husband here?" he asked, looking past her toward the barn.

"Had to go off." She turned her face to look where he looked; then shifted and started on toward the house.

"Got the older boy down there half froze," Jarvis said at the mass of her dark shoulders.

She hesitated, then jerked around. "So *you* got him," she said, still pivoting. "We been late with the milking hunting him. How long you had him?"

"Since daybreak."

"You shoulda sent him back."

"I told you, he's half froze. He come 'cause he was locked out."

"Door don't have a lock." She squared her shoulders and stood up bigger in front of him. The bucket looked light enough to be empty hanging from her hand. Behind her the door of the ell was open. Snow was sifting over the sill into the corridor. The wind moaned deeper and cut at the side of his face as he asked her, "Little boy here? We just got Freddie."

The kerchief was pulled forward around her face like a black bonnet. "Went with Gordon to find his brother. Worried," she said. "Up and down the road looking. That boy worried till he puked, and now come to find out you been keeping him down your place. Had him there all along. We been late with the milking," she said again.

Jarvis turned and, squinting, looked down through the orchard toward the little house. He could barely see it. The snow was swirling around, tossing up in long clouds among the curving, stiff branches of the old trees.

By nine-thirty the day had cleared so completely it was as if the earth had turned a full rotation and come out under another sky. The sunlight glittered on the snow, water dripped from the bright branches of the pines. Viola shielded her eyes as she came down the back steps, raisins cupped in her palm. She scattered them among the robins, pulled her jacket about her, and started up the slope toward the orchard.

Snow was slipping with soft sounds from the trees and making little hollows where it fell beneath them. The cows, standing in the pen beside the barn, had churned the white earth beneath their hooves to mud. The driveway was empty and Viola knocked hard on the closed door of the ell. She could hear voices: a woman speaking urgently, a man softly arguing. She hesitated, then knocked again. And again. The voices went on, louder and faster. Viola went along to the kitchen window and looked in. Marvina was very near her, seated at the table, a magazine spread open before her. A large brown radio sat on the table near her elbow. Viola returned to the door and knocked as hard as she could with the side of her fist. Then she tried it. The door fell back and she leaned in and called, "Mrs. Cord! Mrs. Cord!"

The voices went on but then she could see Marvina coming toward her. "What do you want?" she said, looking down at Viola.

"My husband told me. I'm sorry you were worried about Freddie. He was looking for Daniel. We took him in to warm up."

Marvina's eyelids were thin and half closed. "You bring him?" she asked, looking past Viola.

"He's asleep. He was so cold and tired out he's gone to sleep and he hasn't waked up yet. I'm afraid he'll come down sick, Mrs. Cord."

"Asleep," Marvina said.

"He couldn't find Daniel. He was so worried."

"Daniel done his chores like he's s'posed to." Marvina tipped her head back. She was listening to the voices on the radio.

"Is Daniel all right? Is he here now?"

"His chores are all done," she said, dropping her head to look down at Viola again. "He's gone to the village with Gordon." She pulled the door almost closed so that Viola had to step out into the snow. "Send him back," she said before she shut it completely.

As Viola left, the voices from the radio were following her, insistent as scolding. The orchard was bright, almost blinding, and she bowed her head as she walked through the glistening trees.

Freddie didn't wake for lunch. Viola left him sleeping and called the other children in from the yard. They tromped up the steps, their faces pink, noses running. They were sweaty under their caps. "We need a carrot," Kendrick told her. "And a hat."

"I'll see what I can do," Viola said, bending to unzip Flynn's coat.

"Is Freddie *still* asleep?" Krista whispered loudly.

Viola nodded. "Hang up your snowsuit." She brought their bowls to the table and, turning to look through the window, saw the top of Gordon's truck cab gleaming beyond the orchard trees. "They're back at last!" she said. "I'll tell Freddie as soon as he wakes up."

After the children finished lunch, Viola found an old carrot that had sprouted roots and a sailor hat Flynn wouldn't wear.

"It's ugly," Krista complained of the carrot.

"He'll have a hairy nose like Mr. Cord!" Kendrick told her.

"Noe," Flynn said, following his brother to the door with the hat.

Viola filled a bowl with soup and went into the front room. Freddie was waking up; he turned on the pillow to look at her. "Here's your lunch, sleepyhead," she said, drawing the little rocker over beside the bed. She offered him the spoon and sat forward with the bowl cupped in her hands. "I went up to ask about Daniel," she told him. "He was gone to the village with Mr. Cord, but I see they're back now."

Freddie studied her and the spoon tipped; soup fell in drops onto the quilt. "They were looking for you this morning. They thought *you* were lost." She smiled. "I'll bring you back home after lunch."

He squinted as if he were trying to read something more in her words. A small line of soup slipped down his chin and Viola lifted the corner of her apron quickly to mop it.

Viola helped him with his clothes. He moved slowly, buttoning his shirt with stiff little jerky motions. He was breathing through his mouth. "You get right back in bed when you get home," she told him.

Freddie pulled his hat on. Viola knelt to tie his shoes. He lifted his jacket from a knob on the bureau. She put on her own coat and led him to the door. Freddie shut his eyes: how the world glowed.

"Mou! Dee!" Flynn called as Freddie stumbled down the steps. Flynn was jumping up and down beside the snowman.

"He's real nice, honey," Viola said, nodding toward the lopsided figure. His ball-shaped head was melting. "I gotta bring Freddie home now," she told him, "but I'll be right back."

"Why can't Freddie stay and play?" Krista asked.

"He's got to go home. He's got to rest in bed."

"You okay, Freddie?" Kendrick asked, following after them.

Marvina's kitchen was steamy. A sheet hung on a line strung across the room. The sleeves of her dress were rolled up, and her forearms looked rock-hard and pale as chalk. "You're back," she said to Freddie. "You sick? She says you're sick."

Freddie didn't answer or look at her. He was staring around the room. He bent to peer under the sheet. "I think he's caught a bad cold," Viola said, her hand on his shoulder. "Flynn come down sick last winter and he was a long time getting over it."

"You shouldn'ta run off like you done," Marvina told him, still watching his face. "Got your brother all upset. We was late with the milking." She looked past them at the door. "He come back with you?"

Freddie looked at her. He shook his head.

"He was bound he wasn't going to wait no more for you, so I sent him down to get you since you was so long in coming back." Her voice was almost soft.

"You mean Daniel?" Viola asked.

Marvina looked at her, her eyebrows raised, her lips gently pursed.

"Daniel didn't come down. We haven't seen him."

"Waited and waited, and when he didn't come back"—Marvina nodded at Freddie—"I let him go down to you."

"When?" Viola asked, her voice rising.

"Just now. Well, a little while ago. Didn't notice the time." Her eyes went to the red hands of the clock. "I was too busy."

"Well, he must have changed his mind. He hasn't been down to my house."

"I been right here doing laundry. Door's never locked. He ain't come through it."

"I don't understand," Viola said. "He must be here. We didn't see him." There was the sound of the refrigerator—a husky whir—and the almost stifled voice on the radio, and Freddie's thick breathing just under her hand. "I'll go back and look," she said. "I'll ask the children. They've been right out there in the yard since lunch." She patted Freddie's shoulder. "He's probably down there helping with the snowman right now. I'll go look."

Marvina nodded. "Yes, go look." And she nodded at Freddie. "I just wish you'd sent him back when I told you."

Freddie followed her, silent, his head thrust forward. She didn't realize it until she was partway across the yard, but she didn't argue, just waited for him to catch up and they went through the orchard together.

"Honest, Mum," Kendrick insisted, "we didn't see him."

"I believe you, son. I just don't understand." She looked out across the field. It was beautiful, smooth as sky and the sunlight sparkling on it. "Kendrick, you go run tell Mrs. Cord he ain't here, ain't been here. I'm going to walk down the road to Creeley's. He may have gone by way of the road 'stead of coming through the orchard and just kept on going with the snow plowed so high he couldn't see." She looked again out across the field. It was true: the familiar shape and lie of things was changed. "Then you all look for him," she said, turning back to Kendrick. "Around the house, behind the barn. I'll be back quick as I can." She softly shook Freddie. "You go on up home and get into bed," she told him. "We'll find Daniel, don't worry." Kendrick was climbing into the orchard. Krista and Flynn ran to follow him. "You kids stay together!" Viola cried.

Freddie followed her the quarter-mile to Creeley's. When she realized it they were almost halfway there. Viola wished she had brought him home in the morning and been done with it. They hurried along the edge of the road, the snowbanks rising to her waist. Their feet made crunching sounds. He stood in the dooryard while she climbed the steps and knocked.

"I'll keep a watch out," Mrs. Creeley promised, looking down at the child and then beyond him to her barn and the long field that joined the Cords'. "You tell Marvina to call me when you get him."

They hurried back; they didn't talk. It was warm and Viola was sweating underneath her coat. She turned and took his hand. "I bet they found him," she said. "Out back of the barn making his own snowman." Freddie didn't say anything and they went on. As they neared the driveway she leaned toward him. "I'll bet they found him," she said again. They turned in, went past the fallen porch and around the corner of the house. They stopped when they heard the children calling: "Danielll! Daniellll! Dannnieeellllll!"

Viola left her coat on the railing of the back porch. Freddie followed her and stood in the doorway of the shed. "Would he hide, would he hide, Freddie?" she asked as she shifted the boxes and knelt to reach under the wooden chest. She looked inside where it smelled like old leaves. "Does he play tricks like that?" She turned, letting the lid gently fall, and she looked at the doorway where he stood.

"Daniel don't play no tricks," he told her.

Viola couldn't believe he was hiding in her house but she looked upstairs and under the beds, in the dark cupboard beneath the kitchen counter. There just was nowhere else. She ran around to the front and peered through the busted screen, knelt to dig at the snow so she could look under where the broken boards sagged.

They went out across the field, where the snow was swiftly melting, and up along the wood line beyond the fence. It was hot under their snowsuits; water dripped from the trees and the bright sun caught it sparkling as it fell. " 'Ost, 'ost," Flynn muttered as he trudged, his head dipped down under the blue hood. " 'Ost, Star." He tugged at the back of her coat.

"We're gonna find him," Krista said. "Ain't we, Kendrick?"

He didn't answer her but stopped and leaned his head back and called Daniel's name.

Viola heard him as she struggled to push open the door of the old pumphouse. Freddie turned toward the sound. They were in the hollow behind the barn; the white hills rose up around them. The door hung from its top hinge and rasped on the floor as she finally got it open. Inside, it was empty, the pump itself long since removed. The smell of the earth and the heavy odor of rotting wood filled her lungs.

"I know!" Kendrick cried, and Krista hurried to follow him. Flynn plunged after her, his black boots churning over the pattern of truck tracks in the Cords' driveway.

They waded through the half-frozen bog, they struggled up and up through the trees where the snow was deep. Jays scolded, their tails flashed a startling blue in the white woods; a steady wind tapped the dripping branches together.

Kendrick made his way up the hill through the spruces. "I know he's here!" he cried. "He's gotta be! Daniel! Daniellll!" he hollered. Krista turned to take Flynn's hand and help him up the last of the rise. "Yil, Yil," he gasped. Kendrick leapt for a piece of wood nailed into the oak's thick trunk; he put his foot on the step below it and climbed.

"Yil!" Flynn called again and again as he stood under the tree's long arms and smacked his mittens together.

While Viola waited downstairs in the kitchen Marvina searched through her house. She climbed to the long attic room. They could hear her thumping up there. Freddie was with Viola and they were both staring out the window as they listened to Marvina's feet, dim and sturdy coming back down the stairs. Looking at the naked trees, Viola willed the small form of Daniel to step out from behind the first one. She saw how he would come, his red jacket a flame against the snow. Watching the barren orchard, she felt dread rise in her like an illness.

They stood waiting with their faces turned toward the sky. Then his boots came through the opening, and his legs, and some more of him. He twisted and jumped. Flynn reached for Krista's hand. "He's not there," Kendrick told them. "I thought for sure he would be."

He walked slowly out from under the tree and they followed him. "I guess we better go home. Maybe they found him," he said. They started down the slope single file.

" 'Ost," Flynn moaned as they descended. " 'Ost."

They were in front of the barn, Viola and Freddie; Marvina, coatless and her apron high on her stomach. "We already looked all through the barn," she insisted.

"It's a big barn," Viola pressed. "A little boy could hide."

Gordon's truck pulled into the yard and they turned to watch him climb alone out of the cab. He came toward them with his loose, low-heeled stride. From under the visor of his pulled-down cap he was looking at Freddie's face. He stopped near Marvina. "Ain't gone that way," he said, gesturing with his thumb. "I asked at Vaughan's, Seavey's, they ain't seen him."

Viola came closer to him. He stepped back. "You got to find him before dark," she said.

He looked at her, his eyes flat beneath the visor; he ran his tongue along his upper lip. Then he twisted his neck and looked beyond the low roof of the ell where the colors in the sky were changing. "We better call the sheriff," Marvina told him. "We looked everywhere around here. We need help, I guess, is what it is."

The children sloshed through the bog. Their feet were cold and their noses were running. Krista was crying and Flynn kept tugging on her hand and whimpering. Kendrick drew farther and farther ahead. He climbed onto the shoulder and paused to watch the brown car pass, its tires crunching where the slush had started to freeze. The blue lights on the roof were flashing slowly as it turned into the Cords' driveway.

The sun was going. The fields and the white trees, the barn and the farmhouse, all seemed to be rising to meet it and draw down over them the burning color left by its fall. The wind came slicing from the woods and smelled cold.

"We'll start in the barn," the sheriff said. He was in the middle of the group, a large flashlight in one hand, and he gestured with the other as he spoke. "Temperature's droppin', but we got to move slow and careful. I've known little kids sit there too scared to speak while men were looking not five feet from them on the other side of a bale of hay. I've known of a kid," he said, looking around the circle, "fell asleep in a closet. Looked all night for him. Came out hungry for his breakfast."

Viola moved around the perimeter. Marvina was standing near Gordon. "I've got to feed the children," Viola told her. "I can take Freddie with me and give him supper too."

They hung lanterns. The long golden shadows danced on the round haunches of the cows, flickered toward the lofts, and were lost in the darkness above. As the men began to move, the animals got onto their feet. Shifting uneasily, they turned in their stanchions to watch, their long tails swaying. The barn smelled of their lives: the warm heavy bodies, their urine, the sweet odors of hay and grain. The wide door was open and the cold wind entered in long gusts. Jarvis started in the old tack room. It was filled with abandoned trunks and unused tools, dented milk cans, jars of rusted nails. Hung on pegs, the traces of a rotting harness looped like a sleeping snake. The Vaughans searched in the old stalls. Mr. Creeley started in the ell, its small rooms and the privy. Above, the sheriff and two deputies sought him among the bales of hay. "Daniel," they softly coaxed, "Come out, boy."

Gordon looked in the old mangers. The cows watched him, their heads turned, eyes widened so the whites showed.

Freddie fell asleep at the table, his head tipped toward one shoulder, his hands loose in his lap. The other children watched Viola carry him in to her bed. When she returned she ladled out stew for herself and sat down.

"Why can't they find Daniel?" Kendrick asked.

"They just started looking. We'll probably get the good news before long."

"We hunted for him everywhere we could think of. Everywhere. All our hiding places."

"I know you did, son. I know you tried your best. It ain't your fault if he wasn't there."

"What if they don't find him?" Krista asked.

"They'll look until they do."

"But what if they don't, Mum?" Kendrick sounded impatient.

"They will!" she said in a sharp voice. "Now eat your supper while it's hot."

Krista pushed her spoon around in the stew. "Was I ever lost, Mum?" she asked.

"No! And don't even say it!"

"Star, doe," Flynn scolded softly.

It was close to midnight. Viola stood at the door and drank her tea. The beam of the spotlight in Cords' yard reached into the orchard and shook like smoke over the trees. The front of the barn stood out from the night, the door slid back on its runners. Viola's cheek against the glass was cold and the chilliness spread over her skin and circled inside her. She heard Jarvis's boots crunching on the snow before she saw him.

He walked in past her and sat in a chair. He leaned back wearily and then looked at her. "I'll get you some coffee," she said. "It's all made."

"We went through that barn. With rakes we combed the hay. Seemed like the place he would be. Barn's where kids go." He lit a cigarette and she brought the ashtray to him with his coffee. "The house. The cellar. Every inch of that cellar, Viola, up under the crawl space. The outbuildings. Nothing. Not even a sign he'd *been* there."

She sat down. "It's so cold, Jarvis. Remember that Scott boy?"

He frowned.

"Up in Rumford?"

"Oh, that's right." He nodded.

"He wasn't a hundred yards from the back door."

"That's what the sheriff said."

"What did he say?"

"Said little kids get confused, get lost, go in somewhere and fall asleep. It's too cold they don't wake up."

"Jarvis, he's got to be somewhere!"

"That's what I thought. I was sure we'd find him by now." He got up and poured himself more coffee and sat down with it.

"I got stew I can heat for you," she told him.

"I just want coffee. She fed us sandwiches. She was in there cooking, playing her radio. She's a cold bitch, Viola," he said.

"Some people want to keep busy so they don't think."

"She's a bad woman, Viola. All them kids are is work animals far as she's concerned." He poured milk into his coffee and stirred it.

"You going out again?"

"I'm going back to Vaughan's. They weren't home most of the afternoon. He might have gone up there, no one to see him. Creeleys checked all over their place. Little kid couldn't see over those snowbanks. Wouldn't know where he was. Might of just kept going till he got tired and stopped." He stood and pulled on his hat. "That's the thing, Viola. He might be right here somewhere close. Or he might have wandered off. You think it's going to be easy finding somebody. But it ain't."

"Jarvis, what am I going to tell Freddie?"

"Tell him? He still here?"

"I told her I'd give him supper and he fell asleep, so I put him in bed."

"He up with Kendrick?"

"No. I put him in our bed. I wish I'd brought him up there first thing this morning but I figured it was better just to let him sleep."

"Viola, none of this is your fault, for Christ's sake."

"I know that. I just mean it would of been done with this morning if I'd brought him home."

"Well, I'll put him upstairs with Kendrick. You get to bed. And you can tell him we're still looking. Christ, Viola, we are."

Freddie was as bony and narrow as Krista. He woke and stiffened in Jarvis's arms but he didn't speak. Thin light came up the stairway after them. It was warm in the attic, the heat pressing up through the ceiling. The old dry wood of the rafters smelled sweet. Jarvis lay Freddie down beside Kendrick. He pulled the covers up over him. "Bucket's under the bed you need it," he said. "Give Kendrick a shove if he gets hogging the blankets."

Freddie looked up at him. Jarvis's shadow was climbing the sloping roof, his hands hung big at his sides. Freddie watched as the shadow turned and folded around itself, the head grew longer and thinner, and it all disappeared in uneven jolts down the stairway.

* * *

It was warm in the farmhouse, too. Both the stoves were burning hot. Gordon brought more wood in from the ell; he dropped some of it into the kitchen box and went into the living room with the rest. Marvina watched his back, his head tipped a little to one side, the coat drooping loose from his long frame.

"Feed that stove!" he told her, and she heard the door of the one in the living room clang back.

When she got out of her chair she looked through the window. She could see the sheriff's flashlight coming toward them from the barn. "Sheriff's coming," she called, and opened the stove. She pitched two birch logs into it, and as she closed the door the sheriff was knocking.

He took his hat off.

"You got him?" Marvina asked.

He shook his head.

"You want coffee? It's here on the stove." She lifted the blue pot.

"No, no thanks." He gestured with his hand. "I can't think what drew him off," he said, his face puzzling. "He was going down there," and he swung his hand pointing toward the window. "He was in a hurry to find his brother. Then something happened that was so interesting he went somewhere else."

Marvina shrugged.

"Either that or he was running down there by way of the road and he got mixed up 'cause of the snowbanks." He frowned. "You got to get into the kid's mind and think like he would."

"He ain't much on thinking, that boy," Marvina said.

"What do you mean?"

"Some boys think a lot, some boys just don't." She scowled. "The other one, he's the kind that thinks."

"You mean some sudden impulse caught him and he followed it."

"Yeah. Like that. That's it." She nodded, swung her blue pot toward him. "You sure about the coffee?" she asked.

"Pete Seavey thought he mighta tried to go skating on the bog."

"Ain't ice on the bog." Gordon stepped into the room.

"Musta froze last night."

"Melted."

"There's no skates here," Marvina said. " 'Sides, he's a scared kind of a boy for trying something like that. He wanted his brother was all."

"Bog's lumpy and bumpy from the reeds anyway," Gordon said. "Can't skate on that. Foolish."

"Kids sometimes try, slide on their boots if they don't have skates."

"Well, if he was skating, where is he?" Marvina said, her voice rising, getting a little hysterical.

The sheriff held up his hand. "Now, Marvina."

"Where is he? I coulda looked out my window and seen him skating. Ain't nothing tall on that bog to hide him. I coulda seen him, bright and sunny as the day was by that time."

"But you said you were here in the kitchen doing wash."

"Tenant woulda seen him. Back and forth she's been to my house all day. Looking, looking, she and her kids."

"I'm just going over it again, hoping to see something new. It's late and it's cold."

"We know you're going to find him, Sheriff. We got all our faith in you," Marvina told him.

'OST

6

It was Friday. They had been searching for Daniel since Tuesday evening. Throughout the week the sun had shone brightly, taking much of the snow. The men, seeking him in a wider and wider area, left their coats in the little house or up at the farm and they went through the woods in their shirtsleeves. At night it was cold and the new moon rose late and lay on her back, golden and curved like a cat above the trees. The sheriff went between the two houses, and his face drew in as the days passed; he became short-tempered.

"We got faith in you," Marvina told him more than once. "We know you'll find that boy." But the sheriff wasn't expecting to find him—not alive, not after that first cold night, not after three of them.

"We got to accept it," he said to Viola. He was scowling, looking past her, his eyes on the red handle of the pump. The door to the stairway was closed but Freddie could hear him, his high voice that kept cracking as if he were talking over a sore throat. Freddie was sitting halfway down the stairs. His nose was running and his knees were drawn up under him. "He couldn't have lasted through that cold, not even one night of it," the sheriff said, and he cleared his throat and spoke a little louder. "It's the hardest thing in the world to have to say, but what we're looking for is a body." Freddie could hear a chair scraping, her voice, something that wasn't words. "And I bet everything I know it's close-by."

"Close-by, close-by." Freddie peered down the stairway toward the door. It was dim there like a closet. His mouth was partly opened and his breath rattled in his chest like a tin cup holding pennies. He thought about Daniel, about his body, how it was always moving along beside his own, smaller is all. His mind shifted slowly to consider Daniel's hands, his fingers, the ripped-looking places where he chewed his nails. The scrabbly sound of his feet running after him, his voice low and only Freddie could hear. If Daniel was a body his eyes would be closed and his hands flat at his sides, thumbs resting against the legs of his overalls, his dirty heels bruised by the earth. He thought how those men were looking everywhere for Daniel but it wouldn't help none, because if Daniel was a body then he himself was left so alone that even if he went and lay down on top of him and breathed his breath into Daniel's face, Daniel wouldn't be there. If Daniel was a body he was gone as the sun at midnight.

Viola opened the door and he was sitting there partway up the stairs, eyes closed, his fists shoved between his knees. "Freddie, you're out of bed!" her voice sang, scolding as she climbed. "The men have gone looking in Vaughan's woods," softly, her hands reaching to hold his shoulders. "You come get in my bed," and she leaned back and lifted him, he felt himself aloft, light as milkweed. His fingers on her neck were hot and sticky. "I'll bring you toast, toast and eggnog," her words chanting against his ear, plaiting in his hair.

The state lady's car was in the driveway up at the farm. It was a blue station wagon, the windows rolled up tight. A small woman, thick glasses, her hair brown and curved in a pageboy: Viola had met Mrs. Grant on Wednesday when word of Daniel's disappearance summoned her from Portland. Viola didn't think too much of her; she didn't seem half a match for Marvina Cord, who wouldn't have Freddie back now: it was too much bad luck, it was too much questions, it was too much worry wondering when he'd run off and get himself lost too. Viola shut her door tight and went up through the orchard.

Marvina's kitchen smelled like boiled potatoes and laundry soap. Mrs. Grant was sitting at the table, her heavy blue coat pulled close around her shoulders. Marvina was standing in front of her stove. A buttoned cardigan drooped over the hips of her red-flowered housedress, she held paper towels gripped like an ether mask against her face. She blew hard as Viola nodded to Mrs. Grant and sat down across from her.

"The doctor said he'll have this fever for at least two more days," Viola said. "He told me to keep him in bed and give him fluids, so that's what I'm doing." She turned to look at Marvina but paper towels were hiding her face. Just her eyes showed, moist-looking and dim, and her forehead, puckered so the black line of her brows was twisted.

"We appreciate all you're doing." Mrs. Grant's voice was slow and precise, soft as if she were talking in church or a doctor's office. "We'll get him moved and settled just as soon as we can, as soon as we're able," she told Viola. "And I've put in for a check to compensate you; I hope it won't take more than a week before it comes through."

"Sheriff says he's dead."

Marvina's voice fell on them like a hammer. She pushed the paper towels against her nose and sat down heavily, her knees wide apart. "That's what he said, that's what he told me." She blew hard.

Viola said coldly, "A child just doesn't disappear and not get found."

Marvina's breathing was damp and scratchy behind the paper towels. "Sheriff said," she repeated.

"I think his mother came and took him," Viola told Mrs. Grant.

But she shook her head. "We've been to see her."

"No-good drunk," Marvina said.

"She hasn't seen him for two years. And the weather was so bad she couldn't have gotten out here that day anyway."

"I was hoping that's what happened," Viola said.

Mrs. Grant nodded. "I understand," she murmured.

"Sheriff says he's dead."

Mrs. Grant turned in her chair and looked at Marvina. "Yes," she said. "We know. It's just that it's so hard we don't want to believe it." Then she turned back to Viola. "We lost another little boy. It's five years now. It happened the same way, a cold day and he went outside with his sled. He didn't come in at suppertime. When they found him he was close to home but it was too late." She gestured with her small hand. "I didn't know Daniel. I just got this case from Mrs. White but I feel terrible, terrible."

"They found him, that little boy?" Viola said.

"They'll find Daniel, too; we just can't know when."

The room was quiet except for the ticking of Marvina's yellow clock. "I still don't understand how it happened," Viola persisted. "And it's awful to think of him being out in the cold and trying to find his way. I don't understand. They should have found him."

"Never had a boy get himself lost before. Never." Marvina lifted her face from the towels. "Outta all the ones we had here. Wesley, Chester, Jonathan," and she ticked them off laboriously on her fingers. "Not even the one that was slow, that Warren." Her voice was like stones rubbing together. "Not none of 'em. Gordon's got artheritis getting at his hands. I come down with this cold." She stared into the bunch of paper towels, then looked at Viola. "I sent him down to you," she said, and blew.

"He never came our way," Viola denied fiercely. "My children were outside and they would have seen him. He would have gone right down to them. He never came our way. It was Freddie came down to our house. Early in the morning before the sun rose, while it was still storming. Came because he couldn't find his brother and he was locked out ."

"Door don't have a lock. Daniel was doing his chores. Feeding out hay like he done every morning." She coughed and hacked up something into her paper towels.

"My husband put him in our bed and I let him sleep, he was so cold and tired out."

"There," Marvina said, waving her towels toward Mrs. Grant. "And that little boy all the time out in the truck with Gordon, looking for his brother that he couldn't find, worrying himself so sick he puked up his breakfast."

Mrs. Grant got up from the table and drew her coat closed. "We'll probably never know what happened," she said. "That's one of the things that's so hard about this. All we can do now is the very best we can by Freddie."

Viola came down the stairs with Freddie's dishes. Kendrick held the door open and she stepped into the kitchen. The lamp was lit and its yellow light caught in little pools in the bowls on the table. "Thank you, son," she said, and she went to the sink and set the dishes into it. Kendrick watched her back.

"How long is Freddie going to stay here?" he asked her. "You said he was going to stay till they found Daniel."

Viola worked the pump. When she turned from the sink Kendrick was waiting. "State lady won't put him back at Cords's," she told him. "She's going to find a new home where he can live. He's going to stay with us till then. It won't be too long." She crossed to the stove to get more macaroni for Flynn. "I know it's hard to share, son, and you've been awful good about it."

Flynn watched her. He nodded at each spoonful. "Mo', Mou," he urged.

"I don't mind," Kendrick said. "I like Freddie. He's my friend. I'm just asking you."

"Well, that's it."

"Daniel's dead, isn't he, Mum?" Kendrick was almost glaring at her.

"They don't know," she said quickly, "what happened. They're still looking."

"He froze. Didn't he?"

"They don't know for sure. Not till they find him."

"If he ain't dead, where is he?"

"Kendrick, I told you all I know! I don't want you to keep on at me!"

"Yil, Yil!" Flynn said loudly, looking from her to Kendrick.

"Don't send Freddie away!" Krista cried. She started to get out of her chair.

"I'm not going to send him anywhere," Viola said sharply. "He'll be staying with us as long as he needs to, then moving to a new home. You sit down and finish your supper. Flynn! What's the matter with you kids! Nobody's going to get sent anywhere."

* * *

"What kind of papers?" Jarvis asked again. He was pulling his clothes off. He'd damped the stove down but the room was warm.

"Temporary for him to stay here while she finds another home for him," Viola explained. "She says it ain't easy, they don't have enough homes and she wants him to have a really good one."

"I hope she does better by him than those damn Cords." He wrenched the undershirt over his head. "What kind of papers?"

"I don't understand it, Jarvis. These people, just throwing their kids away, sending them out on strangers that don't care nothing for them." She sat up. "I've been thinking about it. A hen would never let her chicks get lost. Danger comes, she puts herself in front of it and tells them to hide. A mother cat will attack any dog comes near her kittens. You put a gosling in front of a goose, or a gander either, they don't even care what egg it come out of, they'd die before they'd let harm come to it. But people, they just throw their babies away into the world that don't want 'em."

Jarvis sat down heavily on the bed. "Shouldn't surprise you, Viola. Ain't you always figured animals is smarter than people?"

"Well, I guess I have," she said, settling back against the pillow.

Freddie got out of the bed and stood beside it on the bare floor. His heart was knocking around inside him and his teeth were clenched. He could hear Kendrick breathing and he stood there in the dark and listened. Then he took his shirt off the bedpost and put it around him and went and sat on the chest by the window. He was looking out over the front lawn where it led to the road. The moon was up, high above the pasture behind the house. The porch roof made a small shadow, the lawn was pearly grey and then the darker line of the road, and on down the other side where the bog lay under its pale skin of ice. The rise of the piny woods was just a blackness there beyond the stilled water. He watched and watched, his forehead set against the glass where the night pressed cold as a mother's back. He watched and watched but no one came.

There were lengthening days of sunshine and the snow melted into spring runoff, except for patches left in the shadows of buildings, in deep hollows in the fields, far in the woods where the warmth didn't reach. There were cracks worn by running water; it opened the earth and let out the cold, it made mud. Daffodils sent their shoots straight up to the light. The men searched on weekends for Daniel's body. They went through the woods clear to the route road; they looked in every outbuilding on the surrounding farms; they searched with long poles in the narrow river that drained into the bog, and probed there among the greening cat-o'-nine-tails. The sheriff had originally ruled out the possibility of kidnapping but as time went on he began to wonder. A photo of Daniel, taken by the social worker when he first came to the Cords, was sent out over the state. He was standing in front of the open barn door with Freddie. It was hard to make him out; his eyes were almost closed and his face was twisted away from the camera.

Viola kept Freddie home from school for two more weeks. The cold was deep in his chest and he sounded like an old man when he coughed. At night he slept on a folding cot Mrs. Grant had brought out to them; during the day he rested on the couch near the stove. Sometimes when Viola went in he was standing up staring out the window, his hands covered by the long sleeves of Kendrick's pajamas which hung sideways off one shoulder. There was a terrible weariness settled in him.

Viola was washing white clothes in her sink: small things first, children's underwear and socks, their shirts and nightclothes; then her underwear and Jarvis's, towels, sheets. She worked the pump, standing on an old milk crate so her arms wouldn't ache so quickly. She rinsed each garment under the flow and squeezed it into a hard, whorled shape that she piled on the drainboard. Flynn sat on the floor and played with blocks and lengths of wood Jarvis had brought home from the mill, and he talked to the things he built, his voice a little stream of sound beneath the heavy fall of water from the pump.

When the washing was done she piled it in an old apple basket and brought it outdoors to the clothesline. The clouds in the sky were as white as the Easter snow had been, and they were large and moved slowly, the blue beyond them bright and deep. There were little brown wrens flitting in the still-brown grasses that grew in mounds beside the shed, and Viola's tall red hens were pecking in the dooryard. The wind rustled the grasses and fluffed back the feathers of the little birds, and the tall birds, too, to show the soft colors underneath. The cows were spread out all across the field, some almost at the wood line, and they nosed at the earth, impatient for the new grass. The wind grabbed at Viola's sheets and flung them up above the clothesline, where they flapped aloft in a world cleansed of all decay and coldness. She sat on the back steps with the empty basket beside her and looked at the long line of laundry, how it thumped back and forth in the wind, how the clouds swelled and shifted, expanding across the face of the sun to cause a great dancing of shadow over the field and down the sloping roof of the shed, making the grasses sway and tremble, greying the round sides of the cows.

When she came back into the kitchen Flynn was gone, but as she stood listening she heard his voice in the front room. She set the basket in the corner and went to the doorway. He had pulled the small rocker up beside the couch, and on the quilt were all his little blocks of wood, arranged so each had its place. He'd got his little oxen from the crèche. There was one standing on a flat piece of pine and the other was on Freddie's outstretched hand. "Dee," Flynn said. "Dee, baaby," he told him. Freddie held it very carefully; he watched his own hand as Flynn set the second ox in it.

During the last week of May Mrs. Grant came out to the house. The orchard trees shimmered with petals, their perfume rode on the light. The big backs of the cows moved over the tall field slowly, their faces hidden. One had stayed behind in the pen next to the barn and she leaned over the fence, mooing loudly. Her feet shifted back and forth as she pressed her neck into the wire and called. Mrs. Grant stood and watched her for a moment before turning toward the house.

Her low-heeled shoes tapped up the back steps. "How is Freddie?" she asked as she sat down.

Viola nodded and put the sugar bowl and a little dark pitcher of milk on the table. Flynn was following her. "Gant," he was muttering, "Gant."

"He does seem better," Viola said. "He's eating better and he's livelier. I thought he'd mind going back to school but he don't say so."

"That sounds like real progress. You sure are a godsend to that child."

"Well, we all think a lot of him." Viola sat down and Flynn nudged into her. She put her arm around him and asked, "There's been no word at all about Daniel?"

Mrs. Grant shook her head. Beyond the open window the cow's voice sounded over and over. "It's been six weeks," she said. "I thought he would be found by now. It would be better if we could bury him, if we could know for certain. Better for everyone, especially Freddie." She sighed and adjusted her glasses. "Does he speak of Daniel?" she asked.

"No, nothing. But Freddie's no talker." She rocked Flynn. He leaned into her harder and the chair made a soft creaking sound. In the pen by the orchard the cow mooed over and over again, over and over, her voice deep and the sound of it drawn out longer and longer. "They sold off her calf on Saturday," Viola explained. "Poor girl's been calling like that ever since."

"I wondered," Mrs. Grant said. "It seemed as if something wasn't right." She smiled. "Well, I do have good news," she went on. "We've found what we think will be a very good situation for Freddie. His uncle and his family want to share their home with him."

"We didn't know Freddie had a uncle. He never said anything about any family."

"It's his mother's brother but I don't expect Freddie can remember him. He was very young the last time he saw him. They have a nice home and he runs his own upholstery business. They're going to make over a room downstairs for Freddie. They have a son and daughter just a few years older." Up the hill the cow was calling; her voice and the sweet odor of the orchard were coming through the open window.

"Where is it?" Viola asked.

"Out in Windham."

"Oh. Windham."

"This home with his uncle will be permanent. No more moving." Mrs. Grant shifted in the chair. "I think Mr. Pooler's feeling, 'if only we'd taken them in the first place.' "

"No one could know. Pooler," Viola said, her voice deepening into the *l*.

"Poo," Flynn repeated, looking up into her face.

"We like being able to place a child with relatives, with family. It means a lot, to have cousins, to belong."

"Yes, I s'pose so."

"We really would like him to finish out the school year here if you could manage that."

"That will be all right," Viola told her.

"And I've brought your check. I just wish the department could pay more for foster care. You have been a lifesaver to this child."

"Well, he's a good boy and it's a terrible thing to lose what's dearest to you and be all alone in the world."

"Goh boy," Flynn said.

"He won't be alone now."

"No," Viola agreed.

She followed Mrs. Grant to the door and watched her climb the small slope to the driveway. The cow watched her too, pressed against the fence, the wire disappearing into her soft neck. She opened her mouth wide so the creamy ivory of her tongue showed, and she bellowed long and hard.

Viola was quiet during supper and after the dishes were done she walked out into the field and ducked under the barbed wire and climbed the first hill of the pasture. The sky was a very soft blue and a warm light swam slowly through the air. It was that still time when the sun slides and the light changes and the air begins to stir with sweet evening winds. The grass was shiny green and tall, and it swished around her legs as she walked. She went on, leaving them behind her: Jarvis working on his truck, Kendrick and Freddie playing near him, Krista watching; Flynn was on the porch looking out toward the field where Viola had gone. She went on and the cows passed her in a line, moving toward the barn, their tails swaying slowly. She went down the long hollow and up the rise to the far hill. When she reached the top she slipped down into the grass. It rose around her, its sharp green coolness, little bugs walking up the blades, and above her was the sky, pale blue and moving gently toward the long evening. She turned her cheek into the new grass: the freshness of it, how it roared like water from the ground, springs let loose overnight to flood the earth with life. She closed her eyes and just breathed, pulled the sweet air into her. Freddie's going was settled now and would let her back into the real rhythm of her life. It would go well with him—better surely than at Cords'—with these people who were his own blood; he could move past the loss of Daniel. She had done what had come to her to do. And now the day was beautiful, and she settled deeper in the grass, alone as she liked to be, and knowing they were nearby. She looked straight up at the sky. It was still as a held breath, waiting for the sun to finish falling.

His voice came to her now, scurrying through the tall grass like some small creature. "Mou," it said, called, entreated, "Mou!" She lay quietly and watched how light trembled upward from the grass, how the sky pressed closer, how a white cloud appeared across it, drifted like a dropped veil. "Mou!" She could hear his small body now, the grass rumbling and bending as he searched. The cloud stretched thinner and the light was dove grey. "Mou! Mou! Mou!" He ran head down, his fingers set together like a diver's.

Viola let out her breath and sat up.

He laughed and laughed. Held his arms out from his sides and, laughing, ran on until he could push his face into hers, until he could smell the warmth of her hair and the freshness of the grass she had lain upon.

Marvina Cord was watching out her window. "He's going," she said. "That state lady's taking him."

Gordon was on the opposite side of the room, washing his hands in the deep sink. He made a retching sound and got his throat clear.

"He ain't coming back." She was tipped toward the glass, her knuckles leaning on the sill. "He ain't coming back," she said again, and licked her lips. She looked over her shoulder at her husband.

He turned around and his big, wet hands were hanging in front of him. "You got a towel?" he demanded. "Where's the damn towel?"

"Top drawer," Marvina told him, and turned back to the window. "He's going."

There hadn't been much to pack, the canvas bag held it all: some underwear and his battered shoes, two shirts and the pair of Kendrick's pajamas, a winter coat and his black watch cap. He had on new blue sneakers Mrs. Grant had brought and stiff brown corduroys, a green jacket for spring. He came down the back steps, moving stiffly and gripping the canvas bag. The sun stood above the wood line and sent long, soft light across the field. The children were crowded around him. Jarvis led the way and Viola came along behind them all. They went up the slope to where Mrs. Grant's car was waiting in the driveway. "My uncle Bobby," Freddie mumbled.

"Yes," Mrs. Grant soothed, bending toward him. "He and your aunt June are real excited about seeing you."

He chewed on his bottom lip. "My uncle," he tried again.

Viola hugged him. "I have your new address so we can write you. We'll want to know how you're getting along," she said. Krista hugged him, locking her hands and squeezing as hard as she could.

"You don't like it out in Windham you come back here with us," Jarvis told him. "You're a real good boy."

Freddie's eyes slid off Jarvis's face and he looked down the slope at the house, then turned slowly until he was looking back up through the orchard at the farm where Marvina's face was clouding the window.

"Shall we put your bag in back, Freddie?" Mrs. Grant asked him, but he held tightly to it and climbed onto the front seat. Krista started crying.

"Dee," Flynn said, pushing through the others. "Dee," and he reached and dropped a little ox into Freddie's palm.

Then Mrs. Grant was getting in on her side and turning the key and Jarvis pulled Flynn back from the door and shut it. He walked along with the car as it backed down the driveway, and the others followed, raising their arms to wave. Jarvis stood at the road, beckoning with his hand and calling, "Okay, all clear!"

They could see the top of Freddie's head, and his fingers lifted to wave, and then the car was moving forward and they watched as it went faster and followed the wide bend and got blurred by the long gauzy rays of sunlight and went up over the hill by Creeley's farm, and disappeared down the other side and was gone.

Windham, Maine
July 27, 1960

Dear Mrs. Rudge,

I got a letter from you. I got it here to me where I living at the Poolers. She got it out of the box and gave it to me. There house is brown. They got a boy name Roger. Girl Paula. I sleep in a room they got downstares and they put a radio there to. They got a garaj. Bobby Pooler has a truck and he got a car. His truck is red. They got a dog. Its black. Name Tippy. White on his feet.

Youre freind

Freddie Hewitt

Viola read this letter out to the children. Krista jumped up and down. She could hardly believe it. When her mother sent Freddie away it seemed he was gone as completely as the home they'd left in Cornish. Now here were his words on a piece of paper. She held it in her hand and looked at it. Flynn wanted to see too.

"We got to write back quick, Mum," Krista said.

"Mou!" Flynn urged sternly, and he ran to find the pen.

North Royal, Maine
Sept. 28, 1960

Dear Freddie,

We felt so bad when you didn't come to Kendrick's birthday. We would of come and got you if we knew. Then we could see your house where you're living and meet your people. It was a good party. Kendrick says we'll get you the day before next year and then have you for sure. He got a soccer ball that he likes a lot and a new shirt. Flynn gave him a stone that's smooth like an egg. We don't know where he found it. Krista helped make the cake and she saved out a piece for you 'til it turned green and I had to throw it out yesterday. We wonder everything that you're doing and we want to know what your school is like. We hope you write us a letter soon.

From Viola Rudge

Love,
Krista

Windham, Maine
Feb. 16, 1961

Dear Mrs. Rudge,

I got you letter. I wish you didn't move in Portland. I cant see where you are now. Theres no one there cept them. We didn't have school cus of the snow. I shovel for her. Tell Krista they dont have Woolworths here with the booth to take my picktur. I look the same. I went to the dentist. He pull two teeth out. I think about the farm and the cows. I wish you could keep you hens to. I was never there since I was three but theres not hens in the city.

Youre freind

Freddie Hewitt

Windham, Maine
March 17, 1962

Dear Mrs. Rudge,

I was needing one of them shirts like you sent at Christmas. I should a write sooner but what happened is that June Pooler she was sick and then she went to the hospatal and then she died in there. I went to see her and she sit up in the bed and her face was all cavd in like a old lady with no teeth. Her wrist like a chicken bone. They put all June Pooler clothes in a box and gave them away. She had little glass dols on a shelf and they put them somewheres to. Bobby Pooler dont say nuthing. I hope you all O.K. I hope I see you when I am older.

Youre freind

Freddie Hewitt

THE BLUE BUS

7 By the spring Logan Pembroke turned fourteen his body had lost its softness. He'd grown taller and the flesh had stretched and hardened on his frame so he looked like a man and was without the brittle newness of adolescence. There was something unfinished about his face, which saved him from being handsome. Ronnie, three years younger, hardly seemed to grow at all. His voice was squeaky. He fell asleep whenever he had nothing else to do: at the supper table after swallowing; perched on the round stool at the drugstore while his mother chose her medicines—little brown bottles that scraped and clunked against each other in the otherwise empty pockets of her long coat; riding home on the school bus, and his head knocked against the glass of the window. Lumps rose on his skull.

"What happened, Ronnie?" his mother softly asked, her hand going out, the ends of her fingers stiff as November leaves in his thin hair.

He had to think hard. "The bus went over a bump," he told her, and sighed, his lower jaw relaxing.

"Be careful," Linette murmured, her fingers questing cautiously. "You're gonna hurt yourself." Ronnie breathed in as she carefully bent the top of his ear over. "You gotta watch out," she told him, tracing along the back of his neck where the hair stopped growing and it was just bare skin. Ronnie closed his eyes, he nodded. "Your head's all knobbly." Her fingers were pressing the crown. "Feels like you got barnacles growin'," she said, and her hand fell off him, tapped against her own lean thigh. He swayed and half opened his eyes. They were in the kitchen.

Logan was sitting low in the purple easy chair in the corner of the living room. He was staring at the dark console that almost filled the opposite wall. His father had traded half a pig for it; the antenna reared up from the roof like a whirligig spinning the small house skyward. The game show was loud, the clock on the screen was ticking, the small white faces of the audience were strained. Logan turned to look through the wide opening between the rooms. They stood by the table, removed from the accelerating drumming of the clock, Ronnie watching her with his sleepy face, and she, her dark hair falling loose from the pins, was lifting her hand again to touch him. She said something that Logan couldn't hear; when he looked back at the television the clock had stopped, the audience was murmuring sadly.

Logan did not sleep well at night. But he didn't need to sleep, it was a waste of time; he was growing up, he was getting out. He lay awake on his small bed in the attic, his feet hanging over the end, Ronnie's snores breeding in him such impatience that he rose on his elbow to jab him with the broken end of a yardstick. Ronnie started up in a panic, then turned unprotesting to curl on his side, purple bruises hatching on his arm, between his ribs.

Then the silence in the attic hectored Logan's wakefulness like insects under his skin. He heard the mice in the roof and the wind outside, a log tumbling in the kitchen stove, his mother scuffing to the bathroom, the rasping of his father's sleeping body. Logan thought about his father's head thrown back on the pillow of their bed, the grimy neck of his underwear, his face pale where the bones pressed, the stubble of his beard. He thought about a hammer on that face, his own arm raised, how everything could be smashed and made to disappear like sand in water. He thought about the house blown up, burned to ashes, knocked down, the old foundation like a small abandoned quarry where snakes nested.

"No," Logan told him, standing in the yard with his arms poised so he could start running any time. "No, I ain't gonna do it this summer. I got another job." He was half turned from his father but he watched him.

Gage shrieked as if he'd been burned. "Who's gonna help me on the truck?" It was a hot morning at the beginning of June and Gage wore his overalls, his naked shoulders beyond the straps wide and worn smooth like an ox yoke.

"Thumper can help you." Logan kicked at the dirt with the toe of his shoe.

"There's a lot of pigs this year." Gage's voice was loud, accusatory. "I got more people on the route. I got two restaurants."

Logan didn't answer him. His toe dug a deeper hole in the dirt. He could smell the pigs strong this morning. Sometimes it was as if they were inside his nose. A crow flew over the yard cawing loudly.

"*Three* restaurants, goddamnit! Three!" he insisted. "Got that new one over ta Gray."

Logan was watching the road, his eyes squinted, his weight squarely on his two feet.

"This was gonna be my biggest year." Gage leaned closer.

Logan could smell him, his coffee, the bacon she'd fed him. He stepped back and at the same time turned toward him. "You don't pay me nuthin'. He's paying me!"

"You're living offa me!" Gage bellowed, jumping at him. "You eat at my table. You owe me, you little bastard!"

"I ain't going on the truck this summer," Logan muttered as he started down the driveway. He was listening behind him.

"You can goddamn well pay me board then!"

Logan kept moving.

"Don't you ever ask me for nuthin'!" Gage's voice was high-pitched, scratchy. His words chased Logan down the slope toward the empty road.

Logan turned when he reached there and his feet were on the tar. "I'll pay you everything I eat," he hollered back, "and you can pay old Thumper to haul your garbage for ya. Penny a bucket!"

Gage laughed and Logan laughed with him; the length of the driveway lay between them. "You little bastard!" his father called toward him cheerfully. Logan laughed again as he turned and started down the road.

The drive-in was on 196. You came upon it suddenly, a wide tarred break in the woods. In daylight the long screen looked dirty.

The whitish snack bar was in the middle of the parking area, windowless and low like a bomb shelter, speaker poles stretching out in lines vertical and horizontal. Logan arrived for work around three o'clock. The stale smell of the previous night's food hung in the air as he patrolled up and down the broken asphalt, hanging speakers back on their poles, picking up litter and shoving it into the burlap bag he carried in his left hand. His other hand wore an old glove. It disgusted him: mouth-shaped marks of ketchup on thin paper napkins, half-eaten hot dogs in their tattered rolls, the stickiness of soda cups. He found money sometimes, a plastic change purse, the half-ripped pages of a *True Detective* magazine, a baseball hat with a red visor, which he sold to Ronnie for a quarter; once the photo of a naked girl with a towel wrapped around her face, her thin body folded up on a couch. Logan thought she looked like a skinned weasel, but something in the way her arms were raised, hands clutching the towel, attracted him. Unbroken beer bottles he turned in for the deposit, the smashed glass he swept up with a short broom.

Mr. Curran owned the theater and he lived in the lot beside it in a long green trailer home. He was a thin, bald man with a patch on one eye and nervous ways. He could lean over his couch and stare between the blinds in his living room window and be assured of Logan's square figure tromping up and down his speaker poles, stooping at intervals, his right hand going out. Chester Curran had bought the drive-in with money from the accident settlement. His wife, Maxine, sold the tickets. She sat on a tall stool and snaked her skinny head out the open window of the ticket booth, peering into the cars to be sure no one was hiding curled up on the floor. After the night got dark and the first movie was almost over she worked in the snack bar with Logan. He was at the grill, the peaked white cap and apron making him look older. Chester Curran sat behind the cash register, his right leg elevated on a potato chip tin. Chester gave a happy little start every time the cash register rang and the drawer jumped out at him. His eye taking them in, he put change precisely into the palms of the customers, his fingers grasping coins firmly until the last possible moment. There were few customers after the second feature started, and Chester sat outside in a striped beach chair, his right leg stuck out in front of him. He heard small mumblings from speakers attached to car windows. He watched the screen, his white shirt gleaming, a cigarette in his right hand, the skin around his eyepatch pale. He didn't believe what he saw: the kissing, the gunfights, the roulette wheel at Monte Carlo.

It was well into the second movie and Logan was cleaning the grill. He flipped over the three hamburgers he was making for himself and slapped a piece of cheese down on each one. When they were done he set them on the edge to keep warm while he scraped grease into the trough. Mrs. Curran was across the room, seated at the end of the long white Formica counter. She was rolling coins. Logan ate the first cheeseburger with his free hand. There was the clack-clack of the coins on the counter and the scraping of Logan's spatula, the creaking of the fan that shoved the smoky air around. Logan picked up the second cheeseburger and bit into it. A girl had come in and Mrs. Curran was selling her popcorn. She was wearing striped pedal pushers and her hair was blond. Logan chewed and watched her. His french fries were heavy and cold. He licked his mouth.

"Laura," someone called.

Logan looked. He was a tall, sleek-looking boy; his white shirt was open at the throat. He crossed to the girl, and when he got close he smiled down into her face. He said something and Mrs. Curran turned and called to Logan: "Get 'em Cokes!" She watched over her glasses, her chin pointed down toward her coins. He turned and got two cups from the tall pile.

"No! A Coke and a Seven-up!" Mrs. Curran shouted. She tapped the keys of the cash register.

Logan watched them leave. The boy was holding the drinks and Laura had the popcorn. As they went by the grill Logan opened his mouth and belched as loud as he could. It echoed off the metal backing. The girl gave a startled little hop and giggled, her boyfriend shot Logan a grim look and walked faster toward the door. Logan watched them, his weight shifted onto one leg, the spatula half raised in his hand.

Mrs. Curran glared at him. She had bills between her fingers. "What'd you do that for?" she demanded.

Logan turned to look at her. The expression on his face was mild. She seemed small across the room, poised around the cash register. "Couldn't help it," he said. "Had to eat my supper so late it upset my stomach." He kept looking at her, his hand was going out for the third cheeseburger. He didn't need to see across the distance between them; he knew how her mouth was pursed up, her eyebrows shooting together like twin complaints over her nose, and he kept looking at her until she was watching her money again.

Logan was waiting, but when she drove him home that night Maxine didn't mention his burping at the customers. It was after one o'clock and the August night was cool, a long cloud had settled in front of the moon. Maxine was wearing her sweater; her window was rolled up. The car lurched over the crossing and went down the short slope onto the Dunstan Road.

Logan sat beside her, his window open and his arm resting on the frame. His back ached and he smelled like the grill. "Mother of God, roll up that window, Logan!" Maxine said, her eyes on the empty road. He worked the handle slowly, as if it were stiff, as if he lacked strength. He could hear the impatient huffing of her breath.

Some nights the house was in darkness, but this night the light in the kitchen was burning, making a small gray path on the grass. Logan walked up the driveway in the withdrawing beam of Maxine's headlights. He cut behind Gage's truck and went into the thick darkness of pine trees. He moved cautiously, his arm held above him to protect his face from branches. Then he dropped to his knees and felt along the remnants of the old stone wall. It was there, in the hole he'd dug between two flat rocks. He worked out the Crisco can. Inside was the soup can. He felt for his bills that were rolled up there and added thirty-three of the thirty-five dollars Mr. Curran had paid him that night. He put the can back carefully and crawled out from under the pines.

Gage turned his head when Logan came through the kitchen door. Thumper just kept staring at his own clasped hands, his head slightly bobbing. "So you're back!" Gage said, thudding his fist on the table to emphasize the last word.

Logan nodded toward him and made his way around Thumper's chair. Thumper didn't seem to be aware of him. He was lifting his bottle with both hands. There was something hanging from the brim of his hat that looked like cobwebs. Logan was almost to the wide doorway of the living room.

"Where you going in such a goddamn hurry, Mr. Business!" Gage said, lurching halfway out of his chair and grabbing him by the arm.

"To bed," Logan said, stiffening and drawing himself as far away from his father's grip as he could.

"Ain't you forgettin' something?" He grinned at Thumper and looked back at Logan, twitched his fingers against the flesh of his arm. "Huh?" he demanded, his voice deepening.

"I'm tired," Logan said. "I been working hard." He didn't try to pull his arm from his father's grip but his body was stiff.

"You been eatin' hard too," Gage said, and turned to Thumper, his face all pulled wide in a grin.

Thumper laughed, high-pitched, twittery, moist. "Eatin'," he repeated, nodding. "Eatin'."

Logan took the two bills from his pocket. "That's all I got," he said, holding them out. "I ain't had nuthin' but breakfast here all week."

Gage snatched at the money with his free hand. "Two lousy bucks!" he cried, his fingers spreading them like sparse tail feathers. "Two lousy bucks!" He half stood and swayed there, spittle on his teeth. "That all he pays you?" His head bucked as if it would yank an answer out of Logan. "If that's all he pays you you're a goddamn fool!"

Logan drew back until the fingers on his arm pinched and then tightened like teeth. "That's all I got," he said. "I'll eat nuthin' here next week and maybe that'll make you happy." His voice broke. He was tired, so tired he felt dizzy. His throat ached and his eyes felt as if he'd been staring at the sun all day.

"Well, don't cry about it!" Gage jeered, turning again to Thumper, opening his mouth wide, his mocking laughter dropping out. His hand fell from Logan. Thumper was snickering. He pulled a rag out of his pocket and blew his nose.

Logan was in the living room. He reached for the cord, pulled the folding ladder down, and climbed into the attic. His bed showed rumpled in the thin moonlight. The pillow was on the floor. Ronnie moaned and sniffled and coughed. Logan kicked his sneakers off and lay down. He reached the pillow from the floor and put it over his head and fell asleep.

* * *

The drive-in closed at the end of September but Logan quit a week early. He quit to work at the fair, in a booth of the itinerant carnival, and the last day he worked at the theater he brought his father's wire cutters and got himself a speaker. He knew Mr. Curran watched out the window of his trailer, so he took one from a pole on the other side of the snack bar, stuffed it into a burlap bag, and hid it under a pine tree down by the road. Then he went back to the snack bar and turned his grill on, measured butter into the popcorn machine. He told Maxine when she was getting ready to drive him home. "My last night," he said, and lying, "I got a ride."

She was standing in the doorway with her big blue purse slung over her elbow. "You mean you're quittin' us?" she said, her eyebrows darting toward each other.

"Yeah," he told her, "can't do it now. Got too much schoolwork," he lied again. Logan was in the ninth grade and he planned on attending only often enough to keep the truant officer from irritating Gage.

"You coulda give us a notice," she said, her hands going onto her hips, the pocketbook swaying heavily. "You coulda said good-bye to Mr. Curran."

Logan shrugged. "Good-bye," he said. "You tell him." He turned from her and started for the road. She stood in the doorway of the snack bar and watched him until he disappeared into the darkness; just the back of his neck and the white rimming on his sneakers showed, and then he was all gone.

He got the burlap sack out from under the tree and started down Route 196. He didn't mind walking. He was glad to be rid of Maxine, her pursed lips, the heavy smell of her perfume; he was glad to be done with them both. The night was mild. The Big Dipper curved along the northwest horizon, its points bright and sharp as though a scalpel had carved notches in the darkness to let through the light that lay beyond. Logan had struck a steady pace. He watched the road ahead of him; it was silvery and small pines rose dark on either side. The speaker was a comfortable weight nudging his leg as he went, the week's pay was in his pocket. He turned at the crossing and followed the railroad tracks. They glowed warm as old bronze in the soft light of the moon. Logan walked between them, the stones in the roadbed glittering under his feet. The night smells were thick and damp and the tarry odor of the ties wove through the sweetness of dying leaves. The wind blew in small undulations, modulating the night sounds: the small rustlings, a distant owl, the slight tossing of the maple branches where the trees rose beyond the cleared area that ran beside the tracks. Logan was warm under his thick jacket and he stopped to unzip it.

He saw them like a piece of the night moving before he heard the soft thudding of their hooves in the brush. He froze, his hand just letting go of the zipper tab. The doe climbed up the embankment and the fawn, almost as tall as she, moved with his face resting on the rise of her hip. The spots on his back were faint and large. She lifted her feet daintily over the first track.

Logan ground his teeth together. His palm ached for the shotgun he wasn't holding. "Aaahhh!" he screamed, and flung the burlap sack. The speaker thudded against the track as the doe, ten yards ahead, leapt it, the fawn with her—the arch of their forward plunge down the farther embankment tracing but one curve, their feet touching the earth again at the same instant.

"Bitch!" Logan cried. Standing at the crown of the railroad bed, he watched the space between the shadows of maple trunks where there had been for a heartbeat the white flames of their tails. His curse as it fell from his mouth was devoured by the clean night, and only the voice of the owl was heard, long and echoing, clear as the sound of an oboe, rising from the woods where the deer had fled. Logan bent and picked up his dented speaker and started again down the tracks toward his home.

It was hot both weeks of the fair. The bright rays of the setting sun pierced the eyes of the stuffed animals that stood on the high shelves of Logan's booth. They were gaudy colors; the manes of the lions and the ponies smelled singed, the large bears leaned against the thin portable walls with their short arms open wide. Peanuts Burke, who owned the Blue Dream Traveling Show, had hired him. He'd seen Logan hanging around the first days of the fair, and when the man he'd brought with him from New Hampshire quit, Peanuts offered the booth to Logan. Peanuts counted himself a good judge and he knew Persuasion when he met it. The boy had learned so damn quick, even quicker than Peanuts had hoped, but then some are born with it. Peanuts knew that.

Peanuts was a big man. Red suspenders held his pants up. He wore a captain's hat and chewed gum. His voice was low and people stepped closer to hear him when he spoke. The carnival booths were at the very edge of the fairgrounds next to a spindly woods. Then came the rides: the Wild Octopus, the bumper cars, the Ferris wheel, and the merry-go-round. Beyond it was the fair itself: the animal exhibits, the pulling ring, the pens, and the long open-sided buildings where crafts and home-cooked items were judged. Peanuts' duck-shooting gallery was next to the booth Logan ran. There was a plopping sound of BBs striking against the metal backstop behind the ducks, the heavy chain of the machinery rattling loudly as they dropped down to the next row and swam on.

Peanuts liked to listen to Logan work the crowd. He made it sound unremarkably easy, tossing the softballs into those bushel baskets, undersized and tilted at just the right angle. And how agile he was, bending to scoop up the balls, his wrist swiveling as he drew them up behind him and turned, quick as a magician, to place them on the narrow counter before the player. Logan gave consolation prizes—he'd started that the second night—a plastic whistle or a set of Japanese handcuffs, items valued in pennies to players who'd spent dollars trying to win a teddy bear for a girlfriend, a lion for their little girl. "Almost, almooost," Logan moaned, twisting his face as if the pain were his own. And when he'd suffered enough he brought out the consolation prize. They came on to Peanuts with grateful smiles on their faces, their fingers locked around Logan's gifts.

Logan wore a checkered shirt, there was a red change belt tied around his waist. He made a warm, jingling sound as he moved about his booth, leaning toward the crowd, stepping back close to his animals. "Three for a quarter," he coaxed. Holding the softballs in his hands as carefully as if they were eggs, he gestured with them and looked right into the eyes of the people as they walked by. "Easy enough for a little child!" he promised, half turning to look at the prizes. "Win yourself a beautiful trophy."

Logan earned a lot of money for Peanuts. He stole some of it but Peanuts knew that, had a good estimate of exactly how much. It was within bounds and he counted it part of his overhead, like the cost of the animals. He wanted to keep Logan, wanted him to stay with the show when they traveled south again.

* * *

Logan came outside his booth on the last night and scowled down the midway. Peanuts leaned against his own booth, his fingers peeling the paper off a stick of gum. He set it inside his mouth and, chewing slowly, watched the boy. Logan called to a couple coming along eating cotton candy: "Win that pretty girl one of my animals," he urged, his voice shrill. The boy only looked at him a second before he guided his girlfriend toward the Ferris wheel. "Fuck you too," Logan muttered.

Peanuts stepped over and put his hand out. His thick fingers curled over Logan's shoulder. Before they'd settled Logan jumped and twisted out from under their touch. "Take it easy," Peanuts told him. His voice was soft. "It's the last night, bound to be slow. I'll watch your booth. Walk around. See if there's anything you want to take in 'fore we close the show."

Logan narrowed his eyes. He took a step back toward the booth.

Peanuts smiled a little. The gum showed between his teeth. "Don't worry," he said. "Last night's always slow. That's the business." He sighed and smiled at Logan. "Go ahead, go on," he urged. "You've earned any pleasure you find. You're the hardest worker I seen since I was a kid." He laughed and his belly rose and fell, taut as a barrel stave against the red suspenders.

Logan didn't move. "That's all right," he said, his face rigid.

Peanuts laughed again. He reached into his pocket and drew out a wad of bills. He worked the gum to one side and licked his thumb, a long slow movement with the end of his tongue, and he felt the money until he pulled out a twenty. He gave it to Logan. "Here's your bonus," he told him. "Now you go have yourself some fun 'fore the fair closes. Then you come back and see me."

He watched Logan move off. He knew where he was going. He'd seen him looking at the tent, at the men when they came out, at the girls after the show. Nor did it surprise him that Logan went straight down the midway toward the rides. The next time he saw him Logan was at the top of the Ferris wheel, by himself in the center of an orange seat. The wheel had stopped and the car rocked slightly. Peanuts could tell it was Logan by the shape of his head and shoulders, the thick stolid look of him rocking in the sky, the fuzzy lights of the fairgrounds splayed across the night like amber smoke. Peanuts had a few players; he gave a sleepy little blond girl a plastic horse and rider he'd gotten sick of looking at. He turned from her just in time to see Logan going into the tent.

It was smoky and dim and half filled. He smelled the ashes and the sweat and spilled beer. He went past the empty benches, looking at the backs of heads, the crisscross wrinkles in the necks of the ones who were old. He was walking slowly. He paused and then sat down abruptly at the end of a vacant bench. He looked up at the stage, which was a low truck bed. The girls' heads almost touched the roof of the tent. Somewhere beneath their feet a needle clawed at a record; the music, sounding rusty, came in uneven jerks from two loudspeakers mounted on narrow poles in the corners.

There were three of them. Peanuts' niece Lucia was the star. She called herself Blue Iris. She was seventeen and her face was hard and very young. She had a short, stocky body and her long hair was dark. She flung it about as she danced. She painted her mouth and her fingernails and her toenails. They were a bright red that reminded Logan of the tongues and paws of the teddy bears on his shelves. There was a purple heart tattooed on her thigh. She was laughing. She reached up with her hands and flung her hair back to show her breasts. When the men in the audience yelped she grinned and started to twist her hips. The other girls, one on either side of her, were young also. They were thin and blond and cold in the tent in the October night.

Logan watched Iris. His heart was thudding inside him, his stomach felt almost nauseous. He realized his mouth was hanging open and he shut it. She stepped forward to the very rim of the stage and the men in the front row had to tip their heads back. She kept drawing her hands up her body and holding her breasts, and her hips were moving with the tinny music. "Oh, oh," she cried, her face softening, her voice low, but everyone could hear.

They called her name, they nudged each other and laughed. She didn't answer them, didn't even glance down at their faces, but looked beyond them, her eyes half closed. She moved more slowly and the men grew quiet and watched her.

Iris danced. She patted herself. Logan could tell by the way she held her mouth that she was humming. The record got stuck and she laughed and kept repeating the movement of her hips until somebody under the truck bed knocked it and it jumped. Iris jumped too, for a breath she wavered, then her feet thumped hard, one and the other, and she was dancing again.

The blond girls stretched and took off the little skirts that were small pink pleats and rumpled. They dropped them daintily behind them and nudged them farther back with their feet. They had on little shiny underpants and the skin of their hips was pale as a perch's belly. Logan stared at them. He felt sick. He locked his fingers into fists and set them on his knees and rocked slowly.

Iris was talking to the men in the front row. She looked down at them, at the tops of their heads and their uplifted faces, then undid something and the little skirt she had on just fell. She stood taller and turned slowly from side to side, preening like a bird. She touched her hair and her belly, and then she was talking to the men again.

Logan wanted to kill them, to kill them all, and step on the faces of the blond girls and have Iris. He got up and, half crouching, moved forward several rows until he could sit nearer the stage. There was a man seated at the far end of the bench, a blond man who was small and wore round glasses that made his face look younger than it was. Logan barely glanced at him before staring at Iris. Closer now, he could see it was a butterfly tattoo on her thigh, he could see the different tones and colors of her body. When her eyes flickered onto him he felt as if she'd burned him, and then he couldn't look at her and he felt so angry he couldn't breathe either.

Something happened to the record again and Iris turned around and walked to the back of the tent and stood there facing her own shadow. She lifted her hands and ran her fingertips down the canvas. Her legs were short and strong and her hips curved like a basket. Logan couldn't stop looking at her flesh.

The record started again, softer music, and she turned and came forward, to the edge of the stage, and right down the small stairs. Above her the blond girls were still dancing. They looked weary but Iris was smiling like a bride as she came up the narrow aisle. Men were calling her name but she kept on to the fourth row of benches. She squeezed past Logan—he could have tasted her—and she reached her hand out as if she were shooing a fly and took the glasses off the blond man's face. He clapped at the place where they had been but she was away.

She went back up on the stage, her arm uplifted, swaying the glasses above her head like a trophy. Little glints of light shot from them. She turned and held them before her face and blew on them gently several times. Then she drew her hand down her body and slipped them into the red satiny cloth that covered her crotch.

The men laughed, tight static noise; half turning, they pointed at the blond man. His face was pale and apologetic without the glasses. He sat with his head half bowed and his shoulders drawn up. The man on the next bench, thin and long-necked like a young turkey, reached over the space between them to bang his arm. They all laughed at him and watched Iris.

She was tender with herself. Her feet were spread wide and she was smiling down at the blond man. His round eyes blinked. When the music ended she walked again to the very edge of the stage so that her red toenails were tensed over it. "Come get your glasses, sweetheart," she called, waving them toward him.

The men turned and whooped, mocking her tones. He slowly got up and came down the aisle. They pushed at him, urging him on. "She sure fogged you!" one of them yelled, and they laughed and pushed at him some more.

Blue Iris watched him coming toward her, his hands folded in front of him. She looked at Logan and back at the blond man. Laughing, her head tipped slightly to one side, she knelt and her hand reached out, presenting the glasses. After he took them and shoved them in his pocket, she looked at Logan, dead at him, and she straightened her shoulders and stood up.

"Put them glasses on! Put 'em on!" the men were calling and then the lights when out. "Hey!" they shouted as the blond man groped in darkness toward the exit. Logan jumped up, his elbows out should anyone bump into him. When the tent brightened a minute later she was gone, they were all gone, just three little piles that were their skirts left on the stage. But Logan was sure he could hear her laughter as he turned and half ran for the door.

He paused outside and stood blinking. His body felt as if it didn't belong to him, as if he'd gone somewhere else where gravity pulled harder. All the people in the midway looked like midgets. He pivoted slowly, his arms held out as if for balance, then drove himself between the side of the tent and the booth that held the dart game. He was looking at the back of the carnival, dirty and dark and empty. He twisted around and started off toward the low trees where he could see a small light burning. He tromped through uneven grass clumps toward her trailer. It was rounded and silver and attached to a long pinkish Oldsmobile. His fist thudded on the dented door.

"You're Logan, ain't you?" she said when she opened it.

He tripped on the steps. Had he really yelled his name out to her? It was hot inside the trailer. There was one lamp on, rising up behind the couch, the neck twisted so it shone on the low ceiling. He could smell fried potatoes, and the heavy scent of her hair; there was something else, too. He lunged forward and pulled at the smooth green robe she had on, his breath stumbling in and out of his throat.

She acted as if he weren't there, as if she were doing it by and for herself. She gasped and pulled on his hips. Her nails in his flesh were like fire. Her body burned around him like a stretching flame. He felt himself lifted and at the same time his knuckles were sinking into the soft cushions of the couch as if he were falling through sand.

When he rose from her he could smell the sweat in her robe and the sharpness of his own body; his dim shadow ascended the curtain, the breath in his throat hurt. She was pale, the robe where it had fallen from her was dark and rumpled, her knee pressing against his own was bony. He thought her eyes were closed, the shadow of the sofa back fell over her, but then he saw that she was watching him.

The child was watching him also. She stood very straight and still, her face and the white neck of her nightgown visible above the sofa arm. "Mumma," she spoke in a low voice.

Logan stood and grappled with his pants, his fingers working on the belt as Lucia sat up and turned to the child. He stared at her while Lucia's hands guided her around the arm of the sofa and into her lap. "Yes, baby?" she asked, and kissed her hair. The little girl settled close in her circling arms and knees. She looked back at Logan, the expression in her eye solemn.

"What's wrong with her?" His voice in the small space was harsh and loud. His heavy face was twisting so that his lips were pulled down. He backed and his heel was jammed against a metal trunk. He kept looking at the child while he waited for Lucia to answer.

She sighed. He could see how she drew the little girl closer. "Some kinda tumor. Growed right over her eye like that." She kissed her forehead; her soft hair was hiding most of Lucia's face. "Won't go away. Ever. They said if they cut it off it'd grow right back worse. She ain't gonna live long."

"Mumma," the child whispered. She was almost asleep.

"You had her? She's yours?" He bent so he could see her better. Her soft mouth was partly opened. She sighed and he could smell her milky breath; her head turned then and fell against her mother and the ruined eye was looking straight at Logan. His face twitched.

"She's mine," Lucia answered. "Renata." Her white arms were around the little girl, whose open palm lay next to the butterfly on Lucia's thigh.

Logan straightened; he turned toward the door.

"You don't want nuthin' to drink?"

He shook his head. His hand reached for the metal doorknob.

"Uncle Parker wants you to come with us when we go tomorrow," she told him. "He says you could be the best."

He turned. "Uncle Parker?"

"Peanuts." The word was a weary sound.

"He ain't your uncle." He glared at her.

She returned his look, but her face was tired now, or bored. She shrugged. "Well, I always thought that he was," she said, "since I was her size." She moved her mouth across the child's hair, lifted her chin and grinned, amusement moving over her face like light across an ebony mask.

When Logan opened the door he could hear the thin music of the merry-go-round. He stepped down the two narrow stairs and leaned to push it shut, his knuckles scraping painfully against the frame. As he walked through the tall grass to the midway he sucked on his fist where he was bleeding. He could see Peanuts standing in front of the booth, the heavy pull of his belly slung before him like a clinging goblin. He walked toward him. Peanuts was watching him under the dark bill of his hat. "I'll take it now," Logan told him.

Peanuts shifted his weight. "Business is real slow," he said, "but tomorrow we'll be opening in a new town."

Logan pulled the thin door and stepped into his booth. He rubbed the stinging knuckles against his thigh and looked up at his animals. They were all there.

"I'll offer you this booth permanent," Peanuts said, leaning over the counter. "There's still a lotta money you could make 'fore the season ends." He watched him, moving his gum slowly between his jaws. "You can stay with us over the winter. There's room for you." He smiled. "Don't ever snow," and he laughed, looking hard at Logan. "Well, hardly. Then the season starts again 'fore you know it."

Logan lifted two softballs out of the basket. He turned with them in his hands and watched the couple coming down the midway. "Thanks, Peanuts, but I guess I couldn't do that. It'd make my mother awful sad I go away from her young as I am." He laughed and, shifting his gaze from the couple, looked at Peanuts, who was still smiling, his small teeth glimmering in the fuzzy light. "I would like to buy something offa you though."

Peanuts straightened, drawing his hands back until his fingers were splayed out on the countertop.

"I'll pay you twenty bucks for that blue bus you got parked out back." He gestured with his head. He was shifting the softballs in his hands and looking from the approaching couple to Peanuts.

Peanuts had lifted his hands from the counter. He stepped back, looking coolly at Logan. "Don't run," he said softly. "I couldn't sell you a bus that don't run."

Logan shrugged. "Town ain't gonna like it you just leave it here like trash, rusting till next year when you wanna come back."

Peanuts looked woeful. "You been good to me, boy, you worked real hard. I can't sell you a bus that won't drive."

"Ain't gonna drive it," Logan told him. "Gonna park it."

Peanuts leaned back and laughed hard, his gum sitting on his tongue like a boil.

Logan was watching the couple again. They'd been proceeding slowly and now had almost reached his booth. "I'll give you twenty-five," he told Peanuts.

Logan planned it so Gage was out on the garbage route. Jimmy Beasley from the Texaco hauled it right into the side yard and unhooked the wrecker, took Logan's ten dollars, and left.

His mother watched through the hazy glass in the back door. The bus didn't move. It lay under the tall pines in the side yard, still as something at the bottom of a lake. And blue, deep blue. She squinted her eyes. The white letters, wavering along the side said, "Blue Dream Traveling Show." Ronnie's breath was wet on her neck.

"What's he doin', Ma?" He was stretching on tiptoe; it strained his voice.

She shrugged her shoulders, shifting his chin. "Movin' around in there," she answered softly. They could see his shape, darkening the windows, one and then the next. He was at the back for a long time and then the emergency door crashed open and stood out flat from the curving rear. White letters painted on it announced "The End." Logan leapt to the ground, walked the length of the bus, and climbed in again.

Linette opened the door and came out on the first step. Ronnie's fingers were touching her elbow. She shaded her eyes. The sun was very bright. The maples rose beyond the pines red as flames, their dry leaves clattering in the chill wind. She folded her arms so she could hold each elbow, Ronnie pressed against her. They hunched down two more steps. "He got a bus, Ma," Ronnie said hoarsely. He looked at her and rubbed his damp nose on the sleeve of her sweater. She nodded. "A bus," she whispered. They stared while Logan flapped the door open and closed.

Gage got home about one. As he turned off the road some peelings lifted from the back of his truck and settled over the front yard. He came up the driveway fast, the bins and barrels on the back of his truck too loaded to rattle as it lurched between the bus and the house and started down the slope to the pig runs. Logan was unbolting a seat. The inside of his bus smelled like popcorn and dirty clothes. When he heard the long yowl of the brakes he twisted harder with the wrench. Then he rose, opened the door, and climbed down to stand outside.

Gage puffed up the hill, his face red. He leaned forward, his feet spread wide, breathing hard and glaring at Logan. "I thought I was seein' things!" he bellowed. "Lucinatin'!" And he thumped the side of the bus with his fist. "But I ain't! What the hell is this pile of crap doin' in my yard!" He thumped again and started coughing.

"I bought it," Logan said. "Offa guy."

"Well, get the son-of-a-bitchin' thing outta here," Gage told him, gesturing with his finger toward the road.

"It don't drive," Logan said.

Gage paused, pushed his hat up on his forehead. "Then drag it outta here same's you drug it in!" His heavy face was dark, his eyes narrowed and keen as a gambler's. "What you mean it don't drive?"

"Engine blown." Logan stood squarely before the open door, his hand out and just resting against the side of the bus.

"Aaah!" Gage scoffed. "You was stupid enough to buy something with a blowed engine!" He stretched his eyebrows up on his forehead until they pulled at the corners of his eyes. "Or you find it out afterwards?" he demanded, leaning forward and spitting the last word into Logan's face.

"I bought it to live in. I can't drive yet."

"You can drive!" Gage said as if he'd caught Logan in a lie.

"I can't get the license till I'm sixteen."

"So you thought you'd park this lumpa crap in my yard and live in it." Gage stood straight as he spoke, his fingers twining in the pockets of his overalls.

Logan nodded. "I ain't got much room up there with Ronnie." He nodded again and glanced toward the attic.

"You complainin'?"

"No." He looked along the length of his bus; already the tires seemed sunken and settled in the earth. Down the hill his father's truck waited. The pigs were crowded at the fence, their faces uplifted. "Ronnie's gettin' older, gettin' to where he might like his own room," he said, turning to face Gage again.

"Oh, ain't you nice," he mocked. "You park a load of crap in my yard without askin' my permission which I woulda said no, all so your little brother can get his own room!" He swung his face fast as a snake close to Logan again. Logan smiled. He let his face go sheepish.

"Haa! Haa!" Gage crowed, poking his shoulder. "So how much you gonna pay me to let you park your bedroom here?"

Logan looked at him. He was ready for this but he shrugged his shoulders limply.

"What's it worth to ya? Since you're *so nice* to your little brother it must be worth a lot!" Gage licked his lips. The teeth that remained to him were small and square, stained like old shells by tobacco. He laughed hard, then stopped abruptly and watched Logan.

Logan looked vague. In the silence while they waited the brisk swishing of the maple leaves rose up. A headache was pressing behind Logan's eyes like a malevolent hand. He was thinking how he could park the bus at the drive-in and, Curran being gone to Florida, he wouldn't have to worry till spring. But he couldn't park it near the road where it would be seen, and he couldn't plow; he didn't want to have to haul water. "Dollar a month," he said.

Gage grabbed onto his ear as if it had failed him. "Dollar a day more like it!" he shrieked.

Logan shrugged, turned to climb into the bus. "I'll sell it to Jimmy then," he said. "Seats alone is worth a lotta money." He stood on the second step and turned to look down at his father. "Scrap metal man love to get his hands on this bus. Solid iron," he told him.

Gage braced his hands on the door and shoved his head inside. Logan retreated up one more step and looked toward the back of the bus, where the emergency door was still open.

"Fi' dollars a month," Gage said. "Guy that owns all them seats and *solid iron* oughtta be able to pay fi' dollars a month." He smiled at Logan, tipping his head to look at him, one foot lifted onto the bottom step, his palm lying flat on the glass of the opened door. Around his mouth there was mirth but his flat eyes were as eager as any hunter's.

"Not with the kerosene," Logan said, "and the other stuff I need." He started walking. The emergency door was open wide and the blue day hung beyond it like the empty world beyond the moon.

"Well for Christ's sake, how much?" Gage's voice followed him down the aisle like a thrown rock.

"Three bucks," he said, stopping and turning. He sat down and put his feet neatly together in the aisle. He looked at his father, whose face rose just above the floor by the driver's seat. The black orb on the gearshift hung over his head like a descending mallet.

Gage gaped at Logan. "Guess your baby brother havin' his own room don't mean much to you when it comes down to it," he said.

"That's all I got to pay you," Logan told him, lifting his hands and letting them fall against his thighs.

"The day comes I tell you to get this shitbucket outta here you get it gone." Gage pounded his fist on the floor of the bus. Logan felt it under his feet. He looked down at his father and nodded slowly.

"Come help me unload the truck," Gage said, straightening up out of the bus and pulling his hat down over his forehead.

Logan jumped out the emergency door and started down the hill. He could smell the dying leaves, and the garbage, and the muggy odor of the pigs. They were snorting loudly now, shifting their feet and pressing against the fence, pointing their dolphinlike smiles toward the truck.

Logan traded one of the seats for a battery-run radio. He painted the windows black on the side that faced the house. The seats he didn't use to make a bed and a couch and, turned upside down, a table, he sold. He got an old kerosene heater and rammed the pipe through the window of the emergency door. During the winter months he slept near it, grimly satisfied that he needed only a shirt and the worn blanket he'd taken from his bed. He thought of Ronnie up in the attic buried under a mound of blankets like a grub in a trash heap while the wind slapped its way through the roof and shook the glass in the window above him. Logan read *True Detective* magazines, he played poker against himself, he slept better than he had done in the house. His bed was four bus seats pushed together, so it was like being in a long, seamed box, the backs of the seats rising up. He lay flat with his head toward the square heater, the light of the fire flickering through the air vents and dancing around the inside of the bus, beating like trapped birds against the blackened windows and the true night side that faced the pines. The flames breathed hoarsely, the wind when it came bayed like running dogs, snow hissed on the roof and tapped with short sharp strokes on the windows, the blackened and the seeing. Logan lay in the bus beside his father's house like a monk in his cell, clean and separate. Often when he slept he dreamed he was driving the bus, that it was moving through everything in its way, deep mud that spattered the windshield, narrow cliff roads that dropped straight to blackness, over the faces of the people in the house across the driveway. Sometimes Lucia was there, just outside the windows, laughing and laughing, her long hair streaming like seaweed. He went faster, faster; she remained, her mouth flattened on the glass, her eyes blurred, her fingers spread like starfish against the windows; on other nights she was pulled from the glass by his speed, and then she was gone, out behind his bus, small as a bird, her hair a slight mark in the blue of the sky, a shadow in the downpouring rain.

By February the snow rose above the windows, the path to his door was packed ice, and he half slid out and across the driveway to take his meals with them, to use the bathroom, to pay his father the three dollars. His money lay buried under the snow under the old rock wall. He earned more buying and selling things, tools and old tires, parts off the bus, things he found at the dump and patched.

"You ain't froze yet? Or blowed yourself up with kerosene?" Gage demanded regularly when he came in for supper.

Logan looked down at himself and lifted his hands and let them fall helplessly. "I guess I'm still here," he said, and every time Gage howled with laughter.

"You think you're a big shot," he told him, "movin' out on us, but you ain't got far! Shit!" he said, twisting his head around to address his wife. "We might never get rid of him, and then this one," and he jabbed his finger at Ronnie. "This one'll set up housekeepin' in one of them Volkswagen Beetles. He'll be settin' on your front lawn like some damn turtle. You can tell your neighbors, 'That's my boy—growed a shell like a damn reptile.' "

She was serving beans. She spooned them out faster. Ronnie looked from her hands to his own plate. His lids were beating fast so that her fingers and his plate came and went in flashes of light. Finally he paused and looked up at his father, as far as his chest. "But I ain't gonna do that," he said, speaking slowly and severely.

Logan laughed so suddenly he spat out a little milk; his father roared and pounded both fists on the table so the silverware jumped. They laughed and laughed, and the two silent ones drew close together as she spooned out more beans onto his plate and he closed his eyes and breathed slowly, slowly, taking in the hot green smell of the vegetables, the sharp scent of laundry soap in her blouse, the dry odor of her skin.

JUBAL SOPER

8

The Rudge family had moved back to Portland just before Christmas in 1960. They lived several places in the city before finally settling in an apartment on the second floor of a tall yellow house on Brackett Street. That summer when Flynn turned ten Jarvis had steady work at the fish-packing plant. Viola was baby-sitting for Benjamin Griffin. He was nine months old and he lived on the first floor with his mother, Mariam, who worked at the Kresge's on Congress Street.

Flynn was a very small child, he still stayed home with his mother. Krista was thin and all angles: new breasts, pointy knees, shiny shins; her thick hair hung past her shoulders. Kendrick, at fourteen, was suddenly taller than his father, and when they stood together Jarvis looked diminished. Kendrick was a graceful boy, self-contained and serious. His face and his body were changing so that the bones and the muscles, the shape of him becoming, sat on him like a silken coat he was growing toward.

As soon as school got out he was looking for a job. He tried at several stores and at the packing plant where Jarvis was. Then he saw a sign on a utility pole downtown: "Farm Help Wanted." There was a pencil drawing of a basket holding beans. The next morning he waited under the sign, a lunch bag hanging from his hand. The others waiting there, women and teenage girls, were lined up with their toes looping over the curb.

The farm was out in Cape Elizabeth; the sun-soaked fields stretched toward the sea. The sky was hot blue. Kendrick started picking in shoulder-high pea vines; the pods made a soft sound like cat feet when he dropped them into his basket. Mrs. Spivey was in charge. Her dark yellow hair was pulled back onto the top of her head, where it sat in a bun small as the circular pieces in Tinkertoys. She bumped up and down the fields in a golf cart shaded by a red umbrella, which pulled a slat-sided trailer holding gathering baskets. Binoculars hung from her neck on a sweat-stained strap, a thick yellow pencil was tied to her wrist. She wore sagging pedal pushers and her short calves showed round and hard as the heads of tomahawks. Mrs. Spivey's rusty voice could be heard clear as a siren at the end of a five-hundred-foot row. "Doll!" was what she called everybody.

She stopped beside Kendrick and revved her engine: "Don't know ya, doll!" she bellowed.

He straightened. "I want to work," he said, telling her his name. "They gave me this basket," and he gestured toward the road where a little stand stood in a line of oaks.

"Pay per basketful!" she shouted. "On Saturday. No lazing, no stealing vegetables. And that means you don't eat outta the field, doll!"

He nodded. She was vibrating, her golf cart was vibrating, the red umbrella shimmied, small puffs of blue smoke rose up.

"We'll see how you do, doll!" she screeched, grinding into reverse.

By noon the heat was rising off the fields. Everyone stopped work and went to sit under the trees to eat lunch. Kendrick settled on the edge of the group. They were all women and girls and they chatted like birds. He wished he'd brought more lunch, and when the break was over and he got up his back felt old.

The end of the day finally came. The sun cut a great wash of yellow across the plants and Mrs. Spivey leaned hard on the high-pitched horn of her golf cart. They all headed for the line of oaks where she waited to check off their last basket. When it was Kendrick's turn he told her, "I want to buy some peas."

She leaned out of her cart and looked him up and down. "You ain't got nothing stuffed down your pants, have you, doll?" she demanded, watching him with eyes that were pale and lidless like a sleepy reptile's.

"No," he answered after a moment, when he'd figured out what she meant.

She barked her laughter and her two big teeth showed. "You got something to carry 'em in?" she asked.

He hesitated, then started to pull off his T-shirt.

"Hold on," she told him, flapping her hand. "One of them burlap bags will do ya better."

"Thanks," he said, reaching for it.

"Cost three cents. I'll take it out of your wages like the peas," she told him, writing in her notebook.

Viola was out that afternoon, as she was most sunny afternoons, pushing Ben Griffin in his stroller. Ben liked to ride, he liked to frown at everything he saw and then sleep, his head tipped forward and his fist folded on the front of his jersey. Flynn came too, his hand lifted to hold the long bar just under Viola's hand. They went downtown, as they often did, down to the Kresge's to visit Mariam and have a dish of ice cream.

"Here's my sweetheart!" Mariam cried, hurrying from behind the counter. "Here's my baby boy!" she said, her eyes going soft. She was a delicately made young woman with soft brown hair that she pinned up on top of her head while she was at Kresge's.

Ben bounced up and down in his stroller when he saw her. His arms reached. She plucked him out of it and kissed and kissed him. "Do you want chocolate today, Flynn?" she asked, her words whooshing out to stir Ben's wispy yellow hair. Flynn smiled and climbed up carefully onto the red stool.

She walked them to the door when it was time to leave. "Are you going to go by the shoe store?" she asked Viola.

"Well, sure. We always do," Viola told her.

Ben twisted around in his stroller to watch her as long as he could. Mariam was out on the sidewalk waving. Flynn dipped to pat Ben's shoulder. "Okay, Beh , okay," he assured him as they rolled on away from her pink-uniformed figure.

The shoe store was on the next street and Viola held Ben up so he could look at the bright sneakers in the window. His father, Gerard O'Donnell, a married man with three children bearing his name, was the manager. He was kneeling on the floor with his hands around a woman's foot when he looked up and saw Ben in the window. His face took on a dazed expression.

"Nine and a half C," he mumbled quickly and stood. "Red?" he asked before he turned and came straight to the window. "Hi, Ben," he mouthed, waving his hand frantically. "Hi, honey!"

Viola hugged Ben closer and lifted his hand in a wave. Ben frowned. Viola and Gerard never quite looked at each other. It amused her but she kept that to herself. This man seemed almost half-witted to her and she couldn't imagine how he'd stumbled into Mariam and created this beautiful baby. The woman called out from her chair and Gerard turned and almost tripped over a knee-high mirror. He looked back at Ben once more before he hurried to her, and his face was so woeful Viola almost felt sorry for him.

She was surprised when they got home and Kendrick wasn't there. Krista hadn't seen him. She made supper and Jarvis got home and had his shower and Kendrick still hadn't appeared.

"He'll be here," Jarvis told her. "You know how he likes to travel around on his own and look at things."

"He's late for supper."

"He'll be here."

When she finally heard his feet on the stairs she hurried out on the porch. "Where have you been?" she hollered down to him. "Your dad's been home two hours!"

He stopped and held the bag up. "Got a job!" he almost shouted. Then he resumed climbing.

"Why didn't you tell us? Where?"

"Just happened." He grinned. "Working on a farm."

"I thought you'd gotten hurt, Kendrick. Your supper's all dried out. What farm? Where?"

He reached the porch and pushed the bag at her.

Viola opened it and, lifting her face, smiled at him. "Real peas!" she said.

"You're too slow, doll!" It was Mrs. Spivey's voice, clanging out like a dented gong. Kendrick stood up straight. But she wasn't shouting at him. She was at the end of the next row, risen up in the golf cart, holding her wheel with one hand. The other hand was lowering the binoculars. "And you're eating peas!" she bellowed. The umbrella listed to the left, its fringed edges vibrating. "You!" she screamed. "You with the pink shorts! You and the one with you!"

The girls' heads disappeared. The vines shook. Kendrick hunkered down and watched between the round, green leaves. "I'm talking to you!" Mrs. Spivey screeched, and she headed her golf cart down the bare dirt trail between the two rows. It sounded like a motorboat as she bore down on them. She didn't stop and the girls had to jump up quickly to get out of her way. Kendrick picked faster. He heard the golf cart go into idle. "You girls are done!" she said above the rapidly repeating cough of her motor. "This is work, and nobody eats nothing out of this field 'less they pay for it!"

Kendrick started at the top of the next plant.

"We won't do it again," one of the girls said crossly. "We just wanted a taste."

"Taste, nothing!" Mrs. Spivey roared. "You was at it steady, chomping like goats!"

"It's mean not to give us another chance," the other one protested in a high voice.

But Mrs. Spivey tortured her gears into forward. "This is work, this ain't romper room," she said as she started herding them down the row. The taller girl turned and swatted at the golf cart with her bandanna but Mrs. Spivey rolled on as immovable from her course as a planet.

Kendrick stood up and watched until they were heads and a red umbrella, a blue cloud of smoke traveling on toward the road, and then he bent again to his labors.

Mrs. Spivey paid cash after work on Saturday. Kendrick counted it: seventeen dollars and forty-two cents. He put it carefully into his pocket, and when he got home he gave his mother five dollars. After supper he went downtown and bought himself a package of Kool cigarettes and a black felt, broad-brimmed hat with a pheasant feather in the band. When he came walking back home up Brackett Street there was still money in his pocket.

His father was smoking on the front steps and Kendrick settled himself beside him and opened his cigarettes. The cellophane vanished in the twilight and he tapped one out.

"That's quite a hat!" Jarvis told him.

Kendrick grinned and put the cigarette in his mouth. Their smoke sifted into the waning light of the evening and disappeared above the gray street. Jarvis leaned forward and shot the stub of his Camel out past the sidewalk. As he straightened, the front door clicked behind them and Mariam Griffin walked out on the porch. She came down the steps and brought the odor of newly opening lilac blossoms with her. The hem of her green dress swung against Kendrick's shoulder. "Hi," she said to them.

Jarvis looked up and nodded to her.

"Krista's staying with Ben," she told them. "I'm going up the corner for a little while." Her voice was low and tender. As she went down the steps she tapped her fingers on Kendrick's knee. Her open-toed shoes made no noise on the sidewalk, and they were so white they shone above the gray bricks. Her hair swung slowly across her back.

"She can't stay up late," Jarvis called.

Mariam looked over her shoulder and her hand waved back at them, the gesture small and girlish.

Jarvis settled against the step again. "You take some of your money and buy yourself a little notebook and a pen so you can write down the work you do," he told Kendrick. He nudged him with his knee and Kendrick turned. "You write it down where they can see you doing it," Jarvis said.

"I will. I'll buy one tomorrow. I'll go over to the pharmacy." Kendrick turned back to look down the street where Mariam was now a swaying of green and gold light at the end of the block.

Jarvis shifted and reached into his pocket. "The bastards won't like you for it," he said, "but they'll think twice before trying to screw you."

Kendrick looked at him again. Jarvis was lighting a match. He watched him bring it toward his face. His hands were stained and one of his knuckles was split open. Kendrick leaned closer. "You do that?" he asked. "You write everything down?"

Jarvis exhaled a long stream of smoke. "You make sure *you* do it," he said, his voice cracking a little as the harshness slid into it.

The bow window in the first-floor apartment curved out into the porch and Krista could hear her father's voice. Its angry tones jumped through the white curtains of Mariam's bedroom where she stood watching Ben sleep. His crib was across from his mother's bed and he slept on his stomach with his knees drawn up. It was dim in the room and Krista was leaning over the raised side of the crib. She could smell Benjamin's hair, the odors of the powder and baby oil his mother rubbed into his skin with the quick rolling of her fingers around his body. She straightened up then and went quietly across the room to Mariam's dressing table. She sat on the low chair and turned on the lamp. The glow danced in the three-sided mirror. Krista leaned closer and looked at herself, at her two profiles, how the soft light burned in her cheeks. She touched all the little bottles of perfume, held them in her hands, the hairpins, the emery boards, narrow-tipped bottles of nail polish. She set down Mariam's tortoiseshell hair band, rose and went to the closet, opened the door. She ran her fingers down the silky clothes, pulled them forward so the light reached and caught in their colors.

Jubal Soper didn't come on until the beans were ready to harvest. She was the skinniest girl in the fields. Her legs were like a heron's, long and straight; her feet were always bare. Her hair was black and smooth as shadows on stone, worn in one braid that fell almost to her waist and tapered in a fine point like a sable brush. Her arms were bony and long, and between her limbs her body was narrow and sturdy and straight as a candle. Kendrick loved to look at her. It was more than that, he couldn't not look at her. He banged into things, he tripped over baskets, and row hills, and his own feet. He dreamed of her and woke early, not needing any more sleep. He ran downtown early and waited and waited for the truck that brought them to the bean field. Each day it was a kind of agony wondering if she would be there, followed by the bliss of his first sight of her. Gathering up a basket, oblivious of him, she went straight-backed, into the field. He always hurried to get into a row behind her so he could keep her in constant view as he worked, his eyes feeding him with delight.

It was a week before he learned her name.

"That Jubal," he heard the women say as they were walking toward the trees to eat lunch. "She thinks she's special just 'cause Mrs. Spivey's her aunt."

"Snotty little bitch!" another said, "but Indians is like that, snotty and crazy both!"

He rushed to catch up with them, his hands fists. "What do you mean!" he cried. "Are you talking about that girl?" and he pointed toward her reedlike back.

Mrs. Taylor smiled at him. "You didn't know? Her mother's an Indian married Mrs. Spivey's brother." She leaned toward him in an exaggerated gesture. "You got a crush on her, Kendrick?" she mocked in her scratchy voice.

He reared back from her as if she had some crude disease. Then he ran, cutting across the field, hopping over bean plants to reach the trees ahead of them. Panting, he sat down under the last oak.

He sprawled his legs out in front of him, put his hat on the ground and drank from his thermos. As he looked along the row of trees, their wide leaves limp in the heat, he saw the women. They were spread out like colorful laundry. She wasn't there. His mind puzzled with the thought of her being related to Mrs. Spivey in any way. He realized he'd never heard her speak. He drank from the thermos again and rustled in his bag for a sandwich. As he bit into it there was the soft plop of something landing in the grass, just grazing the brim of his hat. He picked up the acorn and looked into the tree. The branches reached unmoving above him, the leaves drooped earthward. He lowered his face and bit again into his sandwich. He was chewing when another acorn bounced off his head.

"Hey!" he yelled, jumping up. "Hey!" He stared into the tree but could see nothing except folded leaves, the thick sprawl of branches, some small pieces of blue sky. He walked around the trunk with his hand testing the top of his head. When he stopped he could hear a quick murmuring sound coming out of the leaves. And then her face was upside down in front of his own, her braid falling to his belt, her eyes level with his and dark as a wild bird's eyes. Then she was reaching her hands onto his shoulders. She pushed herself so she swung from her legs like a trapeze artist. The warmth of her touching him spread right through him to the bottoms of his feet and he stopped breathing. She laughed.

"I didn't hurt you, did I?" she asked. "Your head was just . . . down there," she explained, and his hand went up slowly to his skull again. Her white cotton shirt had rolled up and Kendrick wanted to pull it toward the sky so her stomach didn't show. He moved his hand from his head to reach halfway toward that shirt. He tried his voice.

"Are you really related to Mrs. Spivey?" he asked, and he didn't know if he was booming at her or barely whispering.

She laughed, and lifting one hand out of the air, she put it over her lips. As the sound leapt out from around her small fingers he stepped closer, as if to see it. But then she was drawing her body up into the leaves and suddenly she was on the ground in front of him.

"My stepfather is her stepbrother," she explained, speaking in a businesslike way, "so there's no blood between us." Her head and neck were like a long blossom on a fine stalk.

"Oh." He nodded, narrowing his eyes. His heart was beating so hard he was dizzy. She was the same color everywhere: her face and her knees and her feet. Even the insides of her arms were honey-colored. He saw how she held her hands together, the fingers touching, and then he realized her fingers were trembling. "Oh," he groaned, and nearly caught her hands with his. But instead he stepped back and said almost gruffly, "I didn't think you could be, not really."

The top of her head reached his chin. She was looking up into his eyes and smiling. He was caught there that close to her, and it felt dangerous and blissful at once.

"Thanks," she said, and the word fell slowly out of her mouth batted by her laughter. "I'm trying to cast a spell so that golf cart will take off and just keep going until it's dumped her into the ocean."

He smiled. She was watching: how his mouth moved, the long line of his jaw, how green his wide-set eyes were, the way his neck and shoulder came together, the smoothness of his skin there.

After lunch they started working in the same row—Jubal first, taking every other plant; Kendrick following, reaching carefully among the leaves. They didn't talk, and she was faster, but she waited for him at the end of the row, and when Mrs. Spivey bumped by in the golf cart Jubal just turned and watched Kendrick, her black eyes leveled at the soft, stippled pheasant feather that rose from his hat.

Krista banged on the bathroom door. She leaned her forehead against it. "Come onnn, Kendrick!" she bawled. "I wanna get in there." She tipped her head so she was staring at the stained ceiling, and called his name. Then she listened: he was brushing his teeth, hard like somebody polishing stones. The water was pounding full force. She heard him bang his brush on the sink edge. The water shut off. "Kendrick!" she cried.

The door snapped open and she nearly fell through it. He swept past her and she wrinkled her nose at the heavy pine smell that throbbed in the air behind him. The bathroom mirror was steamed and the floor tracked with wet footprints. She turned and followed him out into the kitchen. He was in motion and working his belt through the loops in his khaki pants. "Where are you going?" she asked.

He paused at the threshold of the living room and put the belt through the buckle. His parents sat on either end of the sofa. They were looking at the TV. Flynn sat between them, laughing at Chester Goode. "I'm going out," Kendrick said.

Viola got up off the sofa. "Where?" she asked, and her nose twitched. She frowned. Flynn left the couch and came to stand with her. He watched his brother. Keen smelled like a whole lot of pine trees. His hair was wet and slick. He looked grand.

Kendrick dropped his weight onto the other leg and stared past them toward his father. Jarvis shifted on the cushion to put his hand into his pocket. "You got money?" he asked. "I could give you something."

"I'm okay," Kendrick told him, tapping his back pocket.

"Where are you going?" Viola asked again. Flynn watched his mouth to see what he would tell her.

"Just out. I'll be back."

"Well, I'm glad to hear that," she said. He was risen up on his toes. He wanted to be there now. "You got to get up early in the morning," Viola told him. "Don't you be late." She turned sharply and looked at Jarvis but he was smiling.

Kendrick was watching to the right of her face, across the room and out the front window, where the evening was beginning to fall around the city. "I won't," he murmured, and turned. He nearly banged into Krista, and Flynn was right behind him; Kendrick dodged quickly around her, yanked open the door, and was gone.

Flynn went right into the bathroom. He shut the door and turned on the tap. He pulled the stool out and stood on it, wetting his comb and slicking down his hair, wetting his comb again and sopping his hair until water was running over his ears and down his neck, so he could look almost as old and as grand as Keen did.

The evening was warm but there was a fair breeze billowing up the hill from the harbor. Kendrick hurried across the bridge and caught the bus on the other side. It left him two blocks from her house. He trotted through little kids riding their bikes up and down the lumpy sidewalk, past hedges and metal fences while through screens came the sounds of people finishing supper. Her house was at the end of a block, small with white-painted shingles and a low hedge. The front door was screened and had an "O'M" worked into the aluminum frame. Her stepfather's name was O'Meara but Jubal still called herself Soper. Kendrick went down the narrow cement walkway that led to the backyard.

They were eating supper outside. Low clouds of smoke lifted from the barbecue. Jubal's mother and her husband sat across from each other at the picnic table, and he turned around to look at Kendrick when his wife called out and beckoned with her wide hand. Jubal was sitting cross-legged on a boat cushion under the willow at the back of the small yard. The tree hung like tangled hair about her. When she saw Kendrick she got right up and went to him. "You're quick as fire," she said. "You couldn't have had time to eat. You want something?"

He shook his head. "I ate."

"Kendrick! Come and have a hamburger!" Mrs. O'Meara called.

"Oh," he said, looking past Jubal and lifting his hand to wave a greeting. Jubal caught at his shirtfront and pulled gently. "You ready to go?" he asked.

"Come and sit down and have something to eat," Mrs. O'Meara invited again, standing up and shading her eyes.

"He's eaten, Ma," Jubal called back. "And we got to hurry. The movie's starting soon."

"You put your shoes on before you go," Mrs. O'Meara said.

Jubal headed down the walkway.

"Jubal!" her mother cried, coming around the corner of the picnic table.

"They won't let you in the movies without shoes," Kendrick said, hurrying after her. "You might step on old gum," he teased. He touched the top of her shoulder. "You might step on a nail or cut your foot."

She stopped so quickly he nearly banged into her. She spun. "Would you carry me home?" she demanded. "Would you?"

He stroked her shoulder. "I would," he said. "You know I would."

"I'd carry you home if you got hurt," she told him.

"You couldn't lift me," he said, smiling at her.

Jubal dipped her knees and wrapped her arms around him. He tried to back up but she had him, her arms locked around his buttocks. Her face grew very still and she lifted.

"Jubal!" he protested.

But she raised him partway off the ground so he was on his toes. He saw Mrs. O'Meara coming toward them. Jubal had him pulled in against her and her breath was warm. He could feel her arms straining.

"Jubal!" he said again, and pushed down on her shoulders.

After a moment she let go and stood up. "I lifted you a little," she told him, rubbing her hands together, "and if you were hurt I'd get my mother's car and bring you home. I'd get that golf cart!" she boasted.

He stared at her. Then she laughed out loud and leaned toward him until the crown of her head just touched his chest. Her shoulders shook up and down. When she'd stopped laughing she looked up at him hard. "You better believe me!" she said fiercely before she turned and started back toward the house.

Mrs. O'Meara stood looking after her daughter; then she turned to Kendrick. "You got a lot of patience with her," she said grimly.

"She went to get her shoes," Kendrick answered slowly, watching where she had passed and, in her passing, stirred up the evening light into shapes and sweet shadows of her body.

Flynn stood behind the chair she sat in. He started at the crown of her head and patted to where the chair curved across her back. He leaned closer, his nostrils working—she was like soap and sunlight on a warm day. "Bell," he called her. Keen put the needle down on a record. "Toot-toot!" the music said. "Now I'm on bended kneeeeeee!"

Flynn watched Keen cross from where that machine sat on the crate by the window: its turning when he stood close to it made him dizzy. The music made him glad. He patted her again. Her voice was like being inside something warm. "Ooohhh-whee!" Keen sat down on the sofa, looked across at this one and smiled. "Just got it," he told her. "Secondhand. The guy gave me those forty-fives with it, but I'm buying some albums."

"Sounds real good," she said. And when she nodded her head, her hair sliding by his hand was smooth as a sun-warmed stone.

"Flynn!" Keen said, and looked at him hard. "Go in the kitchen. Go help Mum." But Flynn ducked down so all he could see was her hair. "Bell," he whispered.

Then she told Keen, "Go get me a scissors and a little piece of ribbon." She told him, "Please." When Keen left she turned and took his hand and led him around to the front of the chair so she could look at him. "I like you too," she said. And when Keen came back with the scissors she cut off some of her hair and tied it with the ribbon and gave it to him.

"Jubal!" Keen was mad. "Now go in the kitchen!" he said, standing there close. Flynn went slowly. Keen was kissing her. She was holding on to his hips. Flynn turned in the doorway and then went along the hall. He looked in the kitchen. His mother was taking supper out of the oven. She set her big dish on the stove. He went to her.

"Good Lord, what's that, Flynn?" she said sharply, lifting his open palm. She touched it gingerly. Then she turned and stared toward the living room. Beneath the loud record she could hear laughter. She led him by the hand to the table where his father was sitting. His boots were off and his legs were stretched out straight and he was drinking a can of beer. "See this," Mou said. She sounded mad.

He frowned at it. "Bell," Flynn told him, his face bright as a kitten's. He patted it with his other hand.

"How'd he get it?" Da asked loudly. "You didn't sneak up and cut if off yourself, did you, Flynn?" Da teased.

Flynn laughed. Mou shook her head. "Flynn's not that good with scissors yet," she said. They all looked toward the living room, where the music was loud and Bell's sweet laughter made Flynn want to go in there and be with them.

42 Brackett Street
Portland, Maine
November 4, 1963

Dear Freddie,

Krista and Flynn made these cards for you. They want you to know we're thinking about you on your day and wishing it's a real happy one. We hope you got a real good year coming ahead of you.

We want to say we're sorry and we know you're missing your Aunt June. I hope the family, your Uncle Bobby and his children, are good. Everyone here is fine and growing so fast I hardly know who they are. Krista wants to wear lipstick all the time. Kendrick has a girlfriend. He met her in the summer when he was working in the fields. We just finally met her. Her name is Jubal. She lives over in South Portland but Kendrick don't seem to mind going way over there to see her. Flynn is going to school now and he's real proud. We want you to put this dollar on something you been wanting.

Happy Birthday from
the Rudge family

LOGAN LEAVING

9 When Logan Pembroke turned sixteen he quit school and went to work in the fish factory over to Leedsport. He cut off the heads and tails and flipped them into a caldron where they were crushed and boiled for cat food. The women in the line beyond him filleted, their hair in nets and their feet in boots, fingers pink and drawn from handling the cold, wet flesh. Logan continued to live in his bus. Its tires had rotted and it listed slightly under the pines, rusted rims sunk in the damp soil. He was saving money for a car; he wanted an Oldsmobile, long and fast, the fenders round and high and chrome so shiny you had to shut your eyes.

Ronnie had a little growth spurt. The tops of his shoulders got pointy and his chin grew long; his mouth was small and dark above it like a bruise. His feet were suddenly too large to walk without stumbling, and his voice cracked and broke like ice on a shallow puddle. He developed tics: his eyes winced in his face, his foot shot out and crashed into things, his knee leapt up and down when he sat in a chair, twitchy as a beaten dog. His friend was Mike, a fat, oily-haired boy. They sat together at the end of a table in the cafeteria, hunched over brown bag lunches, sharing tidbits, the heavy boy and the thin one who vibrated the tabletop with his agitating limbs.

The medicines Logan's mother took made her eyes watery and dim. Arthritis deranged her hands, her fingers were turned and blunted like reptile's toes, her feet bent and folded in her shoes, nails pointing toward the ground. She wore slippers and gave up on buttons, dressed in dingy short-sleeved sweaters she pulled over her head, pants with elastic waistbands. Ronnie opened jars for her, his fingers flapping about the lids like squabbling gulls. He lit her cigarettes, which jutted at crazy angles from her pale hands, and threw away the tattered Kleenexes that fell like trash from her clothes. When he was at Mike's he worried, and as they lay stretched before the TV, eating in the darkened room—cookies, potato chips, sodas, and individual pies—his head ached until he closed his eyes and fell asleep, his nose flattened into the gray rug, his fingertips salty and chocolate in his teeth.

Gage had got thinner and his voice was always hoarse. He developed strange rashes, risen welts as if ants tunneled in his skin as he slept; he drank wine now instead of beer. He and Thumper sidled and lurched around the pig runs, furry and ponderous and unpredictable as bears.

Logan's plan was to save enough to buy his car and move to Portland. In one clean stroke he would sever himself from them forever. And Portland he saw as only temporary. He would move to Florida, where it was always warm. He could chauffeur rich people in their big black cars, the motors smooth as coins, seats soft as chairs in a funeral parlor, the women smelling like money. Five hundred dollars. He was getting close. May had hardly begun when he had four hundred in the can in the sunken old wall.

Gage watched him, his elbows propped on either side of his plate, his heavy jaw resting in his hands. Ronnie's eyes were snapping open and shut, Linette was eating her mashed potatoes with a spoon. Logan lifted the chicken leg toward his face and looked across the table to see his father watching him. Outside the kitchen window the evening was coming down softly from a lilac sky. There were eight pigs in the litter this year and they stood at the rear of the pen, staring into the woods.

"You're up to something, ain't you!" Gage said. His wine was in a red plastic glass.

The chicken was crisp. Logan nipped at it delicately. "Maybe," he told Gage, who had stuck his face across the table, ready to call him a liar.

Gage sat back in his chair, his brows folded down over the bridge of his nose. "Question is, *what*," he pondered slowly.

Logan wasn't looking at him anymore. He ate until he could suck on the bone.

"You better not think you are *ever* gonna put *anything* over on *me*," Gage said. His fist banged on the table, he launched himself forward.

Ronnie snuffled. His heel was clattering on the linoleum. His mother coughed, hauled a rumpled gray Kleenex out of her waistband and pushed it against her mouth.

"I ain't trying," Logan said. He finished his milk and stood up.

Gage stood too, his legs set wide. He raised his fist and shook it. "You ain't fooling me," he said. "You ain't ever going to fool *me*," and he thudded the fist on his own chest.

Logan paused. Gage was between him and the door. His mother raised her face and watched them. She's stopped chewing and her mouth was half open as if she was going to speak. The Kleenex quit her fist and landed balled up into a hard knot on the linoleum. "I can still take you," Gage said, raising his fists and sawing them through the air.

Outside there was a long screech of tired brakes and a truck turned off the road and rattled up the driveway. Linette reached her hand into the air. "Here's Thumper to see ya," she told him.

Gage half smiled, his eyes on Logan. "Get him a plate," he said to her and slowly dropped his hands.

The first shot took out a window in the middle, went straight on and out the other side. The second one hit the roof where it curved up from the glass. The bus rocked; the sound echoed through the pines. The sky was dark, the stars were hidden, it was cold in the new hours.

Logan flipped onto his stomach and crawled around the far side of the heater, dragging his pants with him. He was shaking and his throat was dry and clenched. The fire had burned low, the bus was cold, there was the odor of the cigarettes he'd smoked before going to sleep. The next two shots buried themselves in the motor. The bus heaved like something alive that was dying. Logan reached up and twisted the handle of the emergency door. The end windows fell crashing and clinking onto the floor.

"I'm shootin' high, I'm shootin' high!" he heard Gage yell, his voice quick and reassuring. There were Thumper's words, a few high gasps of laughter. Logan shoved the door open. It caught against the stovepipe and he squeezed through and fell to the ground, his pants in his hand. He could hear a thudding and cracking high in the limbs of the pines as he ran in a crouch down the hill toward the pig shed.

"Time he come back and lived in the house." Gage's voice sounded reasonable, even pleasant in the black night. Logan was hunkered down, his shoulder pressed against the side of the shed. Beyond the thin boards the pigs were snorting in the smell of him. His breath was screaming in and out of his throat, his chest felt clotted with rage. Thumper's voice came thick as a slowed record down the hill to him; his father's, louder and quick, interrupted: "I've had enough of this goddamn bus." The next shots found more glass.

A slow mist was settling through the air as Logan started back up the hill. He placed his stockinged feet carefully into the earth, holding the metal fence post in his two hands, tipping it gently like the balancing pole of a high-wire walker. The mist fell on his face and he put his tongue out to taste it. He could hear them stomping and mumbling, the snap of the breech.

"I don't hear him! I don't hear him!" Thumper's voice insisted. "You lemme go check. You lemme. Put that down now. Lemme check him."

Logan was almost to the top of the hill. He could hear Thumper tapping on the side of his bus. "Logan. Logan," he called in a high-pitched voice.

Logan was behind the house. The mist was making a whooshing sound on the shingles. He could see his father in the light that fell from the kitchen door. Gage was in his stockings too, pitched forward on the balls of his feet, peering across the driveway where Thumper was. He held the shotgun gently in his hands the way Logan was holding the fence post.

"It's awful quiet in there." Thumper's voice squeaked across the driveway.

"Guess we better smoke him out," Gage said. Chuckling, he lifted one hand to pat at his chest for matches. Logan leapt.

The barking of Gage's laughter snapped into a scream. The shotgun thumped softly as it landed on the hard clay of the driveway.

Logan swung the long post again, in a straight, smooth line aimed at Gage's shins. But Gage was crumpling and it took him across his clasping arms. He dropped, shrieking like a train whistle, on the trampled grass of the dooryard.

Logan was past him in one motion and bending to grab up the shotgun. As he ran for the bus Thumper backed from it, waving his hands in front of him. "Jeso, Jeso, Jeso, Jeso," he whimpered, "I tried ta stop him."

Logan didn't even look at him. His boots were behind the driver's seat and he pulled them on his feet. He crunched glass as he moved down the middle of the bus, dragging the fence post, the gun light in his other hand. Gage's screams pitched through the broken windows. The flashlight was near his bed. Logan let the fence post down and shoved clothes into a laundry bag with the freed hand while the other held the gun, and the narrow beam of the flashlight glittered on glass. Outside Thumper crept close enough to see Gage's face, his body curled on the ground and his arms hugging his legs. Logan pulled a sweatshirt over his head. He put on his heavy jacket.

The mist had deepened to a chill rain as he knelt under the pine, the gun beside him, and felt for the can that held his money. Beyond the bus, in the pale light from the kitchen, Gage lay on the ground moaning; high thin curses spat out at intervals. Thumper hovered around him. "It's rainin', Gage, it's rainin'," he kept repeating. Linette watched out the window and Ronnie stood behind her.

"He's gonna get it now," he said into her ear.

Logan put the can into the laundry bag and rose. Rain was holding to his hair and eyelashes, his blood droned in his ears. He shook himself and left the pines. He went down the driveway.

They came down the steps and watched him, blinking in the rain. The laundry bag made a dull white shape a foot above the ground, but the night had hidden Logan before he reached the road. Linette's stiff hand touched her other boy. Gage wailed and coughed on the ground. The rain drummed on the roof of the bus and slipped through the jagged windows. "You help Thumper to lift him," she whispered, twisting to nudge Ronnie's bony shoulder.

It was nine in the morning when Logan got to Portland. He'd been to the city twice before, once with Gage to register the truck and once with Norman Beasley, who'd bought a guitar from a pawnshop. His ride let him out on Congress Street. Logan stood there trying to remember. All the night dampness, its rains and mists, had been drawn up into the sky; it was blue and clear. The stock of the gun protruded from the laundry bag and pressed into his armpit. He was trying to remember where Norman had bought that guitar. He shifted and started walking. After a few blocks he saw a sign that said Cumberland Avenue. The name was familiar. He turned and walked west on the long and dingy street.

The green shade was drawn on the door, the red sign said "Closed." There were some bracelets in the window, an old phonograph, two sheath knives. Logan half slumped against the glass. He was tired, very tired, and his head and the back of his neck felt as if the bones there had thickened and were pressing against all the soft places where the blood flowed. He glared at the greasy window, knowing he'd have to wait. He couldn't walk around the city with a shotgun under his arm. He might be taken for a robber, the police might kill him. He sat down in the recessed doorway, his legs sprawled in front of him, the laundry bag cushioning his back. Across the street a large red building tilted toward the sky. Bricks had fallen from its chimney, the windows that weren't boarded up were empty, weeds grew around the foundation. From where Logan sat it was all he could see. A car, passing in front of him, seemed huge; he was looking at the space between the axles for a long time, and then the stench of its exhaust crowded into the doorway with him, climbed up the glass where the green shade was drawn.

He was startled from near sleep when Mr. Anastacio arrived, jangling the keys from his pocket before he'd turned the corner. Logan stood up quickly, he wasn't sure where he was. It took a moment as he focused on the man and the long ruined building behind him. "You want me for something?" the man was asking. He was small with a full head of gray hair and a narrow black mustache. Logan watched his mouth moving. "You want me?"

Logan sat up against the pillow on his narrow bed in the Y. He was slowly turning in his hands the knife he'd got at Mr. Anastacio's. The black sheath lay beside him on the spread. Beyond the wall, down the empty corridor, a door clanged. The window was open, the long evening light glowed on the sill, he could hear voices from the street below. They had told him there was an Automat downstairs but he was too tired. Sleep pulled at him, drawing him down; it was like melting without fire. His hands relaxed and the knife settled on his chest. He opened his eyes again and looked at the pale yellow wall of his room. He didn't think about anything that had happened before ten-thirty when he got forty dollars for the shotgun, bought the knife for seven fifty, when Mr. Anastacio told him about this place that was called by a letter. It was as if his life had begun again, the life that he would own, the one that would matter.

He was fired from his first job. He was big and strong-looking and they'd hired him on the spot to work as a mason's tender on the new bank that was being built downtown. He was pleased at the way he was so readily taken on to this crew of men, and though it was only minimum wage it meant he wouldn't have to use any more of his savings. But the head mason kept him running, orders coming steadily from his mouth like insults. On the third day Logan lifted the hod above his head, his arms bulging on either side of his angry face. "Do it yourself. I ain't your goddamn slave!" he told that head mason, before flinging the half-filled hod onto a pile of bricks. It rolled, thumping and clattering to the bottom while the other men paused and looked at Logan. They glanced at each other and, shifting away from him, turned to their work again.

"Take your pay and get off this job," the mason told him. "We ain't got time for temper tantrums." He spoke quietly, he was watching Logan, he held the long black crowbar in his hand. "You tell 'em at the shack I said to pay you off."

Logan stomped across the flattened area that would be landscaped later. The small, three-sided shack was set where the dirt ended and the sidewalk began. The woman who paid him put her cigarette down and counted out money from a tackle box. She had a green baseball hat on and her gray hair was frizzy underneath it. She told him to sign in her small notebook. As soon as he turned from her she was reading her magazine again. Logan took a sixteen-penny nail from his pocket and dug it deeply along the green tailgate as he walked past the head mason's new truck and started down the street.

* * *

It wasn't until August that he found another job; his savings were shrunk to fifty bucks, he could see his car traveling down the road without him, the wide, rolling rear of his Oldsmobile growing smaller and smaller, the gray smudge of its exhaust. They wondered at the Y when he'd be moving out, making room for someone else; it was, after all, only supposed to be temporary shelter. At night he lay staring at the ceiling and smoking cigarettes, his thoughts grinding in a rage around the face of that head mason, his heels pressing into the thin mattress. He looked in the paper every morning, he walked the streets staring at windows for Help Wanted signs. The man behind the desk at the Y suggested he go to the employment office. He told him where it was, drew a small street map on the inside of a candy bar wrapper.

The animal shelter was out on Forest Avenue. They interviewed him in a small room with green walls and one narrow window that overlooked a parking area. He told them he'd done factory work and that he was twenty. They believed him—he looked at least that old. David Denton, the dog-control officer, was a little bald man whose green eyes were as round as bottle caps. He spoke so softly Logan had to lean out of his chair to catch his words. Dr. Sampson was thin, with loose, sallow skin. His yellowed hair was brushed back from his forehead. His fingers were stained from his Raleigh cigarettes; the veins and tendons stood out in his narrow forearms. "It's not a glamour job," he told Logan. "You feed animals, clean out cages, and hold 'em when I have to give them the needle. Later you'd probably be going out with David picking them up." He watched Logan as he spoke. "So?" he asked, and drew on his Raleigh.

"You offering it to me?"

"I'm asking you if you're interested."

"What's it pay?"

"Sundays and Mondays off, minimum wage to start. But you get reviewed at three months, six months, a year. You get a raise or you get fired." He smiled at Logan and set the cigarette into the ashtray.

He moved out of the Y with his first paycheck and got a basement apartment in a building on a narrow street off Forest Avenue. Before winter came he'd gotten a bed and a kitchen table, an upholstered chair and cooking utensils. He had a blue uniform, pants and a shirt. Dr. Sampson gave him thick leather gloves to wear. The cats growled and scratched but he only held them tighter. The dogs usually came willingly, wagging their tails, sometimes licking his gloved hands as he picked them up and put them on the table. Often when they felt the drug they bayed and howled; it went on for slow seconds. There was a van he loaded for the dump, tossing the plastic bags with their stiffened contents in an orderly way into the back.

They kept the dogs ten days. Logan noticed her on a Thursday, a small ginger-colored dog with one ear that stood up crookedly and one that lay against the side of her head. She kept to herself in the back of the cage, curled up in a small ball on the cement. When he fed them she was there. With quick snaps she deterred any dog who got between her and the dish, ate her fill and returned to her corner. No one chose her. On the tenth day when Logan went into the pen to get her she bit him, nipped him firmly on the hand, leaving the little dents of her teeth in his skin. "Put on the gloves," Dr. Sampson said quietly behind him.

It took them both, Logan with the gloves on and Dr. Sampson forcing her into the corner with a chair. She growled, low and steadily, as Logan carried her to the table and forced her down on it. His forearm lay across her neck pinning her, his fingers closed around her leg. She growled, watching him and then the doctor as he came with the syringe, the white in her eye showing and her small teeth. Dr. Sampson tightened the tourniquet around her fore-leg. "All right, girl," he said softly.

"I'll take her." Logan spoke quickly. "I'll take this one."

Dr. Sampson lifted his face, his fingers still poised around the rubber tubing. "You want this dog?"

"I'll take her. Yeah. I'll take this one."

Dr. Sampson started to speak; then he lifted his hand slowly and straightened. The dog was still growling, Logan's arm was hard on her neck. "We'd better put a collar on her now," Dr. Sampson said, and he turned to open the drawer in the chest behind him. Her throat vibrated under Logan's arm as Dr. Sampson put the worn red collar around her neck and buckled it. When they let her down she silently went to the corner and sat, her thin tail curled around her haunch.

She went along the sidewalk at the full length of the rope Logan was using for a leash. There were four steps down into his basement room and she wouldn't go. He dragged her. Her nails tore and scrabbled at the stone steps as she dropped down them, her neck stretched awkwardly, the collar yanked up under her jaw. He got her into the hall and reached to turn on the light, tipping his face away from the uncovered bulb. He tied her to a water pipe and went into his apartment, leaving the door open while he cooked his supper. The smoke and the smell of his frying pork chops came out to where she sat at the full length of the rope, small and dark against the pinkish brick of the basement wall.

So she lived in the hall, the rope holding her to the water pipe. He walked her briefly before and after work and before he went to bed, dragging her in and out of the building so she could squat in the dirty grass. She slept on a rug he'd found at the dump. She ate his scraps. He never tried to touch her. She never got nearer to him than the length of the rope. He called her Mutt.

When it was spring again he had his license and a car. It wasn't an Oldsmobile but a 1958 Buick station wagon with busted springs. On the night of his birthday, as on most Friday nights, he drove to Iggy's Tavern and parked in the narrow lot.

It was noisy inside. People were playing pool in the back; the music was country. Logan sat in his usual spot at the curve of the bar and ordered beer. "You wanna check my ID?" he asked Roland.

Roland put the glass down in front of him. "You're an old man," he said. "What would I wanna see your ID for?"

Logan shrugged and, watching him, flipped his wallet open on the bar. Roland looked down at it, then raised it and held it close to his face. Logan grinned. Roland turned to the calendar on the wall behind the bottles. "Yeah, it is the twenty-sixth and happy birthday to you. I guess that gets you a free beer."

Logan smiled at him but he didn't put his hand out for the wallet. Roland's eyebrows stretched up pale and small on his round face. "You don't want your wallet back?" he asked.

Watching him, Logan lifted the beer and drank.

Roland looked down at the license again. "Shit!" he said, slapping the wallet down on the bar. "You mean I been serving you for a year and you ain't but just seventeen!" He spoke softly, almost hissing as he leaned over the bar toward Logan.

Logan was laughing, his lips drawing thin in his hard face. "Where's my free one, Roland? Where's my birthday beer?" he urged, gesturing with his empty glass.

"Get the hell outta here," Roland said. "And don't come back."

"I'm meeting somebody," Logan protested. He was still grinning.

"Not here you ain't," Roland told him.

He waited on the cold sidewalk, stamping his feet. Sheila came along quickly. He heard the hurrying clickety sound of her heels before he saw her. They found another bar, and later she came home with him because her mother was visiting there at her apartment where they usually went. She had kids, they were noisy in the morning. He was uneasy in her bed after making love to her and he wanted to be home in his basement room that smelled like the earth, the dog breathing outside in the hall.

Sheila giggled coming down the stone steps after him; her heels made little tinny sounds. Sheila worked in the furniture factory and her long brown hair smelled of paint thinner and shellac. It was late and the house, rising above the basement door, was dark. He turned the key and went through, reaching up to feel for the light string.

"My God, what's that!" Sheila cried, and giggled again.

"A dog," he said, not turning toward her.

Mutt sat with her face averted, one ear up and alert.

"She looks like a rat. A giant rat or something," Sheila said. "But she's kinda cute," and she bent toward Mutt.

"She bites," Logan said harshly. He was opening the door to his room.

"That why you keep her tied up?" Sheila had drawn her hand back and she held it against her chest.

He turned to look at her then. "I keep her tied so she don't run off," he said. Then he told her, "Come on."

BENJAMIN GRIFFIN'S FATHER

10

It was a night early in December. Snow fell among the buildings with the softest tinkling sound, piling damp and heavy on the roofs of cars, in the curves of tree limbs, on the ice covering the duck pond in Deering Oaks Park. Freddie Hewitt, sixteen years old, drove down Brackett Street, his black 1954 Packard cutting fresh tracks. He held the wheel with something close to passion and he smiled into the night at the snow drifting through his headlights, at the whistling crunch of his tires in the stilled city, at his Packard, so warm on this winter night that he kept the window open. His black jacket was unzipped and he was hatless. Dappled by falling snow, the glow from the streetlights lit his dark hair and his narrow face. He slowed and looked through the open window, peering at housefronts. Down the sloping street they leaned, diminished in the night and the snowfall. The house at the corner showed its numerals, 38, on the white frame. He pulled in at the curb, his motor hummed sweet as trust, he watched the snow come down.

It gathered higher on the porch roof of number 42, covered the steps, buried the small yard. There were lights in the bow window sheltered by the porch; upstairs, in the two windows centered in the wide gable: a small yellow light was glowing on the side porch of the second floor. And then a shadow moved in the gable. Freddie shut off the motor; he rolled up his window and got out of the car.

His boots made fresh marks over the buried bricks of the sidewalk; the heavy snow held to the leather as he went toward the lights. He climbed up onto the porch, where the wind had brought snow almost to the door; his pale shadow lay against the glass. He listened, breathing in the cold air which was clean in his chest, eager on the skin of his hands and face.

He knocked and waited, and then a woman was standing in the opened door. She was small, neat and delicate-looking, wrapped in a thick blue robe, fuzzy slippers on her feet. "Oooo oh," she gasped, and hugged her arms across herself. "Yes?" and she shivered.

"Rudges live here?" he asked her, confused.

"Upstairs," she told him, unwrapping one arm and pointing. "You have to go around the porch"—she gestured again, her hand almost touching him—"and up the stairs at the back." She leaned out of her doorway, one slipper brushed the snow. "Just around," she urged. "And up. That's where they live."

As he turned he could see a little child swaying in the hall behind her, all blue in a sleeper and with pale wispy hair. "Thanks," he said. "Sorry," and he looked at her huddled in her own arms.

"That's all right," she told him, "it's a beautiful night!" and she laughed.

He started across the porch. He heard her say something to the child and then the click of the door. Around the corner of the building it was dark and he went slowly, with his hand on the rail. A light suddenly illuminated the window beside him, and as he went on the next one glowed. He could make out the stairs ahead and then he began to climb toward the small yellow light. The wind was coming from the other side of the house and here it was quiet, just the soft rattling of the snow on the roof above him. He stomped his feet and knocked on the door.

It was Jarvis who answered and Freddie could smell the warmth of the kitchen beyond him.

"Yeah?" he said. He had on long underwear and dark trousers. He opened the door wider. "Who you looking for?" he asked, frowning at the figure who stood on his porch. He could barely see his face, just his hands which were bare beneath the sleeves of the black jacket. The air that swept by him was so cold and clean it was sweet.

"Mr. Rudge," he said, "it's Fred," and he cleared his throat. "Hewitt."

"Jesus H. Christ," Jarvis softly breathed. "Come in, come in!" He pulled the door open wide and reached for him. "My God, it *is* you!"

Freddie nodded. Jarvis's fingers were holding his wrist, his heart was pounding as if his chest had expanded to make more room for it. He shifted in the wet boots and lifted his narrow shoulders.

Jarvis pushed the door shut behind him. "I couldn't see it was you out there. It was too dark," he insisted. "Viola won't hardly believe it! Viola!" He turned and yelled her name down the hall.

"What is it?" They could hear her coming, the TV burbling along behind her.

"Freddie Hewitt!" Jarvis announced, patting his arm and grinning at Viola.

"Well, Freddie. What a surprise," she said, smiling at him.

He grinned and nodded. She looked smaller. The top of her head didn't quite reach his shoulder. "I was coming into Portland," he said. "I . . . I knew your address."

She smiled again. "Come and sit down," she invited. "The kids are going to be real surprised to see you."

So there he was in their midst again, feeling a little dizzy, a little breathless, telling himself yes, it *was* okay, they were glad he'd come. The room was warm and he'd started sweating. They were the same, just bigger children, and Kendrick had grown taller than he himself was. They laughed, they wanted to see his car, Mrs. Rudge made coffee and brought in cookies with it, her voice was still rich and warm the way it had been. In this pleasant chaos he felt so happy he didn't trust himself and he was careful of his words. They were the only ones who knew him back when there was Daniel, when he was part of someone else's life, the head of that small family and not alone, with nothing, as he had been since.

After Christmas winter came down hard. Freddie was working at the garage and many mornings he rose hours before light to plow driveways. He didn't get back to Portland to visit the Rudges until the middle of February when there was a short period of milder weather. He came on a Thursday evening. There was no light on but he climbed the narrow stairs and knocked anyway, shifting from foot to foot while the bare branches of the maple scraped against the porch roof. Waiting, he drew his Luckies from his jacket and lit one. His smoke flattened on the closed door. He turned and went down the stairs with the cigarette in his mouth and his hands jammed into his pockets. He was moving across the porch to the front steps when her voice startled him, stopped him, one boot in the air feeling for the tread.

"They're not home," she repeated. She came closer. She had on a heavy sweater, her arms were folded and her hands stuffed up the sleeves. "But they'll be back soon. They went to something at Flynn's school."

He took the cigarette out of his mouth.

"You're Fred, aren't you?" The porch was dark but her voice was like a warm hand on his chest. "Viola told me about you, that you came to visit. It was before Christmas. You knocked on my door first. I remember you," she told him, coming closer so she could look into his face.

"Yeah. I was here," he said, "before Christmas. Flynn's school."

"An open house. They won't be long. If you want you can wait in my apartment."

He followed her, stood quietly in the front hall while she shut the door. "Come on," she said, urging him through to the kitchen. The radio was playing something soft. An ironing board was set up and there was a yellow blouse on it. She took an ashtray down from the top of the refrigerator and put it on the table. He stepped forward and tapped the long ash of his Lucky into it. "Sit down," she said, a small smile on her face. She took off her sweater and smiled at him. "Would you like Coke or coffee?" she asked.

"Coke'd be fine."

She got two tall glasses out of the cupboard, stretching on her toes to reach. She was small and her hands moved quickly, tapping out ice, filling the glasses until bubbles were leaping into the air. She brought one to him and set her own on the edge of the counter where she could reach it as she ironed. She put the blouse on a hanger and bent to get a red apron from her basket. "I'll just keep on working and we can chat, okay?" she said, and dipping her fingertips into a wide-mouthed glass, she shook water over the apron.

The room was warm, the radiator under the window hissed, a song about moonlight was playing. "I just got Ben to sleep when I heard you knocking up there," she explained. She looked at him, the iron held upright in her hand. "Ben's my little boy. I've always been lucky: he's happy to go to sleep and wakes up cheerful in the morning." She bent her head and moved the iron over one of the ties, set it on its end and shifted the apron. "He's like me," she said. Then she smiled. "You know I never thought about it before, but it's true: he's just like me!" She laughed happily and folded the apron, reached for her Coke. She drank slowly and for a long time, then put the glass down and started on another apron. "I'm a hostess now," she told him, "down to the counter at Kresge's. I was a waitress there five years and now they made me the hostess." She shook more water over the apron. "A promotion, more money too. But I don't really like being the boss of the other girls." She smiled at him again. Her face was small and perfectly heart-shaped. How she could talk, he marveled as her voice ran along free as water, here in her warm, neat kitchen, her little boy in his bed and she was still thinking about him. "Course everything's going up," she said sternly. "Still, Benjamin's father brings us what he can." She gave her head a little shake. "He's already got a wife," she said softly, and brought her iron down on a skirt. He watched her as she turned it quickly and ironed the waistband. "I don't want my Ben to do without anything." Her small face got fierce. "I didn't have much when I was a girl and I don't want Ben to feel like that. Course I don't mean spoil him," she said quickly, her features tightening with concern. "I just mean so he won't worry and feel like his mother doesn't love him enough." She sprinkled water on a pair of small blue overalls. "I don't know what I would have done without Viola to watch my Ben. I never worry, not for a minute." She stopped ironing and looked at Freddie. "I never saw anyone love babies the way Viola does." A look almost of alarm filled her face. "I can't believe it but you know," she said, "my Ben starts kindergarten in just two years." She dropped her head and the iron swept up and down the small legs, pressed out the bib. "I'm lucky," she insisted. "I'm lucky how things worked out."

She folded the overalls carefully and set them down in the basket. "Now, you're older than Kendrick," she told him as she straightened. "I don't remember Viola saying but you must be." She pushed her hair off her forehead and stared across the table straight at him. "You look older. You must be out of high school," she persisted. "Kendrick won't graduate till next year."

He didn't bother to correct her. He sure felt as if he were older than Kendrick. "I'm out," he said. He'd been out of high school since the day that November when he turned sixteen.

She watched him, her head tilted a little to one side. "Viola said you work at a garage and you plow snow and you're the world's best mechanic."

He smiled. "Well, I am a mechanic and I work at a garage," he said. She frowned, her mouth was slightly pursed. "And I plow snow some," he admitted.

"You shouldn't be so modest," she scolded. "My grandfather always said there was no shame in owning up to what you could do."

He smiled and got himself another cigarette. "Guess that makes sense," he said.

She came close and took his glass. "I'll fill you up," she told him. She poured more Coke in her own glass and filled his to the top. "Oh dear," she gasped sadly, looking into it. "I should have dumped out that melted ice." She looked at him. "I'm sorry, Fred." She picked up the bottle. "There's not enough to start again."

"That's okay." He stood up and took the glass from her. "Tastes great." She was standing close, watching him drink, a worried look on her face. The hot-iron smell was all around her. "You remind me of somebody," she said abruptly. "But I don't know who it is." She tipped her head, studying him. "Not the way you look exactly, but something about you."

He stepped back from her. "I don't know," he said.

"Course you don't!" She laughed softly, rocking toward him. "I got to tell you when I figure it out." She smiled. "They say everybody has a twin. Somewhere in the world. You believe that?"

He raised his eyebrows. "No, I don't," he answered softly.

She sighed. "Maybe I don't either, but I kind of like the idea of it. It's as if you're not alone even if you think you are."

They could hear footsteps beyond the wall coming up onto the back porch, Jarvis's voice: "Shoulda left the damn light on, Viola. We'll break our necks!" Their feet tramped up the stairs.

"Guess they're back," Freddie said. He lifted his jacket off the chair, put it on and carefully zipped it.

"You're just going upstairs," she said gently.

He laughed and his hand went to the zipper. He patted his pocket where the cigarettes were.

"I'm glad you came by, Fred," she told him. "Even if it wasn't exactly on purpose." She laughed, and touched his arm.

"Thanks for the Coke, and for letting me stay in where it was warm to wait."

"Maybe you'll come by again." She followed him to the front door. The knob was loose in his hand and he had to turn it and turn it before he felt it catch against something.

"Loose knob," she sighed. "I've been asking the landlord and asking him, but he's as slow as cold molasses."

When he was out on the porch he turned. "Thanks again."

She stepped out after him. "I don't think I told you but my name is Mariam."

"Oh." He nodded. "Good night. Mariam." And he repeated it, a new sound in his mouth. "Mariam."

Kresge's was downtown near city hall. Freddie left the Packard on one of the side streets. It was a warm afternoon in early April, and where the sky showed between the buildings it was silvery blue. Water ran down the gutters, there were birds twittering in the small sidewalk trees. Looking through the plate-glass window, his hand raised to shield the glare, he could see her. She was behind the counter pouring coffee for two men in suits. There was a gangly redheaded girl working behind the counter with her. He opened the door and went inside. The long room smelled of doughnuts and rubber cement and fabric. He moved quickly and sat at the counter. Mariam looked tired and there were stains on the front of her uniform. When she saw him she paused, settled her body in a different way, and smiled as if a kind of lightness had entered into her. She came to him quickly, her hand sliding under the counter for a mug. "Well hi," she said, putting it down in front of him, her hand going up to her face to brush at her cheek. "Haven't seen you for a long time. Sure didn't expect to see you here! How are you?" She watched him, her head tilted a little, her breath caught, waiting for him to tell her.

"I'm good," he said.

Mariam smiled. "You look good."

He frowned and drew on his cigarette.

"You think I'm bold!" Mariam charged, leaning closer to him, then laughing with such delight she had to spin on her thick white shoes. "I'll get you a fresh pot," she told him.

He watched her, how quickly she moved, her shoes clumsy-looking under her delicate ankles. Yes, he did think she was bold; well no, not bold exactly, but startling, unexpected, clean with the truth the way a child is.

He watched her as she poured carefully and gave him the sugar bowl, the small silver pitcher. "Thought you might want a ride home," he said, adding quickly, "Car's just around the corner."

"Oh, I'd love it!" Mariam sighed. "I just have fifteen more minutes, and I'm exhausted. Faye is out sick today and I had to do her job and mine too."

The coffee was horribly hot and he didn't really want it. He watched her as she went to wait on two ladies who had come in. They carried shopping bags, they wore dead animals around their throats, they called out to Mariam in loud, eager voices. She smiled and brought them coffee, doughnuts on a plate, glasses of water. How quickly she moved, how her small hands balanced everything, how her neat body pushed against the flat pink of her uniform. He took out the nearly empty pack and lit another cigarette. Exhaling smoke, he watched her cut a piece of pie, one hand on the knife, the other turning the tin. Then he put down two quarters and went to stand by the window.

As Mariam sorted spoons she kept looking up at him, at his back, the dull black jacket, his long legs in the faded jeans. He was looking down the street and his profile in the flattened afternoon light was sharp, his dark hair curving under the collar of the jacket. She felt he was about to leave, fling open the door, hurry down the street. She fumbled with the ties of her apron, reached for her purse under the counter, her jacket from the narrow closet that held the broom. She kept looking, again and again; he was still there though it surely seemed he would, must, fire himself through the door and be gone. "See you tomorrow, Carol," she called.

He was pitched forward, hand on the door. She saw that the heels of his boots were worn. He went through, holding it open. She was still pulling on her jacket. Outside it was growing cool, the wind was coming up. They walked, careful not to touch each other but close.

His arm brushed her shoulder when they turned the corner. "Car's right down here," he assured her.

Krista came along slowly. She was red from the hot June afternoon and sweaty under her bangs. She paused, leaned against his car, and peered in the window. There was a blanket folded neatly, empty beer bottles on the floor, a wooden box with a battery in it. The doors were locked. The black metal under her belly was burning hot. She flung herself upright, turned, and went faster down the sidewalk.

Flynn was looking at a comic book at the kitchen table and her mother was making shortcake. "You're awful late," she said, glancing up from her board.

"I went down to the park," Krista told her. "We were going to wade in the pond but they didn't fill it yet."

"Have some juice," Viola suggested.

"Naw." She went down the hall to the living room, looking as she passed, but Kendrick's room was empty. Her parents' door was shut because Ben Griffin was inside having his nap. There was no one in the living room. She went back to the kitchen and stood on one foot. "Where's Freddie?" she asked.

Flynn looked up from his comic. "Freddie?" Viola said.

"His car's down in the street."

Viola stopped mixing and straightened her back. "We haven't seen Freddie yet today and we've been right here, me and Flynn." Flynn nodded.

"Well, I don't know where he is then," Krista said, lowering her foot.

"Maybe it wasn't his car."

"Mum, I oughtta know his car by *now*!"

Viola looked at her. "Lord, don't scowl so," she said, and started working the dough with her fingers.

Krista sat on the third step and chewed gum. The afternoon was wearing down dusty and hot. The air was still. Freddie's car was the only one on their side of the street. Its blackness glowed in the hot light. She was chewing so hard she bit the inside of her cheek, and while she was sitting there holding her face and almost in tears from the pain she heard noises in Mariam's apartment, which was supposed to be empty. She half stood, thinking it was thieves after Mariam's television set and her jewelry. Crouching on the step, she looked at the window next to her elbow—Mariam's bedroom and the shade was drawn right to the sill. Somebody in there was sounding upset but not really crying, and thieves wouldn't make any noise but scrabbling through things. The voice came again, somebody desperate-sounding and then a man's voice, too, making noise that wasn't words. Krista did stand up then; her hand flew out to grasp the banister and she turned her head sharply and glared at Freddie Hewitt's car.

Viola had a headache, which she said was from the heat. She lay in her room with the shade drawn. Flynn was with her. Their four bare feet pointed toward the ceiling. They had cool drinks with straws.

Krista was out back watching Ben. He was in his wading pool, round and brown in his bathing suit, a green tugboat in his fist, his eyes very blue behind his diving mask. Krista sat in a chair with her feet in the pool and Ben dove under and was a fish chewing on her toes.

Freddie Hewitt's hand was raised on the screen door knocking when he heard their laughter. He came around to the backyard and watched them, standing quietly on the beaten grass, his arms folded across his chest. When Krista noticed him she jerked her feet out of the water and Ben rose with them, his fingers nibbling at her toes like fish lips.

"Hewitt!" Ben cried.

Krista watched him clamber out of his pool and run, the mask still on his face. Freddie caught him up and held him. "Are you swimming?" he asked.

"Biting Krista's toes," Ben told him in a deep voice.

"That true, Krista?" he called, and then came toward her with the child in his arms.

Krista watched them. She didn't say anything. When Freddie set Ben on the ground he climbed back into the pool, took an enormous breath, and dove under the water. Freddie smiled. "He sure is having fun. I guess you take real good care of him," he said.

Krista nodded. The pool was between them. Splashes of water kept rising from it. Ben surfaced, then went under again.

"You been having a good summer?" Freddie asked.

"So-so." She shrugged.

Ben sat up and started drawing his tugboat around the pool.

"Guess Mariam ain't home yet."

"She'll be home soon." Krista watched his face. He had hunkered down and was bouncing slightly on his folded legs. He took off his sunglasses and hooked them onto the neck of his T-shirt. Freddie looked older to her, more like a grown-up, more like a stranger. He was smiling again, watching Ben.

Ben was sinking his tugboat. He laughed every time it popped up, and reached to sink it again.

"Didn't know she was working late," Freddie said.

"She's not." Krista pulled a pack of gum out of her pocket, unwrapped a piece and pushed it into her mouth.

"Where is she then?"

"She had a doctor's appointment," Krista told him. She was folding her gum wrapper up into a tiny hard knob.

"What's the matter?" He half stood up.

"Ear infection."

"I thought it was getting better."

Krista shrugged. "That's what she told me."

He looked at his watch and then pulled his cigarettes out of the pocket of his T-shirt.

Ben was splashing now. Krista was getting wet but she leaned closer and almost snarled at Freddie, "You can't *wait* till she gets here, can you?" She watched him, holding her breath.

He looked at her quickly. What she had said was so unexpected and so true that he didn't have time to put on a mask. "No," he answered.

Krista jumped out of the chair and ran to him and kissed his cheek. "She'll be here real soon. Honest," she said tenderly.

Krista sat unmoving with her back straight, her eyes closed. In front of her was Mariam's three-sided mirror. The window was open and she could smell the night. It was a Thursday late in August. She could smell Mariam, too, the smell of warm flowers. Mariam stood just behind her, setting her hair in big pink rollers. "You have beautiful hair," she said, and Krista opened her eyes.

It was all drawn back from her forehead in the rollers. Her face looked narrow and startled. Mariam was working on the crown of her head. Her hair was heavy and damp from being washed with Mariam's own special shampoo.

"You can do anything you want with it," Mariam said as her nimble fingers rolled more hair. Her voice was muffled for the bobby pins held in her lips. "You're so lucky, Krista," she said, and their eyes met in the mirror.

"My mother says it's too thick."

"Hair can never be too thick. All the beautiful women in history had thick hair."

"Oh," Krista said.

"Men love thick hair." She picked up another roller. "I'd give anything for hair like yours. Thank goodness my hairdresser knows how to cut it so it *looks* thicker." She leaned over Krista's head to study herself in the glass. Krista watched her. Mariam didn't look displeased. She lifted her hair from her forehead and turned her face; though they were still holding bobby pins her lips pouted slightly. She sighed and started rolling up another bunch of Krista's hair.

"You'll have to sleep on this," she told her. "It won't be very comfortable but you got to suffer a little if you're going to be beautiful!" She laughed and squeezed Krista's shoulders. "Now you come down tomorrow real early and I'll comb it out for you. I got to be to work at seven."

Krista nodded. "I will. I'll come down way before seven."

Mariam tied a yellow scarf around the mass of rollers. "That'll hold everything together," she said, "and they won't stick into you so much when you sleep." She leaned over Krista again, this time to pluck a tube of lipstick from the little tray. "This one," she said meditatively, holding it up. "Precious Pink." She put it into Krista's hand.

The bell rang at the front door, two sharp rings and then a long one.

"My good Lord," Mariam said, turning toward the sound of it. "Krista, is this Monday?"

"No. It's Thursday."

The bell sounded again in the same sequence.

"He'll wake Ben!" Mariam cried. "Oooh! Quick, Krista!" She leapt across the room and flung open the window that gave onto the back stairs. "Go home this way," she said.

Krista stood up from the little stool.

"Quick! Quick!" Mariam urged, beckoning. She pushed the sash all the way up, sent the screen after it.

The bell rang again.

"Krista! Please hurry!"

She climbed up on the chair and stepped through the window, knocking her enlarged head on the sash. Puzzled, she turned once to look back at Mariam.

"It's my sweetheart!" Mariam exclaimed, and laughed. "He's real shy, and I don't know what he's doing visiting me on Thursday." She laughed again and pulled down the screen, the window, the shade itself.

Krista looked toward the street, seeking Freddie's car. All she could see in the blurry glow of the streetlight was a blue Chevrolet and two trucks.

When Mariam opened her front door Gerard O'Donnell tumbled through it. "God," he said. "I was beginning to think you weren't home."

"Hi!" she said and kissed him. "It's Thursday. Why are you here?"

"I can't stay long. I'm visiting my aunt at Mercy Hospital. Gallbladder," he said accusingly, and looked down the hall.

"Oh dear. And how was she feeling?"

"I didn't go yet. I came here first." He stepped forward and peered into the living room. "Mariam," he said slowly, "you didn't . . ." He turned on a light. "Mariam, did you have anyone here?"

She had followed him, and stood staring into her own living room. "Yes," she said. "The girl from upstairs who baby-sits."

"Oh." He took off his jacket and gave it to her. "Where is she?"

"She went. I know you don't want anyone to see you here." She turned from him and opened the closet door.

"That's not true."

"Yes it is," she said, and took down a hanger.

"Mariam, I thought there was a man here. I thought you had someone else."

She shut the closet door and turned to him. "You mean like you have, Gerard?"

"No." He looked at her face. "Oh, God, Mariam," he said, and sat down heavily in the straight-backed chair by the telephone table. "What are you doing to me?"

Krista hurried down the stairway. It was a cold Saturday morning early in October. She had promised Mariam she would stay with Ben while Mariam did her shopping. Before she could ring the bell Mariam opened the door. She was wearing her coat and there were shiny new boots on her feet. "Oh, Krista!" she said.

"Sorry I'm late." She didn't think she was but here was Mariam with her coat on, going out the door. Her coat was red and she looked beautiful, her face glowing above the collar with a joy Krista had never seen on anyone's face before. She stared at her.

"I forgot about you!" Mariam told her, but seeing her expression, she reached and took her hand. "I've forgotten about everything! It's because I'm so happy," she said. "Come in, come in and meet my sweetheart." Before Krista could say anything she drew her into the hall. Then she stopped and put her hands to her face. "I should say fiancé, my sweetheart and my fiancé!" she cried, and flung her arms out to hug Krista. "Come on," she said, and led her toward the living room.

Krista wondered if Freddie had gone down on one knee, if he'd brought her red roses. She looked for a vase on the table but there were only coffee cups and the empty box Mariam's boots had come in. Mariam herself was directing the warmth of her glow across the room. Standing beside her, Krista looked.

A man, a nervous, old-looking man with messy hair, was sitting on the couch with Ben. They were playing with tiny bears who had their own little set of swings.

"Krista," Ben said, smiling and struggling to get off the couch with a bear in each hand. "Krista," he said, "look," and he came to her carrying them before him. "Dadda gave them to me," he told her. "Bears on swings." He was glowing too. Mariam hugged her tighter.

Krista looked at the little bears. She looked at the man. Mariam's arm was burning across the back of her neck.

"Isn't it wonderful!" Mariam practically sang. "We're going to get married! We're going to be a real family!" She dropped her arm from Krista and lifted Ben up in the air. She spun, holding him, and he was holding the bears and they were both laughing.

Krista stared past their spinning, laughing faces at the man on the couch. He was watching them, the grin on his face making him look addled and somehow powerful at the same time. He was holding a bear in each hand too. On the end table beside the couch was a photograph that Krista hadn't seen there before. It showed three children in a fake gold frame; they were dressed in their Sunday clothes and smiling out at the world; they had almost identical round-cheeked faces and the same pale blond hair.

YOUNG MEN

11 The United States Army wanted Logan Pembroke, and when he didn't answer their summons they sent Captain Haney Johnson looking for him. Haney was from Maine, but during the twenty-six years he'd been in the army he'd seen something of the world. In Nuremberg after the war Haney was a prison guard. Later, in Korea, he worked in intelligence. He stayed with that when he went on to Vietnam in the next decade. But the day he saw children amputees hobbling and hopping from their bombed and burning hospital Haney said that's it. When his tour was over he came home to work out of Portland in recruitment. Phyllis preceded him back to Maine by several years. She never had liked the Far East, where everybody got internal parasites and you couldn't eat your vegetables raw. Haney was a tall man, and after he got home he started to put on weight, his hair thinned and finished graying. But he still looked good in his uniform.

Just before Halloween Haney went out to Dunham. It was warm in the middle of the day and Haney kept his window wide open and his jacket folded neatly on the seat. He drove around for a while before he found the post office and got directions.

The air smelled like pine trees and pigs. He recognized their odor when he was climbing the steps to knock on the door. The house was dark and the day was bright and he couldn't see the woman until she came out on the first step, her hand, with its thickened and twisted knuckles, raised to shield her eyes from the day.

"Ma'am," he said, his hat in his hand.

Linette Pembroke stared at him, her face flexing and blinking. When he asked her about Logan there was a long wait and then she said, "He did get some kinda card in the mail. But we didn't know where to send it to. We ain't seen him," she told Haney, clutching a sweater across her chest. "We ain't seen him since . . ." She hesitated, breathing deeply as if she were counting. "Since back in April. April spring afore last one," she explained carefully, licking her top lip.

"And you don't know where he is?" He smiled, watching her closely, but she didn't seem to have the interest or the energy to lie.

"I don't. I don't know where my boy is." Her lips pressed together, she pulled at the sweater again, then turned and looked down the driveway. "I did think he'd come back. Sometime. I thought he would. But he didn't," she insisted. She looked past Haney at the faded blue bus, rust running along the window frames and covering the bracket of the rearview mirror. "I feel like maybe he's way out in California," she told Haney.

"You got an address?" he asked, reaching for the small notebook in his pocket.

"Address?" she said, looking startled. "I just got the feeling that's where he is."

Haney Johnson found Logan the last week in November. He was reading the paper while he ate his breakfast; Phyllis was talking in the background. Haney turned the page and there it was: "Logan Pembroke, age 18; 34 Clifton Street. License suspended for speeding, third offense."

Haney was knocking on his door that afternoon.

"The army?" Logan said, vague as his own mother. He rubbed his palm on his chest. He was wearing a T-shirt and blue pajama bottoms. Mutt looked past them at the first snow falling.

Logan was thick and strong-looking and smelled of sweaty sleep. Haney stepped around him and went down the hall and looked into the apartment. It was small and, except for the open bed, neat. Logan stood in front of the open door, rubbing his bare arms. "Snowing!" he cried.

"I've been looking for you," Haney told him, coming back down the hall.

"Well, you found me. But I'm already doing my duty. I work for the city, rounding up stray dogs, keeping the streets safe." He grinned. "Sunday and Monday is my day off. You're lucky you got me at home."

Stepping stiffly past him, Haney put his hat on his head. "Mr. Pembroke, you're lucky if I don't put you in jail," he said.

The recruitment center was on Congress Street between a sleazy bar and an A&P store. Haney Johnson clapped Logan on the shoulder. "This guy lives at the city pound!" he told one of the other recruiters. "But we'll make a soldier out of him. Somehow," he added doubtfully, then reared back on his heels and laughed loudly.

"Navy," Logan corrected him coolly. "I ain't going to go in the army and get my sweet ass shot off."

Haney stopped laughing. "A sailor. Maybe it's just as well," he said. Then he told him, "You make sure you go see your mother before you leave".

Logan looked at him sharply, then smiled, but the back of his neck stayed red above his shirt collar like a band of sunburn.

"She thinks you're in California," Haney scoffed. "Out there relaxing on the beach!"

Before Logan left in January he sent a postcard to Sheila and he put Mutt in the back of the station wagon and drove down to the waterfront. She sat rigidly and looked out the window. They went along Commercial Street, slipping on and off the train tracks. The late-afternoon light was bright and cold, stiff piles of snow lay on the edges of the sidewalks. The wind came off the water. He pulled over and got out of the car. When he opened the back he reached in with his knife and cut the rope near her collar. As she sprang past him and landed in the street he told her, "I ain't stopping you, bitch."

She went at a fast trot, close to the buildings, her tail low and the piece of rope scraggling from her collar. " 'Bye, dog," he said, and slammed the door.

It was a hot afternoon in June and it was getting ready to rain. Heavy black clouds swept over Portland and hung there. Viola and Flynn Rudge were hurrying down Brackett Street, trying to beat the rain home. "Don't know if we'll make it, Flynn," she said as they crossed Congress and started down the hill. The clouds shook and twisted and the sky drew down dark; the air cooled and surged in eddies. "Here it comes!" she gasped.

The thunder banged, the sky split open, water fell with a rushing, panting sound and splattered on the sidewalk and the street.

"Mou!" Flynn gasped.

He grabbed her hand and they ran down Sherman Street. They were soaked when they climbed to their third-floor apartment. They stood there in the kitchen, holding their arms out from their wet clothes. Sheets of rain pounded the backyard and beat on the dirty glass of the window. Flynn stood holding his cap. When he shook it, it flung off water like a wet dog. Viola lifted her blouse where it was sticking to her skin. They looked at each other and started laughing.

By suppertime the sun had come out again and the sky was washed with light. Viola moved around the small, crowded kitchen filling plates.

"Rain sure cooled things off," Jarvis said.

Viola poured milk for Flynn and sat down. "We were coming home from Mariam's and it hit so quick we couldn't get here ahead of it." She laughed and pushed at her damp hair. "Mariam said they're moving soon's they get married. They can't handle the rent that new landlord's put on either." She nodded at Flynn. "We couldn't believe how big Ben's getting, could we?"

"Beh," Flynn nodded.

Viola leaned closer and cut his meat. "She wants us all to come to the wedding reception," she told Jarvis.

"Who's she marrying?" Krista asked darkly.

Viola looked sharply at her. "Gerard, of course! What's the matter with you, Krista!"

"She's not a true woman," Krista said.

Viola sat up straighter. "She's done the best she could and she's always been a good mother to Ben."

"Can I finish these?" Kendrick asked, reaching for the potatoes.

"There's more in the oven, you go right ahead." She smiled at him and then looked at Krista again. "I thought you liked Mariam?"

"She's not a true woman," Krista insisted grimly.

"Since when are you judge and jury" Viola lifted the wooden bowl. "There's more salad, Kendrick."

But he held up his hand.

She set it slowly back on the table. “Did you invite Freddie Hewitt to your graduation like you said?”

Kendrick nodded. His mouth was full.

“Well, is he coming?”

“He can’t. He’s got to be at the racetrack,” Kendrick told her, and glanced up at the clock.

“What racetrack?” Krista wondered.

“In Scarborough. He’s a mechanic for one of the regulars.”

“Freddie knows everything there is to know about cars,” Jarvis said. “It’s a real gift.”

“He’s a genius,” Kendrick agreed, and got up from the table.

“You going out tonight, son?”

He drained his milk glass, looked quickly at her, and nodded.

Jubal Soper was sitting on the small, round, gauze-covered stool that went with the dressing table her father had bought for her eighth birthday. The child-sized mirror barely reflected the crown of her head as she sat straight, skin blushing from her shower, and watched herself. The open window to her left brought, with the breeze that swayed the curtain, the sharply sweet odor of blooming lilacs. The inclining light cut a narrow path across the room and fell golden on her arm and the side of her face. She could hear children out on the sidewalk with their bicycles, and from the kitchen the sound of her mother. When she leaned forward, bringing her face closer to the glass, the sun struck on the small of her back like a palm. As she straightened and took up her brush the light shifted around her again. She stroked slowly from the nape of her neck; a pan clattered in the kitchen, one of the children made a sound like a crashing airplane. A white waitress uniform lay in a small lump on the floor. A trench coat, dungarees, a red jacket, socks, and underwear drooped off the chair in the corner. A fresh uniform hung on the closet door. Attached neatly to the bulletin board above the unmade bed were photographs of Kendrick, of the two of them together, one of Jubal’s face in profile. She set the brush on the cluttered dressing table, stood, and stretched her arms toward the ceiling. She turned slowly, watching herself in the mirror, her face alert and softly smiling. Then she went and sat on the edge of the bed in the sunlight, her arms crossed so she could hug herself. She rocked her body slowly to feel her hair sliding across her back, and her dreamy gaze went to the window where the lilacs breathed perfume. Beyond, the voices of the children suddenly rose and were loud, and then she heard Kendrick's truck, the noise of his muffler as he slowed down and turned into the driveway.

Freddie Hewitt was out in Scarborough at the speedway. He liked picking up the extra money, watching the races, the noise and the smell, the crazy crashes. He liked drinking beer in the false day of the tall outdoor lamps. He worked for LaVoie DuTremble. LaVoie owned three Fords, their rear ends jacked up high on the axles to lessen drag, and a baby-blue Thunderbird that he drove off the track. For his tile business he drove a panel truck with his name on both sides. LaVoie limped from a motorcycle crash when he was young and reckless. His body lurched down to one side but he was fast-moving and graceful in his way. LaVoie's face was shaped like a brick held vertical, his features were small and tight, black hair rose from his forehead and the sides of his face with the flat gleam of a crow's feathers. He had a low voice and the taut, high belly of a beer drinker.

LaVoie's mother came to the track to watch her son rocket around and around the sandy, grease-stained oval. Ivy DuTremble sat, a small humped figure in the bleachers, crochet hook in her hand, pastel-colored yarn on her lap. She was sixty-three years old but her hair was blacker than his and and curled tightly above her forehead, covered and held firmly with green netting. She loved LaVoie more than anything in the world. She loved the way he chewed the skin at the top of his thumb when he stared at one of his Fords, she loved the sound of him breathing.

His wives came to the track also. The first two, Eleanor and Stella, were small and dark. Between them they had six daughters, whom they left home with two baby-sitters. Their hair was held down by colorful bandannas, bright shorts showed their wiry legs, they wore high-heeled sandals and painted their toenails. They chewed gum and they smoked the longest filter cigarettes made by man. Their pocketbooks were large and their breasts were small. As the night wore on and it grew cooler they put on huge pink sweatshirts, their legs went rigid in gooseflesh. They sat close together below LaVoie's mother and just above where Freddie Hewitt tended the Fords.

The new wife was strawberry blond with little freckles all over her skin. She rode with LaVoie in the blue Thunderbird; she always wore white. She had hazel eyes and a low voice. She was as tall as LaVoie except for his hair, upright as a rooster's comb. She didn't carry a purse; if she wanted some money she slid her hand into LaVoie's pocket. Her name was Corinne but LaVoie called her his cabbage. She sat and watched through the windshield of the Thunderbird, never getting out of it unless he opened the door and invited her, and then he sat her in his lap, her slender legs, covered in the white pants, hanging down over his, her small hand on his thick shoulder.

The old wives, Stella and Eleanor, liked to come right down out of the bleachers and watch Freddie work. He'd pull himself out from under a car and nearly run over their twenty toes. On his back, he'd look up and there were their pointy knees, the folded hems of their bright shorts, the small strain of their breasts against the colorful blouses, their chins and frizzed-out hair. Eleanor would bend down and give him a beer. Her knees always cracked.

"You think he's going to win tonight?" Eleanor asked. Her voice was deep and nervous, her knees were noisy.

Freddie sat up and took the beer she was offering.

"*Do* you?" Stella asked from above them.

"He's going to try," he told them. It was mystery, these women. He couldn't understand it. They cheered for LaVoie. They didn't come to see him hoping for a crash. They wanted him to win every time. They hollered and cursed at anybody who beat him. If they got near to Corinne they patted her as if she were a little doll or a pet animal. They called her sweetheart and baby. They fussed, telling LaVoie she was too thin and he didn't take good care of her.

He patted *them*—their shoulders, their buttocks, the tops of their casually combed heads—his two hands going out, touching them equally. "She eats, she's got appetites," he told them.

"She looks peaked," Eleanor persisted, pursing her lips, the long cigarette jabbing to the right.

"Peaked, hell! She's just made delicate and nothing will change her!" he said, his voice rising, his eyes settling darkly on the short and sturdy bodies of his earlier wives.

* * *

The evening was warm. The falling light flowed in long waves across Portland. Jarvis Rudge yanked open the street door at 14 Sherman and hollered up the stairs: "Time to go, Viola!"

She put her hat on carefully, went out the door and down the three flights. The large beige Oldsmobile was vibrating at the curb. She was shutting her door when Jarvis let out the clutch and the car leapt backward onto the sidewalk. Flynn reached to pat her shoulder as they rocked forward and started down the street. "First one in the family ever to graduate high school," Jarvis told her again, told them all again, as, arm across the seat, he turned to look behind him.

"Keen," Flynn said, and Krista bent to pull at her stocking to make sure it was straight.

After the graduation ceremony they stood outside on the smooth steps of the high school. Kendrick was wearing the new shirt and the belt they had given him. He looked handsome and tall and slightly foreign. Jubal was holding his arm. She wore a yellow dress gathered at the bodice and the night wind caught a strand of her hair and laid it across Kendrick's sleeve. His friend Bruce was with them, his long arms hanging out of the T-shirt he'd worn under his gown.

"You did good going up to get that thing," Jarvis told his son. "First one," he said to Jubal, "first one in the family." He looked up at Kendrick, an unlit cigarette in the corner of his mouth.

Viola was holding the diploma tightly against her chest. "And now you're going to a party?" she asked.

"Mrs. Rudge, we're going to rock all night," Bruce told her. He was leaning off the step, grasping at Jubal to steady himself.

"You be careful driving," Viola cautioned. Her hand went out to touch Flynn's arm.

"First one ever," Jarvis told them.

That evening Freddie Hewitt put a new fan belt in LaVoie's red Ford just before LaVoie ran it into a guardrail, avoiding a five-car pileup.

"Going to take a torch to get it off," Freddie told him when they towed it out of the arena and examined the fender.

"God in heaven, are you all right?" Eleanor cried, rushing up to him. "LaVoie!" Stella shrieked, right behind her. High in the bleachers Ivy DuTremble narrowed her eyes and watched her son, the way he moved walking around the car; then she crocheted a little faster. Behind the windshield of the Thunderbird Corinne looked out at them.

LaVoie shrugged and got in the green Ford. He went around the track fifteen more times, throwing up grit in the faces of his opponents, before his right front wheel fell off and nearly flipped him.

"LaVoie! Don't you think for one single second about getting into your black car!" Eleanor screamed. LaVoie was signaling to the guy with the wrecker. Stella grabbed onto his arm and dug her pointy heels in hard.

"Son-of-a-bitching wheel," he said softly to Freddie. "Why did she want to go and do that?" High in the night Mrs. DuTremble put down her crochet hook. "Get me the Galaxy," LaVoie told Freddie.

"Distributor cap's cracked. You was going to bring me a new one," Freddie reminded him.

"LaVoie! LaVoie!" the former wives were pleading as they pulled on his wrists.

"Shiiiit." He reached over and put his hand on Freddie's shoulder. "I didn't bring it. I forgot," he confessed sadly.

"Maybe it just ain't your night," Freddie suggested.

"That's right, LaVoie, that's it. Listen to him!" the women cried. They were like ballast. Stella, who was the lighter, tugged on his bad side, Eleanor rode the other.

"K Marts will be open," he said. "Will you go get me a distributor cap, Freddie?" LaVoie looked at him, his small eyebrows raised. "If you get back quick I'll make the last few races."

"LaVoie!" the women gasped.

He was reaching in his pocket for his wallet, thin, softened with oil, his and the cars'. He pulled out a twenty. "Take the Bird," he told Freddie. "Key's in it."

"I got my car," Freddie said.

"You take the Bird. I trust you with a car." He narrowed his eyes. "Like I trust Corinne with my love." Just behind where they stood the cars were still circling, the noise of their motors stomping on LaVoie's words. Freddie turned and LaVoie watched him walking away, long-legged, loose and easy-moving like a young horse. He nudged Eleanor and leaned toward her. "You go with him." He spoke low and she detached herself from his arm. LaVoie turned and squeezed Stella. "Go see does my mother need anything I ask you please," he said. He shifted to watch her sturdy figure, wide at the top where her hair bulged, narrowing to her calves and her sinewy ankles. As she started hiking up the bleachers the strange reddish light quivered around her until she was blurry. LaVoie reached a beer out of the cooler and turned the cap. Up above, his mother sat with her knees touching and her yellow crochetwork spreading steadily around her.

The inside of the Thunderbird smelled sweet and light, like the powder mothers sprinkle on babies. Corinne didn't move or speak. "LaVoie wants me to go get a distributor cap," Freddie told her. He was looking straight at the wheel. "For the Galaxy. He's okay," he added quickly. She didn't say anything, so he had to turn his head and look at her. It was like being kicked in the chest. Behind that sudden enlivening blow he felt a slow anger. "You want to get out and stay here?" he asked.

Corinne was looking carefully at his face, studying it the way a child might, curiosity way ahead of good manners. "No, I don't," she told him.

Her voice, and coming clear and strong like that, startled him. "All right," he said, and turned the key.

Eleanor opened the door on Corinne's side. "Got to come with you kids," she panted. "LaVoie said." She slipped right in before Corinne could tip the seat for her. "God, you move fast," she told Freddie. "I was worried you'd get away from me." She was leaning forward so her chin rested near Corinne's head. Freddie drove through the parked cars out onto the road. The Thunderbird moved as if it were ahead of him, as if it knew in advance what he would tell it to do. He had to force himself, he had to concentrate hard, not to drive it too fast.

"Didn't you just want to let it go," Corinne said to him when Eleanor had vaulted out of the car and was jog-trotting across the parking lot, her pocketbook thumping on her hip. "I could feel you wanting to," she told him. She was bending toward him. "Sometimes I feel that way," she said. "But it's not 'cause of a car." She sighed. "I don't know what it is exactly." She laughed but her face was looking sad. Her throat and the narrow V where her shirt opened were pale and speckled like a seabird's egg. They didn't hear Eleanor hollering at them until she hurried back and thumped on the hood. "Get a move on!" she bellowed.

He snapped the door handle. "I'll stay right here," Corinne told him. "I don't like doing a whole lot of moving around for nothing."

Logan Pembroke's ship was lean and close and metallic like his bus. It smelled of the engines and the men, their patterned lives, their sweat and shoe polish. On deck it smelled of the ocean, clean. Depthless and grey, the sea moved steadily like a giant creature breathing. The world was water, water and the sky that touched on its limits and reached upward to hold the heavens after sundown. But Logan did not think of the horizon or of the stars at night, of the diversity of fishes, the grace of whales, the birds in their strength. The ship, he believed, had withered the sea to a road and it carried him to distant places with their entertainments, like Portland in some crazy dream: San Diego and Honolulu and Manila; Tokyo, and he was wearing the most expensive shoes he'd ever owned in his life. They were very young men and far from Pittsburgh or Des Moines or Dunham, Maine, where they could be named; they were unattached, moving; everything could be discounted, left behind. At night they sat in small groups in the narrow, echoing steel bowels of the ship and played cards.

Paul McGinnis tossed down a dollar. "I'll see you," he said to Logan.

It was a calm evening. They were halfway to Honolulu. Logan's eyes flicked off him to watch Carl. "You in or not?" Logan was sitting cross-legged with his back against the bunk, his hands palm down shielding his cards.

"Gimme a second," Carl said. He stared at his hand and his lips worked.

"What you waiting for?" Logan demanded. "Cards ain't going to change while you sit there like a turd." He grinned at Paul.

"Just figuring the odds," Carl said doubtfully.

"Play! Just play!" Logan said. "You wanna see me or not? Cost you a buck is all."

Carl straightened and carefully set his dollar on the pile.

"Lieutenant!" Brien whispered from the doorway. It was his turn to stand guard. They jumped up, shoving their cards in their pockets. Logan swept the money into his hat with the flat of his hand and set it under the blanket on his bunk.

"It's only Frog," Brien said sheepishly, stepping back so the squat, flat-faced boy could enter.

"Jesus, Brien!" Logan glared at him.

"Can I play?" Frog asked.

"We're in the middle of a hand," Logan said, fanning his cards.

"I put mine in with the deck," Carl told him. "They're all mixed up."

"You jackass! I had three kings!" and he pushed his cards into Carl's face.

"Three?" Carl said, stepping back.

"You'll never know now, will ya, you jerk!"

Logan had six hundred dollars in his footlocker. He wore the small key on a chain about his neck; his fingers would go to it when he lay in his bunk at night and around him the ship thumped softly, his brethren snored and mumbled in their sleep. He didn't plan on going back to Maine. He was still thinking of Florida, how it would be warm and easy, how he would take what he wanted there. The cards were helping him, they convinced him he had luck. He loved the slick feel of them in his hands, the bright flashes of color, the profiles of royalty. He loved the tension beating in the air above their small circle. He loved winning, seeing their faces fall, their hands drop, emptying of cards. He loved reaching to draw the money to himself, and did it slowly, luxuriously.

Freddie brought Kendrick a muffler. "Graduation present," he told him.

"Thanks, Freddie. One I got is nothing but rust."

They lay under the truck, their feet coming out opposite sides. "I don't know what kept this thing on," Kendrick said. Chunks of it were falling around him.

"Habit," Freddie grunted. "Muffler's as lazy as anything else." He bashed at it with his wrench, turning his face away. "Get the header," he said.

When Kendrick started the truck it made a soft, comfortable ticking. "Sounds great," he told Freddie. "This was real good of you."

"It's a nice truck. You ought to bring it out to the track sometime. I don't mean race it," he said quickly. "Just come out and watch. It's entertaining."

"Might do that some night. Trouble is Jubal doesn't get off work till late."

"Well, maybe you'll make it sometime. It's a long season."

Kendrick was easing his foot on and off the gas. "You know anything about the draft?" he asked.

"Not much. Just enough to stay clear of it."

"They got Bruce going for the physical next week. When you going to be eighteen?"

"In November," Freddie told him, "but that don't matter. I'm not going in their war. Guys are coming back from there dead."

Kendrick looked at him. "How you going to get out of it?"

Freddie shrugged. "Drop a transmission on my foot. Tell 'em I like boys. Sometimes I think it might be a whole lot less trouble."

Corinne called him. Bobby Pooler stomped down the cellar stairs shouting, "Telephone!"

It was early and LaVoie was in the bathroom with the shower pounding. Her voice over the telephone sounded matter-of-fact. "Yeah," Freddie said. "I know where that is."

Corinne set the phone down and poured herself a bowl of corn flakes. When LaVoie came out of the bathroom he started again. "I won't go, then," she said. "I don't need your mother; I won't go except by myself." He was standing there dripping water, a purple towel tied around his waist. Corinne had an appointment with the doctor that afternoon to find out how come she wasn't pregnant yet. "I mean it, LaVoie," she told him.

When Freddie got there, to the overgrown field off the dump road, Corinne's Chevy was already parked beside a clump of juniper. He got out of his car and shut the door quietly. The morning was still new and it smelled good. His shoes flattened a short trail in the tall grass between their two cars. Corinne didn't do anything but take off her underpants and undo the front of her dress. She slid from behind the wheel over to him where he was sitting in the passenger seat. She sobbed the first time he kissed her. In the tall grass around the car the insects were screaming. Freddie closed his eyes. Her hair smelled like flowers. Her hands were touching him as if he were as familiar and precious to her as her own self.

Kendrick got a notice to report for a physical in July. At supper that night he told his parents, "They want me for a physical. The army."

Viola was bringing Flynn his spaghetti. "When?" she said.

"The eighteenth."

"This month?"

He nodded.

"Patty's brother joined up in the air force," Krista told them. "He says it's safer in the air than on the ground." She watched Kendrick but he didn't answer.

"Is this something you ought to be doing?" Viola asked.

"Mum, it's not like I got a choice."

Viola looked at Jarvis. Flynn watched her. She was still holding on to his plate. "You want to go in the army?" Jarvis asked him. "You got a good job painting."

"No, I don't, but it's happening fast." He got up from the table. His glass was in his hand and he drained it, set it down in the sink and left the room. Jarvis twisted his fork into his spaghetti. It made an angry, scraping sound on the plate.

"Sometimes the army gets them going in a good career," Viola said.

"He's got a good job painting for that guy right here."

"Jubal thinks he can support a wife painting."

"Well, he can. He makes more money than I do at the fish plant."

"It's not steady though. He can't count on it steady." She patted Flynn's shoulder and sat down in her chair. "He'll do what he's going to do, Jarvis. You can't stop him."

Jarvis scowled. He didn't know what he was supposed to do, what he should advise his son who wasn't asking him anyway. He couldn't see, the thing felt way beyond him: he didn't know anything about the army or the government. Kendrick came back into the room. His hair was wet from a shower.

"I'm going out," he said.

Jarvis looked at him. He was a stranger standing there, his voice harsh, slicked-back hair making his face look sharp; he seemed stronger and freer than Jarvis had ever felt himself to be.

* * *

Kendrick drove around in his truck until it was time to pick up Jubal. When she came out of Crosby's Lobster Pound she could tell by the way he was sitting in the truck, slumped toward the door and watching out the windshield toward the wharf, that he wasn't feeling good.

"Hi," she said, opening the passenger door. "I'm sorry I'm late but the last party wouldn't leave. Paul just finally told me go home and he'll give me the tip tomorrow."

He had turned sharply at the sound of her voice and he watched her as she spoke, then frowned and nodded. She slid in, put her hand on his arm, and kissed him. She smelled like butter and smoke and hard work. "You okay?" she asked. "You look upset."

"I'm okay," he said, and turned the key. "Where you want to go?"

"Anywhere you want to take me," she answered, but he didn't smile. She sighed and put her hand on his leg. "Why don't we go swimming," she suggested.

The moon was three quarters and the night as still as a brooded egg. The water shuffled softly by the shore. Jubal had waded in so that all he could see of her was her hair, chaste as a veil, and her two elbows, for which he felt such a sudden tenderness that he stumbled on the sandy beach. "Come on," she called, turning to face him. He waded in; the water climbing his legs was warm and silky. As they went deeper the lake tugged her hair in dreamy reedlike movements behind her. It was quiet, except for the slightest fluttering of birch leaves where the slender white trees leaned over the water. Kendrick flung himself forward and dove, the splash ringing a small echo across the lake. When he surfaced Jubal was swimming with him. They raced. He stroked harder, harder, the pull of his muscles, his body stretched out taut as a spear, the water parting as though to get out of his way. Jubal fell behind; she stopped swimming and watched him, his head tossing just against the rim of light above the water, the bottoms of his feet leaping like fishes. As the breeze rose up, mixing the odors of water and pine, she twisted under the surface and headed slowly back toward shore.

He swam straight out until she couldn't see him, could barely hear him. She crossed her arms over her breasts, hugged her shoulders, and waited while the night air played around her and the water fell with a slow lapping sound against the narrow beach behind her. Finally he swam back, a shifting of the darkness in the water, the splashing of his arms and feet, his breathing in long gasps. He nearly ran into her. She reached out and caught her fingers in his hair, guided his head against her. He hung on to her hips, his ribs arching against his skin; he let his body sink until he was kneeling. She was working her fingers against his bowed head. "I thought you were going clear across this lake," she whispered. "I was getting lonesome for you."

He lifted his face. He was breathing hard. He put his arms around her and, pressing his face into her, pulled her tighter until her bones gave way in a manner as exquisite and natural as the sudden fan and folding of a wing.

"This is getting crazy," Freddie said. It was an evening late in August, Eleanor's oldest daughter's birthday. LaVoie was out at her party and Corinne had said she was sick in her stomach and couldn't go so she could be here now at the cemetery of the Congregational church where she'd told Freddie to meet her. The spire rose up white and luminous from the dark tops of the trees surrounding the church. Corinne, in her white dress, was coming down the small hill past monuments for Civil War dead to get to him. "This is getting crazy," he said again when she was standing in front of him.

"Don't you like it here?" she asked. "It's so quiet and it smells like they just cut the grass." She smiled and looked up at him. "How'd you like to be lying under there?" she asked, tapping the dark grass with her toe, "and be feeling a big lawn mower rumbling over above where you were?"

He looked at her. She was so close to him it meant almost shutting his eyes. "I don't think you'd feel one damn bit of rumbling or anything else under there," he said.

Corinne laughed and touched his chest. "I guess you're probably right," she said slowly.

They were standing near a tall shade tree and the wind blowing made a gentle ruffling noise turning in the long leaves. "What are you gonna do when LaVoie gets old?" he asked her.

She looked surprised. "LaVoie won't ever get old," she said. "He's like Santa Claus or the Seven Dwarfs."

Freddie was angry but he laughed. "It's the truth," Corinne insisted, nudging him. "You might not believe it but it's the truth." She was standing so close that their bodies were touching up and down.

"Then what you want with me?"

He was holding her arm tightly but Corinne didn't flinch. She looked up into the whispering tree. "Oh, you're like the Lone Ranger," she told him, straightening her head. "You come on a big white horse and wearing your mask." She kissed him. "I like it," she murmured into his mouth.

Kendrick had to report for the physical early on a Friday morning. Bruce accompanied him.

"Yeah, they want to make sure you're a good specimen," he said. "They don't want nothing inferior in this man's army."

Kendrick smiled at him and opened the door. The line didn't quite reach the street.

"Good morning," Haney Johnson said, recognizing Bruce. "You so eager you want to sign up twice? That won't get you double pay," he told him, putting out a warning hand.

"You sure?" Bruce demanded, pounding his fist into his palm with disappointment.

Haney leaned back his head and laughed. The line stepped forward one, and the boy who'd been in with the doctor came out wearing a grim expression and bearing documents in his hand for Haney.

"We got you all calibrated?" Haney inquired, turning toward him.

"Yes, sir," the boy said. "I got no secrets from you people now."

Kendrick watched him. It was a kid he'd gone to high school with. He couldn't remember his name. He wondered if he himself was looking as nervous as that.

"Come on," Haney urged. "You men don't want to keep the doctor waiting, his hands will cool off!"

LaVoie DuTremble piled up in the fifth race of the Labor Day Spectacular and bent the front of his Galaxy horseshoelike around the tidy rear end of a Nash Ambassador. "Drove the fan right into the block. She's done," Freddie told him.

LaVoie groaned. His small mouth pursed. "Hate to see this happen to her." He looked up and his face softened. "We'll put a new motor in her," he said. His left hand was on the car, setting tenderly, fingers spread. He was chewing the thumb tip of his other hand. High up in the harshly lit bleachers Mrs. DuTremble could tell that's what he was doing by the tilt of his long head.

"She'll need more than a motor," Freddie said.

The wives were churning around LaVoie like circling wagons. Eleanor's bandanna was bright with flowers, Stella's as yellow as a child's crayoned sun. "Honey, you're indestructible," Eleanor said, patting his elbow. "You're just like some big tree!"

Stella pressed up against the Galaxy and stared at LaVoie's back. "You take too many chances," she told him, her voice shrill. "He takes too many chances!" she scolded Eleanor.

Freddie could barely see Corinne, her face a small paleness behind the Thunderbird's windshield. It looked as if her hand was covering over her mouth but he couldn't be sure.

"You think we ought to junk her?" LaVoie asked.

Freddie ran his hand through his hair. "Can always use her for parts."

LaVoie winced. The Ambassador was nearby. There was a small dent in the thick rear bumper. "Shouldn't have put his brakes on," LaVoie cried. "What in the hell did he want to stop for?"

Freddie shrugged.

LaVoie pushed himself up off the car, parted the two wives, and walked to the Thunderbird. Watching him go, they drew cigarettes from their pocketbooks and lit them. Freddie could see Corinne lean toward him when he got into the car. LaVoie started the motor and put the lights on. They burned sharp as salt in Freddie's eyes but he stared. The wives, watching LaVoie back the Thunderbird and drive away toward the road, could see Corinne's delicate profile turned toward him, her hand raised on his shoulder.

"Well now," Eleanor said softly, "poor LaVoïe must be really sad or else why would he leave before the races are over?"

"We never seen him do that before," Stella said in a hushed voice.

"Hope it ain't nothing long-lastin'," Eleanor worried, stepping closer to her.

They watched him go, the blue roof the lightest bit of anything in the night, the cars roaring about the oval behind them, their cigarettes round glows resting between their short fingers. Freddie Hewitt stood just in back of them, longing for Corinne DuTremble till it made him sick.

Logan Pembroke's ship spent the fall months in escort duty off the coast of Vietnam. There was the banging of the guns, the planes climbing from the carrier, the fires in the dark that showed where the earth was burning. Logan stood on deck in the hot nights and watched, and he thought about that bastard Captain Johnson who'd tried to get his ass sent there.

LAVOIE DUTREMBLE'S EYEBALL AND THE SMELL OF SPRUCE

12 Wordless and scowling, Flynn sat at the table and watched Kendrick eat his breakfast. Outside it was quiet and the sun was coming up. Viola hadn't slept. She was packing lunch for the bus ride: pouring soup into a thermos, wrapping sandwiches in wax paper. Krista paused in the doorway; she looked rumpled and cross in Kendrick's old brown bathrobe. Jarvis was already outside, leaning under the hood of his Oldsmobile, checking the oil.

When Kendrick rose from the table and gathered his things they followed him. They all went wordlessly down the stairs and stood on the stoop: Krista in his bathrobe, Flynn with his fingers pinching the straps of his overalls; the cat Rory was rubbing at Viola's shins and she clutched a dish towel she'd forgotten to put down. It was cold in the shadow of the building.

Kendrick settled the small suitcase and his gym bag in the back seat and got in beside his father. As they went down the street blue smoke throbbed out of the tailpipe.

Jubal lay in her bed, her body curled around the pillow. She'd lain awake since Kendrick left her. The sky had been turning grey then, the birds were twittering in the low bushes around the house. Now they were loud, massing in black flocks on the lawn, crowding onto the telephone wires above the street. Jubal was wearing one of his T-shirts. There were blue paint stains on the shoulder. She pulled it up around her face and fell asleep.

The bus depot was in a long building the color of slate. The sun striking on the gritty frosted windows made them look like ice. Jarvis went to ask again and be sure of the departure time. Bruce came in. He and Kendrick nodded at each other and stood close together smoking cigarettes.

"Seven-fifteen," Jarvis said sternly, coming up to them. He nodded at Bruce. "You got here all right," he said.

"Didn't want to disappoint my Uncle Sam." Bruce grinned. "He gets awful mad when he's disappointed."

Jarvis stomped on the butt of his cigarette and drew another from his shirt pocket. He crossed to the door, flinging the match behind him, and looked out. Turning back to them, he called, "I think it's coming!"

He watched Kendrick as he picked up the gym bag and the suitcase. He moved closer to him. "You be sure you write to your mother," he said in a hoarse voice. "You know how she's counting on it."

"I will," Kendrick said, nodding and starting for the door.

"Be sure," Jarvis admonished, half trotting beside him. "She'll be watching that mailbox."

"I will, Dad. You take care of yourself. And take care of my truck." They laughed and Jarvis told him yes. Outside was the whooshing sound of the bus's brakes. Jarvis put his hand on the gym bag to stay his son. He reached out to shake Bruce's hand. "You come see us when you get leave," he told him.

"You bet, Mr. Rudge." Bruce tapped his forehead in salute, turned and leapt up the bus steps, ducking his head under the doorframe.

Jarvis looked at Kendrick. He still had one hand pressing on the gym bag. The idling motor of the bus made a loud, eager sound. "You take care of yourself," Jarvis said, raising his voice above the roar of it. "Do what they tell you and keep your nose clean."

"I never did know what that means," Kendrick said, grinning at him.

"It means mind your own business. Don't do anything stupid," Jarvis said angrily.

"I'll be okay," Kendrick said. He didn't like the way his father was looking, old and upset and itching to be out of there.

"We're going to miss you," he told Kendrick. "Your mother's counting the days already."

Kendrick hefted the gym bag, pulling it out from under Jarvis's hand. The driver hopped up the bus steps, the brakes hissed again, he revved the motor and the stench of exhaust huffed about them.

" 'Bye, Dad," he said before he turned and climbed the steps.

Jarvis watched the door shut. The air of its motion struck his face. The driver backed rapidly, and he watched the dirty windows without seeing his son as the bus retreated and then shot forward past him and lumbered over the flattened curb. It rocked onto Spring Street, gathered speed, and was turning the corner before Jarvis could take two steps after it.

They were on the bus all through the day and long into the night, stumbling off it in the dark amid the shouts of strange voices, knocking against one another as they scrambled through the door and found their way to the narrow beds, where they fell like uprooted trees. Kendrick wakened because someone, above him he thought and to his right, was crying. And the wet snuffling sound was echoed in other parts of the long room. He felt his own throat draw up tight until it hurt, and he turned on the narrow bed and shifted the flat pillow and wished to God that he were home. It surprised him in his innocence that he could have been such a jerk as to end up in the army.

He looked for Bruce as he made up his bed in the early morning, which was already hot, but he'd disappeared sometime after the bus stopped lurching. With his hair shaved off and his skull showing white as a bantam's egg, in the green clothes that were stiff and smelled unpleasant, Kendrick felt raw and ridiculous and as homeless as an abandoned child. It was then he looked at all the other young men around him.

Oct. 18, 1967

Dear Jubal,

You wouldn't believe this place. All we do is clean toilets and march. I've lost ten pounds and I'm bald. I dreamt about you last night and woke up hollering. I miss you bad. I miss your sweetness and the things we do together. I don't know if I can stand it til my leave when I can see you again. I'd tell you about the dream I had but somebody here reads the mail. I hope you're doing good. I hope you're dreaming about me too. Please write me as soon as you get this. The address is on the envelope. I'll make up all this time we're losing when I get back.

I love you,

Kendrick

14 Sherman Street
Portland
November 8, 1967

Dear Kendrick,

Your adress is about forty miles long. I hope you are O.K. We all worry about you. Mum is hopping somehow you will be home for Thanksgiving. I told her they won't let you home just cause of the holiday. But Mum keeps hopping. The news is that we are moving. Mum dont want to til you come home but dad says he don't want to pass it up. Its mill work and he can get more pay. Its up in the country. I can quit school cause I ain't starting at another one. Every night before supper Flynn goes down and sits in your truck and drives somewhere cause hes steering like crazy. You will like this. Dad found you a side mirror that he says is the esact right kind for your truck. I got to go. He's pounding on the wall for me to put the light out. Everyone misses you.

Love,

Krista

Thanksgiving dinner was at the home of Ivy DuTremble. She lived at the end of a new street and LaVoie lived on the corner. Her dining room was on the north side and she put the lights on early, even before the family arrived. All the leaves were in her mahogany pedestal table and it was covered with a crocheted cloth and laid with her best dishes. Her pies were on the sideboard with the coffee cups and the cut-glass decanter of wine. At three o'clock her granddaughters arrived in velvet dresses with lace collars, their hair curled and firmly anchored by barrettes. Their mothers wore red, were elevated by narrow high heels, noisy with bracelets, and carrying covered dishes heavy with thoroughly boiled vegetables. They mounted the steps together, calling to their girls to hang up their coats, to kiss Grammy, to ask her what was their job. "Don't touch any of Grammy's things!" Eleanor called as they started down the hall toward the living room, a line of six little girls, the oldest pair leggy and irritable adolescents who wrestled with each other to see which would get there first and lay claim to the footstool of their father's chair.

"Where's LaVoie?" Eleanor asked. She was gazing around the kitchen and her nose was working. Mrs. DuTremble was whipping potatoes. She wore her best black dress and a long apron.

"They'll be here soon," she answered. "They're waiting for LaVoie's mechanic."

"Freddie Hewitt! Something happen to one of LaVoie's cars?"

"He's an invited guest," Mrs. DuTremble said, still whipping.

Eleanor looked at Stella. "Oh," she said. Then she opened the oven door and started making room in there for her casserole dish.

"I see 'em coming now!" Stella announced.

Eleanor let the oven door go with a bang and went to stand beside her where they could look out the glass in the back door and see them driving the short distance from LaVoie's house in two cars.

They came up the steps and into the kitchen, Corinne between them, and Freddie Hewitt hanging back to carefully close the door.

"Well, you're a good-looking surprise," Eleanor told him.

"How ya doin'?" Stella asked.

But they were watching LaVoie. Stella took his coat for him. Eleanor patted the front of his chest, which was covered by the new sweater his mother had made. They glanced at each other when LaVoie told Corinne, "You better put an apron on over that dress."

She took the one Mrs. DuTremble gave her. She wrapped the ties around her waist twice. Her dress was white wool and the collar and cuffs were blue. They watched as LaVoie signaled to Freddie Hewitt and they went down the hall to the living room where the girls were fighting and watching television. There was silence and then muffled bursts of puppylike noises as they greeted their father.

Corinne stood in front of her refrigerator with a spoon in her hand. She was holding it as if it might run away and leave her. Ivy turned on a burner. Then she looked at Stella and Eleanor who were standing shoulder to shoulder in the middle of the room. "Which one of you two is going to stuff the celery?" she asked them.

Freddie sat between the very youngest granddaughter and Stella DuTremble. He was feeling this to be a mistake. But LaVoie had pressed him, called him three times, said how they wouldn't be seeing him till next racing season and he wanted to thank him proper. Bobby Pooler was having dinner at his girlfriend's. Freddie was avoiding looking at Corinne, who was five feet away. It was giving him a headache. The tiny girl next to him, raised up to his elbow on a green cushion, was staring at him, her face tipped up on her white neck.

"You want some squash?" he asked, lifting the bowl.

She looked as if she was going to start crying. He passed the bowl the other way and she put her thumb in her mouth and settled back on her green cushion. LaVoie was standing up carving turkey, piling it on the platter Eleanor held for him. He was giving her orders.

"My mother wants dark meat only, Corinne gets a wing, give all these little pea chicks the tenderest white meat you got," he directed, waving the knife in a circle over their heads. He looked at Freddie; the knife stilled in one hand and the other was holding a wing. "What you want, my ace mechanic, my genius, my buddy?" He waved the wing as he spoke, faster and faster; all the little girls watched it. Eleanor was offering the platter for Mrs. DuTremble to serve herself, but Ivy was attending her son, so Eleanor began to spear dark meat onto her plate. Stella circled the table slowly, serving the little girls from the big bowls of vegetables. Corinne was sitting to the right of her mother-in-law. She was very still; just the fingers of one hand moved, picking at her blue collar. "What do you want?" LaVoie insisted loudly, making a wide, wide swoop with the hand that held the wing.

Freddie shrugged. "I like it all," he said.

"He wants it all," LaVoie boomed. "Give it to him." Eleanor hurried to Freddie with the platter. "Take more, take that leg," he demanded as Freddie was serving himself.

"That's good, that's fine, thanks," he protested, nodding at Eleanor.

She returned to LaVoie with the platter. He gestured in back of him with his knife and she put it on the sideboard and went and sat down between two girls. "This looks great, Mrs. DuTremble," she said, flapping open her napkin.

Ivy put some turkey in her mouth and looked across the table at Freddie. If they'd been seated around a giant clock she'd be at noon and he at four. She swallowed. "Do you have a family?" she asked him.

Freddie had to get rid of what was in his mouth. "I live with my uncle," he told her. "He's eating out today. I was going with him but LaVoie asked me here."

She looked dead across the table at her son, LaVoie at six with the very youngest girls on either side of him. Then she looked again at Freddie. Her eyes were dark and small like her son's. "Your uncle, he's a widower?"

Freddie nodded. He was eating mashed potatoes.

"You must have a girlfriend," she said, "a good-looking boy like you."

He didn't respond, but when she kept on staring at him he answered. "Had one," he said, "but she left me for a guy with more money."

Ivy made a small dismissive gesture with one of her hands.

"Well, that's real sad," Eleanor jumped in loudly, putting down her second daughter's knife and fork. "There you are," she told her, pointing her chin at the small pieces of meat. "Now eat!" Then she leaned forward over her own plate, her red beads diving toward the gravy. "Freddie, no girlfriend who'd leave you for a rich man is worth having. You need a nice girl," she said, "love you for yourself."

Mrs. DuTremble didn't even look at her. "You're not very old, are you?" she said to Freddie. "You're much too young yet for the sacred business of marriage. Too busy enjoying yourself. Am I right?" She watched him, her small penciled eyebrows raised.

The room was close, smelling of her furniture polish and the dinner they were eating. He had to keep looking away from Corinne, who was at eleven, her hair in a soft cloud around her head, her fingers gripping her fork. His headache was jumping around to different places in his skull. Mrs. DuTremble waited and watched him, her mouth just a little open. He didn't know what to tell her. He wasn't enjoying himself as far as he knew. Not generally anyway. "I remember LaVoie at your age," she said, "before he married Eleanor and started in on family life." She looked around the table at her granddaughters, and they each sat up straighter under her gaze. She stopped at Freddie. "You're just a wild young boy, aren't you?" she persisted.

"You're embarrassing him, Mrs. DuTremble," Eleanor said with a little laugh. "You're making him real uncomfortable at the table."

"Well, that ain't right now, is it?" LaVoie said, standing and looking down at Freddie. Then he walked around the table until he was behind Corinne. He put his hands on the tops of her shoulders so that his fingers came around her throat. He rubbed the tendons at the base of her neck with his square thumbs. "We don't want him uncomfortable. After all, he's a guest." LaVoie's face looked dark and unnatural as a bruise; his small eyes, watching Freddie, were moist. He bent over Corinne until she was hidden in the fold of his body; his face, inverted, was almost touching hers. When he straightened he was looking at Freddie again. Corinne sat motionless under his hands, her eyes almost closed, her pale neck laced with his dark fingers. "*Are* you uncomfortable?" LaVoie asked.

The little girls, who had been watching their father, turned their heads and looked at Freddie. He'd pushed his chair back from the table and he was leaning forward, his fingertips resting on the white crochet work. "What's going on, LaVoie?" he asked.

The little girls looked back at their father; Mrs. DuTremble watched Freddie. When Corinne shifted just slightly LaVoie moved his fingers and she was still.

"What *is* going on, LaVoie?" Stella asked, half rising from her chair at the three o'clock position.

"Shut up," he told her. She sat down hard and looked straight across the table at Eleanor, her mouth quivering.

"LaVoie," Eleanor protested, "you're ruining Thanksgiving dinner!"

"You can leave any time you don't like it," he told her as he watched Freddie. Then he turned his head to glance at her. "I can throw you out any time *I* don't like it," he said.

"LaVoie!" she wailed, but he'd stopped looking at her. Stella got up and hurried past LaVoie's empty chair to put her arm around Eleanor.

"Anybody hurt my wife," LaVoie said, working his fingers hard so Corinne's head bobbbed back and forth, "I'd kill him." He spoke softly but the little girls stopped staring at him and looked for their mothers. The very youngest granddaughter climbed down off her cushion and ran to press her face into Stella's leg. "Now she don't *look* hurt," LaVoie continued, leaning to the left so he could study Corinne's profile. "Well, maybe a little peaked," he conceded as he straightened and looked at Freddie. "I'm too trusting," he told him. "It's my failing. I ain't quick, and maybe I'm too old to learn different." He sighed. Corinne could feel his breath parting the hair at the back of her neck.

Freddie had risen. He was standing with the chair in front of him, one hand lifted on the carved back. "I'm going," he said.

"But I ain't a complete fool," LaVoie continued as if Freddie hadn't spoken, as if he were mulling something over within himself. He sighed again and dropped his hands from Corinne. He undid his belt, yanking it hard through the loops so it made a harsh slithering sound.

"I'm going," Freddie said again, backing toward the swing door that led to the kitchen.

LaVoie snapped the belt and the little girls shrieked and some of them started to cry. "Take it outside, LaVoie," Mrs. DuTremble said.

LaVoie moved quickly then. He was over the threshold and in the kitchen. The door swooshed behind him. Freddie started backing across the linoleum, raising his arm just in time to protect his face. The wives came hollering after them. The belt cut through the air again. "My God, LaVoie!" they screamed.

Ivy stiffened her spine and lifted her fork. She told the very youngest granddaughter to get on her cushion. Corinne raised her face and looked at her but Mrs. DuTremble wouldn't see her; Corinne was an empty chair she took in for a second as she looked around the table at her granddaughters. "Sit straight," she told them.

Freddie was jammed between the back door and the refrigerator, so he couldn't get out. His arms and ribs were on fire where the belt had struck. LaVoie bent toward him, and grunting, grappled at his arm and his belt and picked him up so he could throw him down again.

"You gotta open the door, LaVoie!" Eleanor shrieked. She leapt forward and tried to pull it open but the bodies of the men were in her way. She shoved in beside LaVoie, her hand going for the doorknob. When he raised the belt again he got her in the face with his elbow. He swung and Freddie thudded against the door and the glass panes rattled. "You gotta open it first, damnit, LaVoie!" Eleanor screamed.

"Oh God!" Stella wailed.

In the dining room the little girls sat silently with their fingers folded tightly into their palms and their eyes downcast, except for the very youngest one, who cried for her mother until Ivy glared her down to sniffling. Corinne almost didn't breathe. She was wishing she could go and kneel and put her head in Mrs. DuTremble's lap and be stroked, feel the ridge of her mother-in-law's wedding ring pressing firmly into her skull.

Eleanor hauled on the door and succeeded in opening it, wedging Freddie tightly against the refrigerator. "Let me out of the fucking house!" he yelled, pressing his shoulder hard into the refrigerator and rising to his feet. He was taller than LaVoie then; he was looking down into his small dark eyes. LaVoie raised the belt again. His heavy breathing smelled of turkey gravy and cigarettes. "Let me out!" Freddie yelled, and shoved hard into LaVoie's chest. LaVoie tipped onto his bad side and the leg wasn't quick enough to get under him squarely. When he toppled, Freddie jumped around the opened door and out onto the small porch. As LaVoie fell, the handle of Ivy's new refrigerator probed deeply into his left eye. He sat down hard on the floor with one leg out in front of him.

Freddie hurtled down the steps and got into his car. He burned from the belt and his eye was shutting above a gouge the buckle had made in his cheekbone. He swung out fast onto the road. Eleanor stood on the porch in the dark afternoon with her feet wide apart. "Son of a bitch!" she screamed after him, while inside Stella was cradling LaVoie in her arms.

"Oh, your eye looks peculiar," she moaned, and tipping her head back as she rocked him, she called, "Eleanor!"

West Minot
December 8, 1967

Dear Kendrick,

Its pretty nice here at this new house. Its in the woods. We got a yard. We dont have to hear nobody else. Mum says youre gonna like it a lot cept you'll probly be all the time down in Soth Portland with Jubal. We got snow. Not much but some. Dad got Flynn two dogs. Abe and Noah. He said if he had known how much Flynn would love these dogs he would of got him one before. Some guy was going to shoot these dogs. But dad got them for Flynn. I'm glad I'm done with school. So thats how it is. The new house and snow and Flynn's new dogs that he loves. I hope you are all right. We miss you all the time. I wish you could send a pickture so we could see what its like there in that place where you are.

Love,

Krista

They came up the driveway slowly, a small group, Flynn and his two dogs. Abe, the old dog, went by Flynn's side, but Noah kept sprinting ahead and rushing into the snowy woods. Bursting onto the driveway, he eagerly watched Flynn's face. Sometimes he went backward so he could keep watching Flynn, his plumy tail raised in the cold afternoon.

Every day they walked down to the mailbox. Every day Flynn picked up a stick and threw it for Noah, and threw it for Noah, and threw it for Noah. Every day Noah brought it back to him, and brought it back to him, and brought it back to him until he had to throw himself down in the snow, his long tongue out panting, his bright eyes watching Flynn. Abe marched steadily, ignoring the behavior of the young dog. He watched the pale world with his cloudy eyes, he breathed in the smell of Flynn. If Noah bounded too close, nosing at the stick in Flynn's hand, begging him to throw it, Abe lifted his long lip and snarled. Flynn threw the stick as hard as he could with one hand, and with the other he stroked the old dog's head.

This day when they got back Flynn knelt in the front room that was like a boarded-in porch and brushed and brushed the dogs' thick coats with an old nylon hairbrush Viola had given him. Abe stood patiently, Noah in his turn twisted to snap at the bristles. "Keen coming, Keen coming," Flynn told them over and over with the strokes of his brush as they stood, the one stoic and the other fidgety, under his slow-moving hands.

But the leave was canceled and Kendrick left the country in the third week of December, flying from California in an army transport. When they landed it was a hundred and ten degrees and Vietnam, green as the first garden, reeked of oil.

Every night when Jubal got home from work she watched the war on television. It was helicopters and fire, helicopters and fire. Thick black boiling smoke. Children crying. People running. Fire. Young men wrapped in bandages, leaning blind on someone's shoulder. Stretchers and helicopters, fire, heads flung back in agony. Dead bodies; they lay on the earth bent and small like something that had never had bones; they seemed to be invisible to the living people who moved among them. Newsmen shouting into microphones held to their lips while right behind them helicopter blades spun, shaking the correspondents' hair, billowing their shirts. They yelled louder. Fire. Children on fire. Jubal couldn't connect what she was looking at with Kendrick. She couldn't really believe he was there with those small delicate people in that small green country that was burning. What if one day he was on the television screen, his face wrapped in a bandage, and she would look and not know him. Not know him: if that could be true then they were already lost. She began to be afraid.

West Minot
January 3, 1968

Dear Kendrick,

I hope you got your package and liked all your presents. We missed you bad. Mum couldn't sleep all Christmas ev missing you. We got lots of snow. Theres more coming tonite. Mum dont want me to write and tell you any bad news. But I figure you should know. Freddie Hewitt got into trouble. Theyre saying the judge will send him to jail. He knocked some guy's eyeball out. They say it might be a long time for Freddie. We say it aint fair. We say what did the guy do to Freddie anyway. Freddie never told us. We would never of know it but Mum read his name in the paper at the landrymat when she was looking for soup coopons. Dad went to see him but Freddie didnt say much cept it was some kind of mistake. We hope you are O.K. We worry all the time. I will write a letter when I know what they are doing to Freddie. Flynn wants me to take a pickture of his dogs and send it to you.

Love,

Krista

Happy New Year!

Freddie Hewitt's defense was pro bono. His lawyer had the time. Warren Ruggles, a short man with fuzzy, thinning hair, had a friendly face. His client was, he decided, of a somewhat diminished capacity, the kind of person who was easily confused and quickly angered. He was clear about the fact that he hadn't meant to do any harm to the plaintiff, but he couldn't or wouldn't explain himself further except to say it had been a mistake.

"Mistake!" Warren Ruggles cried. "They're charging you with aggravated assault. That's a Class B, Fred. You could get ten years!" He studied his client's face. "You got to give me something. What about the wife?" he asked.

"She came to all the races in the T-bird," Freddie Hewitt answered.

The case was heard in Superior Court. Dr. Picone, who was small and neat-looking, had operated on LaVoie. In an aggrieved voice, and aided by three-color illustrations, he explained why he had been unable to save the vision in his patient's left eye. The judge took a lot of notes. Warren Ruggles had nothing to ask the witness.

Dr. Picone's pictures of LaVoie's injury looked awful. Freddie couldn't believe he'd been responsible for such a thing. He'd just tried to push him out of the way but here was this cruel crime. He'd almost made him blind. He'd slept with his wife, and if he could have stolen her so LaVoie never saw her again, he would have done it. From now on LaVoie would have to turn his head this way and that to see everything. His racing days were done. Freddie twisted in the chair to look at the DuTrembles. They were all there.

LaVoie sat between his lawyer and his mother. The black eyepatch shocked Freddie. Evidence of his guilt, it made LaVoie look like an old man. Ivy DuTremble appeared to be wanting to spit out something in her mouth that was too bitter to hold and too foul to expose.

Then came the three women: Eleanor and Stella and Corinne. He wondered what LaVoie had done to her. What he threatened her with. She was looking down; she was looking faded, too, and that felt like a kind of misery to him.

Behind them were the six little girls all dressed up like church. The most he could see of the youngest one was the top of her head.

When the doctor stepped down Eleanor rose from her bench. She crossed the green carpet quickly, as if she'd been waiting a long time to get into that chair. Her short dress had large gleaming buttons from collar to hem. A white band held her hair in position.

"It was Thanksgiving," she told the judge. Stella and then the six little girls nodded. Ivy DuTremble stiffened her spine.

"The family was all together," Eleanor said. She looked at Freddie where he sat next to his thin, worried lawyer, and she lifted her short arm and pointed.

"He came right in and he wouldn't leave," she said. "He kept on calling Corinne's name."

"Calling," Stella's lips whispered.

Corinne lifted her hand from her lap and put it over her mouth.

Ivy DuTremble twisted her fingers into fists and tapped the knuckles together.

Eleanor shivered, and leaning toward the judge, she dropped her voice to a hissing whisper. "I think he went crazy," she said. "Sometimes it happens. To young men." Then she sat up straight and stared across the room at LaVoie.

"LaVoie told him to leave," she insisted. "Told him nice. LaVoie's always been a family man. Always." She squinted, tipping her head a little to one side and wondering how it was that the black eyepatch made him look younger. She sighed and straightened. "And a recreational racer," she added, recalling herself with a sob and looking at the judge. "He wouldn't go. There were the six girls," she cried, thrusting her hand out to point at them where they sat in chronological order. "They were trying to eat Thanksgiving dinner. They had on their new dresses. We got 'em velvet. LaVoie didn't want the girls to see anything ugly."

"Invited!" she said to Warren Ruggles. "Of course he wasn't. Thanksgiving is a family day!"

She glared at Freddie Hewitt as she went back and settled herself, repeatedly bouncing to pull the back of her dress under the backs of her thighs.

"What was he there for? Did he think Mr. DuTremble owed him money?" the prosecuting attorney asked Stella.

"Money?" she pondered. "No, no. He was after Corinne. Crazy like Eleanor said. But LaVoie didn't want the girls to see anything ugly," she insisted. "He asked him nice to leave. And when he tried to walk him to the door that's when he jumped him."

"The defendant jumped Mr. DuTremble?"

"LaVoie! Yes, he jumped LaVoie. He was crazy. Freddie Hewitt might look like a skinny guy, but he's wiry and tough like a cat." Stella looked at him, huddling her shoulders as if she were afraid. "He's lucky. Poor LaVoie is lucky he didn't do even worse to him," she told the judge.

Leaving the stand, Stella made a wide berth to avoid the table where Freddie Hewitt sat with his lawyer. She patted Corinne's hand as she squeezed in between her and Eleanor; then she nodded toward the judge as if she were giving him permission to talk now. Corinne sat very straight on the edge of her seat, her rounded belly firm before her. The bandanna that hid her hair was dark purple, the first three buttons of her black cardigan sweater were buttoned firmly.

Freddie looked at her once more. He felt as if he were in a dream, the kind of dream where you know who people are despite the fact that they are wearing disguises. In this dream you wander, unable to figure out the plot of your own role in it. Freddie wished Corinne would take off her mask. In it she looked harsh and used. She wasn't twenty feet from him but he was having trouble recognizing her. Corinne's beauty had left her like the fate of a heroine in a fairy tale told backward.

When it was over Mr. Ruggles apologized glumly to him. "You sure didn't give me much to go in there with though," he said.

Freddie shrugged. "There wasn't nothing you could do for me," he told him.

On the morning of the eighth of February Viola was wakened early. It was the stillness. She lay on her back in the very dark room and listened to how very still it was. The house seemed to be floating on gently moving water. She smiled and got out of bed when she realized that what it meant was snow.

She made her way through the dark house, shuffling her feet to avoid walking into something. She went down the step into the main room, her hand out like a blind woman's. There was a small red glow in the stove. She kept going until she was stepping up into the front room that was like a small enclosed porch. She felt for the flashlight, opened the door, and aimed the beam high. It didn't reach far; there was no sign of morning yet. Large snowflakes were driving into her light at a slant. How clean it smelled, and it was so cold the snow murmured as it fell. Viola smiled because it was beautiful. Behind her in the stove a log burned through, making a soft thud as it fell into the ashes.

Jubal woke early too. She was confusing the sounds of Ralph O'Meara getting ready for work with the dream she'd been having about the office where she worked filing insurance forms. "I got no socks. I got no *clean* socks." She heard her mother say something. Then, "Oh, in *that* basket," and the sound of his heavy feet going toward the kitchen. "Nadine!" he called back through the house. "It's really snowing! I hope I can get the car out!" Jubal bent the pillow over her head. She was smelling coffee as she dropped into dreaming again.

On the other side of the earth where the evening was coming on, Kendrick lay on his back in a field of new rice and bled. Around him and through the delicate green plants the screaming and shooting went on but he didn't hear it. His own body, his panic and his pain, claimed all his regard. When that left him and he felt himself drawn down wavering and pale like a white flame, he heard his brother, calling calling calling for their mother; his child's voice, high and eager, was moving and modulating as if he were running through trees. And Kendrick thought, "Oh, it's all right then, it's Flynn," puzzled but unable to deny the single unimpeachable identity that was his brother's voice as it came closer, Flynn's fluting through the woods, bringing with it the drenching clean odor of spruce, the sweetness and the sound mixing together, braiding in and out as he attended their drawing near.

THE MESSENGER

13 Logan Pembroke got off the ship in San Diego. It was the twelfth day of February and he had his first year's leave. He went drinking and he started playing cards, and when day came again he found himself on a bus going out of Oklahoma

City. The ticket in the pocket of his pants said Portland. He held it in his hand and stared at it while the bus went on, rocking noisily and steadily through the flat, sand-colored country. "All right, you crazy bastard," he said and went back to sleep.

When he climbed down off the bus in Portland it was twenty degrees. His skin was used to California. He looked about him and considered going straight back there. Slush was rising over his black shoes, the cold air hurt the back of his throat, everything was gray: the street, the buildings, the hard sky. The driver stood in front of him with his duffel bag. Logan took it in one hand and turned up the collar of his jacket with the other. Then he slung the duffel over his shoulder and started up the hill.

Sheila lived just off Brighton Avenue in a square, brick apartment house. He rang the bell and stood stamping his feet in the small cold foyer. Her voice came out of the little mesh of the speaker distant and metallic: "Logan? Logan!"

He climbed up one flight. The stairs were cement and his shoes scraping against them made an irritating sound. She was standing with her door open a few inches. "Jesus," she said softly, watching him ascend the stairs. "You're quite a surprise." Her voice was flat.

"You gonna let me in?" The corridor was narrow and dark. His head ached and his feet were numb in his shoes.

She shrugged and opened the door wider.

It wasn't much brighter in the apartment. He put down the duffel bag and went and sat on the couch and then he looked at her.

Sheila's hair was dirty and drawn back in a ponytail. She was wearing brown pants and a striped smock. She stood under the archway to her kitchen and watched him.

"So how you been?" he asked.

"Been okay," she told him, shrugging her narrow shoulders.

"I forgot how fuckin' cold Portland is," he said. There was a chill going across his neck and down into his chest.

"It's winter," Sheila said.

"Ma."

Logan turned to look at the little boy who came into the room and stood staring at his mother. "I'm hungry," he told her.

"You remember Mike," Sheila said. "He's grown some since you been away."

"Don't look no bigger," Logan said.

"That's Archie," Sheila said loudly. "You're thinkin' of his brother."

"You're having another one," Logan said, "ain't you?"

Sheila smiled a little. She looked down at the boy's face; when she put her hand on his shoulder Logan could see the thin gold ring. "Married Billy Trafford from down to the shop," she explained. "Back in the summer."

Logan looked out the window. "Well," he said, and stood up. He looked at her, his face flat and hard. "So you got married."

She nodded again. "You gonna wish me luck?"

"Sure," he said, moving toward the door.

"You want a cuppa coffee?" She took her hand from the boy. She was looking at the back of Logan, his shoulders stiff as one flat board. "I never heard a word from you," she said. "Not after that postcard I couldn't even read."

He picked up the duffel bag and was in the corridor, pulling her door hard behind him. He went down the stairs fast, the iron rail cold under his hand. He pushed the door open and nearly hit a small boy who was pulling at it from the other side. Logan glanced at him as he shoved past. Then he turned and bent low over the child.

"Your mother wants you," he hissed. "She's real mad." He lifted his hand. "Real mad!"

The little boy had brown eyes. His lips and the skin under his nose were chapped. He looked up at Logan.

"You're Archie, ain't you?" he said impatiently.

The little boy nodded. Snot was running out of his nose onto the raw patches.

"You better get goin' then," Logan told him.

The child moved stiffly, his snowsuit making a swishing sound. He started for the stairs.

"You better hurry!" Logan warned him.

He went down to the Dunkin' Donuts on the corner and sat there next to where the radiator was spitting out heat and got a cup of coffee and two sugar doughnuts.

He felt better when he left, and he caught the Forest Avenue bus and got off one block from Iggy's Tavern. He was wearing civilian clothes; just his shoes were navy, black and wet on his feet, and the dark jacket. It was still daylight but the wind had come up and he hurried with his face pulled into the collar. As he turned the corner there was a harsh flapping sound above him, and when he raised his face up from the dark wool he was looking at the stiff bright flags of a used car lot.

He got to the registry the next afternoon, stood in line behind a large woman, the bill of sale half crumpled in his hand. She took forever, hauling things out of her pocketbook and stuffing them back in. When he finally turned from the counter with the plates he was hailed by a tall man wearing an army uniform who was standing in the next line.

"Seaman Pembroke," the man said, stepping out of his line to speak to him. "You must be on leave."

"That's right," Logan said, wondering who in the hell this nosy bastard was.

"Where are you staying?" Haney Johnson asked him.

Logan hesitated. "The Y," he said, shifting the plates to his other hand.

"I hope you're going to see your mother," Haney told him, stepping back into his line.

"I might. Captain Johnson," Logan said.

Haney grinned at him. "Didn't remember me, did you?" he asked.

"Not right away," Logan admitted. "I've seen a lot of uniforms this year."

"I'll bet!" Haney laughed. His line was moving again. Logan started for the door. "Go see your mother!" Haney called after him. "Good luck to you," he added.

Haney Johnson was awakened at nine-thirty. He wasn't in bed, he was sprawled at an odd angle in his recliner chair in front of the television. The floor lamp behind him shone a half-circle of light on his cheek and shoulder and on the green Naugahyde. He made loud, abrupt snorting sounds through his nose and straightened himself, then lobbed his weight forward like a sack so the chair dropped and his feet hit the floor. In front of him a frenetic car chase was proceeding through crowded streets.

"Haney!" his wife shouted from the bedroom. "Haney!"

He looked around. He didn't know where he was.

"It's one of those calls," she said loudly. She was standing in the door of their bedroom. Her floral-print nightgown covered her feet. Her fingers worked at the small white buttons on her chest. He blinked at her. She turned around, went back in the bedroom, and shut the door. He heaved himself up, stood swaying for a moment, then crossed the rug on thickly stockinged feet, hauling his handkerchief out of his back pocket as he went. In the kitchen he blew his nose, then lifted the receiver.

"Yes," hello," he said. There was a firm click as his wife hung up the bedroom phone. "Yes," he said again, reaching for the pad and pencil. After he hung up he dialed another number, then another.

It took him about forty-five minutes to get to the airport, where Mr. Petersen's assistant awaited his arrival. William Trout was standing beside the new hearse, wearing a black suit like a chauffeur's and earmuffs. They got in to wait where it was warm but Mr. Petersen didn't permit smoking so Haney got out twice and stood in the sharp wind with a cigarette before they saw the plane. It had originated in Maryland and it dropped down from the night and roared up the tarmac. After the passengers got off and their luggage was unloaded, the pilot revved the engines and the plane came on to the freight shed and Haney.

He stood at attention while the wind leapt under the belly of the plane, flapping his pant legs and sawing at the side of his face. Haney saluted as two men guided the thin brown box down a ramp and into the hearse, and he continued to stand with his hand raised to his forehead while the long silver vehicle slid soundlessly across the parking lot and turned left toward Portland.

When he got home Haney turned on the TV and then hung the uniform in the hall closet. He went into the kitchen in his underwear and got the bottle out of the cupboard. He poured three ounces of whiskey over ice, carried the glass back into the living room, and lay down on the couch. He tugged the afghan off the back and spread it over himself. The TV hummed and chuckled. Haney drank his whiskey and felt soothed by the human voices and the tiny human antics on the bright screen.

Phyllis Johnson flipped two eggs onto a plate and held it out to her husband, motioning that he should get off the phone. Haney pointed to the table, paced the short length of the cord, wheeled so it wrapped around his thick body. He was wearing his uniform. "Well, I guess there's no sense to get there before nine then," he said, and turning to free himself from the cord, he slammed down the phone. "Goddamn bureaucrats!" he complained, looking right at her, but Phyllis had her eyes on the cup she was carrying to the table. She had no sympathy she would give him. She put the cup down hard beside his plate, then turned and walked past him.

"You don't have to do it," she said loudly as she went through the door.

Mr. Petersen's establishment was in a handsome old building off Congress Street. There was a navy-blue awning that went from the front door out across the sidewalk. Haney turned down the sloping driveway and parked the truck between two white lines.

"Captain Johnson," Mr. Petersen said softly, extending his long hand. "We're all ready for you."

He turned and Haney followed him, almost colliding at the doorway where Mr. Petersen paused and, shifting his weight onto one foot, dropped his head toward Haney. "There will be no problem in viewing this time," he said in a low voice. He nodded once and then continued into the room. "Fire is our enemy," he explained as he turned the light up higher.

Haney reached into his pocket for the photograph. He didn't want to make that kind of mistake. He studied it and the young man's face as long as he had to, then backed away from the table and turned to leave the room.

"They'll be delivering the uniform in the early afternoon," Mr. Petersen told him when they were in the small parlor. "After that we'll be all ready." He looked inquiringly at Haney.

"I'm going straight out there from here," Haney told him.

It seemed to Haney that most times he was driving way out in the country. And he'd stop in the small village, or at the four corners that was the center, to find someone who could direct him. But it had got so he now drove straight as he could to the poorest part of town, to the shacks, to the rusted trailers with shacks growing out of them, to the places with junk strewn about, lean dogs tied to trees, and he'd find the people he was looking for.

West Minot was a new one on Haney. He'd never been there before but it didn't look that different from a lot of other places he had been. He was traveling into the mountains, and snow was banked up high on the sides of the road. The wind blew fine little swirls of it across in front of the truck, tall bare trees leaned from the woods on either side, and the sky rode along ahead of his windshield and beyond the rising road, a sky almost as colorless as the earth itself, its sun flattened and shrunken.

Haney drove toward that flat sun up a straight-backed hill and the sun retreated higher as he climbed. He dropped down the other side, lost the sun as he went around a slow curve, and discovered himself at a crossroads. He pulled up just beyond the Sunoco gas pumps to give himself a minute. His coat was unzipped. His hat was off. Inside Haney's cab the heater hummed. He bent his head to study the map that lay folded out on the seat beside him. He could see the variety store in the rearview mirror but he decided to trust to the feeling he had. He pulled out and continued on the route road, which dropped steadily until he was crossing a valley with pale fields on either side. A few grey corn stalks stuck through the snow and made narrow dark shadows on its still surface. Haney slowed to bump across the railroad tracks, then took a dirt road that followed them for a ways before curving off to the right. He went by an old farmhouse with the windows gone. He saw in the mirror that the long wall of the barn had fallen in. There was hay hanging stiffly out of the loft. The blue trailer beyond it had a metal sign screwed in beside the front door. It said "Putnam." Haney kept going.

The name he sought was painted on a mailbox hanging from an L-shaped pipe that was buried in a bucket of sand. The wind shook it so that it banged up and down and swung back and forth on the rusted chain. Haney slowed, peered at the name, and turned in. The driveway was plowed a car width and it inclined steadily. There was a thick growth of pines at the crest. Haney couldn't see the house but he kept going, dropping it into low gear to make the rise. A green truck raised on cinder blocks was poised where the driveway ended. Snow filled the bed. Haney stopped behind it. The small house, on rising ground to the right, was almost flat-roofed. It had been added onto in several directions from a central square. Woodsmoke came from a metal chimney that rose up the far side and had a pointed cap like a funnel. Haney eased the stick into park and got out. He settled his hat on his head.

Two dogs, mostly collie, came at him from behind the house. They stopped and barked in high-pitched voices, one standing just behind the other. Haney spoke cheerfully to them and waited. The one in front started coughing; as soon as he could he raised his head and started in barking again. Haney zipped his jacket. Sunlight pale as ice shone in the clearing where the vehicles were, but the house itself was shadowed by tall pine trees. He could see the flash of a blue jay in a tree near the door; then it opened and a teenage girl came out.

Krista thought he was the police. This was something for her father to handle. "Abe! Noah!" she called to the dogs, tapping her hand against her thigh. They looked back at her, then approached closer to the man. "What do you want?" she shouted.

He could barely hear her above the barking. As he went up the path the dogs' voices became more high-pitched. The girl had a narrow face and her hair hung about it like a dark cowl. "They won't hurt you," she called to him.

"I need to see Jarvis Rudge," Haney said. "Am I at the right place?"

Krista didn't answer. She backed up instead, staring at Haney, avoiding his face but studying the rest of him.

"Am I at the right place?" he asked again.

"He's not here," she told him, and turned around.

"You expect him soon?" Haney called.

Krista ran faster toward the house. The dogs followed her, turning around at intervals to bark. She opened the door and shooed them in ahead of her.

Haney stalked back to his truck, his boots making a heavy breaking sound on the snow crust. He kept glancing at the house, but the only movement was smoke rising from the metal chimney.

Krista stood in the kitchen listening, her hands twisting into one another.

"Star, wha'?" Flynn asked. He was sitting in the rocking chair. The dogs had gone to him and he was stroking them.

"It's all right, Flynn," she told him. "It's nothing. Dad'll be home soon."

Haney climbed into his truck. He grew cold quickly and had to run the motor three times before he heard them coming. A muffler echoed as if the world around it were hollow, and then the pale nose of a very wide Oldsmobile poked over the rise and descended to settle almost against Haney's tailgate. Haney shut off his motor, opened the door, and jumped down into the snow.

Jarvis got out of the Oldsmobile. He let his door fall shut and stepped toward Haney. He didn't say anything, just looked at him.

Haney knew him: it was the same face as on the photograph in his breast pocket, the same face he'd seen on the table at Petersen's. There was a cigarette in his mouth and his eye was twisted up against the smoke. His hands were bare and red. "Jarvis Rudge?" Haney asked. He nodded and Haney stepped toward him, holding out his hand. "I'm Haney Johnson," he said. "Could we go in the house and talk a bit?"

He didn't answer. Over his head and the roof of the car Haney could see the woman hefting a bag of groceries from the back seat. She straightened with it and watched them.

"I've got to help my wife," Jarvis muttered, and he turned around and walked swiftly away from Haney. When he reached into the back seat of the Oldsmobile Viola said something to him, but he ignored her and drew out the bundle of laundry she had wrapped in a knotted sheet. He juggled it with his knee until he could lock both arms around it, then kicked the door shut and started for the house, Viola following after him, carrying a bag of groceries and a jug of milk.

"Can I help?" Haney called to her, but she just kept going, so he went to the car and gathered up two bags of groceries and shut the door carefully with his hip.

When Haney reached the house the two dogs were standing in front of the closed door. They didn't even look at him. They waited. Haney waited. His face and his hands and his feet were cold. He finally set the groceries down and reached past the dogs to knock on the door.

They backed away from him and started to bark again, but without spirit, as if they were weary of him and did it out of duty. Haney knocked on the door again. It was almost all windows like a porch door. The room within was narrow and held two large bureaus. He put his hand over his eyes and pressed against the glass to peer in, looked through a door that led to the room beyond, where he could see part of a cookstove. He knocked a third time. A shadow fell across the stove and Jarvis came through into the narrow room and just stood there inside the glass. When Haney filled his arms with the groceries Jarvis jerked the door open and grabbed the bags from him. The dogs rushed in. "I need to speak to you," Haney said.

"Yes," he answered gruffly. "I was helping my wife. You can come in now."

Haney shut the door carefully behind him. He wiped his feet and took off his hat. Jarvis hadn't moved. The bags were almost tipping out of his arms. "I work for the army," Haney told him.

Jarvis wheeled around and went through the narrow room and into the house. Haney followed. He waited by the stove. Jarvis had crossed to a corner and set the bags down beside a metal cupboard that reached to the low, smoke-stained ceiling. He stood beside Viola, who was putting things onto the shelves. A long wooden table was on the wall to Haney's right. Two cats were sitting on it. Another wood stove was on the opposite wall; there was a low, sagging couch beside it and a cane-seated rocking chair between the stove and the table. Flynn had tipped himself forward in the rocker so his feet were on the floor. He was watching Haney, looking from him to his parents and back again.

"You want coffee, mister?" Viola asked. She made it sound like a threat.

But he nodded and smiled at her. "Thanks, if it's not too much trouble."

She went to the sink and filled a kettle from the hand pump. She came near to Haney to put it on the stove but she didn't look at him. Krista stood on the threshold of the little hall that led to the added-on rooms. She was working the thumb of one hand into the palm of the other. She looked at Haney for a moment and then she watched her father.

"I'm so very sorry," Haney said, looking toward Jarvis. Viola made a noise as if she'd been hit in the stomach and Haney rushed on with his words. They sounded in his ears as if they came from outside himself. Keeping his eyes on Jarvis, he could feel her. She seemed to be shrinking, drawing down into herself; she made a horrible cry. Flynn started to rock faster. Jarvis began to pace. Krista ran to her mother, who was bent almost double before the cookstove. It felt to Haney as if he'd started a machine going. There was too much energy for this small room. Jarvis was circling the perimeter, and every time he passed his wife he held, for a moment, her head in his hands and pressed it. Flynn was rocking harder, the dogs whined, the cats leapt from the table and ran through the door into the hall. Krista bent to hug her mother around the shoulders and looked up angrily at Haney.

"You're lying!" she cried. "You come here telling lies!" She looked back at her mother. She shook her. "You tell him," she insisted. "You tell him how you got a letter just the other day."

Viola twisted her head back to look at her daughter. She stumbled to her feet and thrust her hand out at Haney. She didn't grab his arm but just touched it with her fingertips. "It's true," she whispered. "He said he was fine." She looked from him to her daughter and back again. "He said he was being careful; he promised."

Jarvis was still flailing about the room. Flynn banged his chair on the floor, over and over. "No, Viola!" Jarvis yelled.

She started crying then and she charged at him. "Don't you tell me No!" she screamed, and she swung her fists at him. "Don't you tell me No!" And then she was crying hard. He broke from her and her hands hit at the air. Flynn started picking at his head. He rocked and tugged at his hair with the fingers of his left hand. He kept looking at his mother and from her to Haney. His thick lashes screened his eyes like a pony's. He made low noises in his throat. The dogs were moving nervously about his thumping chair.

"I'm so sorry," Haney said again, but they weren't looking at him. Jarvis was still circling the room, touching Viola, backing off from her. Krista was pulling her toward the doorway. As they went through it Krista looked back at Haney and her face twisted as if she were seeing something evil. The kettle started boiling over and Haney jumped for it. Flynn lifted both hands to his hair and pulled hard. He made moaning sounds that climbed and climbed and then dropped before ascending again. Haney set the kettle down and backed to the doorframe. He could hear Viola. She was crying out the dead boy's name.

"I can come back later and help with the arrangements," Haney said in an urgent voice. He wondered if Jarvis Rudge could hear him. The sound of Flynn rose above everything. "I want to make it as—"

Jarvis jerked his head around and looked across the room straight at him and Haney thought, "He wants to kill me." Moving backward, he stepped up into the first room and put on his hat.

Jarvis came right after him. He ground his teeth together so that it almost looked as if he were grinning. He stared into Haney's face. "What!" he demanded, pushing his jaw out as if he were biting the word out of something. "What!"

Haney retreated until his back was against the door with the glass panes in it. He reached behind him to open it. Jarvis's hands were fists and he kept his face thrust into Haney's. They stepped through the door.

The cold air caught Haney like a blessing. He straightened and breathed deeply. Coatless, Jarvis came on after him, his face the color of concrete and his eyes burning. "What!" he said again.

Haney spoke slowly. "He's at a funeral home in Portland," he told Jarvis. "I got the address and phone number written down here for you." He pushed a little card at him and Jarvis curled it between his fingers. "You let me know where you want him buried," Haney said, and Jarvis's face drew one shade paler still, his mouth opened slightly. He made a sound. His hands in fists rose above his head. "I'll call the minister for you," Haney told him. "I'll make any arrangements you want me to; the government pays for this."

Laughter shot from Jarvis's mouth and it was like stones falling out of his face. He stretched forward on his toes and his fists snapped at the cold air between them. "What else?" he demanded hoarsely.

"I'll make sure all his things are returned to you." Haney was moving toward the truck while he spoke, his body still turned toward Jarvis. The woman's cries were following them, the thumping noise of the boy in the chair. Blue jays were screaming in the pines. They were close together on the narrow path. Haney looked up. "Oh Christ!" He'd forgotten. "I'm sorry, I'm going to have to ask you to move the car. I can't get out past it."

Jarvis glared at him, then yanked the keys out of his pocket. They flew from his hand and fell into the snow, and when he bent to retrieve them Haney saw how the hair grew from a whorled place on the top of his head just as it did on the boy at Petersen's. Then Jarvis closed his fingers over the keys and shot up straight. His hands hung at his sides like weights; the silvery key chain dangled from one of them. "I want to give you this card with my number,"

Haney said, digging into his pocket. "I'll be back tomorrow, but you call me in the meantime if there is anything you want to ask me about, anything you want to know, anything you want to tell me." Haney held the card out and Jarvis crumpled it in his fingers with the first one.

He walked past Haney and stumbled toward the Oldsmobile. He went around the back of it and hauled the door open. Haney hurried to his truck and climbed in the passenger side and worked his bulk behind the wheel. As he turned the key in the ignition he watched the Oldsmobile in the rearview mirror. It banged and roared. Smoke gushed and billowed into the air. Then it jerked backward and reared up over the hill, the flat, broad nose pointing for a moment straight up at the noonday sun, which stood shrunken and without heat, balanced round and flat as a saw blade in the colorless, cloudless sky.

ICE

14 The buzzer made a rusty croaking sound like a weary frog. Logan didn't know what it was. He was lying in his narrow bed at the Y smoking a cigarette, a metal ashtray on his stomach. By the light at the window and the sounds in the building he knew it must be well into the morning. He wasn't worried, he had nothing to do. He was going to leave in a few days, drive his new car to California, sell it before he got back on his ship, make a little money on the deal. The buzzer made its high-pitched, hoarse sound again. Logan moved the ashtray to the bedside table and sat up. It kept on; some shithead was leaning on the goddamn button and wouldn't quit. He pulled on his dungarees, stepped barefoot into his shoes, and yanked a sweatshirt over his head.

Captain Johnson was standing by the desk. He was all dressed up in his uniform with his hat on.

"No," Logan said. "I don't want to drive no guy to a funeral."

"*I'm* bringing them," Haney explained again patiently, "I'm just asking you to drive them home because I have to go to a meeting."

"I got a date this afternoon," Logan told him.

"The poor man's motor blew," Haney said, leaning close to Logan. "The sergeant who usually does family liaison with me is sick."

"That ain't my fault."

"I'll give you twenty bucks cover your gas and expenses." Haney reached under his coat for his billfold. He narrowed his eyes at Logan as he opened it. "It's hard to believe you won't help out a fellow serviceman," he said in a cold voice.

Logan shrugged. "I thought you said he was dead." He reached out and took the twenty. "Dead man can't use my help," he said, grinning at Haney as he folded the bill and put it carefully into his own wallet.

Nadine O'Meara brought lunch in to her daughter but Jubal paid her no heed. She lay twisted up in her blankets, her face turned toward the wall. On her pillow were a photograph taken last summer, the clipping from the newspaper, and the short note from Krista.

The cemetery was south of the city, covering about thirty fenced acres of slowly rolling ground between the old route road and a wood. Pitted and mossy, monuments reached up at intervals. Logan waited in the small parking area by the gate. He kept the Chevy running and it vibrated steadily, joggling the dice that hung from his rearview mirror. The heater was keeping his windshield clear as summer. Logan unbuttoned his jacket and lit a cigarette.

They had formed a small semicircle in front of the vault, their figures dark and as separate as the maple trunks that rose up beyond the fence. The hill under which the vault lay was covered with brittle snow; the long black shadows of the winter-shorn trees reached among the headstones like water under ice. The iron door of the vault, low and curved at the top, was open. It was late afternoon, the sun soon would be gone, the sky was the color of tin. The sound of the wind clacking the limbs of the maple trees together was like bare young bones falling on one another.

Logan drew on the last of his cigarette as the small group broke and started walking up the long cemetery road. He could see Haney Johnson leading them toward him.

* * *

Jubal got out of the bed and went through the back hall and returned with Ralph O'Meara's shears. Facing the empty wall, she hacked off her hair. It fell in piles around her ankles. The hair left on her head smelled like oil from her stepfather's carefulness with tools. She put her boots on and her coat and went out of the house. Her mother, downstairs with the laundry, didn't hear her leave. Jubal drove to the cemetery and parked a short distance from the gate. She saw the cars, saw Mr. Rudge sitting in the passenger seat of a station wagon she didn't recognize.

Logan's car was green and there were metal strips on it that were supposed to resemble wood. Their breathing was fogging his windows and he flipped on knobs and switches. He half turned to them. "It'll be clear in a minute," he said, his voice high-pitched, eager. No one answered him. He stepped on the gas and they moved under the wrought-iron archway and out onto the road. The sky to the east was grey and the pale sun hurried down the western sky.

The gravediggers' shed was beyond the vault, down in a hollow near a clump of trees. It was smoky inside where the stove was burning maple. Bodie Graffam watched through the diamond-shaped pane of glass in the door.

"Got this soup heated good," Ezra told him as he lifted the dented silvery pot from the stove and carried it to their table. Carefully he ladled it out into the white bowls. He looked at Bodie's back. Steam was rising from his soup in two little clouds. "Bodie, Bodie," Ezra urged in his small, childlike voice.

"They're leaving now," Bodie said, running his hands through his thick hair.

"Let's eat our soup first," Ezra said. "We got time."

Logan glanced at the man he was driving home. His shoulders were pulled up taut and high and his fist was crushed into the palm of the other hand. He unfolded it in an irregular rhythm to lift the cigarette from his mouth, and the smoke from their two cigarettes floated between them and rose to fan out over the roof of the car. Logan drove fast and soon he'd got them around the city and headed north. His heater hummed and the motor was strong as his own heart beating. He adjusted his rearview mirror so that when he checked for traffic he wouldn't have to see their faces. They cried steadily and wearily, but almost silently, as if something inside them had broken and was leaking. It felt like a fog of female misery spreading from his back seat. All he could see of that strange kid was the top of his head—bald spots as if moths had gotten at him—and bent over the folded flag he held on his lap. He could hear him, indistinguishable mutterings that rose and fell but never got very loud. Logan dropped his hand from the mirror and reached forward to turn on his radio.

Bodie Graffam put on his earmuffs and his railroad cap, which he wore in all weather, and his heavy coat. He bent to open the door of the stove and tossed in his cigarette butt, then reached to turn down the damper. He wrapped the scarf around his throat and pulled on his thick brown gloves. "Come on, Ezra," he said.

Jarvis Rudge said, "Shut that goddamn thing off." He spoke harshly but slowly, so that each word hung between them like something that could be set on a scale and weighed.

Logan sucked air through his clenched teeth and then he leaned into the dashboard and turned the knob. It made an easy, clicking sound. "Thought it mighta helped," he offered, and then said to himself, "Son-of-a-bitch Johnson." He looked straight ahead and stepped down on the accelerator. Though the road was narrow and torn up by the winter his car leapt over it with the sturdiness of a barge. He sat back in his seat and pulled another cigarette out of his pocket. He didn't see a very deep pothole just beyond Gray, and the girl pitched forward so her fingers touched the back of his neck. They were warm and damp, almost sticky.

Ezra shuffled along just behind Bodie in his too large plaid jacket, a visored hat of a different plaid pulled down over his small face. Bright yellow mittens rode on his hands like paddles and he stroked through the cold air as he hurried. They tromped up the narrow way between the stones and approached the vault. It cast a curving shadow across the snow. Bodie ducked under the lintel. Ezra walked tall. It smelled like old dampness inside.

* * *

Jubal wandered among the gravestones. Her head was light; the wind clapped at the back of her neck and curled in her naked ears. It made little rushing tinny sounds around the monuments and in the bare trees. There was no sign anyone had been here, that he was here, stored like an Egyptian until spring made the ground warm enough to dig him a place in it. Jubal sat down hard on a white tomb and started crying. The wind burned where her face was wet. After a time she got up and walked on toward the woods. When she heard voices she thought first it was a new trick of the wind.

They were climbing now but his Chevy didn't hesitate. It felt almost as if they were going downhill it was so smooth. He had made the right choice—screw that shithead salesman and his Buick. The snow was higher on the tree trunks here, the limbs didn't move, the sky was leaden. The girl in his back seat and her mother were quiet now, but he could feel their grieving like a stream of damp air on his neck; the boy mumbled on, the man banged his fist into his hand.

When Bodie came out of the vault and straightened he saw her. She was standing some distance off beside a tall gray monument. He thought it was a boy at first, that chopped hair, but the long unbuttoned coat was a girl's and then she moved and it was a woman's way of walking. He waited there and she came down and stood quite close to him and he realized she was looking at the coffin. "Already had the service, miss," he told her. "They've all gone now."

She didn't say anything, didn't even look at him, just turned slowly and walked back up the hill to the monument where he'd first seen her. He felt Ezra behind him, turned and nudged him and gestured toward her. Ezra peered out from beneath his visor. "She missed the service," Bodie told him. Ezra shrugged his shoulders, banged his mittens together.

Bodie released the brake on the trolley and they began to push the coffin toward the vault. "I can't do it all," he grunted. "Lean into it a little, Ezra, would ya!"

* * *

They reached the top of the hill and pulled around the long corner. The sun was lower than they were. Huge and red, it burned behind the trees, making them deep black, holding their limbs in the flames. The man had his elbows on his knees and his fingers pressed into his forehead; his shoulders were pulled up around his neck. At intervals deep groans came from his throat. He sounded like the buck Logan had shot the November before he went into the navy. He pulled the knob on his lights farther out and pressed his foot a little closer to the floor. The girl and her mother were blowing their noses and coughing—hollow, raspy sounds that made him think of worn-out machinery. He drove faster. They were descending again, dropping below the wall of trees. He jerked his head quickly when something white wavered in the corner of his vision. It was that kid, his narrow chin pressed into the seat top and his hands reaching forward until they touched the man's back. "Doe cry, Da," he gasped. "Doe cry."

When they emerged from the vault the wind had risen, the slate-colored sky was flattened close above the cold earth. Bodie looked for the woman. He squinted to be sure of her: she was as still as the stone. Ezra walked right into him.

"Keepa goin', Bodie," he urged, pushing on his back with his thick mittens. But Bodie halted.

"Should we go speak to her, Ezra?" he asked.

"She's about her own business," Ezra said. He nudged Bodie again. "I wanna go home," he said. "Ma's got pot roast for me."

"But it's almost night."

"You go talk to her then," Ezra told him. "I got to go to where I can get my feet warm."

The big car dropped down the hill and stopped behind the truck that was raised on cement blocks. Jarvis Rudge thudded his shoulder against the door and tumbled out. Logan set the brake and got out quickly to hold the back door for the others, but the man had opened the one on his side and the kid was out and standing with his empty hands hanging and his eyes on his father's face. The mother got out too, her arms folded across her stomach. They turned and started up the narrow path, the snow stretching unbroken on either side. It was too late for shadows and yet he could still make out the yard clearly. They hurried toward the small house, slipping on the path. The girl got out of the door Logan held open and they stood there with it between them, and then she said, "Thanks for driving us home."

He could barely hear her. Her face was all streaked and stamped-on-looking. He liked her hair though. It was long and thick and it looked too heavy for her head. "I'm going soon," he told her. "Back to my ship. Maybe there's something else I can do to help you out before I leave." He squinted and watched over her head.

She lifted her chin. It was a slow gesture. "Can't think of nothing. Thank you though." She had a hoarse, gritty-sounding voice. She went around the car and started for the path.

He shoved the door closed and went after her, reaching to dig a small notebook out of the pocket of his coat. "Tell me your telephone number and I'll call you," he said. "I'll call you and see how you are."

"Haven't got a phone. Use the one down to the store." She paused and gestured toward the grove of pines at the crest of the hill.

"Then you call me where I'm staying." He lifted the pencil. "Shit," he said. "I forgot the number. But it's the Y in Portland. I'll write that down for you," he went on, speaking faster. "You call me in the morning. Tell me how you are." He pulled a crumpled dollar out of his pocket and then he asked, "What's your name?"

"Krista," she answered after a moment.

He put the paper and the money in her fingers. "I wrote my name on there," he told her.

She was backing away but she nodded before turning and starting up the narrow path. She went slowly and her hands kept jerking out to balance her on the ice. He climbed into the car and put it in reverse. He started backing and she paused at the sound and turned, the money and the paper in her bare hand. He looked at her once more before the back of the car rose over the hill. She was caught between the rim of his steering wheel and the top of the windshield, a small brown figure in the midst of the darkening winter night. Her hand half raised, she watched him. Then the car tipped over the crest and started down the other side, and when he looked again he couldn't see anything but the empty sky, rising in layers of greyer and greyer color, and he thought again how this car had been the right choice and he felt so pleased he hadn't let that shithead in the lot sell him the Buick.

Jubal watched them disappear behind the shack and then just saw for a moment the plaid of the small one's coat. When she heard the sound of a truck starting she came slowly down from the monument toward the hill that was curved as though an upturned boat lay beneath it. There were the branches knocking cold against each other and then the quick voice of a chickadee vibrated in the air. She hesitated, listening to the pureness of that living sound in this place. Then she walked on. She walked toward the vault in Bodie's big footprints and over the small ones of Ezra. She sat down and leaned her shoulder against the iron door and stuffed her hands up the sleeves of her long gray coat.

Logan came down from the dark mountains, his Chevy out flat and his radio playing loudly. He was very hungry, he'd had to skip lunch to get to the cemetery. He tapped his short fingers on the wheel and rocked his head with the music.

Behind the vault the trees clacked and moaned, clacked and moaned like sad dead things that the wind tripped through. From the sunken doorway Jubal looked out at the tops of headstones barely separate from the falling night.

Jarvis grabbed the shovel out of the front room and went through the glass-paned door with it. Viola followed him down the icy path. Small, very white stars were high in the black sky. She called harshly, "Jarvis, come back in where it's warm," but he only walked faster. She stumbled as she hurried after him. The wind cut around them both with its sharp edges. "Jarvis!" she called, but he was climbing into the bed of the truck.

"Goddamn son of a bitch," she heard him say, and then the muffled thumping of his shovel as he drove it into the snow.

"Jarvis!"

He couldn't hear her. She stopped on the path. She couldn't see him. Everything was black in front of her. She heard the short, rapid thudding of the shovel and his curses. She turned around and started back up the path.

* * *

"I'm getting her up for supper," Nadine O'Meara told her husband. "This taking to the bed don't do anybody any good."

She went down the short hall to Jubal's bedroom and opened the door. It was dark and her slippered feet went sliding over and through something she couldn't recognize but if pressed would have described as dry water. She kept herself from falling and got to the bed and leaned over it to switch on the light, then turned back to look. She had to kneel down to take hold of bunches of it and raise it before her face.

"Ralph O'Meara!" she called.

He got right out of his chair and went to her but she was already in the hall, standing there crying his name again, and his stepdaughter's hair was hanging from her hands like the pelt of a slaughtered animal.

Jubal half lay against the door. Her feet burned and her hands. Her ears, her nose, her mouth, were gone; there was nothing to see. He lay on the other side of the door in a box, all his young beauty smashed and gone from the world. She whispered to him, her mouth barely moving, and the cold night grabbed up her words and swallowed them. She pressed against the door and could smell its old rusty smell. The wind moaned around them like a tired and irritated beast.

When Logan reached Portland he drove to the Italian restaurant on Congress Street. He ordered a pizza and a pitcher of beer. He ate quickly: the hot dough, the sauce that burned the roof of his mouth, and then the long, cold drink of beer. He thought about his car: it would get to California all right; he thought about the girl: Christine she said her name was, her long mouth and the way her hair was so heavy it could be like a rich cloth in his hands.

Krista came down the slippery path in her heavy coat, a blue hat crammed over her hair. She was shining the flashlight before her. The wind made a low moaning sound as it twisted around the small corners of the house and shuddered in the branches of the wide-limbed pines. Before she'd gone far enough for the beam to reach him she heard the sound of the shovel plowing into the frozen snow, the scraping of the metal on the truck bed. She went close and held the light high so it shone onto his work. He jerked his head up and glared at her for a moment. He bent and dug the shovel in again. She moved her toes inside her boots. She lifted the light higher.

Logan ordered another pitcher and a meatball sandwich. The restaurant was half full, the jukebox was playing, from the game room around the corner came the crisp clunk of pool. He was thinking about getting into a game but the large room was warm and he suddenly felt very tired. He lifted the pitcher and refilled his mug, then started in on the heavy sandwich.

They got out of the car together and walked down the road into the cemetery. Ralph O'Meara shone the flashlight. It was cold and the wind blew and the gravestones seemed to move suddenly into the light that flowed from his hand. Nadine went a little before him, her boots crunching on the narrow cemetery road. "He'll be in the vault," she said, half turning to her husband. "They're not digging any holes this time of year."

Jubal's face looked like a patch of snow slammed onto the iron door. The wind plucked at her cropped hair. "Child," Nadine said, bending to her, reaching to shake her shoulders. The beam of Ralph's light trembled on the snow and on the door and on her face. Nadine shook her hard. "Get up, Jubal," she said, "you're half froze."

The wind rose again and the limbs of the maples knocked against each other, a sharper and sharper sound as if they must break. Ralph pressed a little closer; he shifted in his boots, rubbed his free hand on his thigh. "We'll have to carry her," Nadine told him. He gave her the flashlight and, stooping, put one arm under Jubal's knees and one under the upper part of her body. Turning, he started up the hill toward the road. He'd barely touched Jubal before. Way back when she was ten and angry as hell because he'd married her mother Ralph had respected the distance she wanted between them. She felt light and long-legged; the top part of her body was knocking against him and he realized she was sobbing. He tried to walk faster. Nadine came behind them with the light shining. "You want me to take her legs?" she called.

"I'm okay," he grunted. The wind swooped from the woods and whirled down the small alleys between the gravestones and pushed them along. Ralph lifted her higher on his chest. He could hear a truck going by out on the route road.

Inside the car it was bitter cold. "Thank you, Ralph," Nadine said when she'd shut the door. He was getting out again to clear the windshield. He nodded and shut his door carefully. Nadine reached her leg over to keep her foot on the gas. She looped her arms around Jubal and pulled her close. She stroked her head. "Your beautiful hair," she grieved, her voice rough, a little cold cloud forming from her words. She could see out a little space where Ralph had scraped off the glass.

"I can't stand it, Ma," Jubal said, her voice raspy and worn.

"You ain't got a choice about it," Nadine told her.

Viola lay on the spread in the dark bedroom and wept. The pain had settled in the middle of her body, which knotted every time she thought his name, every time she pictured that Captain Johnson in her kitchen, his bulkiness pressing the room flat, his voice ripping Time in two. To heal the break in the world, to defeat the workings of that savage and piteous moment, she would have to leap into the cold blackness beyond the moon and, standing balanced on the last feather of an angel's wing, push the fiercely spinning planet backward. Viola lifted her arms in the darkness, she rose up from the pillow and roared with rage and, raging, pulled at her fine black hair.

Jarvis sat in the truck. The windows were frosted with his quick breaths, his smoke curled against the cold glass, a small point of heat burned red at the end of his cigarette.

Krista stood behind the long windows next to the door and looked down the path. The light from the lamp in the kitchen sent the long shadows of the bureaus falling across her. She had wrapped a brown blanket about her shoulders, and her hands, holding the ends of it, were pink and raw-looking.

Behind her in the main room the chair thumped and creaked, thumped and creaked, thumped and creaked on the narrow pine boards. Faster and faster and faster rocked Flynn. The cats sat under the stove and watched the runners bang back and forth, their green eyes shifting to follow the movement, their front paws curled under their chests. The dogs lay beneath the table, tipping their heads one way and then another as they watched Flynn. The chair moved across the floor in jumpy increments and after a time he stamped his feet down hard and rose to struggle it back by the stove. He got in and started rocking again. The dogs watched him. The chair jumped and cracked like a lean young tree in a hurricane.

THE LOVER

15 Jarvis went back to work, hitching a ride to the mill with Raymond Bodin. Viola scrubbed the inside of the small house. Flynn walked his dogs and brushed their long coats in the days that followed the death of Kendrick and finished out the bitter month of February. Krista tried to help her mother. She carried the foaming pails of water that sent up a stingy vapor and made her eyes tear; she watched Viola's narrow back and listened anxiously to the gritty sound of her brush on the slanted floors. She helped with the supper, peeling vegetables and setting the table for a meal that was eaten in silence, her father leaning over his plate, his forearms planted hard on the cloth like fences. Flynn ate slowly, sitting on alone when the others had finished, a dog on either side of his chair.

Krista was fifteen, and when she looked in the mirror above the sink in the kitchen she saw a face that was dusky and bony and her teeth that were too long and that gap in the front. She lay in her small bed at night and thought how their family had been broken, how even the strongest could fall into the blackness, how she was alone and could do nothing to change anything, and when she spoke her words went forth like silence, no reply or denial, no echo.

With March came new snow and then bright sun, lengthening days. Krista went outdoors. It was warm by lunchtime, the fresh snow was drops of water falling from pine needles. She walked down the driveway with Flynn and the dogs. One day the mail brought a letter from Freddie Hewitt. Krista held it close to her face to read the address. Flynn was halted beside her, stroking the old dog. "Are you going back now, Flynn, or walking on with me?" she asked.

"Abe tired," he told her.

"This letter is from Freddie." She held it out. "Will you bring it to Mum?"

"Dee," he said, nodding and showing the letter to Abe.

Krista went on down the plowed road. The wind had a sweet, cold taste in it. She was heading for the four corners and the store there. She had thirty cents and she wanted to buy her mother a candy bar. The empty road curved ahead of her, the shadows of maple limbs grey and delicate on the hard-packed snow, the bright sunlight glistening on the new water that ran down the trunks. Krista heard a car coming fast behind her and stepped to the shoulder. Chunks of snow flew up and knocked against her boots as it went quickly past her and disappeared around the curve.

She heard brakes and then the long whine of the car reversing. It stopped abreast of her and he lunged across the seat to unroll the window. His eyes were squinting at the brightness of the day around her. "Why didn't you call me?" he demanded. "I was waiting."

She stared at him. She hadn't been expecting to see him again ever.

"I was waiting!" he said again, frowning at her. "Get in!"

They went on past the four corners and she rode small and unprotesting in the seat with her hands folded in her lap. "I gave you money to call me," he said. "I told you where."

"I didn't know how to call you where you were," she said, picturing that piece of paper folded about the dollar bill on the narrow shelf in her room.

"I *told* you!" he accused.

"I got the dollar saved for you."

She could feel him turning to look at her. His car went along easy and smooth, the radio was playing something happy, warm air was flowing out onto her wet feet. "That's okay," he said, his voice soft. "You can keep it. I gave it to you." He was still watching her. "I came to find out why you didn't call me."

He drove her to Lewiston and they stood by the icy river. "You should see it when the ice breaks up and the rains come," he told her. "River runs right over the street."

"It does?"

"Sure. Where you think it's going to go?" he said, laughing loudly.

Krista stared at the black water that was stilled into icicles hanging from rocks.

"I'd bring you to see it but I'll be back on the ship." She looked at him quickly. "Come on, I'll get you something to eat," he told her. "You look hungry."

She sat opposite him at a small Formica table. He pushed the menu toward her. "What you want to have?" he asked.

Krista picked it up and opened it slowly. "You can have whatever you want," he invited urgently, leaning over the table so his chin rested just above her menu. "I got money."

She started to read it, her lips moving over the words. "What you going to have?" he pressed. She looked. His face was still there.

"A hamburg," she said. "Coke?"

"You want french fries? You can have french fries," he offered, and turning, he called to the waitress.

Krista watched him, watched the waitress move away again, her head bent toward the little notepad in her hand where she'd written what he told her, the bow of her checked apron undone and the ties trailing toward the hem of her skirt. "You ever get a headache?" he asked her.

She looked at him. "Headache?"

"Yeah," he said, leaning toward her again, his eyes bright, his mouth smiling. "From all that hair you got."

She blinked and reached to pull her hat down lower. Her menu skidded toward the floor. She tried to catch it, the other hand still on her hat, but he was quicker.

When he straightened, giving it back to her, he was smiling. "Take your hat off," he said. "Your hair is nice. You just got a lot of it. I like it."

She was holding the menu in two hands, and when he leaned close and plucked the hat off her head some of her hair rose crackling with it.

When he drove her home it was dark and the lamplight showing in the front room seemed far away. "I'll come see you tomorrow," he told her. He was kissing her face. Then he spread his hand over her jaw and kissed her mouth. "You're real sweet," he said as she got out of the car. "I like it that you're sweet."

Krista smiled. Then she leaned into the car and kissed him quickly.

"Yeah, sweet." He smiled as she shut the door carefully and turned to hurry up the path.

"Where have you been?" Viola asked her angrily. She was sitting in the rocker by the wood stove. Only one lamp was burning and the corners of the room were deep shadow. Krista stopped short. Her cheeks were burning and her hat was in her pocket.

"It's lucky your dad didn't come home before you. I've been holding supper for the both of you." Viola got out of the chair and came toward her. "Flynn said you went to the store. Hours ago. It's dark out!"

"It's not late though."

"Of course it is! Sit down and I'll bring your supper."

"I already ate."

Viola went to the stove and bent to take a plate out of the oven. "I got enough to worry about, Krista," she said, straightening with it in her hand. "Sit," she told her again as she came toward her with the plate and put it down hard on the table. "I got a letter from Freddie Hewitt," she said.

"I know. I told Flynn to bring it to you." It seemed days ago that she'd opened that mailbox. "How is he? How is Freddie?"

"He's going to jail," Viola said flatly. "He wrote to say how sorry he is and he woulda been at the funeral but he's locked up."

"I don't believe it," Krista cried. "Not jail. Freddie's good. Freddie's a good person. He must have got a crazy judge."

"Maybe," Viola said.

"What are we going to do?" Krista pushed back her chair and half rose from the table.

"Do?" Viola frowned at her.

"Freddie don't belong in jail. He's good. All alone in jail!"

"You're not alone in jail," Viola said. "That's one thing you never are! You send him letters you want to, send him cards at Christmastime. What else you gonna do, Krista? You can't bust him free!" Viola almost laughed. "He'll get out one day; he's alive."

* * *

The next morning Krista washed her hair. Then she helped Viola, sorting dirty clothes on the kitchen floor, her hair hanging in wet strips around her head.

"You shouldn't have used all that water," Viola told her.

"I'll heat more."

"Your hair didn't need washing." Viola stood outside the circle of laundry. She was making biscuits and the spoon was gripped in her hand. She turned abruptly to listen. "Your dad's back," she said. "Something must be wrong." Krista hurried after her and they stood looking out through the long windows.

"It's that boy, Mum. He's come back to see could he do anything." She jerked the door open and hurried down the path.

"Get back here!" Viola yelled. "What boy?"

Logan stood beside his car watching. He nodded to Krista but he was looking over her head at the house and Viola in the doorway. "Hi," Krista said. He looked so new and bright; it was as if he had stepped in from some other world. She put her hand over her lips.

"You tell your mother I was coming?" he asked.

"I told her . . ."

"What'd she say?"

"I told her—"

"I'll buy you lunch." He looked at her and then nodded toward the house. "You tell her that," he said.

"I was helping my mother with the laundry. I didn't know you were coming so soon."

He smiled. "You didn't know I was coming at all," he said softly. "Not for sure you didn't, if I was coming soon or never." He leaned his face closer to hers. "Did you?"

Krista backed up.

"Well, here I am!" And he held his hands out from his sides and grinned.

She laughed and then hugged herself. "You want a cup of coffee?" she asked him. "I could make you one."

"You tell her I'm going to buy you lunch."

Viola watched them coming up the path. He didn't look like anybody she'd ever seen before. "Krista, you'll catch your death of cold," she said, reaching to pull her into the house.

"Mum, this is Logan. "He . . . Logan Pembroke."

Logan stomped the snow off his shoes and stepped into the house.

"How are you doing, Mrs. Rudge?" he asked softly. He leaned forward to hear what she would answer.

"I'm doing what I can," Viola said, recognizing him. She gestured for them to go ahead of her. "And what do you want here now?" she thought, watching his wide back.

Krista was pushing at the clothes with her foot, trying to get them into a smaller mess. "I was going to make him a cup of coffee, Mum," she said.

Viola had dark socks in the pan in the sink. She was scrubbing them hard. Who the hell did he think he was, sitting down at her table like an invited guest, just about the last person in the world she'd want to ask there. She turned with her hands still in the water and looked hard at Krista.

"I was going to take her to lunch up to Lewiston." He was talking to her and Viola looked at him. "We could take these clothes with us to the Laundromat. Laundromat's right next door to the restaurant I was going to."

Krista started gathering the clothes up into a cardboard box. "It'll save on the well, Mum," she said, looking up at her, "and they'll get real clean."

"Clothes get clean enough right here," Viola said, but she understood he wasn't going to move too fast until he got his own way, and she wanted him out. Shaking the water off her fingers, she went in her bedroom. She came back and gave four quarters to Krista. "We'll dry 'em here," she told her.

Logan set his mug in the sink and followed Krista out the door. Halfway down the path he took the laundry from her. "You better go get that dollar I gave you in case you need it for that change machine," he said.

"I don't write letters." He told her that. But she went to the mailbox every day and looked, feeling her hand way to the back in case something as small as a postcard was lying flat there with her name on it. As the spring came, bringing rain, the driveway grew so muddy that Raymond Bodin didn't chance sinking to his axles but waited down on the road for Jarvis. Krista followed Flynn's woods path. It wove back and forth through half-broken old apple trees and through pines that, quick as crows, had grown up tall in the abandoned orchard. On the way home with her hands empty Krista thought about all the rain, the melting snow, pouring into that river in Lewiston, raising it up until it ran like a bandit down the sidewalk and entered every store. She wished she could see it, the power and will of the river.

And then toward the end of April there was a postcard. It came from someplace she had never heard of, water bluer than any sky, sand white as salt. She held it close and looked at it; her hands were trembling. When she turned it over it said, "I'm here now but I'm coming soon. Watch out!" She read the words slowly several times, then lifted her face and looked down the road. It was empty. It was quiet. The trees were still and the tar was darkened by morning rain.

That night she lay in her narrow bed and listened to rain slide down the roof, taking the last of the snow that lay beneath the pine trees. The postcard was on the shelf formed by the wall stud above her head. Wind drew the rain hard against her window, where it rattled like thrown silver. She could hear her father's voice, raised as it was so many nights. "We ain't never seen him again," he said, accusatory, grieving.

Krista turned on the pillow but still his voice came sawing through the wall. "Never! Since that day he came here. Wouldn't even bring us back home. Sent that fool with the radio!" She heard her mother murmuring and then he got louder. "We got no goddamn flag even. We got no photograph!" The wind lifted the rain and then flung it clattering against the house. "Where?" he demanded, and then the sound of his bare feet hard on the floor.

Krista waited. May, the sweet month, brought nesting birds and soft evenings. The tight buds on the trees plumed and draped the wintered limbs with color. Krista was restless and did not sleep well. Through the open window came the voices of frogs, one night bird, the odor of apple blossoms. She got out of bed and looked to see moonlight sliding gentle as water, warm pools formed by shadows. On the last night of the month the blossoms fell to the ground about the old silver trunks; the leaves revealed were dark as jade.

Krista waited. The sixth of June was a hot day. Her mother was making a garden in the cleared space between the house and Kendrick's truck. Krista could hear her grunt as she stomped on the pitchfork. Viola was tossing up small mounds of dark earth. Beyond her on the ground six thin tomato plants rose out of a tattered wicker basket. Krista got the shovel and followed behind her, lifting the broken earth and turning it again. A thin line of sweat stuck Viola's shirt to her spine. When she'd dug a perimeter she stopped to rest. "What should we plant?" she asked.

Krista was watching where the pines leaned against the sky. "Green beans?" she said, then looked at her mother. "You got your tomatoes. Maybe some squash."

Viola nodded. "I'd like some onions, too," she said. "A hill of cucumbers. It's small but we can train the vines to grow outside the garden."

Krista had turned. She wasn't listening. She was looking over Viola's head toward the driveway. The car nosed over the top of the hill, slid down, and stopped behind the truck. The tailpipe clunked until he turned off the motor. Viola straightened slowly. "It's that boy again," she said, "that navy boy."

But Krista was already going toward him. Earth sticking in lumps to the bottoms of her sneakers made her walk rocky. Viola narrowed her eyes against the sun glaring off his car.

"I'll dig that garden for you, Mrs. Rudge," he called.

"He wants me to. He even got family leave special."

"I don't give a damn what he wants!" Jarvis bellowed. "Who the hell is he? Who in the hell does he think he is!"

Krista was crying. She was backed up against the kitchen door. "I want to get married," she said. Her voice was shrill. "I want to!"

"Talk to her!" Jarvis demanded, swinging around toward Viola. "What the hell kind of crazy fool ideas are in her head!" He glared at his wife, his face red and his hair tousled.

"I'm old enough! I'm sixteen. I'll go with him to California. I'll wait there till he comes back."

"Don't you threaten me!" Jarvis told her, lifting his hand. "Don't you tell me what you're gonna do! Old enough!" he scoffed, and lifted his hand higher.

Flynn came from his bedroom, the dogs' nails tapping after him.

"Now you got him upset," Jarvis told her. "Your sister wants to get married," he said loudly to Flynn. "Thinks she's old enough. Some kind of old lady."

"Star," he said, drawing her name out, his voice soft and admonishing.

"Krista," Viola said, "just wait. You barely know him. You can wait." She pushed her toward the table. "Sit down," she said. She spoke slowly and precisely as if Krista were partially deaf. "You can wait for him, and when he comes out of the navy for good then you can marry him. You don't want a husband who's never here, off in some boat going God knows where. Get smart."

"He's an idiot!" Jarvis bellowed.

Krista sobbed.

Flynn went and stood close to her; the dogs followed him.

"He's been sneaking around here. He's been sneaking around here when I wasn't home and you didn't tell me!" he shouted.

"Way, Star," Flynn urged, picking up her hair. "Way," he said, and he divided it into three and began to braid.

"I don't want to wait anymore," Krista insisted, her voice shaky and wet-sounding.

"Anymore! You just met him at your brother's funeral, goddamnit!"

"Jarvis!" Viola said angrily.

"Where is he, this idiot?" Jarvis asked, glaring around the room. "He should be here asking himself!"

"He wanted to. He wanted to, but I told him no."

"No!" Flynn said, his voice boomy.

"I knew how you'd be," Krista wailed.

Jarvis stood over her with his hands clenched. "What in the hell did you expect!" he shouted. "He's an idiot!"

Viola stepped back by the stove and picked up her mug of tea and drank from it. Flynn braided.

"He is not," Krista protested. "He's good. He's smart. He knows a lot."

"What the hell does he know?"

"A lot! And he knows me! I'll go to California. We can get married there. I'm old enough."

"You're wet behind the ears. You're a child! A brainless infant! You're dumber than he is!" Jarvis stared at her, his face twisting as if she had just developed some nasty foreign habit.

"I want us to get married," she said. "You can't stop us. Please, Dad."

"She's right," Viola said. "We can't stop her, not if she's bound on it."

"Jesus H. Christ!" Jarvis bellowed, and banged his fist on the table.

"People have to take their own chances," Viola said, looking across the room at him where he stood above his daughter and Flynn was carefully putting an elastic around the end of her braid.

Their honeymoon was a long weekend at Old Orchard Beach. The season hadn't started yet and they got a room in one of the shingled guesthouses near the water. When Krista woke up on Saturday she was alone. The empty smell of winter was still in the house but the sun was bright against the curtains of both windows and she could hear birds. The bed frame was painted white and there was a bureau, a bamboo chair with pink cushions, and a floor lamp with a yellowed shade. She stood on the braided rug and tied her robe tightly around her waist. His shoes were gone and the clothes he'd thrown on the chair. She tiptoed to the window and pulled the curtain aside. A fly was buzzing somewhere above the rod. The sky was as blue as the postcard sea he'd sent to her. She pushed her cheek against the warm glass and looked toward the front of the house. He wasn't coming down the driveway. Between the two houses across the road she could see a small patch of the ocean, dark and still beneath the bright sky. It looked higher than the houses, as if it could roll right over them. There was a noise at the door. She started and turned as it was flung open.

"You finally woke up!" His shoes slapped on the linoleum. "We'll go to the boardwalk tonight," he announced, stopping before her. "I'll win you stuff. I know how to play all those games." She smiled. He looked so happy standing there in this strange room. "You want a pink teddy bear?" he was asking. "I'll win you one."

They drove to the bus station on Tuesday. The afternoon was hot. Krista was standing out there on the softening tar, jumping up and down while the bus pulled out. Logan waved once, she could see him through the murky glass, and then he turned to the man next to him. He was ready to go, to get out of that small space where she'd been so near. He would be gone but he'd know where she was, and she'd be waiting for him. He took out his cigarettes and offered one to the man sharing his seat.

Krista got into his Chevrolet and sat crying with the windows unrolled. Sweat was sticking her dress to her, and people looked at her as they went by on the sidewalk. She was there two hours, wiping at her face with a blue kerchief.

When Jarvis arrived he was pale and sweaty. They looked at each other. "Had some trouble getting here," he told her. "Raymond had a fight with his wife and she hid the keys on him."

"Well, thanks for coming, Dad." She was folding the kerchief carefully.

"I said I would." Jarvis shifted around on the seat, lit a cigarette, and turned the key.

They went on for a while in silence and then Krista said, almost whispering, "He'll be gone a long time. Might get home around Christmas, but then he'll be gone again."

The sun was falling. It burned in the windshield. "You got what you wanted, so don't complain," Jarvis told her, and yanked on the visor.

Krista didn't look at him. "How's Mum?" she asked.

"Goddamn son of a bitch got no suspension!" he fumed as they were jolted over a hole in the road. Then he said, "She'll be glad to see you back home."

When they got clear of the city he went faster. The sun slid toward the trees, the air cooled a little. Krista relaxed against the seat and closed her eyes. She was almost asleep when his voice woke her.

"What the hell is all that?" he demanded.

She sat up, looking around.

"What the hell you got back there, a zoo!"

She twisted around. "No!" she cried. "That's for us. Presents! Logan got Flynn the dog and a lamb for Mum and he got me that pink teddy bear." She glared at her father. "He even got you a lighter." She was almost crying. Jarvis drew back. "He thought of everybody. Something for everybody! Something nice."

Jarvis didn't say anything and she settled back in the seat and pulled her kerchief out again.

"I was just asking, for God's sake. I saw something strange out of the corner of my eye. I didn't know what it was. I was just asking you!"

She was quiet but he could see her nod. "Your mother will be real glad to see you," he told her again. "Flynn and her the both of 'em."

PERLEY

16 The world came to her anew early each morning in the sound of his voice. His noises were soft and tentative, then grew more robust, almost quizzical, certainly amused. Krista looked up from her mattress to encounter his face, or his sweet elbow, or the bottoms of his narrow, pink feet. She reached her arm up and tickled him gently, to hear him laugh louder, and she with him, and their joys floated together in the small, white room, rising toward the high ceiling like something alive: butterflies, or birds, or small red-and-yellow kites. She tossed aside the sheet and rose, carried him to the kitchen, riding on the curve of her arm like a small boat on a sea swell, and laid him on the linoleum-topped table, one small hand on his belly, while she reached with the other to wet the washcloth at the kitchen tap, his feet paddling in the air, she reaching for the new diaper, his voice, la, la, la, singing to the morning, to his feet, to her face, turning him to bring the undershirt over his shoulder, his dark hair soft as dandelion seed, rolling him back like a jewel, snapping it over his chest, lifting him to her, again her arm curving like a bough to hold him, and her other hand free, so to make toast and to eat strawberries, lifting them slowly from the green basket, standing before the broad window in that small, white room, her hip against the table, the sweet fruit in her mouth, his warmth, and the roundness of his cheek against her, and then back to the other room to lie in her bed.

He was the same color as her breast. His little fist curled against her flesh was like the flower set against the leaf. His need drew her down into herself, a moving as of quick water to a warm pool; his perfect feet nested on her belly, they were a circle. The morning sun splashed through the wide window and fell over them like a garment, warm, weightless, holding them safe from the world. His tiny limbs seemed more solid, more permanent than her own. His skin was smooth as a feather, as a new twig, as a seashell. He smelled like her own body sweet from a bath. When he stretched, or lifted his head, unfolded an arm, kicked his feet like a swimmer, she knew the tension rippling in her own spine, or her leg, or in the arch of her feet. She felt she'd been born with him, for how new he'd made her, how plump, how full; she hardly recognized her own body, her breasts heavy, her hips rounder, her limbs slower. She seldom left the bed before noon, dozing on and off between the times he suckled, their slowed breathing whispering together in the warm room. There was plenty of time to clean the apartment, to wash his clothes, to cook while he slept, again in his crib, for the first few hours after midday.

They had moved back to Portland in April when Perley was three weeks old. They would be going on in the fall to California where Logan was based. Krista's parents lived upstairs and she had supper there every night. Jarvis was at the fish plant again, but he'd been having headaches and missing a lot of work. He suffered dizziness and cloudy vision and he went to the drugstore and got himself a pair of glasses that magnified a world he didn't want to look at anyway.

Krista went up the dark stairway from her own apartment and opened the door. There was the heavy smell of pork chops frying, the creaking of the rocking chair, the radio was playing country. She shifted the baby higher on her shoulder and smiled at Flynn. When he got out of the chair Noah rose with him. "Purr," Flynn said, putting his arms out for the baby, but Viola hurried through the curtain that hung over the kitchen doorway and took him from Krista. "How is he tonight?" she asked.

"He's good, he's always good," Krista said, but Viola wasn't listening. She was talking to Perley, swinging him slowly in her arms, chuckling as he reached up and tugged on her hair.

"Watch it, he's strong," Krista said, trying to unfurl his fingers.

"Course he's strong," Viola crooned. She sat down in the rocker. "I know all about babies. Don't I?" she said into his face, which was tense and concentrated as he felt her hair and tried to bring it closer.

"Sweet boy," she said. "Sweet baby lamb." She laid him along her legs and rocked him. Perley watched the dark ceiling shifting above him and lifted both hands toward it, opening and closing his fingers.

"Krista, check the chops," Viola said without lifting her face. "Then go in and say hello to your dad."

"Is he feeling any better?"

"You know how he hates the heat."

"Da don't get out the beh," Flynn told her.

Viola looked sharply at him but Perley was reaching for her hair again and she laughed and tossed her braid in back of her and gave him her fingers to hold.

Krista poked at the meat with a long fork. "Mum, maybe Dad should go to a doctor," she said.

"You dad won't go to a doctor and you know it!" Viola said. "I've tried. He will not go!" She bent crooning to Perley again.

Krista went through the curtain into the living room. There were two narrow windows on the wall facing the street, and the evening sun came through them and cast two thin paths across the floor. The doorway at the end gave onto the bedroom. Before she had crossed the threshold Krista was looking at his upturned feet. He had dark socks on, the shade was drawn to the sill, smoke curled above his head. He hacked and brought something up and spat it into the large, rumpled handkerchief he held in front of his face. "Hi, Dad," Krista said from the doorway. He lowered the handkerchief and looked at her. Then he lifted it and spat again. She stepped forward. She could smell his feet and his spit and the smoke from his cigarette. "Want me to open up the window?" she asked.

Jarvis shook his head, moving it slowly as if it weighed too much.

She sighed and reached her hand out to finger the bedspread he lay upon. The room was small and the mirror hanging above the dark bureau reflected the bed and the two of them and the window with its drawn shade. "Perley splashed so much in his bath I got soaked," she said. "Had to change before I came up here."

Jarvis stared straight ahead toward the space between his feet. In the quiet she could hear him breathing, a raspy sound high in his throat. He put the handkerchief down and stabbed out his cigarette in the ashtray on the bedside table. Then he brought his hand back and folded it with the other one on his stomach. "I was just thinking," he said, and Krista drew her hand away from the bedspread. "I was just thinking about how when we lived up to Cornish he used to sleep in the woods at night. Like an explorer," he added breathily. He turned his face toward her. "You were too young to remember," he said.

"I remember, Dad." She spoke quickly. "I remember. He was smart as an Indian."

He nodded slowly, his face still turned toward her. His skin was gray, like the background in a newspaper photograph; his eyelids were a pale lavender. He licked his lips and a bit of spittle glistened as he spoke again. "We were so different," he said. "And I'd get impatient with him. So he'd take to the woods. He always took to the woods. And I could never find him." He coughed and then almost laughed. "I lost a whole afternoon once looking. Later I found out he'd spent the whole time at the top of a pine tree not fifty yards from the barn. All I had to do was look up!" He glared at her as if he'd forgotten she was there and her sudden presence an intrusion. "That boy could sit still for as long as it took and it never bothered him," he insisted loudly.

Krista had retreated until she was on the threshold. "Mum's got supper about ready," she said.

His eyes went onto her. They looked disappointed.

"It's pork chops," she almost shouted.

He lifted his hand in a dismissive gesture, then swung it across the bedside table and folded his fingers around the cigarette pack. "I'll come along in a minute," he said without interest.

Krista took the bus all summer, rising early in the morning to do her chores and traveling across the city to the hospital in the afternoon. She grew thin; she felt time had started up again and was moving fast and reckless, bearing them all like woodsmen riding the crown of a felled tree. On the first Friday in September she cashed the check from Logan and did her grocery shopping and then went back out and up the hill, carrying Perley on her hip and dragging the wire laundry basket. The Laundromat was hot and airless and Perley fussed and then cried until she walked and walked him up and down the sticky gray floor. He grew quiet at last and she sat in front of the churning clothes with him sleeping in her lap.

When she got home she went up to her mother's. The dim stairway smelled of old meals and human sweat and smoke, odors held like dust in the short dry months of summer. Flynn was in a chair in the living room, staring at a noisy game show on the television. The dog lay panting at his feet. Flynn took Perley and settled him and patted his naked back. "In the beh," he told Krista.

Viola lay on the sheet, the thin green blanket rolled unevenly to the footboard. The window was open but the yellow curtain hung motionless. "I'm getting up soon," Viola said. "I didn't sleep good last night."

"Well, you can get a nap now," Krista suggested.

"It's too hot to sleep. You going to the hospital?"

She nodded. "I'm going soon."

"Then I'll go tonight."

The heat sat on them in the silent room, pressed Krista's hair against her head, her feet to the soles of her sneakers. "You want me to get you something? Something to drink?"

"It's in his blood," Viola said hoarsely. "That's why he's been so weak. They explained it to me." Outside in the street a horn started blowing. Viola sat up higher in the bed. "But he don't care," she said angrily. "He's had enough. He's going to go and leave us and he don't care."

Krista stood with her fists folded into her stomach.

Viola looked at her. "You take a taxi out there today," she said harshly. "It's too hot to be on that bus with a baby. There's money in the drawer."

Krista pushed the umbrella stroller up and down the uneven sidewalk. Perley had a white sun hat on, his round legs were bare. She was wearing a sleeveless dress and her hair was pulled back in a ponytail. Krista was worrying the taxicab company had forgotten about them. She pushed her baby back and forth, she could feel sweat running down her ribs. She couldn't see the clock on the bank tower but she knew she was late. He'd be waiting for her, he'd be wondering why she was so careless, he'd be tossing in that white bed he couldn't get out of without two people helping him, and the sheet under him wringing wet. She tipped the stroller onto its rear wheels and turned it around. Perley swung like a gong. "They ain't going to bother with us, Perley," she told him. "We better get up to the bus stop."

They were jolting by a hydrant that Perley reached for, when a brown and white car turned the corner and went by them. Krista whipped the stroller around and they went after it. The man turned his cab in the street and pulled up in front of their building. He tooted his horn as Krista and Perley hurried toward him.

"Are you the cab for us?" she asked, leaning in the window.

He looked at his clipboard. "You Pembroke?"

It took her a moment. "Oh yes, we are," she told him.

The hospital was a tall brick building set back from the avenue. The windows were long and dark. A large yellow hole had been dug for the new wing. "Just you today?" one of the nurses at the desk greeted her.

"Me and Perley. My mother's lying down so she can come tonight."

"Reverend Hall was in to see him this morning," the nurse called as Krista started for the elevator, the baby high on her shoulder. "I think it cheered him right up."

The wide door was closed and she moved Perley to her other shoulder and slowly pushed it open. There was an empty bed and then her father's; long white curtains fluttered in the open window. Beside it was a green chair. There were two tables, one with little drawers and one a flat surface that could be pulled across his bed to hold the tray at mealtimes. A TV hung from the wall so that he could lie there and stare into it.

When Krista stepped forward the door closed behind them with a prolonged whoosh. He lay still, his eyes closed, his head raised slightly by the pillow. There was sweat all along his hairline. His pajama top was open and the bones in his chest stood up like fence posts under snow. His arms, lying still on the white sheet, were bruised and almost as thin as hers.

He groaned softly, sighed for a long time, and slept on. Krista walked Perley up and down between the window and the first bed. Her father's mouth was just slightly open. A delicate white tube was set into his nostrils. It hadn't been there yesterday. She stared at the thin cord that led from it and disappeared into a hole in the wall behind his head. She walked Perley to the window where the small breeze was, and when she turned back Jarvis had wakened. He didn't speak but his eyes were open and looking at her.

"Hi, Dad," she said, going close to the bed. "I tried to keep him quiet so you could sleep on a bit." He didn't say anything. "I better keep walking him," Krista said. "I think he's getting another tooth he's been so fussy lately." She smiled. "I don't want him yelling this place down."

But Jarvis didn't smile. "I was dreaming," he told her suddenly, his voice hoarse-sounding, almost whispery. "When I woke up I saw you. The dream was in Cornish and I thought I was seeing Viola when she was young." He stared at the baby. His eyes were bright and glittery. "You look like her," he said. "More and more."

"I know it." She nodded. Her head was pounding and she felt dizzy. She lowered herself into the chair. Perley just murmured when she laid him along her legs and began to swing her knees back and forth. His eyes were closed. The dark lashes were curves in his face like two small wings. His forehead was sweaty and she blew gently so his hair fluttered back from his damp skin. He smacked his lips and slept. Krista leaned back and pulled at her dress where it was all stuck to her from Perley being pressed so close. She smiled at her father again. "Mum wants to get you home," she said, "so we can take care of you, get you strong again."

He shook his head slowly, then turned so he wasn't looking at her anymore. His eyes closed. Krista began to rock her whole body from side to side to ease the fatigue in her legs. Perley slept on, his fist folded under his chin. The slight breeze at the back of her neck made her even more aware of how hot the rest of her body was. She watched her father's pale, almost luminous chest rise, lifting very slightly, very slowly, flat and still a long time between breaths. They'd been caught by something and it was dragging them forward and there was nothing she could do to get loose from it and there was no way it could ever be persuaded to let go.

"Do you think I'll see him again?" His voice cut like a harsh stroke of light through the room. She raised her face quickly to look at him. His eyes were open now and stared at her, waiting. She stopped rocking and gripped the chair with both hands. "Do you think there's a heaven?" he asked loudly. He struggled to sit higher in the bed. "He mighta killed people; we don't know."

"War doesn't count," Krista said quickly.

The door opened and a nurse stomped in on heavy hospital shoes. She was short and her body was round and wrapped tight in her uniform. Her white stockings made an abrasive swishing sound as she bore down on the bed. Jarvis was staring at Krista, seemingly unaware of the nurse, who took the rectangular basket off her elbow and thumped it down on his bedside table. She picked up his arm and wrapped the rubber hoselike thing around it and went at his vein with a needle. The baby stirred and Krista started rocking her legs again. She heard the nurse click her tongue several times. She kept bringing her arm up and down, up and down. Finally she straightened and snapped the rubber tubing off his arm.

"Not much left there!" she said in an annoyed voice as she crammed her equipment back in her basket and marched out of the room.

Jarvis was still staring at Krista. She could hear her baby's breathing in the silent room. "Fat stupid bitch!" she whispered, and struggled onto her feet. Perley started to cry and she wrapped one arm around him and held him close while she made her other hand into a fist and shook it at the closing door. "Bitch!" she gasped. The baby was sobbing now. His little bones shook. She turned to her father. "Dad, we want you to come home, away from these bad people," she pleaded.

But he was looking past her. "I want to know I'm going to see him," he argued loudly. "I want to know for sure."

Portland, Maine
September 23, 1969

Dear Logan,

I'm writing feeling so bad to tell you my dad died and the funeral was yesterday. They let us bury him where Kendrick is. That's the only comfort we got out of it. Mum's about died too. Flynn don't sleep. That is all I can say to tell you how it is. My only hope is that you will be home soon to take care of us. My only joy is Perley who is a beutiful good boy. It brakes my heart that you've never even seen him except on a photagrafe. Please ask them can you come home now. If anything happens to you I'll walk into the sea. I swear it. I'll bring the baby with me too cause I never would leave him alone in this world.

Your loving wife,
Krista Pembroke

Logan's ship was off the coast of Vietnam when he received this letter. "She don't know nothing about the navy," he thought as he read it. But he sent her mother a card the chaplain gave him, and a second one to Krista. They were purple with a thin silver border. "Sympathy" it said inside. The guns were more persistent now, the planes more numerous; long lines of fire raged at the earth. Logan stood on the deck in the hot nights and watched.

Melly Osbourne joined the ship in January, replacing a radioman whose appendix burst. They flew Melly out from Texas in a transport. He was a tall, skinny boy whose shaved skull was bumpy, whose voice rippled like a young child's. In his pockets Melly carried metal rings, bits of wire, bent paper clips and tiny screws, ball bearings big as aggies, which he held as gently as if they were baby birds. Waving his thin arms, he told jokes and laughed at them in his high, eager voice. He arrived just as they were leaving Honolulu, and his grey eyes looked mournful as he lamented the timing, which did not allow him to touch ground long enough to see "even one bitty dancing girl in her grass skirt."

They teased him, they told him he was too young for naked women. Melly blushed, which made them laugh harder; he protested he could learn. "I'm quick, I'm quick," he told them, his voice arching with sincerity, the ball bearings clacking in his fingers, noisy as hungry nestlings.

They could hear Melly coming along the passageway from his forward berth. He was whistling. He paused in the doorway, clacking two ball bearings together in his pocket. "Cards again!" he said.

"You want to play?" Logan asked him.

Melly grinned. He had little pointed teeth like a puppy. "Sure," he said. "I used to play Go Fish with my cousin Samuel."

Brien snorted. "Go Fish! You play with Logan you'll be gone fishing for your money so you can give it all to him."

Melly slapped his hands against his pockets. "I got no money," he said happily.

"We get paid tomorrow," Logan said. He looked angrily at Brien, then smiled at Melly. "You ain't going to let him scare you offa playing, are you?" Melly shrugged. "I'll advance you a few bucks."

Logan started shuffling the deck in his hands. "You know about poker, don't you?" he asked gently.

"Some, some," Melly said. "Deuces wild!" And he laughed, looking around at their faces in turn.

"Lambs to the slaughter," Tim groaned.

"Shut up," Logan told him. "Make room for Melly."

As Melly hunkered down among them his pockets rang like bells. "I'll play for a little bit," he said. "Deuces wild!"

"Sometimes deuces is wild," Logan agreed. "You can call it any way you want when you're the dealer." He smiled at Melly, snapping the cards under his fingers. "I'll make 'em wild," he said agreeably.

Logan played unevenly; he knew you had to keep hope alive in people. Yet before the arrival of the lieutenant broke up their game he'd won a lot of money. "I'll have to give you my pay after I get it tomorrow," Melly told him as he left. He was looking a little confused. "That's right, ain't it?" he whispered loudly. "That's what I owe you." He looked embarrassed and, bending down, drew a dollar out of his shoe. "I did have this one," he admitted, blushing and holding it out.

Logan laughed and took it. "You're a pretty cozy guy," he said. Then he stepped closer. "Tomorrow, when we get paid," he said.

But the morning broke late and grey, the ocean heaved under the ship in long swells. The sun, a flat white disk, raced behind the moving clouds. The announcement came regularly: "Stand by for stormy sea."

Logan fretted through drill. Once before, bad weather had postponed pay disbursal. He and Paul were cleaning the officer's galley. The stove rocked up and down under them as they scrubbed it. "This is going to be a bad one," Paul said. His face was white, dark rings sat under his eyes like dirt. The ship rose slowly. It kept climbing as if a long cable attached to the bow were reeling it into the sky. They scrabbled to get hold of the railings secured to the sides of the galley and braced themselves. "Jesus," Paul moaned.

The ocean raised the ship like a chalice, the wind howled and banged. The rain beat at the sea as steadily as the sun falls on a field of grain.

Pay was disbursed after the noon meal, which no one could eat except Melly. Logan went in search of him, walking with his feet wide apart, his hand on the rail. Melly wasn't in his berth. People were getting sick. It smelled of vomit; lights were flickering. The only thing Logan could hear was the throbbing of the engines. He turned and started back toward his own berth. Before he reached it Paul came out of the head, his attention concentrated inward. He looked at Logan as if he were far away and small. "It's gusting fifty knots," he gasped.

"You seen Melly?" Paul bobbed in front of him as the ship started climbing. "You seen him?"

"Forget it," Paul mumbled. He started to push past Logan, his arms reaching like a swimmer. "Forget it till it's over."

Logan turned from him and started back toward the mess. The ship was climbing. He arrived at the doorway when it started down the other side. The loudspeaker came on: "Stand by for course change." The ship was descending. Logan started across the floor. The warning came again. He couldn't see if anyone was in the galley. He couldn't remember Melly's detail.

The ship, which had been moving like a running horse over a series of high hurdles, suddenly jumped out from under him. He felt himself being sucked backward like a man in a high wind. The tables in the mess all sheared abruptly to the right as he seemed to gain altitude, his feet left the floor and he felt himself being hurtled forward and slammed into something shaped like a torpedo with a wheel on the end of its nose. He heard things breaking—lights flashed in front of his eyes—bones he realized as the tables continued their journey to the right. Pain filled him quickly, like water gushing into a vase. It pressed against the ends of his fingers and his scalp, the bottoms of his feet, pain that was like an animal trapped and generating a terrible heat as it struggled. It was the legs of the tables he saw moving now, and he heard the voice of somebody moaning, little gasps, little pathetic sounds like an exhausted baby.

Logan lay in the bed glowering at them. They kept telling him: "You're lucky, it's only peripheral damage." It made him furious. He knew if they were the ones lying here they wouldn't feel so goddamn lucky. By this time it was March and he was back in Maine. He lay in a white bed in a body cast in the veterans' hospital in

Augusta. He felt hideous and helpless, the way his legs stuck out of it, like somebody in a pumpkin suit. He remembered it from Halloween when he was in junior high school and they had rolled Bunny Marchette down the long hill by the box factory, his foolish, twiglike legs kicking without effect as his round orange body flung down the hill. The nurse, who was standing just behind the doctor, smiled and nodded. The old bitch. They were full of shit, he couldn't move his legs, it hurt too much. He shut his eyes. When he opened them they'd gone away.

Linette Pembroke climbed the long slate stairway slowly. Ahead of her, Ronnie, on thin legs, his heels jacked up by black motorcycle boots. Below, outside in the truck changing the baby, that girl her son had married. The wide-paned window rose up the stairway beside her; the long blue curtains were dusty. Outside, the hospital lawn was soggy with melted snow, the tall trees were showing new leaf buds. Linette paused and lifted her head. She wasn't even halfway. Ronnie's narrow buttocks in those striped pants. She looked down again. Her heart was thudding like a round stone dropped in a can. She lifted her foot. She'd bought these canvas shoes—in them her feet could bend and twist as need be. She brought the other foot up. Her knee pained as if there were something rusty scraping in there. The banister under her hand was cold as a winter river. It was one thing after another. And Ronnie driving up here today, all that way in the noisy old truck, leaning over the wheel like a maniac at a speedway, and that girl, half naked nursing the baby, though he was a year old and had all those teeth, talking to him in her husky voice, sitting between them, small as a child herself.

She caught up with him. Ronnie was just standing there at the doorway, not budging to go in. She reached her hand out to push him. Her breath was noisy in the front of her throat. "Go in there, Ronnie. This is the room," she complained.

It was a large room and there were four beds, but he was the only one there. The floor was brown linoleum, the walls sand-colored; the bureaus and the beds, the small chairs, were white. They came forward slowly and stopped at the foot of an empty bed. They stared over at him. When he opened his eyes and looked at them they both reared back. She grappled at Ronnie's elbow to steady herself.

"Logan," she said, tipping her head, peering at him to be sure. When he didn't move she came closer until she could rest her knuckles on the end of his bed. "We heard you was here," she told him. "After all that time of hearing nothing." She swallowed the last word and two tears moved slowly on her cheeks. Ronnie was gaping at him.

Logan looked past them at the door. He looked back at his mother. "The old man didn't bother to come?" he asked her.

She jerked her head up and, clutching the iron frame of the bed, turned and looked behind her.

"He's dead. He's dead, Logan," Ronnie said in an eager voice.

Logan looked at him, his eyes narrowed. "You sure?" he demanded.

"His truck run him over when he wasn't lookin'. Honest," Ronnie said.

Logan swung back against the pillow and snickered loudly. They both stepped closer to him. The nurse, out in the hall, heard him and came to the doorway. His face was lifted up, his eyes were closed, his open mouth was flinging out laughter.

Krista heard him as she came along the wide corridor with Perley high on her shoulder. He had a fistful of her hair for balance and he was crowing in a full, high voice. She was repeating the room number to herself softly; her feet were pattering on the slick floor. The nurse turned and made way for her and she crossed the threshold, Perley chirping loudly.

She saw her mother-in-law and Ronnie, the glow of the day through the broad windows; the white furniture, the white man in the bed with his body like a barrel and his head thrown back, laughter coming from his wide open mouth, loud, loud, filling up the large room and pitching out the door. Perley stiffened in her arms, stretched and turned his head to look for the noise.

But Logan didn't see his son. His face was aimed toward the ceiling and his eyes were closed. He laughed and laughed. It was the first thing that had given him any pleasure since they stopped the morphine.

PART TWO

WOMEN, INFANTS, AND CHILDREN

17 Route 110 is narrow, straight in few stretches, and wrenched by potholes. It runs north, connecting Portland on the coast with Lewiston, a river town. Midway, where Route 9 crosses, is the center of New Harris: Palmer's store and lunch counter, the fire barn, the feed store, and a school. Two miles west of the crossing is a brown ranch house with a board-and-batten two-car garage beside it. The front lawn slopes toward the road, where it meets a row of old maples, planted for shade when this property and the surrounding two hundred acres were pasture for dairy cows. It is March and the trees' new leaves are furled tightly and waiting for the waning cold of April, for May's slow warmth. This is where the Pembrokes live now. Logan bought the house the previous year with a VA loan. Krista worried leaving her mother and Flynn behind in Portland, but she persuaded herself that this was a new beginning, that her husband would be happier now, that the country was a good place for children.

Perley Pembroke, eight years old and small, comes out of the house. Perley jumps down the back steps and hurries along the slope, ducking under sheets strung on a line between the corner of the house and the garage. Frayed clothesline holds up Perley's dungarees, he's walked holes in the cuffs. The dark blue jacket he wears is too large and kept closed by long safety pins. He goes into the garage and comes out again, drawing behind him a wooden wagon with a faded red message: "Pepsi." Perley found this wagon in the fall. It was nearly buried partway down the embankment of the enormous sandpit behind their house. It has small rusty wheels, which bounce hard over the frozen ruts in the driveway. He goes under the clothesline, pushing aside a sheet with one hand, and continues up the incline to the back steps. He hollers, "Hurry up, Harmony! I need weight!" Watching the door, he frowns. Around him the morning is raw, the wind gusts, the sheets thump on the line. He hollers again. His voice has a gritty sound like his mother's.

His sister, Harmony, just six, comes out onto the back porch, clutching a doll to her yellow sweatshirt, holding small clothes in the other hand. She shifts everything and carefully pulls the door closed, then crosses the narrow porch and comes slowly down the steps. "Roxanne wants a ride, Perley," she says. Roxanne is large, with one blue eye and lots of holes in her head where her hair used to be rooted. She is wearing purple overalls and a large green sweater. Perley takes her by the arm and puts her in his wagon. "I got clothes for Roxanne Two so she can come with us," Harmony says, showing him the bundle in her fist.

"He's a boy and he don't want to come," Perley tells her, lifting the handle of his wagon.

"Yes suh! She does, Perley! She wants to come." Harmony gets hold of his sleeve and shakes it. "She don't want to sit in there all by herself while we're riding, Perley." She lets go of him to push her hair out of her eyes. Her hair is the same color and texture as his, as their mother's, thick brown hair with dusky afternoon light in it. "Please, Perley!" She steps close and tips her face under his and looks at him. "Please!"

Perley drops the rope and hurries to the garage, to the small pen in the back corner. Roxanne Two is snuffling at the gate. Perley reaches to gather him in his arms. Roxanne Two squeaks and squeaks. His stiff red hairs slant tailward on his pale body. His eyelashes are as long as Minnie Mouse's and orange. He smells like molasses. Perley carries him out into the driveway where Harmony and the wagon are waiting.

"You!" she whispers happily, taking him from Perley. "You one and only Roxanne Two." His legs drape over her shoulder, his pale hard feet flop down her back, his tail twitches rapidly. Harmony turns and sits down in Perley's wagon, the piglet held firmly against her chest. She pulls a pale yellow sweater over his head. Roxanne Two pushes his snout through and squeaks. She ties a stained white bonnet under his jaw. Perley wraps the rope around his fist. Roxanne Two blinks his long eyelashes. Harmony hugs him with one arm and her doll with the other.

Across the yard and around the house they go, once, twice, bumping along the car ruts, slipping on the lawn, which is patchy with snow and brown grass. Perley has to work hard. The wagon bounces. It tilts on two wheels when they round corners, flattening onto four again as they shoot down the yard and under the sheets and rock across the ruts in the driveway. Perley stops in front of the garage and draws his coat sleeve under his nose. He spits. "The new wheels are great, Harmony," he gasps. "It's much easier to pull now." He watches her face, his breath making damp little clouds between them. "It's much smoother. You musta noticed."

"It is, Perley. We did," she tells him.

He pulls the wagon back and forth. "You see how smooth," he insists.

"Real smooth, Perley."

He smiles and lets the handle rest against his chest. Out on the road a dump truck bangs by, the empty bed rattling. A crow flies up from the shoulder, climbs over the maples, flaps across the yard, and settles in one of the small pines beyond the house. The children can hear him cawing there. "Let's go again," Harmony urges, bouncing a little.

Perley turns and starts them toward the backyard at a trot. Harmony giggles as the sheets rise over them. She holds the Roxannes tight. Perley draws them up the slope, past the steps, past the cawing crow, past the bulkhead, beneath his bedroom window. He's almost at the corner of the house when he hears a car slowing out on the road. He turns around quickly and runs, the wagon jolting at his heels. A sheet catches at them and Roxanne bounces out, lies in the snow with her one eye open. "Perley!" Harmony shrieks, looking back for her baby. But Perley runs. They bang over the ruts and into the garage, where Perley yanks the bonnet and sweater off Roxanne Two and sets him back in the pen. Harmony stands with the retrieved sweater and bonnet in her hand, turning to look down the driveway. Perley latches the gate and hurries to stand beside her. They watch as their father's car, a long blue Chevrolet with brown doors, comes to a stop in the ruts beside the house.

* * *

It is summer now and the bright leaves of the maple trees droop in the heat. They drive into the city, leave the children with Viola, and go to the hospital where Krista has an appointment at the prenatal clinic. She sits on a low green plastic couch, as thin as she ever was except for the baby, her hair pulled back in a barrette, her bony shins pale as moonlight on a wall. Logan stands behind the couch and looks out the window. He's thick and solid as a pillar now, he's leaning slightly on his cane and frowning at the hot glass. The waiting room is quiet except for little bells that go off, hushed voices, rubber-soled shoes squeaking on linoleum floors, distant telephones. They have been here half an hour and Logan is like a bomb that's about to be thrown. Krista can feel his rage burning through the couch like a blowtorch, engulfing her spine and the back of her neck. As she looks again at the clock above the doorway a young man leaning on a walker appears on the threshold.

His crooked legs fold toward each other at the knee; he is thin and dark. Lifting his head a little, he smiles and heaves himself forward into the room. A barrel-shaped woman, her gray hair held in a ponytail by an elastic, follows right behind him. She is tugging by the hand a small child whose head is tipped toward his chest like an ill-balanced weight. The thumb of the hand she isn't holding is in his mouth. A nurse walks in, smiles at them, and goes behind a tall partition. The barrel-shaped woman shakes her hand to get loose of the little boy and helps the man on the walker lower himself into a green plastic chair. She grips his arm in two hands and grunts as he lands. Then she picks up the walker and sets it down neatly beside the chair. She goes over to the couch across from the one Krista is sitting on and drops onto it so abruptly that her small feet spring up into the air.

"C'mere," she says, pointing repeatedly beside her. But the child stands near the low, round table between the couches with his head down and works on his thumb.

"C'mere, Ozzie," she says in a louder voice.

Ozzie doesn't move, except to raise his face enough to look at Krista. When she smiles at him he looks down. Behind her she can hear Logan's breath coming out of his face in scratchy, irritated little stabs. The small feet of the barrel-shaped woman hit the floor. She rocks twice, preparing to heave herself onto them. Ozzie jerks around and shuffles toward the couch. He climbs on the end of it and folds his legs. One darkened knee pokes through a hole in his dungarees.

The nurse comes around the partition, a metal clipboard in her hand. She bends over the young man's chair. "How are you today, Chet?" she asks.

"He's doing pretty good," the woman tells her, leaning forward. Chet smiles up at the nurse. He nods.

"Well, come on in and let Dr. Corcoran take a look at you," she tells him. She puts the clipboard under her arm and places the walker squarely in front of him and holds it while he slowly pulls himself up. The walker scrapes across the linoleum and they disappear behind the partition.

"Didn't keep *him* waiting," Logan snarls in her ear.

Krista drops her head, shifts on the slippery seat. He prods the top of her shoulder and she turns to him. "He's seeing a different doctor," she says patiently. "He's not having a baby." She can feel the woman watching them. Logan snorts and straightens up from the couch. Krista looks at the clock again. Ozzie takes his thumb out of his mouth and considers it. Then he puts it back in. Krista hears Logan turn back toward the window. Two phones start ringing.

A very young woman comes through the door. She is blond and round-faced and she has on a white top and polka-dotted shorts. Her legs are sunburned. She looks about to give birth and is chewing gum. She walks straight to the couch and sits next to Krista. "Hi," she says. She leans back and, groaning, puts one foot at a time up on the table. She pulls a Kent out of her cigarette pack, lights it and tosses the match toward the blue metal ashtray on the table.

Krista watches it land on top of *Woman's Day* magazine. The smell of the smoke is sharp.

"This bothering you?" the girl asks her in a loud, lazy voice.

"I'm used to it," Krista says.

But the girls slaps her feet down, leans forward, and jams the cigarette out in the ashtray. Then she throws herself back on the couch, returns her feet to the table, and blows a fat, pink bubble. She crosses her eyes to look at it. When it collapses on her chin she works it into her mouth with her tongue. She smiles at Krista and pats her own belly. "Makes me want to smoke all the more," she explains in a puzzled voice.

"I was the 'xact same way!" the barrel-shaped woman announces. "With the both of 'em." And she gestures toward Ozzie and into the air at the partition behind which Chet disappeared. "And my three girls, too." She settles back, grinning at them, and folds her arms around her belly. She holds it as if it were something precious and tips her head toward Ozzie. "Never had a minute's rest with him," she says. "Always sick to his stomach or an earache. Awful earaches he gets! And fussy! Fussy about his food." She nods with satisfaction. "And of course Chet." She waves toward the partition again. "Born crooked!"

Krista smiles sympathetically at her. The blond girl pops her gum.

"My girls is healthy as horses," the woman tells them. "But I had to quit. Doctor told me my lungs couldn't take it." Ozzie slumps down lower on the couch and puts his cheek flat on the arm of it. "And I figured," his mother continues, "I figured I had to quit. Who would take care of my boys?" And she looks around the room as if for an answer she can refute, then shifts her stomach with both hands.

Krista can hear Logan moving behind the couch. Then he's crossing the room. He stands under the clock looking out the doorway, his shoulders yanked up around his neck. The blond woman is saying something but Krista is watching those shoulders and can't really hear her. Logan turns into the room again and comes abruptly toward her in his rocking, choppy way, flinging the cane out ahead of him.

"You got a bum leg too!" the barrel-shaped woman calls to him. "Course not like my Chet," she says to Krista.

Logan doesn't acknowledge her. He stands with his back to her glaring across the table at his wife. "Do you want to go to the coffee shop and I'll meet you after?" Krista asks.

"Is he deaf, too?" Chet's mother inquires loudly, tipping on the couch so she can look around him and address Krista.

He makes an ugly face and stomps over to look out the window again. The blond girl snaps her gum and asks Krista, "Who's your doctor?"

"I don't always get the same one."

The girl nods and blows a bubble that explodes like a toy gun. Ozzie opens his eyes and looks across the table at her, then closes them again. "I want Dr. MacIntyre to deliver this one," the girl says. "He delivered my boy last year in time for Halloween. I kept him up all night." She laughs. "He didn't mind though." Behind them Logan is tapping his cane against something. "Ma said I get myself in that condition again she'd throw me out. But she didn't."

"You're a lucky girl," Krista tells her.

She nods, chews harder on the gum. "She's crazy about my son. We're hoping this one's a little girl."

"Good to have some of each," Ozzie's mother says.

Krista smiles. "We have a boy and a girl, so this baby could be either, don't matter."

"Long's it's healthy," the woman says, nodding her head. "Course you're going to love it despite anything."

The girl blows another bubble. This one sounds like an elastic snapping on a piece of cardboard. Krista can feel the couch behind her give under his weight as Logan leans down hard on it and speaks into her ear.

"You sure are letting them fuck you over," he says. "You should tell 'em your appointment was for ten-thirty." He nudges her, prodding between her collarbones.

She turns away from the blond girl. "It's a clinic, Logan," she whispers. "You got to wait your turn. That's why I thought it would be easier if you dropped me off and came back. I asked you."

"And what was I supposed to do in the meantime, drive around the fucking block for three hours!"

"You coulda visited Mum and Flynn with the kids."

He makes a noise that sounds like disgust. "You're really letting them fuck you over," he tells her again. Then he steps back from the couch and turns to look out the window again.

"You want a Coke or something?" the girl asks her.

Krista turns her head slowly. "Coke?"

Ozzie sits up. His legs flop out in front of him.

"Yeah. Machine's in the hall. I'm getting one. I'll get you one."

"No thanks," she says. She can hear Chet coming back on his walker. "It's going to be my turn soon."

"All done, Ma," Chet calls in a nasal voice.

"What'd he say?"

"Says I'm doing okay." He pauses and lifts one hand off the walker and taps his shirt pocket. "I got to get some pills, Ma," he tells her.

"Lemme see." She heaves herself off the couch and goes toward him with her hand out. Her other hand is waving. "C'mon, Ozzie, we're going now," she says.

"Mrs. Pembroke?"

"C'mon, Ozzie!"

"Yes, here." Krista gets up and hurries toward the woman in the pink smock whose narrow name tag says "Mildred."

Mildred stands at Krista's head while Dr. MacIntyre disappears behind the paper sheet draped over her raised knees. He sits on a little stool, and the black-rimmed glasses he wears make his eyes enormous. Leaning around her leg he says, "Everything looks fine, Mrs. P.," his voice loud and cheerful.

Mildred pats her shoulder and she quickly pulls herself into a sitting position and gets off the table. "Where's the fire?" Dr. MacIntyre asks, rolling toward her on the little wheeled stool. "I want to see you gain a little more weight," he tells her as she's pulling on her pants. "Are you worried about getting fat?"

Krista smiles quickly at him and heads for the door.

"Hold on there!" he calls. "Mildred, I want you to tell Mrs. P. about the WIC program. We want a nice, fat baby."

Krista smiles at them again and turns to hurry away, but Mildred follows her down the narrow hall.

"Wait, Krista! I need to give you a pamphlet and an application. It will just take a minute," she urges. "And then we can get you started right away."

"Started?" Krista wonders, hesitating.

"With WIC. Women, Infants, and Children." Mildred puts her hand on Krista's shoulder. "It's so you can get extra nutrition, good food for mothers and their little children."

"We eat good," Krista says, stepping back from her. "My husband buys us everything good."

"You heard the doctor. He wants you to have extra. You wait one minute while I get the form."

"I got to go. I will next time," she says and hurries away.

Logan gets a grip on her elbow and starts her for the door. She has to take three little steps to his one to keep rhythm with his rapid, seesaw progress. "They think they can really fuck you over 'cause you're a clinic customer," he spits in her ear.

"Make it fast!" Logan says as he pulls up in front of the large dark building on Grant Street where Viola and Flynn live. Krista scrambles out of the car and starts up the three flights.

Viola has both shades drawn and the room is cool. "What did the doctor say?" she asks.

Krista stands in the doorway catching her breath. "I'm good, he said I'm good. Mum, where are the kids?"

"I needed to get ready for work, so I let Flynn take 'em down to the park with some sandwiches. Come in and sit down, I don't have to go yet."

"I can't, Mum. We had to wait and wait at the clinic, so we're late."

"You're always in a rush. We never get to see you anymore. I made plenty of sandwiches." She looks past Krista into the hall. "Is Logan coming up?"

"No, Mum. It's a lot of climbing for him unless we're staying. I got to go. Thanks for watching the kids. Were they good?"

"They're always good." Krista has backed into the hall. "Now you wait, I'm coming with you," Viola tells her. "I don't want Flynn walking home from the park alone." She follows Krista's hurrying figure down the stairs and out into the bright sunlight.

"How are you doing, Logan?" she asks, shutting the car door carefully.

"They kept her waiting two hours at that clinic," he answers, and pulls rapidly away from the curb.

"But you get good care there. That's what counts," Viola says. "You need good care when you're carrying a baby."

"Two hours! Just 'cause she's a clinic customer."

"You got a good doctor, don't you?" Viola asks Krista.

She nods.

"If she was some rich bitch they'd walk her right into the doctor before she had time to set her ass on that stinking couch." Logan hits the brakes for the red light, then reaches for a cigarette.

"Freddie Hewitt sent Flynn a birthday card," Viola tells them. "He'll be getting out soon. He should of been out last year but something got mixed up."

"Poor Freddie!" Krista cries, clasping her hands together. "When, Mum? When is he coming home?"

"Soon is all he said. He's got no luck," Viola says thoughtfully. "It's like being born with blue eyes, it's a part of you forever no matter what you do."

"He's got luck all right," Logan says loudly. "Bad luck!" He laughs and they shoot forward with the changing light and cross into the park.

"You're not funny, Logan. Mum, we should give him a party when he comes home. Oh, I see them," Krista says, pointing toward the three small figures sitting by the pond, their legs hanging over the cement edge.

Viola and Flynn live quietly. She keeps him close. They mind their own business, they have each other, she likes it this way.

"You coming to work with me?" she asks him when they get home from the park.

Flynn nods. He is filling Rory's water dish.

"We got to go soon."

He bends to stroke the cat. "Okay, Mou," he says.

She locks the apartment and they go back into the street and climb the hill to the store on the corner where she is a cashier thirty hours a week. Flynn usually accompanies her. He sits watching the people, speaking with them as they become familiar. He helps out, straightening the magazines that get pawed through, filling the cigarette rack.

"Who's that?" Logan says, scowling and letting the bamboo curtain fall. He hauls the door open and steps down onto the small cement porch. Twisting his face at the brightness, he lifts his hand to his forehead and holds it there like a visor.

Perley, standing in the garage, reports to Harmony, who is tucked in behind him: "A lady. A lady with a little suitcase."

"A suitcase, Perley?"

"He won't let her in."

Marjorie Hallem shifts her briefcase to her other hand. "Hello," she calls. Logan scowls as she advances, at her thick curly hair, at the light blue dress, the sandals on her narrow feet. "Hello," she says again. Standing below on the flagstones, she introduces herself. "I'm from the clinic," she explains. "I want to talk with Mrs. Pembroke about the WIC program. Her doctor wants her to be enrolled right away."

"My wife's asleep," Logan says, looking down into her face. "I like her to have a nap in the afternoon. She's expecting a baby."

Marjorie smiles. "Yes, I know. That baby is why I'm here."

"She's asleep."

"Well, perhaps it will be all right if I come in and wait," she suggests.

Logan doesn't say anything.

"Would that be all right?"

"You can come in." He opens the door wide. "You can come in and wait. I just don't know how long it's going to be." He closes the door and follows her into the dim room. "You can sit there," he tells her, pointing toward the couch. Marjorie settles herself with the briefcase. Logan stands somewhere behind her. The house is quiet and dark. "Hot day," he says abruptly.

She is turning to say something in response, when she hears feet coming along and somebody is standing where the kitchen and living room come together.

"You wake up already? You got somebody here from that hospital. . . . Kept her waiting two hours," he says to Marjorie Hallem, and then to Krista, "Some doctor sent her out here."

"Hello, Mrs. Pembroke," Marjorie says, advancing to take her hand. "I'm sorry you had to wait so long last time. Mildred asked me to come out and see you and tell you about the WIC program. You didn't have time on Monday."

"Mildred. Oh, Mildred," Krista says vaguely. Then she brightens. "You come on in the kitchen. I got lemonade made. I bet you're thirsty."

Later Logan walks Marjorie Hallem out to her car. "Do we have your phone number in case my wife needs to call you up?" he asks her.

"It's on the upper right-hand corner of the application form. But here," she says, reaching in her pocket. He takes her card and looks at it. "Will you make sure she gets that application right in to me?" She looks back at the door. "I'd be happy to wait while she finishes filling it out."

"I'll make sure she finishes it. She didn't get all the way through school and she don't like people watching her write. I'll help her and then I'll go up the post office tonight and mail it. I got a stamp," he says, nodding.

"Well, I'm glad then. Thank you," Marjorie says.

"Thank you," Logan tells her. "I'm lucky so many people want to help my wife."

The children watch her car turn around in the driveway and head for the road. "He let her in," Harmony whispers.

Perley shrugs. "I don't know what she wanted," he murmurs.

"Maybe Mum's sick. Let's go see!"

"She ain't sick!" He pushes past her. "I'm going down the pit."

In the kitchen Logan is ripping the WIC application into long strips. Krista is sitting at the table. He steps closer and keeps on ripping. "What the hell did you tell 'em in there?" he demands for the third time. "You tell 'em I don't feed you or something?"

"I didn't. The doctor did it. He wants me to have this WIC because of the baby." She is looking at the white strips fluttering past her face.

"It's none of his goddamn business!"

"That lady was nice."

"The hell she was! She was a nosy bitch!" He looks at her, his eyes narrowed, measuring. "She came out here to see just how bad I'm starving you. She thinks we're too dumb to feed ourselves."

When he settles in the living room to watch the TV Krista goes outdoors. She hesitates on the porch before going down the steps into the backyard. "Perley!" she calls. "Harmony!"

Hearing her voice, Roxanne Two stands up and looks over the top of his fence. He is tall now. His forefeet tap on the top board. He strains his snout upward and Krista reaches to scratch behind his ears. Her hands are still trembling and it feels good to be working them hard against his bristly body. "Where'd those kids go?" she asks him. Roxanne Two pushes against her hand. His eyes close. Krista looks into the piny woods where the sun is setting in long shafts. "Are they down the pit?" she asks him. She scratches extra hard for a minute and then leaves the pig and goes on past the garage and down the hard-packed path. She can hear them whooping before she gets there.

They are more than halfway to the bottom and Perley is jumping, landing on two feet buried almost to his knees, extricating himself and leaping again. Harmony lies down, stretches her arms above her head, and starts rolling. Faster and faster she goes, spinning past him, hurling on and on to the bottom. Krista watches apprehensively until she gets to her feet and sways there. "Kids!" she calls, waving at them. "Kids!"

They look up at her. How small they are, how small, way down there, standing close together with their faces upturned.

"It's Mum!" Harmony says.

They both start scrambling.

Krista watches them toiling upward. They have to stop and rest three times before they get to her, and she waits, standing where the sun falls bright on her, lifting her arms toward it, her eyes closed, hearing them coming nearer, their efforts and their panting breath. "Lord!" she calls, "come easy, come easy. I'm waiting. I won't go."

But they just climb harder.

And finally they stand there. "Mum," Perley gasps. "We saw a lady."

"With a suitcase," Harmony puffs. "Are you okay, Mum?" She grips Krista's dress.

"What did she want?"

"She was a nice lady," Krista tells them. "She just came out to see how I am."

"What did you tell her?" Perley wants to know.

"I told her I'm just fine 'cause I got the very best kids in the whole world!"

"Oh, Mum!" They are still panting so hard they can barely speak and their faces are red as fire and sweaty.

"You come home now so I can give you some lemonade," she tells them. "I got it all made for you."

The evening is hot. Krista cooked pork chops and her kitchen is over ninety degrees. She's started washing the supper dishes and she's slow at it. She feels tired all the time, worn out to the bone. It's not just the heat and it's not just the baby. She didn't feel like this with Perley, or with Harmony. She thinks maybe she's got some secret disease that's getting her real old real fast, a disease so sly no doctor can find it. She puts glasses into the water. Loud TV noises come from the other room where Logan sits in his gray Naughahyde chair with his two feet up on the attached footrest, a beer in one hand and his cane in the other. Perley watches his mother crossing the floor again, going to the refrigerator to get down the ice cream. His hands are folded into fists, there's a thing like a pain in his chest. She stands for a moment at the open freezer, her face thrust forward.

"I'll get it," Perley tells her. "You sit down and I'll bring you a cold towel so you can put it on your forehead."

"I'm getting you your dessert, Perley," she says, turning with the box in her hand. "I'm getting you a real big dish." She smiles at him. Perley watches her face, every little movement that the smile is making in it. "It's worth waiting for, fudge ripple is," she tells him. She fills a soup bowl until it's round as a globe and Harmony, bearing it in two hands, takes it in to her father. Then they sit at the table with their bowls. The sun falls toward the pines, the supper plates soak in the sink, the TV makes loud stupid noises in the living room. They tip their bowls and work their spoons over every last bit that melted there. They lick their spoons and their lips and the corners of their mouths. Then Krista stacks the three dishes and takes them to the sink. "Son, you won't forget that bucket for the pig. I got it ready by the door," she says.

Perley nods, getting off the chair slowly. He's wishing he could have his ice cream in a big soup bowl piled round and full as a globe. He goes down the back steps and crosses the yard with the bucket. "Hi, Rox," he says, standing on the bottom rail and straining to look into the pen.

Krista lies on the couch with her bare toes pointing toward the ceiling. A wet paper towel is plastered to her forehead. Her arm hangs down to the dark floor. "It's really moving tonight, Logan," she says. "This might be a baby that comes early." She pushes herself up into a sitting position. The towel drops off onto her belly. "Logan, I'm wondering if this is an early baby." She leans on one elbow and lifts the towel up and sucks water from it.

"Baby will come when it's ready." Groaning, he shifts in the chair, pulls the damp T-shirt off his chest. He turns and looks through the door into the kitchen. "Harmony," he calls. His voice is soft. She comes and stands on one foot at the threshold. He beckons her closer. She blinks, pushes her hair out of her face. Logan keeps flapping the fingers of his left hand. She comes and stands beside the arm of his chair. "You wipe the dishes?" he asks sternly. She nods. "You break any?" She shakes her head. His right hand goes into his pocket. He unwraps the chocolate patty. He holds it toward her. "You want a bite?" Harmony nods. He breaks off a portion and gives it to her, puts the rest into his own mouth. The candy is softened and gluey but it tastes so sweet. Harmony chews slowly. She looks dazed and concentrated. He watches her. "I can't lift you," he says.

Harmony climbs over the footrest and pulls herself up into his lap. She turns and sits so she is looking at the TV but not blocking his view. "It's *Laverne and Shirley* next," he tells her.

When Perley comes back from the yard he runs the tap in the kitchen and drinks two glasses of water. The TV is loud, somebody on it is giggling. He looks through the doorway: Harmony and his father, and beyond them his mother's feet, her belly, her palm flat open and her fingertips resting on the floor. He circles behind his father's chair and goes to sit beside that palm.

"Perley, Perley," Krista says, almost whispers. The palm lifts up and her fingers press into his shoulder, knead carefully along the back of his neck where he aches. "Perley," she says. "I figure this is a brother for sure. He kicks like you did. He doesn't want to sit still and be. He's like some kind of cyclone," she whispers. He tips his head back to look at her but all he can see is her belly where the cyclone whirls. He stares, then drops his head. Her fingers work up and down the back of his neck, but unevenly, as if she's thinking about something else.

"I was a kicker?" he says, looking toward her again.

"Honey, you were a champion. Grandma used to say you were impatient to get out in the world and start doin'." She is softly stroking the top of his head. She pulls gently on his hair before letting her arm go slack. Her fingernails make a soft tap as they hit against the bare floor. He hears her sigh. The light of the TV glows brighter in the darkening room, laughter burps out of the speaker. He looks at Harmony. Her back is very straight and she is staring solemnly at the screen. Her bare feet hang in the air between the chair and its footrest. She is carefully eating something. Perley closes his eyes and lets his head fall against the sofa, against his mother's thin hip. He can hear her breathing, the gurgling of her stomach. The fuzz on the upholstery itches his chin and he puts his forearm under it, his fingers nudging at her a little.

"It's hot," she gasps softly. "Don't crowd me."

Perley sits real still.

HOMECOMING

18 Frederick Hewitt stands on the shoulder of Route 1 in Waldoboro amid a row and in the shelter of turning maples. The rain, which caught and drenched him farther east, has slowed to a light shower tapping softly on the leaves. The sky, so lately shrouded in storm clouds, is visible now, steel-colored, ivory on the horizon, and still. Frederick's sneakers squeak among fallen leaves. His plaid work shirt sticks to his narrow shoulders, his rain-darkened hair is plastered to his forehead. When a blue Nova approaches he lifts his arm straight from his body. The car shoots by him, the driver's head held rigidly forward. Frederick's face doesn't change expression. He lowers his arm and reaches in the pocket of his shirt for the pack of Camels. He pokes inside, considering the contents, then puts one between his lips. He turns and starts walking.

The air around him is quiet. The sun comes out in the west, sending long lines of yellow light reaching through the yellow trees until they glow. Birds start singing. He hears one note over and over, growing fainter behind him, coming louder from somewhere up ahead. As he passes between the trees the golden light flows all about him, softens the lines and angles of him, swarms on his hand and the side of his face. The wet earth smells of rot and the wet road of asphalt. Birds are calling now, there are many voices. A black flock rises from the field to his right and turns in the sky at the same instant, as if they were the feathers of an individual creature being lifted by the wind. A pickup truck comes over the rise behind him. His thumb goes up as he turns. The red Chevy passes him, slows, and pulls over. Frederick drops the stub of his Camel, runs and catches the door handle. "Thanks," he says, and, "How far you going?"

"Damariscotta," the driver tells him as the Chevy bounces back onto the road. He is a large man and his thick neck is strung with warts like barnacles growing on a pier.

Frederick nods. Damariscotta won't do him a whole lot of good but it's something. This Chevy isn't new but the motor sure sounds sweet. "Motors last in Chevys," he thinks, "it's the transmissions turn to shit."

"So where you headed?" the man asks. "You sure got wet," he tells him before Frederick can answer.

He lifts the shirt off his shoulders and says, "Portland."

"Well, I guess this'll be some help to you," the man decides.

"I appreciate it." Frederick leans his head back against the seat. His blue eyes, half closed, watch the darkened road ahead of them and the short rolling hills on their right.

The man leans forward and turns up his radio. "Ain't she something," he says, nodding toward the sound of Dolly Parton's voice, singing about infidelity.

Frederick says, "Yeah."

Sixty miles an hour, south on U.S. Route 1, this red truck is bringing him home. It's not an address or anything he owns or belongs to; it's some thin memories, some attachments, mostly failed, and the letters of Viola Rudge and her daughter, which, coming to him through the years have assured him that his existence is being noted as a continuous event by someone perhaps surer of that than he himself often is. On he comes, through late-afternoon October light, beneath a sky whose perfect blueness betrays no remembrance of the sudden hard rain so lately falling down.

The television casts a thin purple light into the bedroom. It falls like dust upon socks, underwear, a rumpled rag rug, flicks shadows on the dark paneling of the walls. Logan lies on his stomach, elbows propped up on a pillow at the foot of the bed. He's watching a special with magicians. "Dumb fuck," he mutters. Krista laughs a bit. "I'll change it," she offers, but he shakes his head. She is squatting across the small of his back. Her small hands knead his spine, gently massage the long white ridges that run like snakes from his shoulders to where she sits. She leans forward so her belly pushes into him and reaches to rub his shoulders, softly works them back and forth. Logan lowers his head and rests his chin on the back of his hand as she pushes her fingertips into the vertebrae and follows them down, straightening as she goes. There are commercials and then the participants gather onstage for the finale. "Get off," Logan says softly.

Krista scrambles onto the sheet and shifts to face the headboard. The bed heaves as Logan gets to his knees and turns to her.

The last ride leaves Frederick in Leedsport. The night is cold and clear and the moon that was rising while he was traveling south is now high in the sky and white as a skull. There is a bus, they tell him at the paper store where he sits and buys a cup of coffee; it goes into Portland but he's missed it, they tell him. Twenty minutes ago. His clothes have dried out but he's stiff and cold and damn tired. The guy sitting next to him at the counter, the one who told him he missed the bus by twenty minutes, says, with the same slow, stupid smile on his face, "Too bad you ain't going to New Harris."

Krista lives there, on the route road. Somewhere, he's got the photograph they sent him. It was taken from the road, by Viola he supposes. They are standing against the house so small and far away they look like any four strangers grouped under a picture window. On the back it said in Krista's cramped writing: "Hi, Freddie! Our new house, June, 1976." Maybe she'll let him stay the night.

So he leaves with the man, who drives like a bat out of hell, everything underneath the car rattling like hooves over stone. He slows long enough for Frederick to jump out where Route 9 crosses. He starts walking past dark fields smelling of cows and smoky with moonlight.

The TV is off and she is sound asleep, curled like a child under the yellow quilt. Logan lies on his back looking steadily into the dark empty space before him. The house is still. Within the room there is the papery sound of Krista's breathing. Outside, the wind cuts in gusts around the corners of the house, rocks the branches of the pines.

Frederick goes over a railroad bridge, past long berry fields stripped for winter, past new houses and a thin maple woods. Finally he reaches Palmer's Corner Store and Lunch Counter, very dark except for one little light left on so anyone going by can read "Breakfast" in the window. He climbs a long slow hill and goes into the wide valley beyond. He's checking mailboxes for her name and is almost surprised when he finds it, for her reality is something he hasn't been sure of for a long time, knowing nothing is real unless it's standing there where you can touch it and speaking your name. He looks up the driveway. The house is dark; he can see the outline of the roof and the black shape of the garage. He walks quietly up the long driveway.

Before the tapping on the front door ceases Logan is on his feet, groping to the end of the bed, fumbling for his pants. He leans against the mattress and puts them on. The tapping sounds again, soft but persistent.

"What is it, Logan?" Krista asks, blinking at the darkness.

"Shut up." He's listening, his head tipped. "Don't touch the light!" he warns, and groaning, he kneels to reach under the bed.

"Someone's knocking. I hear someone!" Krista whispers.

"I said shut up!"

He stands with a long unsheathed machete hanging from his hand. "Come on, and keep your mouth shut," he tells her. He goes down the short hall to the living room, setting his bare feet as quietly upon the floor as a big cat. She follows him, tying the belt of her bathrobe. The knocks sound louder. He pushes Krista toward the door. "Say 'Who is it?' " he whispers.

"Who is it?" Krista calls. Then louder: "Who's there?"

"Frederick." It comes through the door like a foreign word.

Logan presses against her back. "Who?" she asks again.

"Frederick. Freddie Hewitt."

Krista turns to Logan, her voice suddenly warm. "It's Freddie Hewitt. Freddie! He's come back!"

Her voice is familiar beyond that door. It sounds like Viola.

Logan pushes her aside. "What do you want?" he says.

"Christ," Frederick mutters. The cold air is jumping down his collar and gripping his fingers, settling into his bones now that he's stopped moving. "You shoulda gone to Portland, man," he tells himself, backing down the steps.

Inside Krista is whispering, "Please open it, Logan. It's Freddie."

"That bad-luck boy. What the hell is he doing here?"

"Let me turn on the light."

"No!" Logan opens the door and looks into the night, his fingers locked tightly around the handle of his machete. The moon is hidden, the night is black, his breath hangs in the cold air. "Turn the light on, for Christ's sake," he tells her. He looks down at the thin man who is standing, now lifting his arm against the light, in his front yard. "What do you want?" Logan says.

Frederick half smiles, makes a gesture with his lifted hand. "To come in," he answers. Squinting into the sudden light, he sees them, just a part of Krista behind the thick man, and then the knife hanging from his hand. All the muscles in his body draw down tight and he thinks of the lie of the driveway he came up. "What the hell?" he's thinking but he says, "Sorry to be waking you folks. I was going to keep on to Portland but rides didn't come like I hoped." Logan hasn't moved. Krista has stepped to the left so she can see Freddie better. "Maybe I could stay over in your garage," he says. "Or I'll keep going if that don't suit you."

"It's so cold," Krista murmurs. "Please, Logan."

Logan looks down at him. "You can come in," he says. "Come on." Frederick climbs the steps again. Logan swings the machete and grins almost sheepishly. "Didn't know who the Christ was out here at this hour," he explains.

"I can't believe it's you." Krista doesn't quite touch him. "But you look just the same!" She laughs a little, reaches then to touch his arm. Logan shoves the door closed. They are crowded there in front of it. He lifts his machete and uses the tip of it to shut off the outside light, leaning close to Frederick as he does so.

"I'll make you some coffee," Krista says. "You must be cold." He starts to follow her toward the kitchen. "Where were you coming from?" she asks, turning to him. Before he can answer she tells him, "I'll bet you'd rather have hot chocolate. That's what I'll make you."

Logan follows them. "Guess I can put this away," he says. "You don't look too dangerous."

Krista laughs a little. "Freddie's one of the family, he's not dangerous!" She smiles at him.

Frederick sits down slowly on a kitchen chair and watches, his eyes passing from her blue form at the stove to the refrigerator, the window above the sink, the back door. "Mum's going to be so happy to see you," Krista tells him, turning from the pan, her face lit up.

"Viola's been awful good to me. Writing to me at Christmastime. She sent me a picture of this house."

"I know." Krista laughs. "I wrote on it."

"Oh, that's right, yeah," he says and smiles at her.

She stirs her pan again. "Almost ready."

"I wrote to tell her how sorry I was when your father died, Krista. I couldn't believe it. He wasn't an old man."

"She told us about your letter. I read it." She steps toward him. "It seems so long ago, but I remember everything that happened, everything." Her eyes are wet; then she smiles quickly. "Freddie, Flynn's never forgot you. When Mum tells him there's a letter, or mentions your name, he says 'Dee' like always." Still stirring it, she brings the mug to him. "You drink this. You must be froze. And take off those wet shoes." She crouches to untie them before he can stop her.

"I'll get 'em, I got 'em," he says, pulling his feet away.

She stands up slowly. "I used to think I would never see you again," she says, studying his face.

"I hope I'm a good surprise."

Krista smiles. "You sure are," she tells him. Then she grins and she looks like a kid again and he can laugh too.

"You're having a baby," he says.

She looks down at her belly and sets her hand on it. "My third baby," she says.

She is close to him and he can smell the laundry soap in her bathrobe and the bed she lately left. He leans back in the chair a little and lifts the mug. "You got a real nice house here," he says. And gesturing with the mug adds "Good cocoa, too."

She smiles all across her face this time. "Logan did it. The VA helped him. They owed him that much. He said he'd get us a house and he did." She smiles quickly toward the wide doorway where Logan's been leaning. "I was telling Freddie how you got us our house."

"Oh yeah."

"Must be real nice having your own place."

"Yeah," Logan says, "it beats paying rent to some asshole."

"Logan, you want cocoa?" Krista asks.

He shakes his head. "Bet you didn't like it too much up there, a little fellow like you," he says slowly.

"I can't recommend the place," Frederick tells him, and Logan laughs a short loud laugh.

"Logan, I thought maybe Freddie could sleep on the couch. We got an extra room," she tells Frederick, "but all it's got in it is a crib."

"He's no baby." Logan laughs. Krista watches his face. "Yeah, he can sleep on the couch. You can sleep on the couch," he tells Frederick.

Krista starts down the hall. "I'll get some blankets," she calls over her shoulder.

"I'll give her a hand. She ain't supposed to be reaching too high."

Frederick stretches his feet out. His damp socks are clamped about his cold toes. He rubs his feet against each other to warm them and drinks the cocoa. He is exhausted and his head is aching but it's good to be somewhere, to be stopped where it's warm and people know who he is. He hears the bedroom door clunk shut.

On the other side of it Logan is watching Krista drag the chair over in front of the closet. She climbs on it and reaches to the shelf to lift down a blanket and an old quilt. "I guess there's no pillow up here," she says, stretching to feel around before carefully climbing down off the chair.

Logan steps forward and grabs her by the hair on the back of her head. He forces her face down into the mattress. "How did he get here? How did he know where to come?" he demands.

She turns her face so her cheek is bearing into the sheet, but his hand holds tighter. "Don't, Logan!"

"How'd he know where to come? In the dark? In the middle of the night?" His hand twitches with each question.

"We sent him a Christmas card, same as every year," she gasps. "Him up there all by himself. I think Mum even sent him a picture to show him the nice house you got us to live in. Told him how we were in the country and about the yard."

He turns his hand as if he's opening a door. "Don't you ever tell nobody nothing! You ask me first!"

"It was a Christmas card!"

Their strained breathing rattles in the dim room. "You don't know much," he says, and then stands up away from her.

Krista pushes herself to her feet and draws the belt of her bathrobe more securely. His breath blows against the hair hanging forward on her cheek. "You go bring him those blankets now," he says.

She has a headache and it keeps her from sleeping and she lies on her back and thinks about Freddie, remembering the little boy he was and how he took care of Daniel. Long, long ago: that life seems like something on the other side of a door that she's traveled so far away from it's as gone as a dream or something made from magic. And she thinks of later when Freddie came to them on Brackett Street, how handsome he was then with that wildness in him and sleeping in Mariam Griffin's bed on hot summer nights. He's thin now, and quiet, held back like somebody waiting for something. And when she does sleep he comes to her and he's touching her arm and telling her something and she makes everything slow down and wait so she can keep feeling that hand touching her arm.

Frederick wakes up looking at a small boy who is looking at him and asking, "Who are you?" The plastic bamboo shade holds out the sun but the kitchen light is on and he can see the child, his faded overlarge pajamas, hands hidden by the cuffs.

"I'm Frederick Hewitt," he says. "I lived with your mother's family for a while. We was kids together for a while." The child watches him. Frederick can see Krista in the narrowness of his bones, his thick eyelashes, the way his hair grows up from his forehead. He sits straight, pulling the quilt up with him. "I came late last night when you were sound asleep," he explains.

"I'm Perley," he tells him, and steps closer, studying Frederick's face.

"I've heard about you from your grandma."

A girl who looks like Perley comes out from behind the big chair and stands there pressing up against the arm of it. "This is Harmony," he says, pulling her by the pajama sleeve. "She's my sister."

"I've heard about you, too," Frederick tells her. She doesn't look at him past his knees. She whispers something to Perley.

"We got to get ready," Perley says, " 'cause the bus is coming soon."

Frederick lies still and listens. Their soft careful sounds make it seem as if they are far away. The refrigerator door opens, there is a slight clinking of glass, a spoon scraping. The boy says something in a loud whisper; he can hear slippered feet and then her voice: "Are you all ready?"

"Mum, I can't find my red shirt."

"Shhhh, don't wake your dad. And Mr. Hewitt's sleeping on the couch."

"He ain't sleeping. I saw him."

"I saw him too."

"Shhhh. You let him get back to sleep then. He's real tired. I got to wash your red shirt, Perley. I got another one here for you."

Krista scoops french fries off the cookie sheet and puts them in the yellow bowl. Perley carries it to the table where the men are seated. Logan breaks the legs off the roast chicken, flips one onto his plate, one onto Frederick's. Harmony follows her mother to the table and sits down in the chair beside her. She watches Mr. Hewitt's hands as he spoons french fries onto his plate. Men fascinate Harmony. She likes the strange way they smell and the rumbly sound of their voices. Perley watches his mother. She has been so quiet lately, she has been sleeping a lot; in the evenings she lets him rub her ankles while she lies on the couch. But tonight she's not sleepy and her feet are quick. She laughs and lifts her hand toward her mouth.

"I helped Mr. Hewitt change the oil today," he tells her.

She nods. "I know, honey. They put new oil in your car, Logan."

"Found it in the garage," Frederick explains. "Figured it wasn't doing your car much good sitting in cans."

"The oil was *real* dirty," Perley says gleefully. Logan raises his eyebrows. "You got to change the oil regular or you ruin the motor," Perley tells him.

"That so? You got any ketchup?"

Krista glances at Perley and he gets up and goes to the refrigerator. He brings the big bottle to his father. "You got to undo this little bolt underneath"—Perley demonstrates with his fingers—"and then the dirty oil comes out. We drained it into a big pan." Logan is whomping the bottom of the ketchup bottle. Perley gets back in his chair.

Krista smiles at him. "Mr. Hewitt knows all about cars," she says. "Knows 'em like he invented them."

"Ain't much ketchup in here." Logan whomps the bottle some

more. He sets it on the table and looks at Perley. "I guess he's a pretty smart fella," he says. "You going to be a smart fella like that?" he asks him, twisting his thumb toward Frederick.

"Yup." Perley grins and looks around the table.

Krista laughs and says to Logan, "That'll be good if Perley can help you with the car. So then you won't have to be getting under it."

"I don't get under nothing." He looks at Frederick. "You want more meat?"

"I'm all set, thanks."

"Freddie was always good with machinery. He could fix lawn mowers, broken doorknobs. You fixed Mrs. Cord's old toaster. Remember? Dad always said he never saw a boy like you for talent with machines." She turns to Perley. "He said it all the time. 'Some people got the touch,' your grandpa said."

"Like me," Perley brags. "I got a wagon and I put new wheels on it myself," he tells Frederick.

"That's good, Perley."

"Well, I found 'em in the sandpit so they're not really new."

"New to you," Frederick tells him, and Perley grins.

"Perley is good with machines," Krista says eagerly. "He likes 'em. My dad said, 'Some people got a way with machines, some people are all thumbs.' "

"I remember him saying it," Frederick agrees.

She leans toward him, her hand half raised. "It was like Kendrick having that special way in the woods. Dad said he could never get lost. He'd notice how the trees grew, he'd smell his way back like an animal could, he said."

"My uncle Kendrick," Perley tells Frederick. "He was killed in the war."

"Mr. Hewitt knew him, honey. He was his friend."

"You were?"

"Sure. I knew him a long time. He had a beautiful truck he fixed up himself. A '56 Studebaker."

"Freddie, Mum had to sell it when Dad got so sick and we went back to Portland. I don't remember the man who bought it. It made Mum feel terrible and Dad left and wouldn't come back home till the man had took it away."

"I wish Grandma didn't sell it."

"She had to, honey, else she wouldn't."

"You got any more potatoes?" Logan asks.

Krista looks at him. "We ate 'em all. I'm sorry. I could give you some bread." She starts to get up.

"Forget it." He leans back in the chair, pushes his empty plate from him. "Harmony, get my ashtray," he says, reaching in his shirt pocket.

"I made dessert, Logan."

"So get it on the table." He strikes the match, and when his cigarette's going he reaches in his pocket again and offers one to Frederick.

Frederick goes into Portland the next morning. The city smells. He'd forgotten—smells of the packing plant down at the wharf, of car exhaust, of filth. All the buildings are brown or gray with black slabs of glass. The only color is women, women in bright coats, tapping along the sidewalk in their high-heeled shoes, looking rich, looking as if they're going somewhere he can't even imagine. He walks downtown and sits in the small park in front of the courthouse. The sharp wind coming up the hill from the water blows trash around, blows an old man in black laceless sneakers into the park from Congress Street. His long coat flaps about his ankles, his head is bare, he's carrying a small cardboard suitcase. He sits on the end of Frederick's bench. His skin is caught in bunches around his empty mouth, gray whiskers stick out from it. He rears back his small head and spits a brown hunk of saliva onto the walkway in front of him, then opens and closes his mouth, making a dry smacking sound. Reaching into the deep pocket of the coat, he draws out a little packet of saltine crackers and works at it. The clock on the courthouse starts striking. Frederick counts.

"You get it open you can have one."

Frederick stands up. He feels the day falling away from him like something lost out of his pocket.

"You can have one you git it open."

He starts walking rapidly toward the courthouse.

"Fuck you too," the voice behind him says.

His parole officer is a sleepy-looking young man named David Oulette, who has an office in the basement of the courthouse. He ushers Frederick in between two tall file cabinets and gestures him toward a chair. The office is lined with overloaded metal bookshelves. Frederick can see feet going by the small window high on the wall.

"Welcome to Portland," David Oulette says. He looks down at the paper on his blotter. "Or welcome back. I guess you were born here." He takes off his glasses and smiles at Frederick. He has very round, very blue eyes, so blue it looks as if he's wearing tinted contact lenses. "Have you family here?"

"No."

"Well, I guess what you need is work and a place to live."

"That's about it."

He goes up Congress Street to State, turns and goes along the block to the hospital. Nothing's changed here. The person behind the counter is a nun, her face almost as white as her clothes. She has narrow lips and steel-rimmed glasses. "How can I help you?" she asks.

"I want to sell some blood," he tells her. "AB."

She leads him into a small room. He sits on a wooden chair and waits. Wheels glide softly by in the corridor; somewhere an elevator begins to rise, humming like a flying saucer in an old movie. "Sister said you wanted to give blood," a woman says, walking briskly into the room. She smiles at him. She is not a nun. She seems to fill the space with her blondness and her round, pink flesh. Her voice is even and slow. Her white stockings make a swishing sound.

"I want to sell it," he corrects softly.

"Yes." She smiles again, and holding a clipboard, she perches on the edge of the table. "Let me ask you some questions, Mr. . . ."

"Hewitt," he says, and spells it. He gives her the address of the rooming house his parole officer suggested, Mrs. Pulham's.

He goes into a narrow luncheonette on Congress Street and sits on a low stool. It's after one-thirty and there is only one other customer, an old man settled around a cup of coffee. The waitress is squat and middle-aged and her neck is thick. She brings him Camels from a tall plastic case above the grill, then an apple muffin, a cup of coffee. She doesn't look at him when she slaps the thick crockery down. As soon as she can she leans back against the shelf on which the thick white cups are piled and lights herself up a Pall Mall. She looks out the window while she smokes it. The muffin is lousy, it tastes like sawdust, but he likes being able to sit here eating it. And the coffee is hot. He sips it slowly, his knees crammed against the counter. He starts another cigarette with the last of his coffee. The waitress lifts the pot from the burner and gestures at him with it. Behind her, smoke rises from the ashtray. He shakes his head.

"Second one's free," she tells him flatly.

He hesitates, but shakes his head again, pulls the bill out of his pocket and rests it on the counter, his finger holding the edge of it.

City Welfare is in the basement, and in the manila-colored windowless room Frederick sits on a blue plastic chair in a line of blue plastic chairs. There are several other men but most of the people in the room are women with infants and small children. Everyone has a coat on. There isn't much talk but the voices he hears are tired, peevish. The woman in front of him has a baby who is standing in her lap and looking over her shoulder straight into his face. The baby has black shadows under his long eyes and he's working hard on a pacifier while he stares at Frederick. After half an hour the baby's eyes start closing, his face slackens. The room is hot. Frederick gets sleepy also. Time slows and stretches, it begins to feel as if he might be here forever, as if they all might be, here in this windowless place, waiting with their coats on. But then something happens. A pretty woman in a purple dress comes in and, smiling, beckons to the woman in front of Frederick. She and her baby rise and follow the pretty woman through a thin door. He never sees them again, but the woman in the purple dress comes out after a while and gestures to him.

"Mr. Oulette called about you, Mr. Hewitt," she tells him when they are seated in her little partitioned cubicle. Her glasses are enormous. The cubicle smells smoky and stale but she smells of perfume. "We've just got some forms to fill out and then I can give you the food stamps and the voucher for Mrs. Pulham's," she says.

Twenty minutes later he's going to the Salvation Army. It's not far, a long dark building that used to be a furniture warehouse. "I'm

Bob Guyer," the short man behind the counter tells him. There's a dusty light settled all over the long, open room, over the racks of clothes, the shabby-looking upholstered furniture, the tables holding kitchenware and utensils. "I need some pans to cook in, dishes to eat off. Just a few things," Frederick says.

Mr. Guyer nods his head and comes out from behind the counter with a cardboard box. "Dave Oulette call about you?" he asks.

Frederick looks sharply at him; then his face relaxes and he nods.

"He said you needed a winter coat." He points to a rack. "We got a pretty good selection just now."

"I get a job I'll buy one in a store."

Mr. Guyer shrugs. "Well, you're welcome to get one here to tide you over if you change your mind." He lifts up a frying pan, and when Frederick nods he puts it in the box.

He carries the box up the hill to Mrs. Pulham's. It's a long, long brick building on a corner. He climbs the steps and rings. The front room, to his right, is curved out in a bow so he could look right in the window if he wanted. He rings again and someone raps on the window from inside. It's difficult to make out the face through the greasy glass. "Come in," a voice is calling. The image shifts and flutters. "It's open!" A hand is waving.

He steps into the entryway and opens the inside door. He's standing in a hall lit by one naked bulb that hangs from the high, cracked ceiling. A long stairway rises in front of him. A hallway runs along it toward the depths of the house. A wide doorway opens from it. "Come on in," the voice calls.

He steps through the doorway into the dining room, where it's very hot. The big table is covered with stuff: unfolded clothes, a pile of plates, some paperback books, a tower of jigsaw puzzles. Steam hisses from the tall silver radiator between the two windows. The room smells of sickness and dirty clothes and fried fish. "Come on in," the voice insists. He steps across the faded green carpet and goes through another door and he's in the front room, where it's even hotter. Steam spits and burbles from the big radiator between the two windows in the front. This room smells too, sharply, of sickness and dirty clothes. "Hi," she says to him.

Frederick shifts the box on his hip and nods to her. She is sitting on an upholstered chair in front of the bay window. She's wearing a short-sleeved cotton dress, little cotton socks, and red sneakers that don't touch the floor. Her hair is waxy-colored and pulled back tightly from her round, pale face. She wears blue-rimmed glasses. She smiles so broadly at Frederick he wonders if she knows him from somewhere. He steps a little closer. "I'm Frederick Hewitt," he tells her.

"I know it!"

"I got a paper for a month's rent here."

"I know it!"

He pulls it out of his pocket and hands it to her.

She takes it but keeps looking at him. "Got you a room on the third floor," she tells him, and the thick mole on the right side of her upper lip rocks up and down. "You don't look like you'd mind stairs."

"No." He shakes his head.

"Tamara!" she bellows, and he leans back from her. "I'll have my daughter show you. Kitchen's downstairs. You get a cupboard with a padlock. A key. Got to take your chances in the refrigerator, but the people who live here ain't none of 'em thieves." She's still looking at him, and with the frankness of an innocent. "I don't believe you'll have any problems 'less you make 'em."

He nods.

"Tamara!"

Someone groans and he starts and turns. In the opposite corner of the room, beyond the wide, unmade bed, an old man sits in a wheelchair. He's all slumped forward toward the floor and would topple to it but for the brown cloth belt tied around his waist and attached to the back of the chair. His large hands are the color of flypaper and spill across his thighs. His blue and white striped pajama top is dingy. He groans again. "My father, Mr. Begert," Mrs. Pulham tells Frederick. "He's got a cancer," she says loudly. Frederick looks at him again quickly. "Eatin' through his stomach to his bowels. I feed him baby food," she explains proudly. "I'm keepin' him to home, I don't care what nobody says. Tamara!" She leans forward in her chair.

"Stop yelling, Ma! Whaddya want?" She is round and short like her mother, but she has lots of brown hair and it's let loose to fall all over her polo shirt. She has thick, brown-rimmed glasses on her wide nose, and her eyes behind them are slightly crossed.

"My daughter Tamara," Mrs. Pulham says. "This is Mr. Hewitt."

They nod at each other. "I want you to show him the kitchen and then show him his room." She shifts in the chair and pulls a key out from under the seat cushion. She holds it toward her daughter. "I'm giving him number ten now that Mr. Celestino's left us."

"He'll be back," Tamara forecasts without enthusiasm.

"Well, he won't be back in number ten," Mrs. Pulham says serenely. "It's Mr. Hewitt's now."

"Thanks," he says, and turns to follow the girl out of the room.

"Mr. Hewitt!" she calls, stopping him on the threshold. "I don't have many rules. I only make 'em 'cause I mean for 'em to be obeyed: No guests in your room after eleven, no hot plate in your room ever, no messes left in the bathroom or kitchen." She holds her chubby white hands open wide to indicate that is all.

"I'm not a messy person," Frederick tells her.

"I didn't take you for one but I got to tell everybody the same."

The kitchen is a large room giving off the dark corridor at the foot of the long flight of basement stairs. The light is faint and watery; tall ocher cabinets cast strange shadows about him. Somewhere on the floor above, Tamara Pulham's radio is playing rock 'n' roll. Frederick is alone. He finds a can opener in the top drawer and opens the beans, dumps them into his small saucepan and sets it on the stove. He puts a slab of butter in his frying pan and turns the gas on under both burners, then sets the table, which wobbles so badly he bends to shim the shortened leg with a matchbook cover. As he is straightening from this task there is the sound of someone coming, jumping from step to step and landing with both feet. Moments later a young man shoots into the room and heads for the refrigerator. He stops short when he sees Frederick's pans and spins around. His mouth is open, he has a few teeth, he is a young man with a very big lower jaw and bright, true yellow hair. "Hello, hello!" he says loudly, as if Frederick were far away, across a parking lot. Then he pounces, thrusting out his hand. "I'm Junior Small," he says. "Yes, yes, Junior Small." He holds fiercely to Frederick's hand and pumps it up and down, up and down. Frederick can hear his butter snapping in the frying pan. Junior has a small frame and his head is big and his hair stands up in a shiny pompadour. "How you like it here? How you like it? You like it? You like it?" he asks loudly, bringing his face close to Frederick's, his head slightly tipped. He smells like chewing gum.

"I can hear my butter burning," Frederick says.

"Yow-eeee!" cries Junior, and lets go of his hand.

"Whatcha cooking? Whatcha cooking?" Junior wants to know, standing at his elbow while Frederick drops three hot dogs into the dark butter.

"Whatcha got there? Whatcha got cooking for your supper?"

"Beans and hot dogs," he tells Junior Small, pushing at them with a fork.

"That's what I got!" he hollers, and then laughs loudly. "I got the same! The SAME!"

"Quick meal," Frederick says, stirring the beans.

"Yeah, yeah, quick meal. Quick. Quick." Junior is breathing down the length of his arm.

"You're too close," Frederick tells him. "I need elbow room." And he steps back and forth.

Junior jumps. "Oh yeah," he says, "oh, that elbow room. Elbow, elbow," and he's flapping his own.

Frederick spoons out the beans, forks the hot dogs. He rinses both pans and brings his plate to the table, Junior dancing along beside him. He gets bread from his loaf, pours milk from a carton on which he's written "Hewitt" in the dark red ink of the Flair pen he bought that afternoon. He puts mustard on his hot dogs and sits down. Junior slaps his hand against his thigh with satisfaction and rears back. "I'll cook mine!" he fairly shouts. "I'll cook mine and eat with ya!" He whips a long string out of the pocket of his blue pants. From it hang many keys. He chooses one and charges at his cupboard with it, thumps the padlock, springs it open. "Beans!" he yells triumphantly, turning to Frederick with the can in his upraised hand. Frederick nods and Junior Small rushes to the stove, then clatters in the cupboard for his pans.

A woman slips into the room. So quiet is she that Frederick hasn't heard her come down the long stairs. He looks at her feet as Junior slams his dented frying pan down on a burner: little red shoes like slippers. Junior dances to the refrigerator. She is a large, soft-looking woman and she is carrying a grocery bag, her two arms locked around it as if she had just tussled with a would-be thief. Her hair is black and straight and chopped very unevenly and generally below her ears. The front is jerked back off her forehead and pinned by a yellow barrette of Minnie Mouse. She watches inside the bag and walks in a slow shuffle to her cupboard.

"Pam!" Junior shouts as he leaps back from the refrigerator with his hot dogs in his hand.

She scowls at him and draws her key out of a very large, nearly flat, black plastic pocketbook that is looped around her neck. She watches him over her shoulder, presses against her cupboard so no one can see, and undoes her padlock.

"It's Pam!" Junior tells Frederick. "Pam! Pam! Pam!" And he points to her curving back, his finger punching at the air. Frederick scrapes up the last of his beans and rises from the table. Junior trots beside him and stands, tipping forward on the balls of his feet, while Frederick washes his dishes. "Whoa!" Junior cries, slapping his forehead and hopping back to the stove to stir his beans. Pam shifts her shoulders so her back is to him. She's rustling things out of her grocery bag and slipping them into her cupboard.

"Boy, you eat fast, you eat f-aaast!" Junior says, and his hot dogs sizzle. Frederick can smell the burning butter. "Guess I better turn it down, turn it down," Junior says, yanking the pan from the heat, shaking it like popcorn. Smoke drills toward the high ceiling.

"Catch you later," Frederick calls to him as he hurries for the door.

"Catch you! What's your name! Catch you! What's your name?" Junior cries, dashing after him with the pan held at arm's length.

He stops, turns, and gives him a salute. "Frederick Hewitt," he says.

"Fred. Fred. Fred, Fred, Fred," Junior sings after him as he climbs the stairs. He's almost at the top when he hears, "Hey, Fred! You fixed the table! Pam! Pam! He fixed the table! He *fixed* it!"

He writes them in a small spiral notebook he keeps in his pocket, the garages where he goes to ask for work. But Mr. Oulette knows a man in South Portland needs somebody on his evening shift. He walks out of his office and down the corridor with Frederick. "Just be cool," he tells him. "This guy knows as much as I had to tell him and he's willing to see you." He grabs his hand to shake it. "Let me know how you make out," he says urgently before ducking back into the courthouse basement.

The garage is out by the mall between two fast-food outlets. Allen Kirby is a small man with sandy hair. He's pumping gas when Frederick gets there. He is bundled in a thick brown jacket and he dances back and forth in his black boots, thumping his mittened hands against his biceps while the little dials twirl on his gas meter. "Hi," he says to Frederick. "Go on in where it's warm. I'll be right there."

"Ain't you cold in that little shirt?" is the first thing he asks him.

"It's only November," Frederick says.

"It's damn cold out," Kirby insists. He sits down in his chair. He's still wearing his mittens and smacking them together. "You're looking for work," he says.

Frederick nods.

"Man told me you got experience."

"I've worked in garages, worked on racing cars, rebuilt motors, done front ends, transmissions, just about everything."

"Well, there ain't nothing big-time like that here. Just pumping gas mostly. Thermostats, oil pumps, shit like that. Oil changes, lube jobs," he adds quickly.

"I done all that."

"What I need is someone here three to eleven Tuesday through Saturday. You interested?"

Frederick nods. "Sounds good."

"Fine, fine." Kirby rubs his mittens together. "Only fair to tell you the meters keep a record of the gas so I know what to expect in the drawer."

"I'm no thief," Frederick tells him.

Kirby waves his hands in the air. "All right, all right," he says. "Just wanted you to know how everything works."

He gets up early Sunday morning and hustles up to the bus stop. The November sky is as grey as an old pan. It's his day off, but on Friday he towed a guy who left his truck; took the plates off it and said he wasn't coming back for the son of a bitch. It's an old Dodge, used to be red.

The station is quiet. Kirby is sitting in his swivel chair reading a magazine. He has earmuffs on; a thick white cup sits on the plastic blotter in front of him, steam rising from it. "It's your day off!" he cries when he sees Frederick.

"I wanted to get going on the truck. It needs a lot of work."

Kirby's eyes widen.

"Guy signed a bill of sale," Frederick says, reaching in his pocket. "One dollar."

"I know, I know. It's yours, it's yours. Just . . . how long you think it's going to take before you can get it out of here? It ain't the best advertising, you know," he says with a grin.

Frederick's studying it: big old Dodge, she'll get him through the winter. "I'll have it out of here by next week," he tells Kirby.

"Guess you're a miracle worker," Kirby says, and laughs. "Oh, I got your pay, no sense to waiting till Tuesday."

Frederick stands at the bus stop with the money in his pocket. The wind gallops across the wide parking lot of the mall and slams into his back. He'll be able to get the radiator hoses, pay a week's rent. He's going to buy supper which he'll bring to Viola, whom he hasn't seen yet. Maybe he'll get the jacket.

At Mrs. Pulham's the hall is dark and the TV is booming from the front room. Climbing the stairs, he can smell all the different odors rising from the basement. He's planning to get a bath before he goes to Viola's; it's a good time now with everyone eating supper. He climbs quickly. Mrs. Pulham has said with the next vacancy he can move down to the second floor. As he starts up the final flight Junior Small bolts out of his room. Through the open door his TV is blaring. "How ya doing? How ya doing?" he cries, leaping to grab Frederick's arm. "Come on in! Come on in! The movie! The movie!" He smiles into Frederick's face. He smells like french fries. "The mummies!"

"I'm going up for a bath," Frederick tells him.

"Mummies! Mummies!" Junior hollers happily.

"Sounds good," Frederick laughs, "but I got to get my bath."

"They eat you up!"

"I got to go." He pulls away from him. "Another time."

"Another time. Another time. Mummies!" he says, making his voice go deep. He waves and waves as Frederick climbs the stairs.

The light hurts his eyes. He thinks how tomorrow he'll buy a shade. His room is narrow and the ceiling is high. He gets the clean clothes out and sets them on the bed. He keeps his toilet things in a large plastic tub Mrs. Pulham gave him. Lifting it from the bureau, he takes his towel off the hook on the door, and steps into the hall.

The bathroom is occupied. It must be Clara, who lives next to him in a room filled with sun-starved plants. He can hear water sloshing. He leans against the frame and lifts his knuckles to tap lightly. "How long you gonna be, Clara?"

Except for the sound of shifting water it's quiet behind the door.

"Clara, how long?" He can't picture her in that bathtub. It's a small tub on raised feet and Clara is big, too big, he feels sure. Maybe she just stands and washes herself in midair. "Clara, you're s'posed to be downstairs eating now."

"I ain't eatin', I'm washin'!" Her voice is a barking voice. It is followed by a loud sound of water.

"Che-rist!" he says, and goes back down the hall. He lies on the bed. The ceiling is so high and the room so small it's like looking up an air shaft. He stares past the hanging bulb and then looks at the window. Green plastic curtains nearly cover it and what he can see of the world beyond is a thin black vertical line. It's close to six o'clock and too late now. The Italian market where he wanted to shop is probably closed and they've most likely eaten already anyway. He'll go tomorrow night. He lights a cigarette and thinks how he'll go out somewhere and get a couple of beers, a pizza. He smokes impatiently, listening for the lock to turn on the bathroom door.

He's dressing in his room, his hair slicked down and his skin smelling like soap, when he hears someone hollering for him. "Mr. Hewitt! Mr. Hewitt!" Feet are pounding up the stairs. "Mr. Hewitt!" He opens the door and she stumbles through it.

Tamara Pulham, so close her hand flings out to hold his arm, panting hard after two long flights, her face bunched up around her glasses, wearing her yellow T-shirt that says "ELVIS !!!" in green letters. "Ma wants you to come—it's Grandpa!" she tells him, her voice high with breathlessness. She spins off him and runs. "Hurry! *Hurry!*"

He goes after her down the stairs in his clean black socks, doors opening at their passing.

"What? What? What?" asks Junior Small, coming out into the hallway in his underwear. He looks after their descending heads, slaps his hands on his nearly naked chest, and jerks back into his room.

"I got him!" Tamara cries, rushing into the front room and stopping short. The radiator is rattling and hissing and Frederick starts to sweat the minute he steps across the threshold. There is only one light on, a metal lamp, the flexible neck of which is twisted to focus on the ceiling. The TV is shrill. He doesn't see anybody in the shadowy room. Tamara has retreated into the dining room, where she stands with her back pressed up against the table. He hears, above the hissing radiator and the steady noise of the television, "Daddy, Daddy." And then Mrs. Pulham stands up on the far side of the bed. "Come help me lift him," she says.

Mr. Begert is on the floor between the bed and the wall. He's slumped forward on one shoulder, and his knees are caught somehow underneath him. Mrs. Pulham is almost naked in her pale blue nylon nightgown and her face, without the blue glasses, is naked also. "Can't lift him," she gasps. "I been lifting him for eight months and now I can't lift him."

Frederick comes around the end of the bed. "Tried to get him on the bedpan and he tumbled right off onto the floor," she explains. Her fingers open and close on her hips, puckering the nylon. In the dim room all Frederick can see of Mr. Begert is the grayish stripes of his pajamas. He bends closer and almost gags. "Help me," Mrs. Pulham says again, stooping to lock her arms under her father's knees. Frederick gets him under the armpits and they lift. The old man hangs like a long, starved cat between them.

"What's wrong? What's wrong?" Junior Small demands from the doorway.

"Call Medcue, Junior," Frederick cries hoarsely. "Call 'em up on the phone."

"Number's aside the phone in red ink," Mrs. Pulham moans.

"Red, red," Junior says, plunging back into the dining room, where the phone sits on top of a stack of old cookbooks.

They lay Mr. Begert on the bed and his arm falls off the mattress, so fast and so stiffly it seems it must have snapped. Mrs. Pulham picks up the hand and holds on to it. Mr. Begert has very thick eyebrows and beneath them his eyes are pale points. Frederick steps back and then draws the covers up over his feet and legs. Underneath the blankets his shins feel sharp as chisels.

Junior lifts the receiver and dials with authority. "Mrs. Pulham's," he tells them loudly. "Mrs. Pulham's, ninety-two Winter Street. 'Mergency!" he bellows.

"I don't think he's breathing," Mrs. Pulham says, laying her head down on his chest.

"Ninety-two Winter Street. Nine two, nine two. Winter Street. Winter Street!" He slams the phone down and runs back to the front room.

"Medcue is coming," Frederick tells her, looking around, looking toward the doorway and finding Junior standing there with his plaid bathrobe belted tightly and Tamara behind him, peering into the room. "You get 'em?" Frederick asks.

Junior nods vigorously. "I got 'em, Fred. They're coming. Medcue, Fred. I called 'em," he shouts, gesturing behind him with his thumb. "I told 'em. I told 'em. On the phone."

"Good work," he says, and looks back. She still has her head on his chest. The television is still droning on. The radiator is wheezing and spitting. The TV gets louder. Mrs. Pulham is moaning. They hear the high steady sound of the siren.

"Siireeeennnnnnn!!!" Junior whoops, holding his arms up like a triumphant boxer.

Later Frederick lies in the narrow, dark room and stares at the ceiling. "I got to get the hell out of here," he thinks. Around him the tall house is quiet. The city beyond the green plastic curtains is quiet also. He has a headache and it keeps him awake and in the darkness his thoughts circle around inside his skull, gaining speed, banging into each other like crowded animals fighting for space.

PIG KILLING

19 Perley wakes in the night. He sits up blind in darkness, hears Harmony breathing across the room, then hears his mother on the other side of the wall, her voice worried. Something is wrong.

He listens and the door opens and they go down the hall. His father says something, he is impatient, his feet hit hard on the floor.

"You got to call the doctor," his mother says. "He told me to call him and then come right in."

"You call him. I'll get the car."

Perley opens his door and he can see her, she is in the kitchen and the living room both; her arm in the yellow sleeve of her big sweater is bent to hold the receiver. He starts down the hall toward her, squinting at the bright light hurting his eyes.

She hangs up. "Perley," she says, "you should be in bed."

"What's wrong?" he whispers.

"Nothing's wrong. The baby's coming is all. Dad will take me in to the hospital and then come back. You watch out for Harmony, okay?" She holds his face for a moment and kisses the top of his head and then the horn sounds and she is gone and cold air is filling the kitchen, left behind her opening the door and going through it and shutting it.

Shivering, Perley runs into the living room and kneels on the couch and pushes the curtain aside. The car is backing down the driveway through the blackness. Then it turns into the road and the taillights are flickering between the maple trunks, rising and curving with the road, climbing over the railroad bridge. Gone.

Perley stands in their bedroom and looks around. He squints at the hot circle of light burning from the shadeless lamp on the bedside table. The covers are rolled back and hang onto the floor; the imprint of his father's head is stamped into one of the pillows. Perley goes into the closet where it is dark and crowded. He slips between his mother's green sundress and the long folds of her bathrobe, leans his cheek into the skirt of the robe, and rocks so it rubs softly against him. It smells of her and of coffee and smoke from his father's cigarettes. He works it off the hanger, wraps himself in it, and lies down. Above him are legs and the folds of her clothes, around him are shoes and the old smell of feet. He curls up like a caterpillar and shuts his eyes.

The windows are lighter patches high on the wall and a voice is calling his name. It calls and calls at the other end of the house. He hears the front door, then someone running through the living room to the back door. "Perrrrlleeyyy! Perrllleeyyyyyyy!"

He unwraps himself from the robe and gets onto his knees.

"Perrlleeyyyy!!" She is calling louder.

He stumbles to his feet and goes into the hall. "I'm right here," he says, his voice slow with sleep.

She comes toward him from the kitchen, her mouth hanging open. The house is cold and she is huddled around herself, her hands holding her elbows. "I couldn't find you," she says. "You weren't anywhere." She is still moving and she doesn't stop until she is right in front of him and he can see sleep in the corners of her eyes.

"Mum went to have a baby. He drove her."

"Mum."

"Come on, we got to get ready."

"Mum. I couldn't find you."

"Hurry up," he says, starting for the kitchen. "Get ready."

"Perley," she says to his back, "Perley, is Mum going to die? Is she?"

He turns and charges at her, shoves her into the bathroom. "Mum ain't going to die!" He pinches her arm. "She ain't! You're a real jerk, Harmony!" He backs out into the hall and pulls the door shut over a rumpled pink bathmat. Harmony rubs her arm where he pinched it and cries quietly.

As they get off the school bus that afternoon they see the long blue car and a rust-colored truck parked in the yard. "Mum's home!" Harmony cries.

They run, Harmony's clothes flopping about on her narrow body. But when they get halfway up the driveway they hear Roxanne Two screaming from behind the high, uneven walls of his enclosure. Harmony runs harder, the plastic bag that holds her thermos whacking against her ankle.

"Get the rope on him!" they hear their father holler, and then his short, round head and thick shoulders rise above the top rail. They fling themselves onto the fence and climb.

Roxanne Two is backed into a corner; his narrow eyes glitter like eyes caught by flashbulbs. His head is low and his round sides heave in and out, making sudden hollows. In the opposite corner is a tripod with a short chain hanging from it. The chain has heavy links that barely rock in the November wind. Smoke rises from a fire beyond the pen and is swallowed by the grey sky, which presses close above the pine trees. For a moment Perley could stretch his hand out and touch his father, but then Logan is rushing in, a lassolike rope held before him. "Get it on him, for Christ's sake, Hewitt!" he yells.

Mr. Hewitt is slinking along the side of the fence, quiet as dust. He has a rope too. When their father jumps at Roxanne Two, Mr. Hewitt throws his rope and draws it tightly around Roxanne's back feet. Then he leans hard and pulls.

"What are you doing to her?" Harmony shrieks. But her voice is nothing to the pig's.

High, piercing, and terror-filled: he screams and screams and screams. The men are dragging him toward the tripod. His forefeet scramble in the ridged dirt of the pen, his voice goes on and on and on. Harmony is screaming too but nobody can hear her. She is still screaming as she pulls herself over the top and drops into the pen. Perley is about to follow her, when he sees on the maple stump the long, thick knife that lives under his father's bed.

"We got him, we got the bastard now!" Logan exults as Harmony stands up and rushes at them. "Leave her alone Leave her alone!" she cries, banging Mr. Hewitt on his hips. "Leave her alone! You're hurting her!" Frederick is straining with the body and the terror of the pig and Harmony's fists don't mean much.

The wind gusts up, drawing the burning wood smell over the pines, making the day colder. "Get her out of here!" his father bellows, twisting his head back to look at Perley. Then he braces himself against the rope. "You get that winch turning, Hewitt!" he shouts.

Harmony spins off him and runs at her father. The screams are higher and higher. There is nothing else but the terrible voice of the pig. It shatters the space enclosed by the pen and fills the sky above it; it leaps out to encompass the house and the yard and everything that Perley can see until it is as if all the sky is pressing down on them to hold that screaming here forever. Perley knows they are beaten and he watches from a small stillness as Harmony wraps herself around their father's leg and bites him. Holding the rope in both hands, he is braced against the animal, his weight and his screams and his struggles. Harmony's teeth are sharp as a puppy's. "You got it?" Logan bellows.

The winch is making a steady creaking sound, shortening the

slack on the rope. "Faster!" Logan orders, and he drops the rope and bends to loosen her teeth from his flesh. Swinging his arms in an arc, he tosses Harmony over the fence; his eyes find Perley on top of it. "Get her in the goddamn house!" he snarls.

For a moment, when Logan releases the rope, Roxanne Two runs on his front feet, dragging the hobbled ones behind him, but then the winch catches up with the slack and his screams, suspended by that brief release, sound again, louder, more panicked, more frenzied. The winch groans as Frederick turns it; the cold wind moves smoke through the needles of the pine trees.

Perley locks his arms around Harmony's waist and drags her toward the house. "There's nothing you can do," he gasps. "Nothing!" Her stomach muscles are hard as a book and her booted feet kick at him.

"I want Mum," she sobs as her heels bang his shins.

"Cut that out!" he tells her, and squeezes hard. They've almost reached the back steps. It's shadowed by the house here and cold. As Perley starts to climb there is a shout from his father and the screaming beyond the fence changes pitch, gets glutted-sounding. "Watch the feet!" his father yells in a high, excited voice. Perley scrambles faster, dragging Harmony up the stairs.

Perley has slept, slumped against the closed bedroom door with his legs sprawled, slept and wakened, grown a headache like a red, blinking light. Across the room on her bed Harmony lies asleep, her breathing rattly and clogged. He feels dizzy and hungry and his belly hurts. There is laughter coming from the kitchen, and his father's stomping, uneven stride. Pans slam down on the stove. Perley gets up slowly and opens the door.

He can smell meat frying, onions. The odor of cigarette smoke rolls down the hall. "Jesus, once you learn something like that you never forget it," his father booms. "The right moves just come to me. My old man was the best, slick as shit with a knife."

Perley, crossing the hall to the bathroom, hears Mr. Hewitt say, "It's quicker and easier you shoot it first."

"You trying to tell me my business?"

"Just a suggestion."

"Here, have another beer and shove your suggestion." There is laughter and Perley shuts the bathroom door.

When he's done he goes quietly down the hall. They're sitting at the table, leaning toward each other, their hands out. Smoke floats in the air above them, smelling of cigarettes, of burned butter. His father is wearing a hat. Laughing, he tells Mr. Hewitt something, and as Frederick nods and laughs in response he sees Perley in the doorway. "Hi, Perley," he says, lifting his hand in a wave.

His father shifts in his chair to look at him. His hat is tilted on his head, like a gambler Perley thinks. "You come out to eat?" he asks.

Perley shrugs, shifts his weight onto one foot.

"That mongrel with you?" his father demands, thrusting his neck out and looking around. "Bites just like a dog." He swings his head toward Mr. Hewitt. "You think I ought to get a rabies shot?"

"She didn't know you raised that hog to eat?"

"What in the hell did she think it was for?" He looks hard at Perley.

Perley looks at the floor and shrugs. Then he looks up at his father. "Is Mum okay?"

"You got another sister."

"Oh." He can't do much with that information. It is as if his mother is gone from the face of the earth. He can't picture her in a hospital, having a baby. He can't picture her anywhere he hasn't seen her. "Sister" means Harmony.

"Get yourself a plate," his father tells him.

On Monday late in the afternoon Frederick drives downtown to the Italian grocery. This truck he's resurrected is running all right, though it burns oil and rust flakes off the body like old skin. The cab is warm and it gets him where he needs to go; he's riding, he's not walking or waiting at a bus stop like a schoolkid.

It's warm inside the grocery and the small store smells like celery and cheese. Produce hangs over the bins into the narrow aisles. He goes to the back and looks into the deep white case. He wants to get something very good. The dark man and woman who stand behind it are talking to each other in their own language. He decides and the man gets him six pork chops, the woman slices cheese. The door opening and closing up front keeps sending cold air back to where he's waiting, and the cold sharpens the odors of the vegetables and the cheeses.

Outside the remaining light is dun-colored; a few people hurry by. He drives up the hill and crosses Congress Street, goes partway down the other side. The address is in his pocket, written in her round, looping letters. At the stoop he hauls it out and checks to be sure.

For a moment he thinks he's made a mistake, knocked on the wrong door. This woman is old; her hair is gray, there are deep lines in the hollows of her cheeks. He steps in farther, urged by her smile; it's Viola's voice. "Freddie, hello. We've been watching for you. We didn't know what to think."

"I would have come sooner, but I had to get settled, get a job," he says quickly. "Transportation."

She nods. "Well, we're glad you're here." She moves forward and embraces him. "You grew up," she tells him. "Come in and sit." She draws him into the small room and closes the door. The walls are green; there are two windows at the end. While she goes ahead of him to pull a chair out from the table he sets his grocery bag down. She is wearing slippers and they scuff along the bare floor. "Walking like an old woman," he thinks sadly.

"Flynn!" she calls. "Flynn! He's having a nap," she explains, turning to him.

He thinks how beautiful she was, how quick she used to move, bird-quick, how she ran across the field faster than all the children when Flynn cut himself on the wire and stood screaming in the tall grass.

She gestures him to the chair. "And is it working out?" she asks. "The place, the job?"

"Yeah." He nods. "I'm getting along okay." He's not going to tell her about Mr. Begert, not going to bring death in here with him.

She sits in the chair opposite. "Well, you look fine. Krista told me you did and she's right."

"They got a real nice house. Nice kids. I've been out there," he says.

She is nodding. "Krista told me. Said you were starting in on a new life."

"I would have come sooner," he repeats. "I was trying to get settled and the truck took all my money."

But Viola doesn't look concerned. She smiles. "You and your trucks."

He grins. Her words are still praise. "You got a new granddaughter," he says. "You must like that."

"I do. I like it a lot."

"Hi, Dee." Flynn is standing at the threshold of his room. His hair is sticking up on the back of his head.

"Hey, Flynn!" Frederick jumps up and they shake hands. Flynn has a very small mustache but to Frederick he looks like a child still, a serious child. Flynn nods and pats him.

"Dee," he says again.

"He's grown, my son has." Viola stands up with them. "He's all grown now." And he is taller than his mother.

"I brought something for supper," Frederick tells them, "seeing as how I'm a surprise. If you ain't had it yet," he stumbles on, then turns toward the grocery bag. "Pork chops."

"I got a meatloaf all made, Freddie. And you know you're always welcome at my table."

He steps back. "But I . . . pork chops."

"Well, I'll just put the meatloaf in the refrigerator and we'll have it tomorrow. Tonight we'll have a real treat!"

"There's potatoes and green beans," he tells her.

"You brought the whole meal, Freddie. You didn't have to do that."

She doesn't sound pleased and he's embarrassed and he thinks about the ice cream that's starting to melt in the bottom of the bag. "I just didn't want to make any extra trouble for you," he explains.

They eat in silence at first. It's dark out and the small room is softly lit and warm. "Good, Dee," Flynn says, grinning and holding up a green bean on his fork.

"Sure is," Viola agrees, "even if is is the cook saying so."

They laugh then. "You always cooked real good," Frederick tells her.

"You got to when you're cooking for a family. Besides, I like to eat!" She laughs again and leans toward him. "I dreamt of the farm two nights ago," she says. "Maybe that was some kind of sign we'd be seeing you."

"Cows!" Flynn leans back in his chair and moos softly.

"I went back there," Frederick tells them. "Last week soon's I got the truck on the road. I wanted to see Cord bad, but at first I thought I was lost. You wouldn't believe it, Viola: your house knocked down, gone, and a new one in its place. New houses filling up the field where the cows used to be. Ell gone, what's left of the house painted bright blue. Swimming pool where the barn used to be."

"A swimming pool!" Viola snorts. "Whatever for?"

He shrugs and drinks from his beer bottle. "Anyway, I went down to Creeley's, asked 'em where's the Cords."

"Creeleys are still there, then?"

"Yeah. They're there. Ain't got much pasture left though. But the Cords," he continues, his voice getting louder. "He dropped dead. Heart. She went to the nursing home." He leans closer to Viola, his face puzzled. "She weren't that old. I know she weren't."

"Health might have gone on her all the same," Viola says. "Happens more than you think."

Flynn nods. " 'Appen," he whispers.

"I sure as hell feel cheated. Cord dying like he did 'fore I could get to him." He looks at her but she's lifting her tea mug and watching it come toward her. "I owed him."

Viola sets the mug down. "It's good to let the past go," she says briskly.

He doesn't hear her, not really. "Cord needed a much harder death than that, Viola. He needed to see it coming a long way off and feel it feasting on him like maggots in garbage."

Flynn gets out of his chair and steps close and puts his hand on Frederick's shoulder. "All right, Dee," he says, his voice almost stern. "Okay now, okay." He stays there patting him while Viola gets up and gathers their plates.

"You want dessert now, Freddie?" she asks.

"Sure," he says. He feels dismissed. He gets up and lights a cigarette, looks around for an ashtray.

When Viola comes back with the bowls of ice cream she tells him, "Krista's bringing the baby home tomorrow. Flynn and I are going up to the hospital to see them off. Flynn's an uncle three times now."

"Nuncle," Flynn says, nodding gravely.

"She's the biggest baby we've ever had in the family."

"LaLa." Flynn smiles, folding his arms like a cradle and rocking them.

"Perley and Harmony were delicate as baby birds, but this Lila!

Round as a partridge." And she laughs and shapes her hands like a ripe fruit.

Frederick, watching her face, sees it transformed, lightened by this talk of the new baby. She looks the way he wanted her to look when he came to her bringing the nicest meal he could think of. He feels this, but he doesn't think about it. He picks up the bottle and drains the beer.

"LaLa!" Flynn crows, laughing and making his arms a cradle again.

It is dusk and the first snow is falling. It piles on the bare branches of the maple trees down on the front lawn, it clings to the soft limbs of the pines. The children are sitting on the floor in front of the couch, quiet and still as they watch their mother, who isn't looking at them. She is looking at their sister Lila, set across her lap, her pink neck straining to lift her dark head. Lila stares out over the couch arm, her face serious, as if she is looking at one particular thing. The bottoms of her feet, her fat pink toes, point toward the ceiling as she arches her back. She makes little sounds: "Omph, umph, omph"; one hand stretches forward. Their mother's palm, placed on the middle of her back, steadies her. Harmony gets up on her knees to peer closely at the baby's face. "Hi, Lila, hi, Lila," she calls loudly. She touches the outstretched hand but Lila paddles her fingers free.

"Such a strong girl, such a *strong* girl," their mother croons in a voice they almost don't recognize. She bends her head and blows softly into the baby's hair. Lila stretches so hard she almost jumps herself up and down, her body as taut as a leaping fish's. Perley watches his mother's bowed head, her pale hand on the baby's back.

"Hi, Lila," Harmony calls hoarsely, tipping her head to peep into the baby's face. Lila stares toward the window, her mouth slightly open, both hands reaching.

KEEP YOUR HANDS TO YOURSELF

20 Fern Wallace leans on the horn. One, another, and a third blast. The deep bell of the school bus cuts through the frozen air and echoes off the pitch of the garage roof. Her bottom lip pressed between her teeth, Harmony peers between the steering wheel and Mrs. Wallace's broad bosom. "He's coming," she says. "He's coming."

"We'll give him another minute—you go sit down, honey," Mrs. Wallace tells her. She sticks her hand out the window and waves two cars by. Their rear ends first shift to the left, then swing hard to the right as they accelerate down the icy road. Mrs. Wallace watches in the long mirror above her while she digs for a pack of gum in the pocket of her plaid shirt. "You keep your hands to yourself, David Fisher!" she bellows as she unwraps Juicy Fruit. She pats her new perm, pushes a curl back into the mass of it, and slides the gum into her mouth.

Harmony sits down and presses her face against the window. She watches for Perley, who is crouched astride the tall black tank beside the house. He is pouring kerosene from a two-gallon can into the funnel his mother holds over the opening. Krista is on the porch, reaching over the railing. This is the last of it. She jiggles the funnel and then removes it. Perley screws on the cap. They hear the horn again. He drops the empty can into the snow and slides off the tank; he starts to run.

" 'Bye, Perley!" Krista calls, and he turns a circle waving to her and is gone. She blows on her cold fingers and stomps her black boots across the porch. She can hear the baby crying before she opens the door.

The rims of Perley's ears are deep red and his nose is running. He gasps, "Thanks," to Mrs. Wallace and heads down the aisle toward his usual seat. She flips the handle, the door closes with a whoosh, and checking her outside mirror, she starts the bus down Route 110. Perley drops into the seat with Michael Reed and pulls the sleeve of his coat under his nose.

Michael has brought a different matchbox every day since vacation. Perley wants to see the dune buggy again, shiny blue with black roll bars and thick double tires. But Michael holds up a black and white car that says "78" on the doors. He gives it to Perley and Perley chases Michael's red car named "Spitfire" all over the back of the seat ahead of them. Mrs. Wallace pulls over and opens the door for the Anderson kids.

Rosemary gets on first, her brothers following, elbowing each other. "None of that!" Mrs. Wallace growls, and they stop until they get well past her. The Pierce twins arrive panting at the door.

Their coats are unzipped. Their heads are bare. As they board they haul tiny purple hats out of their pockets and stretch them over their narrow skulls, crushing their short-cut spiky black hair. Moira is first and Mildred so close behind her Moira can feel her breath on her neck. They are thin and they wear identical white-rimmed glasses; their voices are high. They love Harmony, who can tell them apart because Moira has more freckles and Mildred talks much more slowly. They sit on either side of her. Moira takes out a small pink brush and starts brushing her hair. Moira works steadily; Mildred watches; Harmony sits, eyes closed and unmoving, while her hair sparkles and crackles in a halo around her head. Mildred slips a tiny baby doll with tight fuzzy hair into her limp hand. "She's yours," she whispers, her words coming out in breath that smells like Kix cereal. Harmony smiles and rocks the baby doll back and forth while the bus lumbers up the long hill on Cott's Brook Road.

Louise Sample is short with wide hips and a long, sweet face. She has taught fourth grade for ten years, and each June she mourns the loss of her class, her kids. The summer is a restless time for Louise, overlong. She rejoices each year when Labor Day finally comes.

"That's very good, Perley." She beams, bending over his math sheet. She puts big red check marks on each problem. "These are all correct," she praises, then pauses at 4 × 4. "What's this one again, Perley?"

Perley hunches over the page. He uses his fingers. He works his eraser back and forth until it makes a hole in the paper. Then he writes 16 next to the hole with the end of his very short pencil. Perley spends a lot of time at the pencil sharpener and he has about six stubs lined up in the indented tray on his desk. "There you go!" Mrs. Sample applauds. "Just try to work a little more neatly," she urges as she straightens up. "I'm coming now, Harold," she calls to a boy who is chewing shreds of paper and spitting them out on his desk. But she bends once more to Perley. "Come see me before you go out to recess," she tells him.

Congregated under the coat hooks, the children are hauling on snow pants, zipping their jackets, sitting on the floor to pull on their boots, wrapping scarves around and around and around their necks. Perley is standing beside Mrs. Sample's desk. She has Kleenex and unshelled peanuts and colorful stickers. She has ivy in a white pot shaped like a frog, she has a purple cyclamen. There is a picture of her little boy and her husband. Books and papers are arranged on her desk in neat little piles. He knows that in her drawers are pencils and chalk and paper clips, more books, rubber bands of many sizes, cars she has confiscated until June, her tiny indoor shoes that look like slippers, her rubber boots that fold up small, her pocketbook, her lunch bag, extra peanuts, saltines, fruit. She smells like flowers, when she laughs her head goes back and her eyes get shiny, and her hair is so short it barely moves. Sometimes she hugs him and he holds his breath to concentrate on her softness and her sweet smell and her voice singing inside her chest like a bird.

The door keeps banging as children leave for recess, and Mrs. Sample offers Perley saltines spread with peanut butter. He is hungry and while he holds one in each hand she spreads two more; then she bends to the bottom drawer and brings out a black watch cap with a hockey decal sewn onto the front of it. "I thought this might suit you, Perley."

He stops chewing and smiles at her. He holds the cap carefully in two hands. "Thanks, Mrs. Sample," he says, and puts it on.

"Looks great!" she tells him.

"Thanks a lot. I needed a hat. My other one got lost."

"Oh, Perley," she thinks, loving this child, whose struggles and griefs she only half perceives, and who is nothing less than gallant in her eyes. She puts her hand gently on the hat on his head. "You are very welcome, Perley," she tells him.

When the weather is good the children eat fast so they can get out to recess. If it is cold and stormy, as it is today, they don't hurry. The noise in the lunchroom is louder; there is laughter, and sometimes arguments, tears and occasionally fights. The tables fold down from the wall and the tall room is cold and drafty. They line up by grade and pass in front of the rolled-open window of the kitchen, overseen by teachers who are always urging them to be quieter. The ladies behind the window are dressed in white and their hands move quickly. Mrs. Chalmers puts two rolls on Harmony's tray, pinches salad with her tongs. Mrs. Forbes puts a plate of spaghetti square in the middle, Mrs. Vine serves up sliced peaches in a small blue dish. Harmony's chin reaches the countertop; her eyes move, watching their hands. She carefully lifts her tray down and walks with it toward her table, her fingers curled tightly around the edges. As she crosses the slippery gym floor she watches the red sauce slide back and forth, climbing toward the lip of her plate. She is not careful enough and some slops over the edge onto the tray itself. Her fingers clench more tightly and she slows down. Chad Creighton's tray bangs into her spine, she almost drops her own tray, the plate slides off onto the floor where it breaks in three pieces, the salad flies down, two thin slices of cucumber and her roll travel under a table.

"Why did you stop! You shouldn't have stopped!" Chad Creighton screeches at her. "You almost made me spill my lunch!"

Harmony can't move, she can't look at her lunch on the floor, she hunches her shoulders against the sound of his voice.

"You clumsy jerk," he says loudly as he moves past her. "You're a jerk and you smell like an old furnace."

Her hair has fallen stiffly over one eye, her face looks old and worn; she could be a middle-aged midget with her dress that doesn't fit and her tired, stained face. Children point to her disaster. Teachers sigh; she is one of the poor children in this school and it is expected that unhappy, inelegant things will happen to her. Someone steps on her lettuce.

Chad isn't three paces from her, holding his tray high and still sneering, when Perley is on him, leaping onto his back and locking one arm around his throat, punching wildly with the other fist. Chad's tray is gone too now, his dishes are crashing and breaking, red sauce splatters on the new sneakers he didn't take off after gym class. He's grappling at Perley, swinging his body to rid himself of the smaller boy. They go down. Perley's knee thuds hard on the gym floor; he punches, both fists swinging.

Then Mr. Hyde has Perley's arm, his fingers clenching as if they're going to lift those arms right off, leave Perley a two-limbed boy holding the stub of his pencil in his teeth. "That's it! That's enough! Perley!" Mr. Hyde bellows.

"Shitbum!" Perley screams, kicking at Chad's legs while Mr. Hyde lifts him up high in the air, feet swinging.

When he goes limp Mr. Hyde sets him on the floor and marches him out of the lunchroom, his hand hard on the back of Perley's neck. They go down the long hall to Mrs. Thorton's office and sit outside on the pale bench. Perley's thinking about how he just jumped Chad Creighton. He didn't know he was going to do it. Suddenly he was doing it, punching him, kicking him; suddenly he was doing it and it felt good.

Harmony stares at the door Perley went through, Mr. Hyde's fingers bearing like pincers on his neck. "Come on," Miss Weir says, stooping to put an arm around her. "You come sit down, Harmony, and I'll get you a new lunch." Under her hand Harmony's shoulders are shaking. "It's all right, honey. It was an accident." Weeping, Harmony follows her to the table. "You sit here next to Mildred," Miss Weir tells her. "I'll be right back with your lunch. It's all right," she says again, puzzled by such grief over a spilled lunch.

Mildred hugs her. "That creepy Chad," Moira squeaks, breaking open her roll and feeding it to Harmony.

Perley spends the afternoon in Mrs. Thorton's office, seated at the round table in the corner, head bent low over his work, a pencil that started out long a stubby end in his fingers. This is what he writes:

Chad Craytin hit my sister in the lunch room. With a tray. He call her dirty. Clumsea. I hit Chad Craytin. I jump on his back. He ain't specting it. I hit him. I call him swars. I was bad. No hiting at school. Chad Craytin hit my sister. He call her dirty. I hit Chad. I chop him. I kick him. He swing and miss. I am in truble. My mother says its my job to take care of Harmony. I hit Chad hard. Chad Craytin is a bum.

They climb down off the bus. Mrs. Wallace watches in the outside mirror. She waves good-bye to them, her jaws moving steadily over her gum. They walk slowly up the driveway in the tire tracks. The wind is coming hard; it batters its way between the bare maples and pours across the lawn, going right through their coats. Harmony struggles forward and catches onto Perley's sleeve. "Mildred gave me this new baby doll," she tells him. She holds up the small, fuzzy-headed figure but Perley keeps walking.

"Perley, I can keep her. Mildred said so." His blue back plods on. "Perley!" She runs. "I'm sorry you had to go to Miss Thorton," she calls.

He stops and turns. "I don't care," he says.

She's close now. "You got Chad good," she tells him.

He looks down at her. His grin is a bit lopsided.

They stomp the snow off their boots at the back door and go in. Lila, in her playpen on the kitchen floor, is holding herself up and drooling. Their mother is rolling dough on the counter. She stamps out biscuits with the bottom of a Flintstone glass and flips them onto a baking sheet. Her dungarees hang off her narrow hips, her sweatshirt is faded green. She is working quickly, she barely nods at them. They stop beside the table, suddenly wary, for the presence of tension and danger in the room is as irrefutable and life-threatening as a pillow held over the face. Silently they hang up their coats, leave their boots in the corner on the newspaper, and start down the dark hall toward their room.

"So there you are!" he says.

He is sitting in his chair in the living room. There are no lights on and he is little more than a shape and a voice. They stand just inside the room, waiting. "I got a call from school today," he says, and launches himself out of the chair. "Principal tells me you was fighting and saying dirty words." He speaks slowly and almost casually as he stares down at Perley with his delicate eyebrows raised.

They are silent.

"I don't like getting telephone calls from school," Logan informs them loudly. "They wonder what the hell kind of kids you are."

"A boy hit me with his tray," Harmony says. "A creepy boy in the lunchroom." When her father doesn't say anything she goes on. "He called me names, he made me drop my whole lunch on the floor." Fear makes her voice loud.

"I don't like getting telephone calls from school." He says this to Perley and then his eyes slide onto her. "I told you, girlie, you better learn to quit dropping things."

"He . . ." Harmony begins; she is whispering now.

"Well!" Logan says, and he leaps forward with surprising agility and twists his fist into the front of Perley's shirt, lifting him. The first button flies off and pings against the baseboard. "Just what the hell do you think you're doing!" Logan yells into his face, enunciating each word. "Are you crazy?" he shouts, banging him against the wall.

Krista gets a hold of Perley's arm and tries to pull him down feet flat on the floor. "It won't happen again, Logan," she says. "It was a mistake, for God's sake!"

"Mind your own business, lady!" He shoves her hard and twists his hand again in Perley's shirtfront. Pulling him close so their bodies are touching, he stares down into his face. "I'm not having those candy-asses down to the school calling me up and telling me you're a jerk!" He bangs Perley against the wall by straightening and flexing his arm in several quick motions.

"Logan! Stop it!" Krista gets a hold of that arm and hangs on to it with the weight of her body. "Leave him alone!"

"Leave him alone! Leave him alone! Leave him alone!" Harmony cries, almost chants, while the baby starts to scream.

Logan shoves Perley down the hall toward his room, dragging Krista after them. He batters at the back of his head and shoulders. "Watch what the hell you do!" he says. "I hear from that school again you won't like it!" He shoves him through the door and turns on his wife, grabbing her by the shoulders and pushing her down the hall backward. She's half holding him up while he yells into her face. "Don't you ever tell me what to do," he says. "And don't you ever interfere between him and me again!" Harmony is getting shoved and trampled along by the two of them. They end up in the kitchen, Logan panting and glaring down into Krista's face, Harmony backed into the table. At the end of the hall Perley shuts his door. His radio goes on, playing softly. Lila pulls herself almost to her feet in the playpen, looking up at their tangled forms and wailing.

"You be sure and have your bath after supper," Krista tells Perley that evening. He nods and spears his fish stick. She brings him another one, brings jelly for his biscuits, pours him more milk. Logan gets up and stomps into the living room and turns on his TV. "I got cake for you," Krista tells Perley.

"Me too?" Harmony wonders.

"A big piece for you," Krista tells her.

Krista opens the door quietly and steps into the bathroom. She closes it. It is warm and steamy. Perley isn't aware of her at first. How small he looks in the white tub, the white walls around him, his dark hair, his narrow arm. A blue boat sits on the lowered cover of the toilet seat. His towel is on the floor; she goes forward and picks it up. Perley looks at her, his face guilty and then wary. He draws his knees up against his chest. Krista makes room for the towel on the toilet set next to the boat. She holds out a jar. "Perley, I got some special cream for you," she says softly.

He shakes his head, scowling. He isn't looking at her anymore. She takes another step toward him. "Perley. Perley."

"I'm trying to take a bath, Mum," he says in a high voice.

"I just want to put this on you." She gestures again with the jar. "It's special for muscles. It's like what athletes use," she says, her voice fading.

He reaches for his boat and drops it into the water.

"Perley, you can't reach by yourself."

He makes the boat roar up on the side of the tub and into the water again. "Bruuuummmm, bruuuummmmmm," he growls.

"Are you all right?" she asks him, whispering.

He nods, "Bruuummmm, bruuuuummmmm."

"Perley, I'm sorry what happened. There ain't no excuse. But he loves you. He just wants you to do right so he can be proud of you."

She waits but he says nothing. "He's got a bad temper, Perley. That's not your fault."

But he still won't look at her. He keeps busy with the boat, his lips forming the sound, bruuummmm, bruummmm. He wants her to go. She waits for a while and then she does.

When Perley comes into the room the next morning Mrs. Sample is writing at her desk, her head tipped to the side and her lower lip caught between her teeth. Perley glances at her, then puts his lunch box on the shelf and starts for the door. She looks up and calls to him, "Good morning, Perley. How are you today?"

"Good," he says.

"Come here for a minute, please." She sits back in the chair, smiling at him as he approaches. She is holding out an orange. "This came all the way from Florida," she tells him as she digs her fingernail into the rind. It makes a tearing sound like rich cloth ripping. He can also smell her perfume and her freshly sharpened pencils and her shampoo. "I understand you had some trouble in the lunchroom yesterday," she begins, and drops rind into the waste basket.

"Miss Thorton already punished me," he says, and turns from her.

"Perley, I thought it was brave of you to stand up for Harmony. But you got to do it a little differently. Maybe with words, don't you think?" She puts her hand on his arm, so he turns back and she gives him a section of the orange. He puts it in his mouth and the sweet juice squirts along his cheek. There are wide dark circles under his eyes. She gives him another section of orange and asks, "Were you up late last night?"

"We were watching TV. A good movie, so my mother let us see the end." Perley smiles quickly and puts more of the sweet fruit in his mouth.

"It takes a good night's sleep to be a good student," she reminds him, pulling off another piece of orange. Perley shrugs and chews. "So if something like that ever happens again, like what happened in the lunchroom, you'll go to the teacher on duty. Okay? He or she will help."

Perley nods. "But if there's no teacher I'll have to do it myself," he warns, mumbling around the orange.

"There's always a teacher." Mrs. Sample sits straighter in her chair and looks at him sternly. Perley swallows and she smiles and leans close to him again. "You've worked very hard this year, Perley, and I'm so proud of you. I don't want you to spoil your good record by fighting."

He nods again and she stands up and hugs him. "Good for you," she says, but he winces and pulls back. Putting her hands on his shoulders, she looks straight at him. "Perley, is something wrong? Did you hurt your back?"

"I'm okay," he insists brightly, and steps away, freeing himself from her touch.

"Perley, I can tell you've been hurt."

He doesn't look at her, he looks past her at the blackboard that has her wide neat letters on it. He grins quickly. "I was sledding yesterday with the kids, Mrs. Sample. We went sledding in the pit and I crashed into the pine tree." He's moving his hands to show the sled and then the tree and the two coming together. "You should have seen me! Pow! Goin' like lightning and then wham! into that pine tree! Twisted the steering all up. Twisted my back," he says, his tone conveying satisfaction. He looks into her eyes for a moment to check how this is going over. This story is coming out of him so fast it's like something wild that got loose. Words: jumping from his lips before he knows they're in his brain. He looks at her chin. "My mother says I'll be sore for at least a week. She had to put some special cream on me."

"I'm so sorry you were hurt." She strokes his head.

"I got to go," he says. "I told Michael I was coming."

"Be careful out there!" she calls to him. Perley turns to wave. She watches him leaving the room, walking rapidly, shoulders jerking he's taking such long strides, scuffing in his overlarge boots.

He hurries from her, from the lies he has told this person he values so much. But he could never tell the truth; he would never betray them, he is theirs. And he would never shame himself, or Mrs. Sample for her good opinion of him, by telling what is true about his life.

HANNAH NILES

21 The second winter Frederick lives at Mrs. Pulham's is a cold, hard winter and it snows often. His truck does not like to start. On the floor are jumper cables and an extra battery, which he brings in at night. It is late on a Thursday in February and he's about to lock up the garage, when a woman appears between the two islands of his gas pumps. Her back is bent under a child and she is leading a big black dog by a piece of clothesline. Frederick rises from the wooden chair and stares through the glass at her. Behind him the radio plays. It is snowing lightly and they are all dusted with it. The woman pushes the glass door with her elbow and steps into his station. She stands there, feet apart, breathing hard, and asks him, "You give me a tow?" The dog sits down. The child peers at Frederick between the line of his yellow winter hat and his mother's shoulder.

"Where's your car?" he asks, lifting his jacket off the chair back.

She has a wide face and wide features, her curly hair sticks out under her hat; the child's mittened hand pins some of it to her coat. "Not far," she says. She straightens abruptly and the child clutches at her throat. "Loosen up, James Ewan," she says, patting at his hand.

Outside it is very still. Snow melts as it touches their faces. He motions to his tall red wrecker and they cross the asphalt single file. He waits until the motor is warmed up and then asks, "What happened?"

"I filled the tank," she says. Her voice is a slow voice, clear and even. "We were going along fine and then nothing. Dead."

"You try to start it?"

"Course I did," she says, her voice lifting a bit. The child is in her lap, watching the lights on the dashboard. The dog is pressed against Frederick's thigh.

"Wouldn't even turn over?"

"Nope. Damn car. I hate to depend on a car."

It's out by the food warehouse, a light green two-door Plymouth with rusted-out rocker panels. Frederick holds his hand out for the keys. "I'll be right back," she tells the child. "Stay, Paris! Watch James Ewan." They don't move. The child's face is pale and there are delicate smudges under his eyes. The dog is panting in the heat of the cab. She follows Frederick back to her car.

He's got a pretty good idea it's the coil but it might be points. He unlocks the door and slides in. The car is full of stuff. There are boxes crammed into the back seat. The floor on the passenger side is piled with toys; there's a big rawhide dog bone on top of them. A clothes bag hangs over each back window. He puts the key in the ignition and turns it. There's a clicking sound, nothing more. He gets out and lifts the hood, shines his flashlight over the connections, wiggles wires. Nothing seems pulled loose. "You wanna try it?" he asks her.

He watches and sees what he expects to see. It's the coil. He shuts the hood and goes back to her open window. "I could jump you," he tells her, "but the same thing will happen again. Maybe tonight, maybe not till next week, but it will happen."

"What's wrong with it?" she asks, narrowing her eyes at him.

"Your coil's shot."

"You got one?"

"Can get you one tomorrow. I'll leave the boss a note."

"Can you tow it to your station? Get it off the street."

He looks at her. She's got strange eyes, narrow and long and green like an ash leaf. "Sure," he says. "Were you going far?"

"California," she says, and he leans back from the window. "But we were stopping in New Hampshire first."

He looks up and down the length of the car. "You think this will make it that far, even with the new coil?"

"New Hampshire?"

"No. California. With a new coil it should get you to New

Hampshire no problem." It takes him a moment to realize she's laughing, and when he does he takes another step back into the snowbank.

She winds up the window and bangs the door open. She slams her feet into the snow and slams the door. But the latch won't hold and she slams it again and again. "You bastard car!" she hollers in a thick voice. "You son of a bitch bastard!" She kicks the door repeatedly.

"You'll dent the hell out of that door," he tells her softly. He steps forward and lifts it so it closes and locks.

They are silent as they drive back to the garage, the Plymouth riding behind them like something dragged up from the bottom of the sea. The child is almost asleep, pressed against his mother's shoulder with his mouth open. Paris is squeezed in a large ball.

Frederick backs her car into the bay. "Your stuff will be safe," he tells her. "I'll leave my boss a note and he'll get you a coil and put it in tomorrow. I don't work in the morning."

She nods. "Thank you."

"You want a ride somewhere?"

She smiles. "How 'bout New Hampshire?"

He considers. Snow is still falling. "I can take you into Portland," he tells her, "or South Portland, or anywhere around here you came from. I can take you back to it. But New Hampshire. No. Sorry. Couldn't do that tonight."

"Well, I can't go back," she says, looking past him, out toward the road, where large flakes of snow fall and disappear into the slick tar. She lifts the child higher on her shoulder. The dog stands.

"You want to call somebody?" He looks around. There are no cars on the street; the outdoor lights of the mall gleam fuzzily on the empty parking lot. The lights of the round hotel across the street blaze and he hears a car start somewhere over there. "You could spend the night there," he says, gesturing toward it.

"Don't think they'd take Paris," she decides after a moment.

"I could keep him in the station for you," Frederick offers. "He's housebroke, ain't he?"

"Course," she says quickly. She looks at the dog, gnaws on her lower lip.

"It stays pretty warm in there at night," he assures her.

She pats the dog's head. "Could we all stay there? Sleep in the car?" She takes a breath and looks straight at him. "I put everything I had in the gas tank. Filled it. And two quarts of oil. To get us to New Hampshire. My sister's there. I held out a dollar for the toll."

And then he thinks how she owes him for the tow and there's to be a new coil, the labor; Kirby will shit.

"I know I owe you," she tells him quickly. "But I can get money in New Hampshire and send it to you. I'm an LPN," she says.

He doesn't say, "A what?"

"I don't do things this way," she insists. "Not usually. It's just that I'm going through a bad patch right now. I don't like owing people," she says firmly.

He nods, looks at his truck. "Maybe my landlady could put you up over the night."

"A dog!" Mrs. Pulham says as she leans back from the front door. Her feet are shoved into fuzzy pink slippers and she has an afghan patterned in purple roses wrapped around her shoulders.

"He's Paris."

"Oh." Mrs. Pulham frowns and looks closely at him. Paris sits down.

"I'm Hannah Niles. I'm so sorry to be disturbing you." The child lifts his head off her shoulder and starts to whimper. She sways back and forth, rocking him.

"How old is this child?" Mrs. Pulham asks sternly.

"James Ewan is three and one half," Hannah tells her.

Mrs. Pulham mouths his name silently as the child's head falls against his mother again, one hand drops from her shoulder and hangs limp. Mrs. Pulham, reaching to squeeze it, can barely feel his fingers through the thick mitten. "Georgianna Gregoire's back in the hospital," she says, and raises her pale eyebrows at Frederick. "Front room, second floor, view of the Holiday Inn." She gently swings the little hand. "One night wouldn't hurt I guess." And then her voice deepens: "Georgianna's got a lot of stuff up there."

"We will be very careful not to touch anything," Hannah Niles tells her. She looks at Frederick for a moment and then up the long staircase. "Thank you both for being so good to us," she says.

It is three days before Frederick is carrying Georgianna Gregoire's boxes and bags and suitcases down the two flights to the basement and Hannah's boxes and bags up one flight to Georgianna Gregoire's room. Mrs. Pulham stands in the front hall and watches.

"Last time she was gone six months," she frets. "I'm losing money every day."

Frederick drops a little blue suitcase, and Georgianna's hair dryer uncurls along the dark floor. "Oooph!" Mrs. Pulham grunts as she bends to stuff it back in its case. "I think Mr. Robichaud will be moving out before long and Georgianna can have his room when she gets back with us," she decides and works the hair dryer under his arm.

Frederick sits across from James Ewan and watches him spoon corn flakes into his mouth. James Ewan doesn't look like his mother; he's a narrow child, tall for his age. His skin is pale and his eyes are brown and his hair is black and very straight. Frederick wonders who it is he does look like. Paris sits next to James Ewan's chair and watches him eat. James Ewan makes precise movements with his spoon and he never puts more on it than can comfortably fit in his mouth. Frederick has seen his mother peel and eat an orange, sliding the sections one after another between her lips, juice dripping down her wrists, cheeks rounded out like a pumpkin. "You want peanut butter on your toast?" he asks.

James Ewan considers. He nods his head once. Frederick pushes down the toaster and then unlocks the cupboard and gets the jar of Skippy.

After breakfast they go out food shopping. Frederick got a new truck in April, a 1970 Ford that runs well. In the pocket of his shirt he's got his list and he's got her list, which is in the envelope with her money. He drives to Shaw's out at the mall. They have to leave Paris in the truck, and even though Frederick locks the doors and opens the windows four inches he doesn't like it. "That dog won't let anyone steal him," Hannah has said, has told him several times. But he doesn't like it. He knows letting your guard down is a draw to ruin, which is always waiting like a hungry beast at the gate.

James Ewan rides in the grocery cart facing Frederick, his slim legs hanging straight as new trees. Sometimes he leans forward and pats Frederick's hand where it rests on the metal bar. When he does this Frederick feels as if his chest is being opened by a too deep breath, his poor heart made naked as a new-hatched bird fallen in the wide-open pathway of this thorny world.

Back in the basement at Mrs. Pulham's they unpack the groceries and have lunch. They build something and then they nap, James Ewan in the small bed in the corner, and Paris on the braided rug beneath the window, and Frederick in her bed under the shiny slippery spread she bought, his boots upright by the door.

Hannah gets off at three and comes down the hospital steps in her white uniform with the white stockings that remind him of something wrapped in tissue paper. She climbs into the cab and hugs and hugs James Ewan. She pats Paris and kisses his wide nose, she sets James Ewan on her lap and feeds him bites of her chocolate bar, and she smiles at Frederick. "Hello," she'll tell him, and she smiles at him until he has to look away and straight out through his windshield. Just her voice alone makes the cab seem smaller, warmer. And when she throws her head back against the seat and sighs, hugging James Ewan to her, Frederick feels held in that embrace also. He drives them to Mrs. Pulham's door; he has to hurry to work. "I'll be missing you!" Hannah tells him, standing on the sidewalk, waving. "I'll be missing you," James Ewan echoes in his high child's voice, perched on the curb before her, her hands pressing him close. "Hurry back!" Hannah cries. Feeling slightly foolish, he waves to them. He's never known anyone happy the way she is; it's a marvel and a mystery, one he can't begin to understand.

And he does hurry back. She's waiting in his room, or finishing up her bath, padding along barefoot, pink from the hot water, her damp hair falling about her neck. When she leaves, to check on the child down the hall, his bed and his room smell warm from her, and he lies on his back and smiles, rejoicing at his life, listening for her coming back up the hall to him. Returning, she will smile down into his face, tenderly as when she looks at James Ewan.

One day when Frederick is up at the Laundromat with James Ewan, Viola and Flynn come in. Frederick doesn't see them right away because he has his back to the door and is shooting a metal car to James Ewan. Around and around and around their clothes go. The place hums and is hot.

He sees something in the child's expression and turns. It is Flynn, knowing him from the back of his head, coming to them still drawing the laundry basket, and calling softly, "Dee!"

"Hi, Flynn! How are you? It's Flynn Rudge," he tells James Ewan, who has picked up his car and come to stand where he can press close to Frederick's leg.

"Hi, Viola. We came by but you weren't home." He frowns. "Couple of weeks ago."

"This must be the little boy," Viola says, smiling. "Krista told us you had a lady friend and there was a boy."

"James Ewan." He bends over him. "It's Mrs. Rudge and Flynn," he tells him. James Ewan watches them. "Yeah. Hannah," he says, straightening and looking at Viola. "Hannah is at work at Mercy Hospital. She's a nurse there," he adds.

"Pretty child." Viola smiles. "You got a family now. That's good."

He swallows and nods. "Yeah, she gets off at three," he explains. "We'll start our laundry and then we can have a chat."

Flynn holds up James Ewan so he can put the money in the machine.

"It makes sense," Frederick argues, shifting into third gear. It is July and they are on their way to the beach after James Ewan's birthday lunch at the park.

"Yes, but you know I'm saving money to go to California," Hannah reminds him.

Frederick grips the wheel and drives faster. She touches him but he won't look at her. "Goddamnit, Hannah," he says softly. "I'm tired of living in rented rooms. I've been living in rented damn rooms my whole life."

"I'm sorry, sweetheart." She puts her hand on his arm again and leaves it there.

"Then you'll do it."

"I didn't say that. I like living at Mrs. Pulham's. This has been a good time for me, a happy time. But it's been my dream to go to California. You know that. I want to start my life again. I want to choose what happens. I want to do it right."

"You said you were happy."

"I am, but that doesn't mean I'm not going to make plans for my life. I never liked Maine much. It was my husband wanted to come here."

"I don't want to hear about it."

Hannah watches him. Paris sits between them, panting and looking out the windshield. "You know I'm saving to go to California. If I get an apartment with you my money won't build up as fast."

"I'll pay for the damn thing!"

"I don't want you doing that."

"I don't mind. At all."

"I do. I'm not going to live that way again." She is sounding angry now. She waits, watching out the window. Then she turns to him again. "Look, I know Mrs. Pulham's is provisional. But I like it. It's just what I need now."

"What do you mean, 'provisional'?"

"Provisional is something that's just for now, for the meantime."

"That's what I am for you. Provisional," he says. "Your provisional sweetheart." He spits out the word bitterly.

"I'm hoping you'll want to come to California with us," Hannah tells him.

"First I've heard of it," he says after a moment.

"I hope you'll think about it. I hope you'll come. Fred, in California it's never cold."

He stands on the sand in his dungarees while Hannah and James Ewan and Paris run into the sea.

"I want to leave before the weather starts getting cold," Hannah says.

"You going to thumb?" he asks, his voice cold. He's lying on the spread with his hands folded under the back of his neck. She is sitting at his feet, one leg curved under her.

"I bought a car today." He doesn't answer, but she feels him stiffen on the bed; then he draws himself up into a sitting position.

"You bought yourself a car," he says flatly. "How big a piece of junk you get yourself?"

"I had a garage check it out before I bought it." She leans toward him, putting her hand on his foot. "I know you're the best mechanic in the world, but I also know how you feel about this so I thought I shouldn't ask you."

He's looking past her and she straightens, her hand sliding off him. He doesn't say anything and what they hear in the silence is Georgianna Gregoire's radio playing gospel music, and her voice singing high just ahead of it. "I don't want to leave you," Hannah says. "But I am determined for me and James Ewan to go to California and start a new life there."

"What kind of car you buy?"

"Haven't you ever had a dream for your life?"

He looks at her, softly for a moment, and then his eyes harden. "Let's get the hell out of here. It's my damn day off. Let's do something, for Christ's sake."

"Have you thought about coming with us?"

"I got the feeling it was something you planned on doing alone. Your 'dream' for you and the boy."

"I know it's scary. I'm scared, but I want to take the chance."

"I'm not scared."

"Do you want to come with us? Do you want to *be* with us?"

"I've told you how I feel."

"No, you haven't. But I guess that's one kind of answer." She stands up. "Yeah, let's go out. I'll just ask Mrs. Pulham to keep a listen for James Ewan." She turns at the threshold. "Fred, they don't have winter out there."

He puts his cigarettes in his pocket. "California is for crazy people," he says harshly.

Hannah smiles. "We're pretty crazy," she teases. "We'll fit right in."

"Can I stay with you tonight?" she asks him when they get back. But lying beside him on the narrow bed where turning means untangling from his limbs, Hannah feels like someone bereaved. His hard back is to her and his breathing is deep and slow; his hand is thrown across the pillow so his fingertips rest against the wall. She lies still and listens to him and thinks how he never will come with her after all. She is awake for the dawn that shows frailly in his meager room and she rises and goes down the hall, where she is greeted by the long thumping of Paris' tail and the snores of James Ewan.

* * *

Hannah's car is a 1969 gray Rambler. She loads it up and leaves after breakfast. Frederick stands on the quiet street and watches them go. Inside he is feeling as if he is breaking apart and will die.

"I got to find somebody who's lost," he tells Kirby that afternoon. He is standing in the door of a phone booth with the toe of his boot holding it open. "I'll be back. I just got to find them."

"I can't hold this job for you. I need a man on here. A dependable man! Jesus, Hewitt!"

"I got to go. I'm sorry."

"You got somebody lost you call the police," Kirby tells him, almost shouts into the phone, but Frederick is hanging up and leaving the booth before Kirby gets his advice out of his mouth.

His second day and he's in Virginia. Virginia doesn't mean much to him but it's somewhere closer to California than Maine is. His truck is running well. He's watching the side of the road for her Rambler. He stops beneath a tall wooden Texaco sign, the winged horse faded to rose, in a place called Ashland where the fall is coming sedately in yellow with none of the passion of autumn in stony New England.

"What can I do for you, sir?" the man asks him. He tips his head like an alert, listening bird: a thin, blond man with a worn neck, a soft green hat on his head.

"Would you fill it," Frederick says, and he gets out and walks stiffly to his hood and opens it, pulls his handkerchief out of his back pocket and wraps it around his hand before he loosens the radiator cap.

"Clean your windshield?" the man asks him. The gas pump whirs softly.

"Thanks, that'd be a help."

"You come a long way," the man says. "I never been to Maine."

"I have to get to California."

"Whew," the man whistles as the pump clicks off. "Then you got a long way to go yet."

Frederick steps toward him. "You sell maps?"

His office smells like old wood, oil and grease. He spreads the map over the worn image on the card table. "Most folks take what they call the southern route," he says. Frederick nods; yes, she called it that. The man pushes his green hat up high on his head and places his penpoint carefully on Ashland.

It's dusk, a red, red dusk, when Frederick arrives in Stamps, Arkansas. He's looking for a place where he can get something to eat cheap. He pulls into "Marilyn's Roadside Diner and Gifts." Marilyn's is a small wooden building crammed against the side of a cliff that rises to nowhere. He sits on a yellow stool at a low counter and looks at the menu, which is such a frail, faded page that he makes a rip in it when he picks it up. A woman wearing a flowered apron sets a glass of water in front of him. "Evening," she says. He can feel her looking him over. "You're welcome to wash up in the bathroom," she tells him.

Food rises high on his plate, and though he is tired through to his bones he picks up the fork quickly; Marilyn keeps his coffee cup full.

He figures to press on to the Texas border before he'll let himself pull the truck off the road and sleep, but on the edge of Stamps he sees the Rambler. It's parked in front of a low, whitish building called the Highway Hotel. He is past before he realizes what he's seen and he backs up while the horn of a semi blasts at him and his hands tremble on the wheel. The car is just parked there in front of one of the doors, no flat tire, nothing. He stares at it. The lights of the Highway Hotel are lit although it is not yet true dark. Insects shimmer around their yellow glow. Stringy red letters, "Va ancy," flash like a carnival. The Rambler is parked in front of the second door in a line of doors, and it sits low. It is so loaded all she can be seeing in the rearview mirror is her belongings. He backs the truck until it's opposite the ninth and last door. His heart is banging about his chest as if it got worked loose. He shuts off the motor. He watches and imagines her sitting back against a pillow looking at a tiny TV screen, James Ewan sound asleep beside her, his knees curled up, the big dog lying on the linoleum floor panting with this sealess, southern heat. The night draws down: grey, then purple, then soft black; the insects batter at the light bulbs, small shadows against the ash-colored building. Cars, trucks drone and rattle and rumble on the lean highway. The biggest ones, heaving by, shake his truck. Warm air, smelling like dust and gasoline, and faintly of manure, sifts through his windows. He takes the key out of the ignition and quietly opens the door. His boots crunch on gravel.

Just as he draws abreast of the car the white door to number 2 jerks open and a short, skinny woman comes out. She spits in the gravel and then unlocks the passenger door of the Rambler. She lifts out a large teddy bear. She shuts the door hard and turns. "Won't go to sleep without Bear-Bear," she tells Frederick.

He stares at her, at the bear she's slapped under her arm. Watching her scuff back into number 2, he thinks he's going to vomit. Her hair was so pale it looked white in the Highway Hotel's neon, her voice was exotically southern. He hunkers down and squints at the license plate on the low rear end of the Rambler. Behind him three semis bang by on the highway; the stench of their exhaust and the hot rubber smell of their tires wrap around his crouching figure like fire around air.

Amarillo is a sunken city, loud, garish, and angry. The dry plain above it smells like death. In the camping area run by an old couple from Wisconsin cars sit on the flat earth looking as worn and abandoned as junks; plastic tents gleam like survey markers raised over rubble. Frederick draws the truck up just beyond the boundary of the camp and sees, he is almost sure, James Ewan swinging on a metal swing set and pushed by a big girl in flowered pants. He steps forward, squinting his eyes to watch that child flash back and forth, his toes pointed toward the sky, his hair hanging toward the earth as he rises through the still, shimmering air of the evening. Frederick goes closer until he is pressed against the two-strand wire fence. The tumbling sun sends burning shards of light through tents and between tires, hard into the weary earth, causes Frederick to shade his eyes and struggle to keep in view that small boy swinging in the hot light who is, he does believe, James Ewan. James Ewan, or the image of the child his will sent forth through his eye until he could see no other. He watches and watches, trying to be sure of this child who climbs the sky. But it may be that the whole world is gone from him and he is tangled in his own brain like a crazy man.

Later he sits on the truck bed, his legs hanging over the open tailgate, and eats the McDonald's food he bought on his way up out of Amarillo where, from the drive-in porte-cochere, he could watch for the grey Rambler. He listens to people rattling their tin dinnerware and smells meat charring, hears voices, some laughter, car doors banging. He crumples the red cartons into the white bag and lights a Camel. A breeze comes up with the night and flutters around him like a flock of finches. It rustles at his clothing and soothes his hot, dirty skin. He stubs the cigarette out and yawns widely and the headache, which began with the Texas border and is like a band of steel through the middle of his skull, eases slightly. He half leans against the side of the truck bed, then slides off it to relieve himself beside the tire, his water hissing against the dry earth, the warm smell of it rising to him, the night dark and growing cooler around him, the odor of death that seeps across Amarillo stirred by the night wind and brought against his face in irregular waves so that he coughs and spits and, coughing again, stumbles to the wide door of his cab and opens it.

The dawn is early, blood-red and still. The sun comes across the empty earth like a thrown mallet, hurtling over Amarillo as if it were a dull stone. Frederick struggles into a sitting position and focuses out the window. A short woman is stepping from a bright green tent beyond the Rambler. Inside the car it is quiet and he imagines Hannah curved into the front seat with one bare foot set against the door and James Ewan rocked in her round arms. He turns the key and backs down the road and onto the highway. He heads in the same direction the sun pursues, the day around him filling with glare thrown up from the hard, dry earth. He knows the route, how she will come—the man in Ashland marked truly with his red pen—and he hopes to find a gas station before the city limits so he can buy some oil, ask leave to use their bathroom to wash his skin, clean his teeth.

In Albuquerque he rents a seven-dollar room in the O'Leary Tavern. At eight o'clock, when everyone else is downstairs, he takes a bath in a tub so small his legs have to hang outside of it. He washes out his clothes and changes to his other set and walks out into the strange black night. He makes his way several blocks and stands in front of a yellow adobe hotel. It's the kind of place she'd stay in, quiet-looking, where they serve breakfast, but he doesn't see a Rambler from anywhere on the streets surrounding it. He goes back to his room and lies flat on the thin, smelly mattress and stares at the ceiling until he sleeps. Wakened past two by the man who stumbles into the next bed, he lies with his head aching and thinks of them in the yellow hotel: Hannah in her white nightgown with her legs careless, her tumbled hair; James Ewan curled neat as a puppy, his lips soft about his thumb.

He stands in the early dawn under the tall sky and watches the yellow hotel. The mountains hold back the sun, and when it comes it is with the suddenness of an alighting hawk. The tilting city wakes. The door of the yellow hotel opens and a cat comes out on the porch. She walks with delicate steps. A small tortoiseshell cat, she moves down the flattened sidewalk away from Frederick with her tail held straight in the air.

He goes to Flagstaff, but there are no grey Ramblers pulled off the road, no flat tires, no boiling-over radiators. He drives in the pathway of the long red sun, his dark glasses on his tired face, the headache settled deep in his skull, a dullness like slow-starting pain burying itself in his chest. He goes on, on to Los Angeles, where he drives down freeways that he can't get off until he decides that this is no place that Hannah would ever be and he finally takes an exit to the north.

THE CIRCUS PEOPLE

22 Logan Pembroke does not think about a thing, forgets it totally, if it is not in his life at the present moment, affecting him like a knife point or a plate of cake. When he leaves a thing, it's gone, it might as well be dead. He does not think about his time in the navy although he carries it on his back, or the people he knew then, or the things he did. He doesn't think about Frederick Hewitt now that he is gone, although in his loneliness Logan had wanted his company when seeing him was possible. He doesn't think about his parents or of himself when he was a sad and angry child; he does not think about his brother, Ronnie. But Ronnie thinks about him, and he comes back one day with his new family to visit Logan and perhaps make adjustments on the Logan who lives inside his head.

It is a Monday morning in May and they arrive quite suddenly and in two vehicles: the black Ford truck with the overlarge plywood camper hulking above the bed, and the Volkswagen bus painted yellow. They pull in close to the garage and get out. This takes a while. Betty Pembroke is driving the Ford. She descends slowly, stomping down on her long legs in the heavy way she does everything. She's got her little dog, Wade, tucked under her arm. Her teenage daughter, Midge, almost as tall as Betty, slides past the wheel and gets down after her.

Logan is watching out the kitchen window. "What the hell!" he says, and starts for the door. He doesn't see Ronnie climbing down out of the Ford. All of the doors on the Volkswagen open and from it emerge the entire Dooley family plus Blind Edgar Moss. It's all three generations of Dooleys, everyone, and they are small people; Edgar Moss drives. The seats in back have been removed and all the Dooleys ride there on child-sized green and white lawn chairs: Grandmother Dooley first, then the two mothers, then the Dooley fathers and the children, while the babies are in little baskets in the center of the circling green and white chairs. Only Francine Dooley rides up front, elevated by a green boat cushion and holding her cat, Carleton LeRoy Dooley, who weighs seventeen pounds and jumps through a red, white, and blue hoop when Francine asks him to.

Logan's hanging off his back porch gaping at them. "Krista!" he yells. "We got a circus here! A whole circus took a wrong turn!" And then louder, "My God, it's Ronnie! Ronnie raised up from the dead!"

"I do remember you, Ronnie," Krista says when they are all in her kitchen. "Of course I do. It's just that it's been . . . well, years." Krista feels for the first time in her life clumsy and oversized: none of the Dooleys is as big as she is. They patter around her kitchen as soft and as supple as cats. When Francine sits on a chair the furry form of Carleton LeRoy hides her except for her feet and their little purple slippers with silver beading.

"Is that a cat or some other kind of a thing?" Logan asks her, standing back a distance.

"Carleton is a coon cat," Francine says, "and he is the very best cat in all the world." Her hand comes out and strokes his spine. Francine has a high, musical voice and her words emerge with great delicacy, like individual flowers chosen for a bouquet. Carleton purrs very loudly.

But Logan presses closer. "Looks too big to be in a house," he says. He nudges Krista because he wants her to do something about it. Francine settles behind his fur and only her fingers show, stroking and stroking. Lila is staring from her highchair, enchanted. Her hands reach and reach, fingers moving like Francine's.

"I'll make coffee," Krista says, stepping away from Logan. "Do you all like coffee? I got Lipton's, too." For a crazy moment she thinks of Harmony's tea set with the tiny pink cups that Viola gave her for Christmas. She gazes at the row of heart-shaped faces, the curly black hair. "I got juice for the children," she tells their mothers.

They stay to lunch, bringing forth from the yellow Volkswagen and the Ford camper sandwiches and hard-boiled eggs, juice in thermoses, grapes and oatmeal cookies. They move in a line, Edgar Moss carrying the red cooler, and they take their provisions to the backyard and eat in the sun at the picnic table. Afterward the Dooleys curl up in piles like puppies under the pines and nap. Edgar Moss stretches out like a stripped log. Ronnie and Betty stay on at the table with Logan and Krista. Midge is there too, stringing wooden beads into a necklace.

"I wanted to meet you," Betty tells them. "We're on our way to Canada for a whole season, but I told Ronnie, 'It's time I met your brother.' I've heard about you," she says to Logan, but her face isn't giving anything away. Ronnie sits beside her, his cheek pressed against her bicep.

Logan looks right back. Betty has a broad face and there are broad spaces between her teeth. She has a lot of reddish hair piled up on top of her big head. Logan is both fascinated and repelled. He can't imagine Ronnie with this giant of a woman. "I used to be in a carnival," he tells her.

"Oh, and what was your talent?"

"Parting people from their money," Logan answers, laughing loudly.

"And what did you give them for it?" Betty wants to know.

Ronnie leans around her. He's watching Logan with his mouth a little bit open. Logan laughs again. "I gave 'em a real screwing," he tells Betty Pembroke.

"Betty is in charge of the merry-go-round horses," Ronnie interrupts proudly. "And she reads the cards too." He nods gravely, his chin rubbing against her arm; then he leans toward Logan. "Ma died in December," he tells him, and sighs as if he's finally put down his load.

Logan has to concentrate hard to conjure up his mother and to remember the last time he saw her: in the hospital; she had come to him in the hospital and he hadn't known her, had thought she was her own mother and not his, had come to him there when what he'd really wanted was his father.

"She was the sweetest soul," Betty says into his face. "She made the popcorn."

"I called her Gram," says Midge Masterson, looking up from her beads.

Her mother smiles fondly down on her. Midge is leaning against Betty's other bicep. "We buried her in Florida," Betty tells them. "Linette loved the sun and the warmth."

"There wasn't time to call you," Ronnie says.

Logan shrugs.

"She went quick. She wasn't complaining. She was ready." Betty sighs and pats her daughter. "I sure miss her though." Ronnie nods and his chin makes a little dimple in her sturdy flesh.

Perley and Harmony can't believe it when they get off the school bus. They never knew they had an uncle Ronnie, an aunt Betty, a cousin by marriage named Midge. And all these Dooleys and the little trick dog, the cat who weighs seventeen pounds.

There are about six Dooley children and two babies. Other than the babies it's hard to tell their ages. At first Perley and Harmony are afraid of hurting them, but the Dooleys are acrobats. Following the oldest brother, Merle, they fly into space, do somersaults down the sides of the sandpit. At the bottom they form pyramids, balancing each other on their shoulders, the littlest ones at the top. They tumble and stand on their heads, patiently showing Perley and Harmony how to do it. They juggle little stones and do magic tricks; they can climb trees as quickly as squirrels do; they seem to have a language of their own. They are delightful companions, highly skilled but they do not brag.

While the children are playing the two mothers are in Krista's kitchen making a barley soup, standing on stools to stir with their wooden spoons. Grandmother Dooley sits to make a green salad; there is fruit salad, bread in round loaves. Lila watches them, and the Dooley mothers feed her little pieces of what they are making: a bit of tomato, the thinnest slice of cucumber, part of an orange section. They pat her round cheeks and say how beautiful she is.

"You have such a nice big family," Krista says. "I think you're so lucky to be living all together."

"We married brothers," they explain.

"Samuel is a genius with machinery," the smaller one says. "He keeps everything ticking tip-top."

"My Maurice gets shot out of the cannon," the wall-eyed one tells her, "and he does the wire-walking."

"We ride the ponies," they say almost in unison.

"Ponies!" Krista exclaims, clapping her hands with delight.

"They're beautiful, with silver manes that Edgar Moss shampoos with camomile," the small one tells her.

"The ponies have been sent on ahead and Edgar is pining for them," the wall-eyed one explains. "He used to be married to Francine's twin sister, Claudine, but she was young and light-headed and she eloped from Edgar with the man who ran the rocket ride."

"Young people don't know enough," Grandmother Dooley says.

"We're just hoping and praying she comes home safely," the wall-eyed mother says in a low voice while her hands are buttering bread. "We're leaving messages at all our stops sending her on to us."

They move quietly out of the kitchen, carrying food and plates, another low, long line. One husband helps the grandmother down the steps of the back porch, the other carries two babies. The evening air is soft, the sky is pink, they can hear peepers calling from the reeds around the pond way down in the sandpit. Logan is inside frying chicken and drinking beer. Still, he keeps going to the window to look at them. "Can you beat that!" he demands, laughing and turning to Perley. "Can you beat it!"

"They can do *everything*, Dad," Perley tells him, his eyes wide.

"Oh yeah," Logan says. "They can't stand five feet high!" He laughs again and prods his meat with the long fork.

The Dooley children come down from the pine trees and line up with their bowls. One of the mothers ladles out soup, one serves them bread and salad. Logan comes out on the porch with his plate. Betty Pembroke shifts her tiny dog to her other armpit and fills Ronnie's bowl with soup. She sets it in front of him firmly. "Eat some bread," she tells him, "but watch the butter." She turns to look up at the porch where Logan is. "You have trouble with cholesterol?" she calls to him.

"No. And they've tested me for everything." He frowns at his sister-in-law, who sitting down or standing is bigger than he is.

Betty smiles and gives him a wave. "Come and join us!" she booms.

Krista gives Lila a bone to suck on and brings a chair up near Betty. The Dooley children file past and sit down on a blanket, balancing bowls on their folded thighs, conversing softly among themselves. Nearby one of the fathers is feeding the smallest baby with a silver spoon. He talks to it softly. "Ooohhh, you're beautiful," Krista hears him say. She looks at his neat little mustache and at the perfect baby resting in the short curve of his arm. Lila bounces hard in her lap, trying to get down so she can make her way to Francine and Carleton LeRoy at the other end of the picnic table. "Mum! Mum!" she shrieks.

Krista gets a firm grip on her waist and, turning to Betty, asks, "How did you and Ronnie meet?"

"It was Ma," Ronnie tells her, leaning around Betty. "I was taking her to the hospital for her appointment. And she fell down on the ice."

"It was January 1974, and I come up to Portland from our winter quarters in Florida on account of my uncle Luther was in the hospital dying there," Betty explains.

"Betty picked her up," Ronnie says proudly.

"She didn't weigh any more than Francine's cat," Betty demurs, speaking gently.

"She carried her to the clinic where we was going when it happened. For her arthritis she was going, Logan," he says loudly. Logan can hear him. He's come down into the yard and stands holding his plate in two hands. He can hear them all. He thinks about his mother's hands, how they were thick and twisted and always dropping things.

"Nothing was broken," says Betty, "even where she hit so hard." Logan watches her, her red hair and her big breasts.

"She hurt awful though," Ronnie insists.

"But didn't the Florida sun do her good," Francine says carefully from down the table.

"Ma loved Florida."

"I think she died happy to be there," Betty says.

They are gone in the morning before anyone in the household is up or even hears them driving away. No trace, no little hats left behind, no slippers. "Jesus," Logan says, looking out the window at the driveway empty of everything save his Chevrolet. "Did I dream Dooleys or were they here?"

Krista laughs. "They were here all right. I wish they'd waited to say good-bye." She shifts Lila higher on her hip. "I never thought we'd see Ronnie again, and here he is living with all those good people."

"A bunch of freaks!" Logan says, and laughs. "But come to think of it, Ronnie was always hanging around with freaks."

"They're good people," Krista argues. "And I'm happy for Ronnie." Lila is tipping out of her arms, stretching to look through the window as her father is doing, watching the driveway forsaken of Dooley vehicles.

"Where *are* they?" Perley demands when he gets up and finds them gone.

"Oh, Mum, I was going to take Merry to school with me," Harmony wails.

"Dools!" Lila laments, leaning farther back in her mother's arms and raising her hands toward the ceiling.

Across the nation in San Francisco, California, Frederick Hewitt is living in a rooming house and working for a janitorial service that caters to hospitals. The money is good, much better than in Maine, but he spends a lot of time in bars, so it leaves him. In the hospitals he cleans great kettles and ovens, countertops long as bowling alleys. In the bars he drinks beer and whiskey, socializes a bit with the other men. He stays through two snowless winters, through summers of no heat; in the fall the bay waters tense in a steady chop and the wind wails in the dry hills. He does not find Hannah Niles, whose name is in no phone book, whose warm shade visits him in his sleep, whose departure from his life is something he should never have let happen.

In February, toward the end of the month he's walking along Mississippi Street, a slight, dark-haired man who lately grew a mustache, long and curving down his face like a bandit's. It is his night off and he's thinking about getting himself a pizza for his supper and then going to a bar he knows where the beer is cheap and they have live music. He pauses to stamp out his cigarette and, glancing up, sees across the street a tall black man with a big black dog whose skull is as broad as a bull's. Wheeling on the toe of his boot, he watches them, then starts across the street, moving faster and faster until he has nearly caught them and can call, "Paris! Here, Paris!"

The man and the dog stop and turn toward him.

"Paris!" he cries again.

The man tips back his broad-brimmed hat and looks at Frederick. "Man," he says, "this is *San Francisco*. Shit," he adds softly, and the dog sits down on the sidewalk. "You okay, man? You okay?" he asks.

"I'm okay," Frederick says. He clears his throat and stands up straight. "I'm okay."

"You sure?"

He nods and the tall man salutes him and begins to drift away, the dog rising to follow. Frederick turns and bolts back across the street. He runs. He's breathing hard when he starts up the second flight to his room. There isn't much to pack: his toilet articles, a few clothes, a small radio, towels. A black plastic garbage bag takes it easily. He lies on his back in the street and changes the oil in his truck. On the door of his room he tapes up some words written on a torn piece of grocery bag: "I'm gone now."

It's night when he leaves the city and climbs into the mountains. Darkness drops around him; the world is alien, its strangeness discovered by the narrow reach of his headlights. The early hours find him in the desert, empty and silent as a moon. Just before dawn a coyote passes in his lights: tawny, lithe, and hungry, the slanting eyes, the long patient face; the creature looks directly into Frederick's eyes before disappearing like wind across the grey earth.

It is late. The news will soon be on. Mrs. Pulham dozes as she lies low on the pillows and watches the screen, her blue-rimmed glasses overturned on her chest, her small feet lifting the lavender spread in two small points partway down the big bed. The room is dark except for the TV's bluish, filmy light. When he looks through the window Frederick can see her, a shape like a little dried-up mummy. He steps back quickly and knocks on the door, shifts his shoulders and waits. Up the street a steady March wind blows, smelling of the winter still. He knocks once again. She thrashes and straightens in the bed, fumbles to put her glasses on her face.

She pushes the switch for the hall light and clunks her blue rims against the glass in the door. She stares and stares, then jerks the door open slightly, her small foot poised behind it. "Is that really you?" she whispers in a loud and cracking voice.

He shrugs his shoulders. Who else can he be? She peers up into his face, squints to see how it's thinner, how his beard is half grown around the long mustache. She sighs and, dropping her hand from the door, says with satisfaction, "You look like the wrath of God."

He smiles at her.

"Did you just land in town, or what?"

"Just landed," he tells her softly, his eyes glittery and tired.

He follows her into the dining room, glancing up the long stairway where it is dim and quiet. She pushes a pile of socks and underwear toward the center of the table, pulls out a chair, and sits, drawing her robe tightly around her and folding her arms. "Last time I set eyes on you, you was tearing out of here like a crazy man, chasing that woman, that nurse and her little boy."

He nods. "I've been traveling."

She sits up straight, narrows her eyes behind the glasses. "You catch 'em?"

He shakes his head, lifts his hands and rubs his eyes with the tips of his fingers. He can hear the news mumbling anxiously from the front room. He lets his hands fall into his lap. "How you been?" he asks. "How's your girl?"

"We been doin' okay 'cept Mrs. Gregoire's up to the hospital again and you won't know Tamara. Thinks she's all grown up. Taking a secretarial course, got a boyfriend, says she's gonna get married."

He leans back in the chair. "Guess I have been gone awhile."

"These girls don't wait for nothin' today," she tells him, shaking her head so the mole on her upper lip vibrates. "Jump into marriage quicker than they change their hairdo." She pushes out her chin, watches him. "In my day we was a bit more cautious. Marriage ain't no bed of roses, I don't care what they say. More like thorns. No, no," she says. "More like them burr bushes, you know? The ones that hang on to you and won't let go. Come out in little pieces. You got to pick and pick, you can't get rid of the whole damn thing at one pull."

Frederick blinks at her.

She gives a laugh that sounds like a rooster beginning to crow. "Course you ain't gettin' married," she says. *"I* know that. You're one of the *real* cautious ones, hang back till the very last minute when you get worried about dying alone." She leans forward over a pile of sheets and hisses, "As if marriage makes any difference." She straightens and waves her hand with disgust. "She won't listen to me, not to one blessed word, so I guess she can just go on ahead and find out for herself." She nods at him with satisfaction and her face softens for a moment and she says, "She will be a pretty bride though." Then she snorts and slaps her hand on the table: "I guess! Bought herself a weddin' dress worth a month's rent!" She sits back sighing, and gazes at him over the sheets. "Got a Mr. Batchelder in your old room. Quiet gentleman, used to work at photographing. Got a room on the third floor though. Front. Mr. Howle left us sudden last Monday morning."

"Thanks. That'll be fine." He gets his wallet out of his back pocket. "I expect you've gone up some."

"Not as much as I should," Mrs. Pulham says.

JOSEPH

23 Today Perley Pembroke is eleven years old and the red-winged blackbirds have returned to Maine. They call and call with their creaky voices down in the maples by the road; they rush through the grey sky in a spade-shaped band, flap down into the naked limbs of trees. When Perley lifts the plastic bamboo curtain and looks out the picture window he can barely see them and the road is all gone, because the world this morning is wrapped in a tender sea of fog. Freed from the earth's hold, the glistening trees seem to be slowly moving, the birds are dark as soaked leaves. Beyond the vanished road the long line of field drifts in and out of the fallen sky. Perley runs to the kitchen and opens the back door but the pines are hidden, the garage is gone.

"Happy birthday, Perley!" His mother hugs him and kisses the top of his head. "Happy birthday! Happy birthday! You're growing tall, Perley, you're getting awful big!"

"Mum, it's all fog," he tells her. She runs to the window to look, her bathrobe swinging around her ankles, her small feet bare. She turns to smile at him—how happy she looks today, how light.

"Ooh, it is," she says. "Fog comes with the spring, Perley. It's the south wind bringing the warmth to us. We'll have the new grass and soon the cold will be like a dream we can't even remember."

By midmorning the fog is gone; the sun came through suddenly like a lifted lamp and took it. The birds fling through the sky, down into the soggy field where the stubble of last year's corn shows pale as willow bark. Their voices ceaseless, they rise up again, whirling in one motion quick as a school of fish. Perley is riding his new bicycle down the road, pedaling as hard as he can, strong as any young creature. His father bought him this bicycle for his birthday. While Perley was eating his breakfast Logan went down to the Western Auto where they were keeping it and put it in the trunk of his car and brought it home. "Go out, go out," his mother urged him. And there it was, shiny green, aslant on its kickstand in front of the garage, the ribbon she had tied to the handlebars fluttering. His father, studying under the raised hood of his car, heard Perley cry out, the sound of his feet as he ran. Logan was feeling both powerful and irritated, which is what giving does to him, for no one is ever grateful enough. He half turned his face from the car when Perley came close, wheeling the bike.

"It's what I wanted most," Perley said.

"That's good, Perley."

"Thanks, Dad."

"It's no cheap model, you know," Logan told him, narrowing his eyes and looking hard at the gift. "You better treat it right. Don't leave it out in the damn rain."

So now Perley is riding this bicycle, and with all of him welded in the sweet work of it. How fast he goes: the wind leaps into his hair and down the sleeves of his jacket; the birds start before him, rising from the roadside grit, from the puddled earth.

His mother stands in the driveway, Lila large and scowling on her hip, and watches him. "Oh, Logan," she says, turning so the hair blows across her face. "Perley's been wanting that bike so bad. I was bursting to tell him, 'Well, your dad got you one.' " She comes closer and touches his shoulder. Lila, swinging her feet, kicks the fender of his car.

Logan lifts his face and looks between the raised hood and the fender. He watches Perley for a minute. He's flying up the hill. "Perley!" Harmony shouts, jumping up and down in the driveway. Perley disappears over the crest.

"Well, he ain't done nothing too bad this year," Logan says before staring down at his carburetor.

"Perley!" Harmony runs halfway to the road. She can see him again. He's going flat out on the long stretch that climbs slowly to the railroad bridge. "Perley!"

"He'll be back, he'll be back, honey," Krista calls. "He's just trying out his bike. He's just having a *great* time!" she exults, whirling around with the sturdy child in her arms.

"Oooooohhhhhhhhh!" Lila cries like a long siren.

It's almost nine that night when Frederick Hewitt arrives with Perley's present. Perley's watching TV, sitting on the floor with his back against the couch, Harmony slumped against him. Logan is out, driving Viola and Flynn home. Krista is finishing up the dishes; she hears feet on the back porch, thinks how it can't be Logan back already.

Frederick smiles and steps into the kitchen. He is holding a box to his hip. "How are you?" he says.

"Freddie, it's you!" she cries, half waving her dish towel at him. She doesn't take the box. "I thought we'd never see you again," she tells him almost angrily. "I thought you were gone and not coming back this time. Mum said, 'No, he'll be back.' But I didn't believe her. I thought you'd been gone too long this time." Now she steps forward and hugs him. "I'm awful glad to see you," she says, "but I sure wish you'd stay put!" She stands back and smiles at him. Freddie looks good. He's getting real handsome now. He is one of those men who get handsome when all their being young is gone.

"I brought this for Perley," he tells her, holding out the box that cans of oil came in. "It is his birthday, ain't it?"

"Yes. How good you are to remember Perley." She takes it carefully and looks inside. "Oh my Lord, Freddie!" she cries.

The puppy is just waking up. He is very small and brown, all ears and belly. Krista puts the box on the table and lifts him out, brings him close to her face. "He's beautiful, Freddie. Oh, he smells so good!" She laughs and holds the puppy close. "Perley!' she calls, turning her head. "Perley! Come see who's here! Who's here and brought you a present for your birthday!"

Frederick folds his arms across his chest and watches her. She still looks like a girl, a tired girl, pretty despite her fatigue, and possessing what to him is the dearest thing in the world, her familiarity.

Joseph soon outgrows his box. Perley gets him a bigger one, puts it beside his bed padded with two old towels his mother gave him. Joseph grows longer and leggier. As soon as he's able Joseph climbs up onto Perley's bed and sleeps there. Joseph moans low in his throat when Perley goes off to school. He has a houndlike song for when Perley comes home again. His mother says Joseph is the smartest puppy she has ever seen. Perley loves Joseph. He loves Joseph because he belongs to Perley, a part of himself he's proud of.

The spring is slow in coming, then arrives sudden and hot. Joseph is four months old. In the long evenings after supper Perley takes him down to the pond in the floor of the sandpit behind their house, where Joseph wades and splashes and brings back sticks. Perley has a rope he's using as a leash until he can get the real thing. On this evening his father is gone when they return from the sandpit. Perley dries the puppy's coat and feet before they go in. Perley gets a banana and goes into the living room, Joseph at his heels. His mother is on the couch looking at a magazine, Lila is playing with plastic blocks. "Joseph was swimming for a minute tonight," Perley tells his mother. "He really was over his head."

Krista smiles. "Don't rush him, Perley. He's a real young puppy still. You don't want to force him, might scare him off it for life."

"I don't force him. I say, 'Joseph, you want to swim in this water?' And if he wants to, he does it."

"Mine!" Lila says loudly, climbing up on the couch and reaching for Perley's banana.

"No, Lila, get your own." He goes down the hall with Joseph and shuts the door of his room. Lila jumps off the couch and hurries after them. "Mine!" she demands. "Mine!" But Perley has taken the doorknob off so she can't get in. She bangs on the door and hollers for a while before going back to the living room and standing in front of her mother, her face aggrieved.

Logan is not home this evening because he is driving around. He slows at lots and looks in dooryards, seeking red signs: "For Sale." He figures he needs a new car. He's got two hundred bucks in his pocket and the Chevrolet he's driving, which never will get another sticker. He stops briefly at several places, talks with men who lean against fenders with their arms folded across their chests, their hats pulled down against the setting sun—sons of bitches Logan won't even haggle with, wanting six hundred bucks for a crapbucket.

The sun has gone and it's the soft lilac light of evening when he pulls into a grassless backyard in Gray. The dog whose chain is tied to the corner of a fallen-down chicken house barks twice, then lies down so he's facing out across the field. This guy's got four cars: a Chrysler wagon, a Volkswagen bus, a Nova, and an Oldsmobile Toronado. Logan gets out of his car and starts circling slowly. His cane makes little pock marks in the dirt. He keeps away from the Toronado because that's the one he wants. He hears a screen door whack and then Billy Barrow comes around the corner of the house, pulling on a shirt. He has greased-back blond hair and a potbelly, a narrow face, narrow eyes, and a tight little mouth. "How ya doin'?" he asks Logan.

Logan nods, gestures with his cane. "I was driving by and saw the bus. Been lookin' for one."

Billy nods enthusiastically. "Just picked her up. She's got seventy thousand. Runs good."

"You wanna let me drive it?"

"Well, sure."

Logan drives the Nova, too. Billy Barrow rides beside him, his small red lips holding a Tareyton. "Christ, she got nothin' when I step on the gas," Logan complains.

"Six cylinders," Billy says, shrugging. "This is a lady's car. Low mileage. Don't burn gas. Dependable. Buy this car for your wife. This car ain't a speedy car, this car is a woman's car."

Logan puts on the lights, the high beams, the directionals, bangs on the horn, accelerates and slows, accelerates and slows. "Go for it!" Billy applauds, slapping his hand on the dashboard. "This car won't run away with you but this car can take it!"

They get back in the yard; lights have come on in the long, weathered house. "So how much you askin' for it?" Logan says.

"Gotta get six fifty," Billy tells him.

Logan nods; he revs the motor. "Well, you better wait till the right lady comes along," he scoffs. "I got to have a car with guts."

"That'd be the Toronado," Billy says softly. "She's got over ninety thousand, but the guy I bought it off gave her an engine job; she really moves out." Logan puts the keys to the Nova in Billy's hand. "Goes like a son of a bitch," Billy says, letting the keys settle gently in his palm. "What the hell, we might as well give her a spin." He opens the door. "You want a beer first? I'm gettin' awful thirsty driving around with you."

They drink their beer leaning against the Nova, facing the Toronado. Billy has switched on his outside light, and moths flutter around it; the TV is playing inside the house. The Toronado is black and blunt-shaped. "Got a teenager," Billy says, lifting his beer can, "wants that car so bad he'd offer me his sister if he had one. Comes by every week making promises. I can't eat promises I tell him. I just deal with cash." He turns his head enough to look at Logan. His skin is gray in the false light. He smiles. "Makes it simpler."

"You don't trade?"

"Oh sure, if I like the deal. Some guys want you to trade a car that's just about made it to crawl in here and die. Sure I'll trade on a decent car. I just don't want no paper and no promises." Billy pushes himself up off the Nova. He pulls the key to the Toronado out of his pocket and gives it to Logan. "Take her out while I get us another beer," he urges. "You'll see what I mean about guts."

Billy finishes the beer and has to go get himself a third before Logan returns. "Thought you wasn't coming back," he says, speaking slowly, his face puckered around the eyes.

Logan gets out of the Toronado. He has a pain in his stomach that's worked its way through and climbed up his spine he wants it so bad. "Took a wrong turn," he says, laughing. "Thought I was back here and I was at some other house. Almost went in and gave 'em your key." He laughs again and hands it to Billy, then turns and starts for his own car. He pauses. "She got a lot of miles," he says. "Almost what I got on my car that I'm trying to trade up from."

"Couldn't give you much on your car," Billy says. "It's about done. You must be burning a quart of oil every hundred miles. Smoke was hanging in the air twenty minutes after you got here."

Logan doesn't know how much oil he burns. He buys it by the case and dumps it in regularly. All he knows is he wants this Toronado. And he hates this little bastard who is insulting his car and trying to screw him. His hands are trembling. He leans back on the cane. "What you think you might give me on it?"

Billy pushes the beer at him. "Hope this ain't too hot. I've been holding it for you a long time."

Logan grabs it and takes a long drink. "What'll you give me?" he asks, lowering the half-empty can.

Billy lifts his arms, his own beer can shining in the sharp light.

"Couldn't sell it to no one. Just have to junk it. Get forty bucks if I'm lucky."

Logan doesn't say anything. He drinks the beer. He feels dizzy. This little bastard with the girl's mouth is dragging it out, teasing him. What he'd like to do is hang him out a third-story window by his ankles.

"I'd have to get five hundred. And your car," Billy says.

Logan frowns as if he's thinking hard, considering. "Well," he says, "I guess I can't do it. Not for a car with that kind of mileage, I don't care what kind of engine job he *says* he did on it." He looks at Billy, narrows his eyes. "Know a guy sell me a Malibu, seventy five thousand miles, for four hundred."

Billy shrugs.

Logan moves closer to his car. He balances on his cane and turns to look over his shoulder. "You better hope that teenager finds some blind man to buy his sister." Billy laughs. Logan gets into his car and turns the key. "See ya," he says, inclining his head through the unrolled window. He drops the empty can and steps down hard enough to churn up dirt and little stones in Billy Barrow's driveway.

Krista sees the lights and hurries to open the kitchen door. Moths come in while she waits for him to climb the stairs and cross the small porch. She's studying the way he's moving so she'll know what's going to happen next. "I've been worried about you," she says.

"Oh yeah." He looks straight at her and comes through the door. She has to back quickly out of his way. "You afraid your meal ticket ran out on you?" he demands, glaring at her. She moves around him and shuts the door. Four moths are circling the ceiling light. "I can't hear you," he mocks.

"I always worry when you don't come home."

"Like I said. You worry your meal ticket's gone and ain't coming back." He reaches out for her arm. "Don't you!" he says softly, bending to bring his face close to hers.

"I worry you might get hurt."

He looks at her, his face still inches from her own. "I'm riding around in a goddamn shitbox 'cause I got to spend all my money feeding you people," he says. "I even got to feed a goddamn dog.

That bastard Hewitt was quick enough to load me up with something else." He watches her, his face not quite so hard, a question forming on it. "He ain't brought you out no dog food. Has he?"

"Dog food?"

"Yeah. Dog food." He shakes her arm. "That dog is eating and shitting everywhere. Can't come in my own goddamn house without stepping in dog shit."

Krista looks at his feet and behind where he came in and there's nothing on the floor but linoleum.

"I told him to clean up after that dog or it was going."

"He does. He's awful good about it. You know he is."

"I don't know nothing about him and don't you tell me I do." His voice is getting loud. He's twisting his hand to make her arm more uncomfortable. "All I know is I got shit on my foot!"

Krista looks again. The floor is clean. He seizes her shoulders and launches his weight onto her so he can pick up his right foot. "There!" he shouts.

Krista stretches to look. The gray rubber sole is worn but unsoiled. "Well, sit down," she says, "and take off your shoe and I'll clean it for you."

He puts his foot onto the floor and stands hard on it. "You're always trying to protect him!" he says with disgust. Pushing on her shoulders, he turns and starts down the hall bellowing, "Perley!"

Perley was asleep until he heard his father yelling in the kitchen. He sits up straight. Joseph, who was lying with his chin on Perley's hip, sits up too. The feet stomping down the hall get close and then he's pushing on the door and then he's banging. "Where's the goddamn doorknob!"

"It's broke," his mother says. "It's broke. Just wait a minute."

Logan throws himself against the door. These are cheap hollow doors. He practically falls through it.

The door leans hard from its bottom hinge; Logan stands over the bed. "Get up!" he shouts. "There's dog shit out there. I told you to keep it clean or this dog was going!"

Perley's out of the bed; Joseph, behind him with his back feet on the pillow, is smelling Perley's fear. The hair on his spine stands up in crooked little waves. "I cleaned it," Perley protests. "I cleaned it after school and when I took him out last time before bed."

Logan lunges at him and threads his fingers in the V neck of

Perley's pajama top and lifts. "I got shit on my foot!" he yells into his face. He puts him down hard so the bedpost slams into Perley's ribs. "Get out there and clean it!" he screams, shoving him toward the door. Joseph barks short, sharp barks, his front feet dug into the edge of Perley's mattress.

"Logan, it's late. He needs to be in bed. We'll do it in the morning."

He shoves Perley hard into her. "Get the hell out of the way, you. He'll do it NOW!" He kicks Perley and they are all moving down the hall. The door to the girls' room opens. The puppy drops off the bed and slinks after them, making little, anxious sounds. The third time Logan kicks at Perley, Joseph leaps and grabs onto the ankle of the foot that's still on the floor. He braces himself. Logan turns, screeching for the pain of Joseph's narrow teeth.

Joseph pulls hard, tugging backward, growls vibrating his bones. Logan twists and seizes him by two legs, front and rear, and throws him.

The puppy hits hard on the splintered doorframe of Perley's room. He makes a thick, warm sound and one cry and he falls and lies there. In that moment before he starts yelping they all stop. Then Perley hurtles past his father. He kneels; his open hands lifted above Joseph don't quite touch him because Joseph is screaming now. Perley turns and looks for her and cries, "Mum!" Joseph shifts himself, weight on his elbows, hind legs extended. Perley puts his hand on his head and the puppy whimpers and then starts screaming again.

Krista stumbles past Logan and kneels.

"You better shut him up," Logan tells her.

"Let me see him," she urges. "Come on, Joseph, come here, boy." She hoists him into her lap. Joseph's tail that's always wagging hangs behind him like a string. He yelps and pants in harsh, quick breaths.

"You better shut him up, Krista!"

"What's wrong with him, Mum? What's wrong?"

"He'll be all right. He's just frightened. It's okay. Easy, Joseph."

"Shut him up!"

"You hurt him. You hurt Perley's puppy." Harmony stands in the hall in her nightgown. She's staring at her father, her jaw thrust out.

"Mum! Mum!" Lila calls from her bed.

"Harmony, you go back to your room," Krista says. "You hush Lila. It will be all right."

"Mum!" Lila shrieks.

"But he—"

"You want some?" Logan lurches toward Harmony with his arm raised and she ducks quickly back into her room and shuts the door.

Joseph screams sharply when Krista stands with him in her arms. "I'm going to put him in a blanket, keep him warm," she says to Perley. "You go get some water, son." The puppy is making long sounds almost like human sobbing.

"You better shut him up!"

Perley twists past him, and those words come down into his hair like fire. In the kitchen he hears more words. "He's hurt, Logan. You threw him hard."

"The little bastard was biting me. Look at my ankle!" Perley turns off the faucet. His hands lifting the bowl are trembling. "He's just fussing. I'm the one that's hurt! Look at my damn ankle."

"I think it's bad, Logan."

Perley feels as if the inside of him has opened up in some awful way.

"Christ, I'll have to get a tetanus shot!"

Perley can hear his mother murmuring to Joseph as he starts down the hall with the water.

"You shut him up! I'm going to bed."

Perley maneuvers past the broken door and holds the bowl out to his mother. The TV goes on loud in the bedroom. "You hold his head, son," Krista says softly.

Joseph's head fits in his hands just as it always has, but the expression in his eyes is different. His mother dips her fingers in the bowl and pats water onto Joseph's lips. He laps at her hand. "There, he took some," she said, and fills her palm. Joseph refuses it, and he's panting louder now. Perley wishes he could go to sleep where he stands or fall down dead on the floor and have this not be happening. He takes his hands slowly from the puppy and curls them into fists.

"Mum, what's wrong with Joseph?"

"We're taking care of him. Go to bed, Harmony."

"But what's wrong with him?" She stands at the foot of the bed staring, her face knotted up with tears.

"Nothing's wrong with him!" Perley screams. "Nothing is wrong with him!"

"Mum," Harmony protests.

"Shut up, alla you!"

"Go to bed, Harmony." Krista stands up and guides her to the door. "He needs to sleep so he'll feel better in the morning. I'll come check on you in a while. Go."

It is quiet now. All they can hear is the TV in the other room and the rapid hoarse sound of the puppy's breathing. Perley touches his paw. His pad feels hot and hard; his head is stretched forward and his eyes are almost closed. Perley sinks down on the floor so his cheek is pressing into the side of the mattress, so his eyes are level with Joseph's. He doesn't look at his mother. He's aware of her tucking the blanket more tightly around his puppy. People on the TV are laughing. Perley wishes he had some sort of special remote control so he could blow up that TV and everything in the room with it into tiny, tiny pieces that nobody could put together again ever.

When Krista comes in around two-thirty she can hear Joseph's breathing before she crosses the threshold: short, shallow breaths as if he can't or won't expand his lungs very much. The light from the hall shows him lying as he was, his chin on the edge of the mattress. Perley is slumped on the floor and she can hear him breathing too. The raspy, openmouthed sound tells her he's asleep. He looks uncomfortable but she does not want to awaken him. She slept a few hours on the couch, and, waking, she came in to check, hoping Joseph would lift his head and greet her. But he doesn't seem to know she's here. He looks very small, as if all the growth he gained in the last two months has left him. She turns and bends into the closet to get the afghan from the floor. She folds it carefully over Perley.

"Mum!" Perley whispers, tugging at her sleeve.

The new dawn has lightened the room. Perley smells sweaty and tired. "Mum! He's worse, Mum." His voice is scared and bitter.

They stand by the bed. Joseph hasn't moved. His breathing is shallower. At intervals he makes a long moaning sound. "We'll take him to the doctor, Perley. You wrap him in that blanket tight and carry him gentle."

"I'll put him in the wagon."

"No. I'm driving you in the car."

"You can't drive."

"Perley, get ready quick."

Logan is asleep on his back, his arms outflung. Krista gets the keys from his pants. She takes five dollars, too.

"Mum, how is Joseph?" Harmony stands in the doorway watching her.

"We're taking him to the doctor, honey." Without being quite aware of it, Krista puts her finger to her lips.

Krista carries Lila, wrapped up and sound asleep in a blanket. Perley carries Joseph. His arms are aching. He's trying to carry his puppy so lightly it won't hurt him and so carefully he won't fear to fall. It's a soft morning. There are birds, there is a sweet smell in the air.

The car grinds when she starts it. She has to sit on the very edge of the seat. If there were a clutch it would be hopeless. As it is her heart is thudding when she pulls the gear down until the arrow is pointing to R. They go in little jerks out of the garage and all the way down the drive. They pause at the end and then move in a rapid arc out into the road. Krista puzzles and puts it in D1. They go down the road in uneven little spurts, the rusted tailpipe scraping on the tar. She keeps the Chevy almost in the middle where it feels safest. The wheel is never quite still. She wobbles it back and forth to give herself the illusion of control. Lila sleeps in the back seat with her head in Harmony's lap. Harmony can see the top of Perley's head and she watches that. Some of his hair is all stuck down. She can hear Joseph. She tries not to make any noise herself. She tries not to cry. Mum is driving his car. He is going to kill them all when he finds out.

"Do you know where you're goin'?" Perley asks her once.

"I've been by it. I've seen the sign." Krista doesn't take her eyes from the road. "It ain't far, Perley. You keep him warm."

* * *

Dr. Herman opened this practice a year ago. He goes out to farm animals two days a week and sees pets at his office the other three and Saturday morning. He's in the barn talking to his horses and drinking a cup of coffee when the battered-looking Chevrolet turns into his long driveway and keeps coming. It stops on the outer curve of the circle. The motor quits and the driver's door is opened. Dr. Herman puts the mug in the wheelbarrow and leaves the barn. Only the police come this early, bringing him dead dogs found in the road if they have rabies tags, so the owner can be traced. This sure isn't the police. A small thin woman is getting out of the car. This is going to be something real bad.

"Good morning," he says, approaching her. If he had a hat on he'd be lifting it, he's that kind of man. She is standing by the open door. She looks like a woman brought by some kind of disaster, burned out of her home, or flooded out, everything she owned carried off by river water, fired to ash.

"It's our puppy hurt bad, Doctor," she says. "Can you help us? He's my son's," she adds in a softer voice, leaving her door open and walking around the front of the car so she can open the passenger door.

The child looks like her, like her face and as much of a refugee as she does. At first he thinks the dog in his arms is dead. "Let me take him," he says, looking into the child's eyes and lifting gently. "You come right in with me," he tells them.

When he lays him on the table and unwraps the blanket he knows there is nothing here but death he must hasten. But he gets out the stethoscope, he listens to the lungs, he gently feels the body and limbs. "What happened?" he asks. He takes the instrument from his ears and looks at them. A girl who must have been in the back seat is here, standing just behind the boy. Nobody answers him. They are all staring at the dog as if now that they have got him here they have done everything they can do. "Did a car hit him?" he asks.

The woman nods slowly. "An accident . . . didn't mean to," she whispers.

Dr. Herman bends to the puppy again. But there are no reflexes, his hind limbs are paralyzed, there are contusions, internal bleeding. "It didn't happen just now, did it?" he asks. He touches the hind feet again but there is no response.

The boy is staring at the dog. He doesn't look at anything else. Pressing closer, he sets his hand on one of the paws.

"Last night," the woman says finally. "We didn't know how bad it was. I shoulda brought him last night."

"It wouldn't have helped if you brought him last night. Don't think that it would. I'm sorry," he says. She still won't look at him, none of them will. "I'm sorry. But his back is broken. There's other damage."

"You could give him a cast," the boy says quickly. He's still staring at the dog. "I'll take care of him. You could put him in a cast," he repeats, his voice getting higher. "Like they do with people. Like they done with him," he says, turning his head slightly toward his mother.

"I would if I could," Dr. Herman says. "If it would do any good. But it's damage to the spinal cord. He can't move," he tells Perley, bending close to him, setting one hand carefully on the dog. "He won't ever get any better." The boy doesn't look at him, doesn't say anything; his hand clenches. "He's dying, son," the doctor says. "I don't think he's in pain anymore, but the kindest thing is for me to put him to sleep. I'm very sorry."

The little girl starts crying: slow, muffled sounds. "Do you want to leave him here?" he asks the woman. She doesn't answer. "Or bury him at home?" She still doesn't say anything. He starts to ask her again, when she steps closer to the boy and touches his arm.

"Perley, the doctor can't help Joseph. We got to leave him here. He's going to put him to sleep. It's gentle." She looks at the doctor. "It's gentle, ain't it?" she asks.

"Yes," he tells her. "He won't know anything but that he's going to sleep."

"It's gentle, Perley," she repeats. The little girl is sobbing. She steps behind her mother and presses her face into her. "Son, we got to go and leave him here."

"I had to put my old dog to sleep last month," Dr. Herman says, "and I buried him out in the orchard. I'll put your puppy out there with him if you want me to," he tells Perley. Perley's fingers are slowly stroking Joseph's paw.

"It's nice in an orchard, Perley," his mother says.

The room is quiet except for the little girl. Then Joseph growls. It's soft but he persists. "You don't want to make him wait, son," Dr.

Herman says. "You don't want to make it any harder on him. I know you don't."

Perley turns and runs through the door and out into the yard and the gravel of the driveway. He gets into the car and folds his body up so his knees are pressing into his eyes, and he wails.

"You did the right thing to come; I just wish I could have done more to help you," Dr. Herman tells the woman. He gathers Joseph up. "I'm sorry this happened."

She nods. She looks at him once. "Thank you, Doctor," she says, and pushing her hand into her pocket, she brings out the five dollars.

He shakes his head. "You don't owe me anything, ma'am. I'll go take care of this puppy now." And he steps through into the inner office with Joseph and closes the door behind them.

Harmony clings to her as they leave the building. The sun has come through so bright Krista has to squint and raise her hand as a shield. She stands swaying with the child pressed against her. It takes her a moment to realize that the strange sound is Perley. As she starts toward the car Lila comes around from behind it, her hands full of flower heads. She hurries toward her mother.

"Lila. Where?" But she can't repair whatever garden Lila has throttled. She gets the girls into the car and softly shuts Perley's door. Getting in behind the wheel, she reaches for him, "Perley," but he jerks his arm at her touch and continues rocking, his knees dug into his eyes, hoarse sobs coming from his throat. She turns the key and the car starts; she puts it into D1. They get out onto the road. They are the only car. They go by a field full of cows, they pass another field where a horse is running, his tail lifted like a sword. Krista, her hands high on the wheel, drives them down the middle of the road in this old car on this June morning, the sweet odor of the flower petals strewn across the girls rising from the back seat, the nearer stale old smell of the upholstery and cigarette butts, Perley with his knees gouging his eyes, her own dear child with his raging, broken heart, she who is not a driver in this car which is not her car and may, if she is not totally vigilant, drive itself off the road and kill them all. And the narrow white needle is tapping at the E; they are almost out of gas and there is nowhere to go to but back home.

* * *

Logan is pacing in his empty driveway, listing like an ill-laden ship, his cane forgotten back in the house. When he awoke they were not there. His first thought was that they were hiding on him and he began to look: he opened closets; groaning, he bent to peer under beds, his cane held ready to poke at them for taunting him in this way. But they were nowhere. The silence, which he had never before experienced, was so awful that he turned on both televisions, he muttered as he sought them, he opened windows to let in sounds. When he went outside to look in the garage and discovered that his car was gone, a dizzying rush of rage drowned his panic and he had to sit down hard on a sawhorse or he might have fallen. Who the hell had taken his car, had driven them all off, quietly in the night like thieves or people who'd been owing on the rent money too long? Who the hell did she know except her mother, and Viola couldn't drive her way out of a wet paper bag, and how would she get in here anyway unless he himself went and got her? He stood up off the sawhorse and went out into the driveway. It was early, he couldn't see where the sun was; it didn't stare like an eye, there was only the light. He thought, Freddie Hewitt. That little bastard had walked out here plenty of times when he didn't have a truck. Or he might have broken down and she let him take the Chevy. But what the hell did they all go for? He went back into the house and looked at the telephone. Viola didn't have one. And he couldn't remember the name of the woman downstairs where she used the phone, or where Krista kept that number. It was when he was walking toward the bedroom to look for it that he remembered the puppy. He pushed the broken door of Perley's room wider. He saw what he hadn't seen when he was looking before, the red plastic water bowl on the floor by the bed. That was it, no other sign of a puppy; it didn't even smell like dog.

Logan went back through the house from the sound of one television set to the sound of the other. He got himself juice and a bowl of cereal and ate it standing up in the wide kitchen doorway, staring out through the picture window at the road where, between the line of maples, he could see the sand trucks that were beginning to pass.

And now he is pacing the driveway, his blood rattling along in his veins like BBs, feeling short of breath and as desperate as an innocent man awaiting judgment. If they do not come back by nine o'clock he will call the sheriff and report his car stolen; he will not mention a wife, a betrayer, a mocker, a thief. Let the law catch them. He pivots, almost falling, and glares at his deserted house. It looks dark and haunted, like something in a dream, recognizable but alien. When he shifts to look at the road again he sees his blue Chevrolet turning slowly into the driveway. It balks there and then comes creeping toward him. It looks empty. He lunges, peering to see who is driving his car. It is not until it's almost upon him that he realizes it's Krista and not the man he's been waiting for. When the car stops she opens the door and gets out.

"Where you been? Where you been?" he demands breathlessly.

She turns her back and opens the door for the girls. They climb out. Petals drift by them and settle. Krista half turns. "I had to take the puppy to the doctor, Logan," she says.

"Joseph's dead. You killed Perley's puppy," Harmony sobs. "You did! You killed the little puppy!" She runs around him and heads for the house. They hear her feet on the back steps.

Logan reaches for Lila and picks her up. "Bad dad," she chants, hitting him with her fist. "Bad dad, bad dad. Bad, bad, bad." He grabs her fist and holds it tightly but he doesn't squeeze any harder than he has to.

"I didn't mean to hurt him. He was biting me," he says to his wife's back. "Nothing would have happened if you did what I told you. You don't listen, you get into trouble." She shuts the door. "He was biting me, for Christ's sake!"

The passenger door opens and Perley gets out of the car. He doesn't look at his father or anyone else. "Perley," Krista says, coming around the front of the car toward him. He starts running. "Perley!" she cries. He's past the garage and ducking under the pines.

"Bad! Bad!" Lila says.

Krista walks wearily toward the house. He follows her. "Bad!" Lila tells him, sticking out her chin until it presses into his cheek. He carries her carefully. It makes his back ache. When they reach the steps he puts her down and looks toward his wife. She's going into the house. The door will close behind her. He hurries, lurching past Lila and jerking the door open.

"Where are my damn keys?"

She still doesn't look at him. She puts the keys and the five-dollar bill on the table. "Ain't much gas," she tells him, her voice hollow, disinterested.

He snatches the keys up and shoves them in his pocket. She's crossed the kitchen and is leaning against the sink. She gets herself a glass of water and drinks it slowly.

"I'm hungry, Mum."

"You go in your room. I'll get your breakfast in a few minutes and I'll call you. You go now." She sounds so fierce and so different that Lila goes.

Logan picks up the five-dollar bill. "You stole money too," he realizes.

She puts more water in the glass. "You killed the puppy," she says before she drinks it.

"I told you I didn't mean to hurt it." He steps toward her. "You took my car. You can't even drive. You ever take my car again and I'll break your arm."

She turns slowly and it's worse than when she wouldn't look at him. "What did you mean to do then, Logan?" Her voice is low and weighted and weary but she is looking at him straight, and he shifts his eyes. "You don't love us," she says flatly. "You don't love us. Not at all." She laughs and it turns into a hoarse sob. "I used to just think, I used to tell myself you was just rough and you had a quick temper. Blamed it on your back. On me being clumsy. But you don't love us." She turns again and runs the water and fills her palms and throws it against her face.

"What the hell are you talking about?" he demands, looking at her back, feeling scared and angry and disgusted at the same time. "What the hell are you talking about!"

She pauses. "You don't love us," she says dully, and then she throws more water on her face.

It is evening and Perley is on the floor of the sandpit with his bicycle. He's smashed out the lights and the reflectors and the basket with a large rock. Logan is standing at the rim of the pit, watching. It is dark purple where Perley is with his lifted arm and his hoarse cries, but on the top the long red rays of the sun run right through Logan, he's glowing like a coal in a furnace. He stands at the edge of the long drop engulfed in fire, huge and tipped on his cane like a maimed god. Perley is smashing spokes. He climbs up on a boulder and heaves his rock down, dives to retrieve it, and throws it down again. He goes on and on and on. Logan can feel it inside himself when the rock strikes. Perley has a long piece of broken glass and he stabs at the seat, at the tires. Logan sees him crouched way down there, small and destructive, his arm moving.

When Perley has done all he can do he leaves the bicycle and starts to climb the tall embankment. He has to go home now. He is hungry and frail with exhaustion, he wants to see his mother or at least be near her. He is climbing slowly, watching his feet; his hands are helping too. He doesn't see his father standing there until he pulls himself over the top, almost touching one of his shoes.

Logan looks at him as Perley stands. He's got an ugly sneer on his face. Perley is afraid but Logan doesn't lift his hand. He just speaks. "Well, now you got nothin'," he says, his words spat out slowly. "You're even dumber than I thought you were."

ZORRO, A GYPSY, AND A CLOWN

24 Tripp Duffy is driving his 1968 Chevrolet truck down Route 110, his foot almost to the floor, his arm out the window, his lips locked around a Marlboro. Tripp is a thin boy, eighteen years old; he works in the auto parts store for his uncle. His reddish hair is wavy and already receding, his skin pale and freckled. He is his mother's last child and he lives with her in a very small blue house beyond the dump. Tripp is on his way to see Perley Pembroke. He has never had a friend before. Ridiculed by his classmates since third grade as small and spotty and stinky and stupid, he has never had a friend before.

Perley is fourteen and a half. He is standing by the road in the fading light with his denim jacket over his arm. His long dusky hair drifts over his eyes; his face is narrow and sharp. Perley has headaches and stomach cramps, nightmares and despair; he's older than he ought to be but he hasn't grown much. Tripp's Chevy slows, a sound like coughing comes through the tailpipe, it pulls over onto the shoulder. The lights blink like small heartbeats as Perley runs around the back of it, opens the door, and climbs in.

Tripp eases the volume down on the radio. He offers Perley one of his Marlboros and lights one for himself. They don't talk much. They have been friends since the winter and they have never talked much. They ride. Tripp knows all the back roads, and what he doesn't know they discover, ending up unexpectedly in Lewiston, finding themselves halfway to Augusta, following the river down from Lisbon Falls. Perley can feel the six-pack under his shoe; he moves his foot: yes, there's another one. Tripp buys beer from his cousin Dexter, who is twenty-two and charges him for the service. Perley leans back in the seat and smokes the cigarette, he listens to the radio, he half watches the world outside: light leaving the sky and the trees erupts in concentrated little pools inside houses; there is the harsh blooming of television screens in darkening rooms, the sudden view of families seated around tables. Perley sighs.

"Open a brew," Tripp invites.

Perley reaches to the floor, gives Tripp a can, gets one for himself. They snicker at the popping sound and Perley settles deeper into the seat. They are heading inland, the radio plays country; they could be in Spain, so completely have they escaped where they've come from. As the beer goes inside Perley everything blurs and softens. Fears and worries that hound him all day long disappear as wonderfully and completely as rabbits down their holes. He stretches his feet out and laughs, turns the warmth of that on his friend. O kind beer: it's as if he doesn't have to be who he is anymore.

Harmony is at her friend's house. She spends a lot of time with Audrey West. Audrey lives with her mother, whose name is also Audrey, and her three half sisters. Audrey's mother works at the fish plant, and her boss is the father of the three youngest girls. Albert Bishop is going to marry Audrey when his wife, Rosemary, dies or divorces him, whichever comes first. Meanwhile Audrey packs fish at minimum wage.

Harmony's friend Audrey is wild. She smokes and drinks and has lots of boyfriends. The last one was thirty years old but he's in jail now for something unrelated to Audrey. Audrey is too young to have a license but she frequently drives her mother's ancient Buick, and Audrey has a heavy foot. It is her wildness that attracts Harmony; it makes Audrey seem powerful and independent; it makes her seem invulnerable, a condition Harmony can't imagine but deeply envies.

They are sitting on the floor of Audrey's small room. They are eating candy and smoking cigarettes; the radio is playing loudly. They are reading magazines with articles entitled: "How to Tell if You Are Addicted to Sex," "Your Hair!!!" "What to Do When the Boss Makes a Pass."

"I ought to give this one to my mother," Audrey says. She twists her mouth into a little sideways pout so smoke comes out in circles. "Too late now though." Audrey has long dark hair and a thin, long body. Her voice is deep and makes her seem older than she is. Harmony listens carefully. What else will Audrey say? She knows all her mother's secrets. How can she know so much?

"Anyway," Audrey says, slapping one magazine onto the floor and picking up another one. "I'm glad he's not *my* father." She makes a face. "Imagine doing it with somebody that old."

Harmony giggles.

"I'm serious. My mother's no spring chicken but she looks a whole lot better than he does."

"Maybe they don't do it anymore."

Audrey rolls her eyes. "He still comes over here. And it ain't for her cooking, which is lousy, or to see how his girls are. I have to take them and go to the mall before he gets here. We have to stay there for hours. It probably takes him that long to get it up." She grins at Harmony and crushes her cigarette in the ashtray. "I mean it! The guy looks like he's been dead for three months." She grabs up her magnifying makeup mirror and studies her tongue, then she frowns and tosses the mirror onto the bed. "My mother gets all excited though. She's got her red dress on and her blue eye shadow. She looks like hell and she acts like she's in junior high school. And I'm telling you, if a cop ever stops me I won't lie. I'll tell him my mother sent me to the mall with those girls so she could spread her legs for her decrepit boss." She glares at Harmony, who is trying to decide if Audrey is serious, if she'd really tell on her mother to the police.

"I mean it!" Audrey insists. "I ain't taking no rap for her."

* * *

Lila brings it home, all damp and crumpled from gripping it tightly on the bus ride. "They said to give it to you, Mum," she explains.

"Parent Information": a message from the new principal—lunches, clothes for gym, unexcused absences. Then it says they want to hire someone to work in the kitchen because Mrs. Vine left suddenly when her husband had a heart attack. "We'll miss YOU, Mrs. Vine!" it says in wavery purple mimeograph ink across the bottom of the page.

Krista reads it over and over, keeps it in the cupboard near the cereal boxes, folded small. It is like a talisman in there behind the closed pine door. She wonders what will happen to her if she goes and says, "I want that job please." They will ask her did she graduate, where has she worked before, who will speak in praise of her. But if she had a job he wouldn't worry so much about money, she could buy things for the children, she could buy a toaster that wouldn't set the bread on fire.

She stands in the picture window and watches Logan's car go down the driveway and turn right, flashing rust red between the trunks of the maple trees. The morning is still cool. In Hallum's field the nighttime frost has paled the emptied cornstalks. Krista is wearing the dark gray skirt she wore to Kendrick's funeral almost sixteen years ago. It was large on her then and it still is. She is wearing red sneakers and carrying a large, almost empty pocketbook. It's a walk of less than two miles.

She feel dizzy standing by the counter in the front office waiting for the secretary to help her. Krista shows her the rumpled piece of paper. "I was wondering about that job," she says, her finger shaking as it points to the words.

"I'll take you down to Mrs. Bernier in just a moment," the woman tells her crisply. Then she goes back to typing.

Krista follows her down the hall past all the closed doors. This woman has on high-heeled shoes. Krista thinks about her red sneakers and her toes curl under.

Mrs. Bernier is wearing thick white shoes. Her hairnet makes her look wonderfully, almost mysteriously old. "I can cook," Krista says. There are sinks two feet deep and it's steamy back here in the kitchen where they are preparing a hundred and fifty hot dogs.

"Come on in my office," Mrs. Bernier tells her. "We'll talk. It's got to be fast though. Lunch is coming up."

"You what?" Logan says. It's three days later and he does not believe her. Krista hardly believes it herself.

"I got a job," she repeats. "Down to the school. Cooking lunch for the kids." She is standing beside his recliner chair. The TV is loud. She is anxious about his reaction but she can't keep her delight from showing. "It's true, it's true," she tells him. "But it's all right because I'll be getting home before Lila does."

He glares at her, rapidly tapping his fingers on the chair. "Ain't you full of surprises," he says.

"I'm lucky. There were two other women wanted the job. Mrs. Bernier chose me though 'cause she says I look like a hard worker."

"You sure fooled her."

"That's not funny, Logan," she says, stepping back from his chair. "I *am* a hard worker."

He studies her as if he's measuring her for a suit of clothes. Then he smiles. "How you getting there?" he asks. "And back again?"

She looks confused and he settles back in his chair. "I was hoping you'd drive me," she says.

He nods slowly. "I don't remember you asking me."

"There wasn't anything definite to ask you about till now."

He purses his lips, nodding slowly.

Lila is excited. "I'll see you at lunch, my Mum?" she asks again.

"You sure will!" Krista tells her, zipping her jacket. She follows her out the door and watches her go down the driveway. Lila is the only child at this stop; the high school bus goes much earlier. She is little standing down there by the maples. Bending to look closely at something on the ground, she is smaller still. She straightens as the bus comes down the hill from Perrault's and then she is gone.

Sitting behind the wheel of his car, Logan looks furious. Krista opens the door and gets in quietly. She wasn't able to eat breakfast and her empty stomach keeps turning over. She sits silently and waits. She doesn't want to have to deal with Logan, she just wants to get there and try to learn her job. He turns the key and backs the car down the driveway in quick, jerky motions.

The women are nice: they help her, they laugh when she makes a mistake and tell her about their own goof-ups. "Goof-ups" they call it, an expression Krista has never heard before.

"I was washing all the dishes in the sink," Mrs. Forbes tells her. "Mattie came in to see what was taking me so long. I'd never seen a dishwasher machine!" She laughs and laughs. She is a big woman, soft arms, soft eyes. "You'll be just fine," she assures Krista, giving her a hug. "My goodness, you're as little as a bird!" she says.

Krista gets out of work at three o'clock and she waits and she waits and she waits. The buses roll out. She is worrying that Lila will get home before she does. She's afraid to start walking in case he comes from the other direction and is mad because she is not here. The teachers leave, driving off in their small cars. The day turns cloudy. She is hungry and tired and her head is aching. All the joy she was feeling in the day going so well has left her. She decides to walk. Maybe the car wouldn't start. She gets abreast of Palmer's store when he pulls up behind her and brakes hard. "I've been waiting at that school for you!" he yells before she has the door all the way open.

"I didn't see you."

"How in the hell could you see me? You weren't there!"

"But I waited and waited. I've been worried, Logan, about Lila. Is she all right?"

"How the hell do I know? I've been up at that school waiting for you!"

"But she's been home more than half an hour."

They are sitting there in the road. A truck has to swing way out to go by them. He watches her. "*You* told me four o'clock. Where the hell were you!"'

"I told you three, Logan."

"Like hell. You said four."

"Let's just go." Maybe she did say four. She can't be sure. She was thinking about so many things at once.

* * *

"Lila, are you okay?" she asks, hurrying into the house.

"I saw you at lunch, my Mum," Lila tells her. She's made herself a sandwich. There's jelly all over the table.

Krista smiles. "I saw you too."

She is late for work two days out of five. The car won't start or there's no gas; once, Logan is sick and can't get out of bed and by the time she starts walking it's late. The women cool toward her. Mrs. Bernier gives her a warning. "We got to count on you," she says. "Or someone else has to carry your share of the work and that's not fair.'"

"I know. I'm sorry. I'm trying to save for a better car," she says, not able to look straight at Mrs. Bernier, her eyes tearing. "I like the job. I'm trying to work hard for you."

"When you're here you're great. These kids won't wait, you know. They want to *eat!*" She smiles but without the warmth she used to show.

Krista wakes up earlier and earlier, worried, wondering what's going to happen, will she get to work on time. "This job is too much for you," he says. "You look like hell. I'm sick of supper being late every night."

"I'm going to walk to work from now on," she tells him on a Sunday night. "You won't have to bother about taking me and you can stay in bed extra and get a good rest."

"What do you mean?"

"Well, everyone is saying how you ought to exercise more. Walking is good exercise and it's not far."

"You're always trying to insult me. Aren't you?"

"I'm not insulting you, Logan. I just want to walk."

"You want people to say I won't drive you. Poor little you has to walk."

"What people?"

"Those old bags you work for."

"They're not old. Mrs. Bernier's the oldest and she's younger than Mum."

"Jesus Christ," he says, stomping up close to her. "Most women argue as much as you do woulda got their teeth knocked out a long time ago."

Krista walks. He starts getting up earlier too, but she walks anyway, leaving just after Lila does. It's a dry time of year. It's not until well into October that she gets caught by the rain. Logan watches it come down. "Now she'll learn," he tells himself.

Krista goes into the bathroom when she gets to school and tries to dry herself off, but her hair is soaked and it's gone through her jacket so the shoulders of her blouse are darkened.

Mrs. Bernier considers her, her bottom lip rolled out. "Going to be winter soon," she says.

"I like winter."

"Your husband has health problems, doesn't he?"

"He does," she admits softly, not quite looking at Mrs. Bernier. "His back hurts him most of the time and he has to take a lot of pills. It's real hard on him," she says.

"Why don't you ride on the school bus with your little girl? You can help out the driver, keep those kids in their seats and half behaving."

"Would she let me ride?"

"Won't know for sure till you ask, but I can't think of a reason why not."

It's Halloween and Lila is wearing long underwear down the front of which Krista has sewn red pompons. On her head is the largest pompon of all, held on by a thick elastic. She is carrying a Windex bottle filled with water and a black and white dog with one plastic eye. Her nose is a Ping-Pong ball sliced almost in half, reddened by a Magic Marker, held on by a large hunk of bubble gum. The fist of the arm that holds the dog is squeezing the handle of a shopping bag. It rustles around her ankle as they go down the road, she and her mother, the new moon rising from the pines on the far side of the sandpit. "Candy," Lila chants. "Candy, candy, candy!"

They go on up the hill where lights are blazing in the farmhouse from the front room to the last window in the ell. "Oh my Lord!" Mrs. Perrault cries, opening the door wide, bending to look into Lila's face. "Jim!" she calls, straightening. "Jim, come see this little clown!"

* * *

Harmony and Audrey are wearing their costumes. They're on their way to the dance but they've stopped off at the store. Audrey is a black cat: black leotard, white face, little pointy ears and a long tail. Harmony is a Gypsy girl with crystals around her neck and gold in her ears. Audrey orders cigarettes and while Mrs. Gale turns and reaches, Harmony steals candy bars and a *TV Guide*. They go giggling out of the store and get in Mrs. West's Buick.

Perley and Tripp are going to the dance also but first they go up to Lewiston, driving the curving river road slowly. It is warm for the end of October; wind rattles the trees and takes their leaves, tosses them onto the shiny road, onto the blacker water. Perley leans his elbow on the open window and watches the river. It moves lithe as an animal beside them; trees grow up from the banks to be shed like horns in the spring floods and rushed downstream, jamming one against the other like naked bodies where the river runs hard in its narrowed bed. He holds the empty can between his knees and leans farther out the window. The water gleams like oil, blue-black, dense, as if he could stand on it. Perley laughs and leans farther still. Tripp resists reaching for him and says instead, "Why don't you open a couple more beers."

Perley brings his head in the window and grins at him, his teeth shining under the Zorro mask.

After Logan gets into the car he sits behind the wheel staring at nothing. Krista waits, Lila in her lap chewing on a Three Musketeers. The wrapper crackles loudly, and then Lila begins to jounce on Krista's lap. "Let's go, let's go," she commands. "My grandma is waiting for me."

"I feel lousy," Logan says. "What the hell did you put in that casserole?"

"Nothing. Nothing but what I always put." He turns the key. "Are you all right?" she asks.

"I told you I ain't." He grinds it into reverse. Krista looks out the window where the night leans black as Herod.

"Who is this wonderful clown?" Viola cries, clapping her hands together.

"It's me, my Grandma! It's Lila!"

Viola bends closer, peering into her face. "Are you sure?"

"It's me! It's me! It's Lila!" She brings her thumb down on the Windex bottle.

Viola shrieks and jumps back. Ross hisses and runs under the couch. The end of his black tail sticks out, twitching, and Lila heads for it.

"Don't rile that cat!" Viola cries. "He's a witch cat!"

Lila spins around then and squirts Viola's slippers. She makes her dog bark; she runs forward and does a somersault on the rug in the middle of the room. Ross hisses from under the couch. Lila staggers to her feet, the pompon hat twisted over one ear. "Come here, you clown!" Viola says, bending with her arms out. Lila runs to her.

"Grandma, I got Three Musketeers and jelly beans and gum and Mary Janes and Kisses." Viola kisses her cheeks. Lila giggles and hugs, calling out, "Red hots! Candy corn! Sugar Babies!"

Krista arrives at the door, Lila's coat over her arm and Logan behind her, breathing hard and gripping his cane. "This clown is wonderful," Viola tells them. "Come on in and sit down. How are you?"

"You better slow her down," Logan tells Krista.

"Lila, you stop and come here!"

"Sit down," Viola says to Logan. "I'm sorry you have to climb so many stairs to get here."

"Lila!"

"Well, I got coffee ready and"—she turns toward Lila whom Krista has captured—"special Halloween cake."

"Cake! Cake!"

"Oh, Mum, she's already crazed by sugar."

"A little piece," Viola mouths over Lila's head. "Lila, you come help me serve it and tell me if you saw any ghosts tonight."

"Oooooooh," Lila moans, "ooooohhhhhh."

"Mum, where's Flynn?"

"He's downstairs helping Mrs. Neelar." Lila tugs on her hand. "She doesn't get around well and she was nervous about tonight. He'll be up soon's he can."

"Cake, my Grandma," Lila demands, butting Viola with her head.

"I thought you were a clown, not a billy goat," Viola says as they go into the small kitchen.

"I'm a clown *and* a billy goat," Lila tells her.

Logan doesn't speak for the first part of the ride home, but Krista knows he is seething. It's in his body and the way he holds the wheel, the sound of his breathing. She feels it as a sharpness in her bones, all her muscles pulling tight to bear this load he's passing on to her as something he won't carry alone. Lila is asleep, slumped against her, the clown suit stained with orange frosting.

"You always like to insult me in front of your mother, don't you?"

It's almost a relief now that he has finally spoken. "I don't do that," she says.

"Telling her you have to ride the school bus."

"I do ride the school bus. It's working out fine."

"Telling her we couldn't pay for Christmas unless you was working."

"I didn't say that. She said how it would be good having the extra money at Christmas."

"She ought to mind her own goddamn business."

"She didn't mean anything bad. She was just happy for us is all."

"You told her I wouldn't drive you to work."

"I didn't say that."

"The hell you didn't!"

They've woken Lila. She leans forward toward her father. "You quit talking mean," she says to him.

"You shut up, Big Mouth!" he tells her, lifting his hand from the wheel.

"Hush, Lila," Krista admonishes, pulling her close. "We'll be home soon."

"You're a Mean Mouth," Lila says, and Krista pulls her closer still and gently puts her hand over her lips.

They aren't at the dance very long before Audrey decides to leave with Otis Farleigh. "We'll come back and get you, give you a ride home," she tells Harmony. "I'd invite you along but we ain't that perverted." She giggles.

"It's okay," Harmony tells her. "My brother's coming and I'll get a ride home with him."

Audrey studies her face a moment. "Well, okay. If you say so. Just watch that Tripp. He wants you!"

Harmony makes a face and then watches them leave. Audrey is twirling her cat's tail and whomping Otis's arm with it.

By the time Perley and Tripp arrive it's late and they stand in the doorway almost leaning against each other, wearing their Zorro masks. Harmony has been ready to leave for a while and she hurries over to them and suggests it.

Perley looks hard at her. "It's you," he says. "It's Harmony." And he nudges Tripp.

She takes off her gypsy bandanna and her hair falls down around her face again. Perley's grin is lopsided. Tripp's eyes, centered in the black mask, are watery and weary. "You want to go home now," he says, "we'll take you." He looks at Perley. "We'll take her." They shuffle through the door and find the truck. The night is very black now and a thick mist streams past them. "The cab's real warm," Tripp assures her as they climb in.

It smells of beer and cigarettes and boys' hair in Tripp's cab. She settles between the two of them, slips off her shoes, and rests her stockinged feet on the dashboard. They pull out of the parking lot and into the dark street. Perley opens a beer and offers her some.

"It's hot!" she complains, handing it back to him.

Perley shrugs. "It's beer. You want one, Tripp?"

Tripp was going to say no; he's had enough and he knows that. But because Harmony is here he changes his mind. He offers to share it with her, and as they go along she drinks from both opened beers, her Gypsy bracelets tinkling.

Tripp takes the long way: none of them is in a hurry to get home. The radio is loud, they laugh and sing with it; they pass few vehicles; the night is dark and soft about them. Tripp feels delicate and tender with happiness to have both of them in his cab. He keeps turning to see their faces, mysterious and beautiful and close in the light from the dashboard. He's never been this near to Harmony before. He can smell her lipstick and the faint powdery odor of her sweat. He wishes they could all go somewhere and live together, somewhere far and exotic like Hawaii, where they wouldn't speak the same language as the other people and they would be everything to each other.

When they go around the next wide curve they are moving too fast and the truck leans hard and in the quickest possible moment—a moment in which Tripp can say, "Oh shit!" and fling his arm out toward Harmony—it rolls over twice and ends up on its side with the tires spinning.

It's so quick they don't have time to be afraid. They disentangle themselves from each other and Perley pulls himself through his open window. He stands on the door and reaches in for Harmony and pulls her out. Tripp follows. They get down carefully and stand on the ground. They're looking at two wheels still slowly spinning. They touch themselves and look at each other. They are bruised and bumped and their hands are shaking but they are all right.

"Jesus, I'm sorry," Tripp groans. He stumbles toward the front of the truck. "Come into the light," he says. He looks them up and down, afraid to touch them, in the strange parallel pattern of the headlights.

"We're okay," Perley says. "You're all right, aren't you, Harmony?"

"I think so."

"Are you sure?"

"I banged my knee, but I'm okay. No blood or anything." She giggles.

"You okay, Tripp?"

"I am. I am. Where are we?" he asks, and pulls off his mask.

"In a cow pasture," Perley tells him, and they start laughing. There are house lights back down the road where the black shape of the field ends. "If we could get it righted I bet it would drive fine," he says, hanging on the tire with all his weight.

"You can't," Tripp tells him. "Don't worry about it. I'll get the wrecker tomorrow. We better take the beer cans out of it before a cop comes."

Perley goes back in through the window, and Tripp holds him by his feet. He piles the cans into the bag they came in and hands it up. "Good thing we drank it all," he says, climbing out. "It stinks of beer in there but they can't arrest you for a stink." They laugh, Perley rattling the beer cans, and then they look at each other.

"You're okay. You are, aren't you?" Tripp asks them again.

"Sure we are, honest, Tripp." Harmony steps closer; she's shivering. "But we got to get home. If we're too late and he finds out about this"—she gestures toward the belly of the truck—"he'll kill us."

"I'll go to that house and call my mother," Tripp tells her. "I'll tell them I ran out of gas so they won't call the cops. Don't worry, she'll come quick and take you home." He gives her his jacket and starts down the road.

Perley takes up the bag of beer cans. "I'll hide this in the woods over there," he says, shaking them so they clatter and grinning underneath his mask.

LOGAN AND LILA

25 Logan lies on his side in the dim, smoky bedroom. He broods on the pain in his back, which is something with a separate life sent to ransack and curse him. His gaze shifts from the wall to the narrow window where the late-April rain falls, pattering like hands against the pane. The rain turns the air shiny and pale, makes the earth boggy, traps puddles in the fields, darkens and polishes the bark of trees. It makes wildness in the rivers, and they will leave debris—broken branches and beer cans—clinging high in the limbs of trees, flapping like tattered clothing after an assault. Logan hates the rain. He shifts on the pillows and, grunting, half turns onto his back. He has grown stouter, his body thickening rather than turning soft, and there are pouches under his eyes because he does not sleep well. Krista opens the door and peers into the room. "You're awake," she says.

"I don't sleep. You know damn well I'm awake."

She steps back into the hall. "Do you want your breakfast?" she asks through the doorway.

"That'd be nice," he snorts. "Must be almost lunchtime."

"It's seven-thirty, Logan," she says. "I'll make you eggs. And pancakes." He doesn't answer. She retreats, pulling the door closed.

He moves in his halting way to the television and turns it on, then gets back in bed and scowls at it. Quick items of news spit at him. Commercials go on and on, shiny-lipped, overly excited women selling things nobody needs. "Jesus Christ," he complains with growing impatience each time one ends and yet another comes on.

When Krista enters with his tray Lila is following her. She walks right up to the foot of the bed and stares at him, watches while her mother sets the tray across his legs. He's staring at the TV. "Why ain't she in school?" he asks.

"It's vacation, and besides, she has a stomach ache," Krista says. "Threw up her cereal."

He takes his eyes off the screen and looks at the child, into eyes that are round and dark like his own. Her hair is fine and dark like his and red barrettes hold it back from her large face. She looks strong and healthy. As he is thinking that, she draws the sleeve of her bathrobe under her nose. "Something's going around at school," Krista says, pouring milk into his coffee. She straightens up. "You think that's going to be enough syrup?"

"Better get me the bottle. She don't look sick." He puts his fork into the pancakes and spears half of one up into his mouth. Lila watches, the fingers of one hand curved over the footrail. Logan keeps eating—pancakes, fried eggs—drinking coffee in quick sips, draining the juice glass, watching the TV.

"What's wrong with you?" Lila asks him, leaning over the footrail.

He drops his fork hard onto his plate and looks at her, scowls, and his face is dark, darkness around the eyes and in his unshaven jaw. He makes a harsh sound in his throat and works something off his teeth with his tongue. She keeps staring at him, her eyebrows, delicately curving like his own, slightly raised. He keeps scowling at her.

"Huh? Huh?" she inquires, patting at the spread with impatience, almost nudging his feet. "My mother says there's something wrong with you. I want to know what is it."

"I got a fire in my back," he says, speaking slowly, their eyes locked. "Burning red, hot as . . . this coffee." He gestures with the mug. "Hotter."

She frowns and her eyes grow dark as his. She walks around the side of the bed, looks up and down the length of it. "I don't *see* no smoke," she tells him.

He laughs in a short bark, then leans out of the bed toward her. His plate slides on the tray; he grabs at the coffee mug in time. "It's all inside," he explains in a loud whisper. Lila makes a face. Her nose is twitching. He straightens in the bed. "You look like a rabbit," he tells her as the door opens and Krista comes in with a plate of toast.

Lila turns to her. "He told me he was on fire." She looks disgusted, glances back at him, then marches to the door. She turns, looking dead at him. "No smoke," she says, "I don't *smell* nooo smoke," and she walks out of the room, lifting her hand to scratch the back of her neck. The rain comes down harder on the two narrow windows. Krista sets the small plate on his tray. He's watching the door. "She's the only one of 'em takes after me," he says as he reaches for the toast.

Two weeks later at three-thirty in the afternoon Logan is dodging up and down the living room, turning on the point of his cane. His face is flushed and there's sweat all along his hairline. His stomach churns. Everyone stays out of his way. The older children have left altogether. Lila is in the kitchen wiping dishes, her cloth going in the uneven rhythm of his feet. Krista is in the bedroom checking his suitcase again. "She's here!" Logan yells in a high voice. Krista hurries into the living room with the suitcase. "I left money for you in the drawer," he tells her. "I paid the light bill yesterday." She nods. "She's here," he repeats.

She is Mrs. Oliver, the social worker who is to drive him to Togus Veterans' Hospital so they can look at his back. She takes up his suitcase as if it were light as a box of Kleenex and, putting her other hand under his arm, guides him down his flagstones and into her Subaru car. Logan walks more quickly than he's accustomed to; he carries his cane in the air.

Mrs. Oliver unrolls her window and nods at Krista. Lila is standing behind her mother, staring at the woman, looking from her to her father and back again. "Three days of tests and observation," Mrs. Oliver says, "see if they want to go in and operate again." And she's turning her key; the motor makes a high-pitched thrum.

Krista looks frightened. The wind, which has blown hard all the sunny morning and dried up the lawn, whips at her hair and snatches the sweater back from her body. "They'll call you from the hospital, Mrs. Pembroke, if they decide to operate. Probably they won't; they'll give him exercises to do, try a new medication, see how that goes."

Krista nods, bends to look into the car at Logan. "You have the car. You have money?" Mrs. Oliver asks her.

"Yes, I have money. I don't drive but my son does."

"I don't want him touching my car!" He looks at her then. "You remember that!"

"How long they keeping him?" Perley asks at the supper table.

"Three days," Krista says. " 'Less they decide to operate. They might operate on him, Perley." Perley feels remote, he doesn't care; he must be really bad not to care if they cut his father open.

"He *says* he's got a fire inside him," Lila informs her brother.

Perley looks at her. "Oh yeah?"

"It could be real serious," Krista says.

"He wants them to stinguish it," Lila tells him.

Perley laughs so suddenly he almost chokes.

"Perley, it's real serious," Krista cries.

He's still laughing; half choked, he holds out his hand toward her. Harmony nudges him, makes a face that means "Cut it out."

"He's afraid of an operation, afraid it might make him worse."

"Worse?" Perley says.

"Paralyze him or something." Krista's watching Perley but he doesn't seem to react to that. For a moment she sees her husband sitting in his recliner chair unable to move, yelling, demanding things, waving his cane, and herself rushing about to do for him in his suffering and his rage. "Perley, a family's got to stick together," she insists. "That's the most important thing."

"I don't think he's really got a fire inside of him," Lila says. "You're all wet inside—a fire would go out." Perley's grinning at her but she frowns. "*I* think it's teeth," she speculates, gritting her own. "I think it's extra teeth he growed on the inside that's biting and biting."

"One more day of peace," Perley says at the supper table on Thursday. It's been quiet with Logan gone but they've all been edgy, half holding their breath, waiting for what's missing so they can go back to normal.

"It's just lucky they didn't have to operate. Least they haven't called me," Krista says.

"They would have called you, Mum, if they were going to do anything serious," Harmony tells her.

Krista looks gratefully at her. "No news is good news," she says.

"No news is no news," Lila tells her, tipping her head and watching her mother. She repeats it, mouthing the words.

"Well, you must admit it's kinda pleasant with him gone," Perley says.

"I don't admit it." Krista's cutting Lila's meat, she doesn't have to look at him. "He's in the hospital and he needs his family now. You know he's always had bad trouble with his back." She sets the knife down and turns to him. "Family is what you got in this world, Perley, and that's if you're lucky. And you hold on to it and you don't throw anybody out. It's what you are."

He gets up quickly and pushes in his chair. "If that's what I am I better quit right now," he says.

"A noodle is a noodle!" Lila proclaims loudly, hoisting one on her fork and waving it toward Perley who's heading for the door.

Krista is settling Lila in bed when Frederick Hewitt arrives and knocks on the back door. "You stay right there!" Krista says, but Lila jumps up and runs out of the room and down the hall.

"It's Mr. Hewitt!" she calls, jumping up and down.

"It can't be."

"It is! It is!" And he's standing in the door Lila pulled open.

"Freddie, I don't believe it! What a sight for sore eyes. Come in, come in," she says, reaching for his hand.

"I recanized you!" Lila tells him.

"I thought you were in Florida."

"Got back last week." He looks into the child's bright, round face. "How you been, Lila?"

"I knew it was you!" she tells him again.

"Come and sit down. Lila, you say goodnight. I'll make you coffee. Are you hungry? We just had supper and there's plenty left."

"Noodles!"

"I ate, thanks. Coffee would be good though." Lila sits down at the table with him while Krista is filling the kettle. "You sure grew," he tells her.

"I'm nine."

"Lila, not till November. And you're s'posed to be in bed."

"I'm almost nine," she persists.

"Almost nine's a good age." But she shakes her head. "How come?" Frederick asks. God, she looks like Logan.

Lila studies his face. "You can't do stuff," she complains. "You can't do what the big kids do. Everyone says, 'No, Lila.' "

He can't help laughing. "Well, 'fore you know it you'll be ten and then eleven and on and on. You don't like one age you wait a little and you'll be another. Then when you get as old as us they all blend and you got too much to do all the time." He looks at Krista. "Right?"

"Well, it sure goes fast. Faster and faster. Perley's already talking about joining up in the navy and leaving us. Harmony's tall as me."

"Where are they?" he asks, looking around. "It's kind of quiet here."

"Perley's out with his friend. You remember that Tripp Duffy? That nice boy with red hair." The kettle starts a low shriek and she turns to get it. "Harmony's out baby-sitting," she says, and fills two mugs.

"My dad's in the hospital."

"What happened, Krista?"

"He's been having a real bad time with his back, Freddie, worse than usual even. They wanted to examine him up at the hospital. Maybe operate." She comes toward him with the coffee.

"He says there's a fire burning inside him."

"Lila, it's bedtime," Krista says sharply. "They're going to help Dad."

"You believe that, Mr. Hewitt?"

"I expect that's how it feels to him."

"Fire?" she asks, moving closer and studying his face.

Frederick nods. "It's what he thinks of hurting most."

"I know they'll really help him this time,"Krista says. "It's got bad enough they'll have to do something that works. I'm sure of it," she insists. "Come on, Lila, it's bedtime. You say good night to Mr. Hewitt."

Lila keeps turning to wave as they leave the room and go down the hall. He settles back and drinks the coffee. He can hear Lila talking and the door closing and Lila still talking. In a bit the door opens and Krista comes back in the room.

"No," she says, turning. "I won't. Lila has to have the hall light on," she explains.

"She doesn't look like she'd be afraid of nothing," Frederick says.

"She's pretty tough," Krista laughs. "But she wants that light on." She sits down and drinks her coffee. They can hear Lila humming in her bed.

"You got your hair cut off," he says.

She passes one hand over her head. "Mum cut it for me." She shrugs. "It just seemed like time."

"Looks good on you."

"You mean off me." They both laugh. It shows the lines, where they'll come in her face, and she looks both younger and older. "You got your beard growed out," she says, "now that everybody is shaving every single hair offa them."

He smiles. She looks pleased at this. "Are you home to stay this time?" she asks.

"I am till next winter. I'm living the way the rich people do, Krista. Maine in the summer, Florida all winter long. Course I'm driving their cars, bartending their liquor." He laughs harshly.

Krista shakes her head. "I just wish you'd stay home. It's better to be settled in one place. You started all that moving around when Hannah went away."

He shrugs. "Maybe I did. I don't remember." He lights a cigarette, then offers the pack to her.

"Freddie, you know I don't smoke!"

"Just offering. People change."

She laughs. "I'll just never be a smoker."

"Probably a good thing," he says, putting them back in his pocket. "That Lila sure looks like Logan."

"You think so?"

"Oh yeah. Tough like him too."

"Well, she's not like the other kids when they were little. Perley and Harmony were almost like twins when they were small. Then Lila, coming along so much later."

"Kids are all different. You were all different.'

"We were?"

"Sure."

"Kendrick could do anything and Flynn was good."

"You were pretty good yourself."

"Well, but not like Flynn."

"Except when you were fourteen. Then you were pretty rough."

"I was?"

"You were a little hard to get along with."

She laughs out loud. "I was jealous," she says, reddening.

"Of what?"

She makes a face. "Mariam Griffin."

"Mariam Griffin! What for?"

"You were crazy about Mariam Griffin. You were together the both of you and I was alone."

"You were a kid living at home."

"I was alone though." She sighs and then leans toward him, her hands sliding along the tabletop. "You and Daniel were different too."

Frederick stiffens in the chair as if his arm had been twisted up behind his neck.

"You were so grown up and so serious and Daniel was little and shy like me. He was my best friend in second grade. I missed him so much. Then you went away and I was lonesome for you."

He's looking at the tabletop. The room is quiet but for the now far-off sound of Lila humming and the gritty noise of the hands moving in the clock above the stove. "I shouldn't of let anything happen to him, Krista," he says, his voice hoarse. "He counted on me." He looks up at her. "I never know, I never know for sure if those goddamn Cords just shut him out or if they hurt him first." He stares past her. "They beat him up, I'm sure of it. That was how they always done. Maybe he ran away from them and got lost. Or they shut him out. I'll never know what it was. What it was exactly."

"But Freddie," she cries, getting up out of the chair, "what could you know, what could you do? You were a little boy yourself then. Little as Lila. Nothing was your fault. You were little as Lila!"

"I was bigger than him."

"I made you meatloaf," Krista tells him, "and I'm frying potatoes. I got a pie for dessert."

Logan sits at the kitchen table watching her. He feels as if he's been away from home a long time; he wonders what's been going on. He looks around the kitchen. "What did you do while I was gone?"

Surprised, she turns to him. "Went to work, took care of the kids, the usual stuff."

"My Mum made cookies with me," Lila tells him. She's sitting at the table with him, holding two dolls.

"You save me some or you eat 'em all?"

"Ate 'em."

"You didn't save me out one?"

"Nope!"

"You ain't very nice."

"Nope!"

He laughs and looks at Krista again. "I bet you were on the phone to your mother the whole time."

"Mum? No. By the time I get home Mum's at work. I hardly ever talk to her on the phone."

He shrugs. "I bet you called her at that store."

Krista blushes. "I did call her. But we just talked a few minutes. I told her about you." She starts taking the potatoes out and spreading them on a paper towel.

"What'd she say?"

"She was worried about if you would have to have the operation and if we would be alone here without you."

"I couldn't have the operation. They could screw up and paralyze me." He tips forward, leaning his elbows on the table. "You get my pills?"

"No. Pills? No."

"She told you I had to take three kinds of pills every day. Three times a day. Weren't you listening? You musta left 'em in my suitcase. Go get 'em. I'll show you." He taps on the table with the fingers of his right hand. Then he stops and picks up his beer. Lila watches him, the tapping fingers and the lifted bottle.

"What happened to you?" she asks.

"A lot of lousy things."

"Like what?"

"They took a lot of blood out of me."

"Was your blood hot?"

"You bet it was. Those nurses couldn't get near it!"

Lila scrunches up her face, studying him. "What else?" she demands.

"They X-rayed me. A lot."

"What's that?"

"That's when they take pictures of what's inside you with a special camera."

"What did they see inside you?" She leans closer. "Did they see a fire?"

He laughs and almost spits out beer. "They saw a fiery furnace," he tells her. "They had to turn off their camera real quick 'fore it melted!"

Krista returns with three large vials. "That's them," he says. "Put them high in the cupboard, high so this girl can't get at 'em."

"There sure are a lot." Krista shakes the vials gently.

"Build up my bones. Take away some of the pain," he tells her. Then he looks at Lila. "You touch them pills and I'll take my belt to you."

She gets down from her chair, a doll in each fist. "I don't want your damn pills," she says. "I don't like pills. And I don't like belts. And anybody try to hit me I'll burn him up!"

She flounces out of the room and he laughs and shakes his fist after her. "Who said you could swear! I'll wash out your mouth with soap!" He looks at Krista. "Who taught her to swear?"

The door opens and Perley and Harmony come through it. "Well," Logan says, grinning at them, "ask a question, get an answer." He lifts his emptied bottle toward them in a salute.

"You're back," Perley says.

"Yeah. You disappointed?"

Perley shrugs, moves farther into the kitchen.

"It's just that we didn't know, Logan." Krista puts a hand on Perley's arm. "The lady said they would call. We didn't know for sure until you got home."

He doesn't look at her. Harmony goes on down the hall. Logan watches Perley. "You think you get rid of me you'll be in charge here," he says, "the *big* man."

"I'm going in the navy," Perley says, "soon's I'm eighteen. I got no reason to want to be here, whether you're here or not." He pushes by his mother and follows Harmony out of the room.

"That little girl's the only one of you cares a damn about how I am," he calls after them.

* * *

He starts bringing Lila with him on his long rides. Sometimes he picks her up at school. Sometimes they're gone most of Saturday. Summer comes and they're gone on weekdays, too. It makes the house they've left behind peaceful. They ride around, the way Tripp and Perley do. They get ice cream cones, they drink sodas, they get M&M candies in a giant bag. It travels on the seat between them, their two hands going into it, his left one on the wheel and her right one holding a doll.

"Don't be a goddamn fool," he tells her.

"I ain't," she says, her new-moon eyebrows tightening.

"Don't tell people how much money you got," he tells her.

"I never tell," she says, indignant, her lips closing up like a snapped purse.

"Where you going to put this quarter I give it to you?" he asks, holding it out.

"Somewhere," she says, looking straight at him. "Somewhere ain't none of your business."

"Haa!" He grins and slaps the wheel. She puts her palm up for the quarter, and when he drops it she closes her fingers quick and slides her hand under her.

"What you going to buy with that?"

She shrugs.

"What you going to buy? Candy?"

"You buy my candy." She reaches into the M&M bag.

"You going to put it to a new doll?"

"My grandma buys my dolls."

"Well, you just about got it made, ain't you!"

Lila smiles and chews on M&M's.

One hot Saturday in July he takes her out to Dunham. "Why are we stopping?" she wants to know.

"That's where I used to live," he tells her. "From when I was a kid littler than you up until I left."

She stretches taller in the seat to look past him. "You didn't live there," she protests, suspecting he's trying to make a fool of her. "That's an old junk house."

And it is. Weeds are growing up past the smashed windows, and part of the roof has collapsed. Juniper has risen around the rust-colored, rust-fragile bus. "I told you. It was a long time ago. I'm old," he says, turning the wheel and pulling in where the driveway used to be. They get out and she's up to her waist in grass. She turns and sets her doll back in the car before closing the door. Looking at him, she's squinting into the hot sun; there's chocolate ice cream stuck to her chin. "Let's go see if there's any ghosts," he tells her.

Lila follows him. The windows are high and dark. Logan never touches her; twisting his hand in her overall straps where they cross her back, he hoists her like a crane lifting a package. She hangs there at the end of his hand, her feet swinging slightly, and reports back to him: "Got junky old furniture."

"You see any ghosts?"

She looks hard. "No," she answers, a little uncertain.

"Lemme look," he says, dropping her abruptly. He steps closer and shades his eyes with his cupped hands. The chairs are gone, except for the purple upholstered one in the corner his father used to occupy. Mice have ripped out most of the stuffing and it sits in little cloudy piles around the legs. The sink is there. The stove is gone but he can smell his mother's greasy cooking. Tipping his head back and breathing deeply, he can smell pigs. He moves along the front of the house and looks in the living room. There is no furniture and half the floor has fallen into the cellar. There is more evidence of mice, empty beer bottles, cigarette butts. The blanket hanging over the door to the bedroom is grey and chewed on.

"You got a father?"

He turns and she's right behind him, grass scratching at her elbows, and looking straight up into his face. "Dead," he says.

"You got a mother?"

"Dead."

She frowns, watching him closely. "You got a brother?"

"Joined the freaks," he says. "You met him, only you were too much of a twerp to remember." He pushes past her and starts toward the car.

Lila twists her face up trying to recall. It would be such a victory. "What's he a freak for?" she yells, following him, swishing through the hot, itchy grass.

Logan swings around and bends so his face is close to hers. "Two heads," he says. "He has two heads." He starts walking again.

"I don't believe you!" she hollers, shrill, annoyed. "Nobody got two heads. The doctor woulda cut one of 'em off!"

He whirls on her again. "Which one?"

"The stupidest one," she yells, sticking her jaw out.

"Jesus!" he says admiringly. "All right," he tells her. "All right. He has no head." He plunges through the grass again.

"No!" she screeches, rushing after him, slapping at little bugs that are jumping out of the grass and landing on her bare arms. "No way! There's nobody hasn't got a head!"

He opens the door and gets in the car. Already the plastic seat is hot. He watches her red face as she hurries around to her side. She gets in and glares at him. "He's got a head!" she yells.

"All right, all right." He lifts his hands from the wheel in submission. "But you can't really count it as a head, more like a pimple with a little piece of bone in it."

She draws back in the seat. "Yuck," she says, wrinkling her nose. Backing the car in little bursts, he laughs all the way to the tarred road.

FALLING TOWARD THE MOON

26 "Well, so, you're going in the navy." Logan smiles and leans toward him. "You could do worse."

Perley is sitting across the table from him. He's very straight in the chair, a small frown on his face.

"He'll look all right in a uniform," Logan says, leaning back and turning to address Krista.

"Yeah, all I need is you to sign for me, Mum," Perley says.

"Don't be in such a hurry, son. Once you leave home you don't ever come back, not in the same way."

"I'll go in March soon's I'm eighteen anyway. I'm not going back to school."

"What's the matter with you? I'll sign,"Logan says, lifting his hand toward Perley. "You got it on you?"

"Perley, there's a lots of other things you could do. You got that job with Mr. Holland."

"Mum, I don't want to spend the rest of my life in a dump, for God's sake."

"I didn't mean that, Perley. I just meant there's other jobs. And you should finish school. It's important."

"I hate school, Mum." He stands up and puts his cigarettes in his pocket.

"You think he's too good for the navy? I was in the navy!"

"Perley, going in the service is dangerous."

"There's no war on!" Logan says impatiently.

"You never know. They're always starting something," Krista worries.

"That's the stupidest thing I ever heard!" Logan says scornfully.

Krista has a dish towel in her hand and she twists it up into a knot. "After what the navy did for you, Logan, you shouldn't want it for Perley."

"Jesus Christ!" he roars, standing up out of the chair. "Don't you tell me! Don't you ever tell me! And don't you interfere between me and this boy!"

"I don't want anything to happen to Perley." She backs up against the counter, still twisting her dishcloth.

"Forget it!" Perley says, and goes through the back door.

"If he spends the rest of his life hanging on to your apron, nothing will!" Logan pushes past her and sits down in his recliner chair, picks up his control and snaps on the TV. "You want him to be like your brother Flynn, living with Mumma till he's too old to care!" he yells above the commercial.

Lila comes down the hall in her pajamas. She is holding Mary Alice Stanford high on her shoulder with one hand, and the other hand is holding her new piggy bank, cradling it like an egg. "Ssssshhh," she tells them.

Mary Alice Stanford has on a white nightgown that reaches past her porcelain feet. "You're keeping Mary Alice awake and she has a cold and she needs her sleep. You quit your shouting!" Lila scolds, setting her piggy bank carefully on the small table so she can make a fist and shake it at Logan.

Logan sits back in his chair and lowers onto her his full attention.

"Since when are you in charge, missy? Since when are you giving the orders?"

"I'm in charge of Mary Alice Stanford and Mary Alice needs to sleep."

"Tough shit on Mary Alice Stanford," he mocks, grinning at himself and at her.

Lila presses the doll against her and covers its ears. She stalks up to Logan. "*You* got a dirty mouth!" she tells him. "*Your* mouth ought to be washed out with Ivory soap!"

"You big enough to do it?" he says, half rising on the cane so he's leaning over her. He opens his mouth wide and sticks out his tongue.

Lila looks up at his tongue, the edges of his small white teeth. "One night you'll be sleeping," she tells him, backing two steps, "and you'll wake up blowing bubbles."

"Ohh?" he says. "Well, I'm glad you warned me. I'll be watching for you. I'll be sleeping with one eye open." They are alone in the room. They have been for several minutes. Logan leans toward her. "That's where you made your mistake, missy. Don't ever warn anybody if you're going to do something to 'em. Just do it. Sneak 'em quick, 'specially if they're bigger than you." He settles back in his chair. "Now if you want to you can put Mary Alice Shitford asleep on the couch and watch some TV."

"Stanford!" she hollers, her face red. She settles her doll on the end of the couch under the afghan.

"You bring that for me?" he asks, looking at her piggy bank.

"No!" Lila snatches it from the table and runs down the hall to her room. She turns at the doorway. "I'm coming right back," she calls to him. "Don't you make any more noise!"

Perley is working at the dump for Mr. Holland and he doesn't come home much. He stays there overnight in Mrs. Duffy's little blue house. Mr. Holland looks like Elvis Presley: the narrow face, the rising shiny hair, the higher-on-one-side mouth; the only difference is Mr. Holland's lips aren't so swollen and he has a limp from a motorcycle accident. He's in his forties now, but he's still a pistol. He likes Perley, who works hard and doesn't jabber.

It's a hot Thursday in September and Perley's working in a T-shirt. He hoists a stove with Mr. Holland and they rest it on the tailgate and slide it forward into the truck. They are sweating as they raise up an old doorless dryer, an oil tank punctured by BB gun shots, two rusted barbecue grills. Mr. Holland steps back and hikes up his pants, nudges his brown fedora off his forehead. "We'll take this to the scrap place on Monday," he says. "It's too late to do it today." He clears his throat and spits, then looks back at the dump road. A long, light blue car is turning in. It pauses before it gets to the little shack. A small hand comes out the window and waves. The motor purrs.

"See you later, kid," Mr. Holland says as he starts toward the car, his body tipping to the left, his hat jaunty on his head.

Tripp comes through the juniper and the new poplar trees between his house and the dump. He's got a bag on his hip. He and Perley sit slumped in a burned-out station wagon parked at the edge of the gully and drink beer. Looking through the glassless front of the car, they watch the dump, which is almost pretty in this light. The earth drops suddenly, falling where they can't see it; the pines rise again on the other side of the ravine. Sea gulls hang between them and the falling sun; only the ends of their flight feathers are illuminated, their bodies are black as shadows.

Harmony is at Audrey's this same afternoon. She is often at Audrey's. They are watching soap operas and eating. Audrey's little sisters sit carefully out of the way and crane their necks to watch too.

"She keeps taking him back, taking him back again," Audrey says, pointing with her potato chip at the screen. "She's a jerk, a first-class jerk." She slumps back on the well-worn sofa and glares at the woman on the screen as if she had personally set out to disappoint Audrey.

"Ma's coming," announces one of the girls.

"It's too early," Audrey says, without looking at her. "What do you think of him?" she asks Harmony, pointing with her chin at the screen, where a young man stands punching buttons on a phone and looking about him, fearful of being overheard.

"She's here! She's here!"

"Bullshit." But Audrey gets up off the couch and goes to the window to look. "Jeez," she says, frowning and turning to Harmony, "something must be going on."

They can hear the door shut and Mrs. West's scuffy shoes coming across the kitchen linoleum. She's making little moaning sounds. She stops—there's a break in the sound of her scuffing feet—and blows her nose for a long time. Then she comes on and she's standing in the doorway looking at them, looking at Audrey.

"He's dead," she gasps, and comes into the room far enough to sink down on the edge of the couch, where she starts wailing.

Audrey leaps off it as if a hot match had been set on the back of her leg. "Who's dead?" She says it like a challenge, facing her mother with her hands on her hips.

Mrs. West can't speak, she can't answer. The three younger girls have crowded around and are patting her. She raises her face toward Audrey. "Mr. . . . Mr. . . . Mr. Bishop," she gets out and then howls openmouthed, tears spurting from her eyes, one hand clutching a Kleenex, the other reaching toward Audrey.

Audrey steps back. A grin pulls half of her mouth down. "What happened?" she asks.

Mrs. West rocks on the couch, her narrow calves pressed together, her feet making little tapping sounds as they rise in the air and then hit the floor again. "He said he didn't feel good . . ."

"I guess he knew what he was talking about," Audrey says.

Mrs. West starts coughing, and one of the girls pats her back softly and then harder and harder until she stops. "He went in the men's room," Mrs. West tells them, her voice rising and then disappearing in a squeak on the last word, and she's crying again.

"And that's the last anybody ever saw of him!" Audrey thunders, bringing her fist down on her thigh.

Mrs. West stops crying and looks brightly at Audrey. "Alive. Yes. How did you know? Who told you?"

Audrey roars with laughter. This makes her mother start wailing again. Although her hair is quite short and frizzled and her face weary, she and Audrey look very much alike, "What-t-t am-m I-I-I going to do?" she sobs, and the three younger girls crowd even more closely about her, squeezing gently, giving Audrey mean looks.

Audrey rears back on her heels. "Did they have to break down the stall to get him out?" she demands, slapping her thigh again.

"Oh, Audrey, you're not very nice," her mother sobs.

* * *

When Harmony gets home Tripp's truck is parked in the yard and Perley is sitting at the kitchen table drinking coffee, his legs thrust out in front of him, a cigarette in his hand. He looks older already from his dump work and his life away in the little blue house. Her mother is at the stove. She's got her hunched-up, worried look. "Are you staying to supper with us, Perley?" Harmony asks.

"I was. I'm not so sure now. How you doing?"

She hears her father's voice coming from the living room. The wall is between them but she doesn't have to see him: he is in his recliner chair, his cane held ready in one hand. "I asked you, how much you paying your mother?"

"And I told you, I ain't paying her nothing. I don't live here." Perley leans back in the chair to throw his voice around the wall.

"Way I see it, you got back rent owing, mister."

"Jesus!" Perley looks at Krista. "Mum, you want some money?"

She looks at him, shakes her head, then turns and lifts a pot off the stove. "Logan, supper's almost ready," she calls. Then she smiles at Harmony. "Did you have a good time with Audrey?"

"Her mother's boyfriend died."

Krista looks at her. "Are you serious?"

"Yup. Audrey thinks it's funny."

"Harmony, you shouldn't say things like that."

"All right, I'll lie." She starts to leave the room.

"What you got going on over there to the dump?" Logan is leaning in the doorway now, watching the back of Perley's head. "You got something going with Mrs. Duffy?"

"Oh for God's sake."

"I'll bet you pay *her* plenty." Logan is grinning; he's having fun but Perley's angry. He jerks himself up out of the chair.

"I'm going, Mum. I'll see you some other time."

"Perley! I got your supper ready. Come back and sit down, son," she calls, turning from the stove and following halfway across the kitchen with a saucepan in her hand.

He pauses at the door and gives her a little salute. "I'll see you some other time, Mum," he says, and goes through it.

Logan glares at the door. "Touchy, ain't he," he says.

"He can't stay you tease him like that. You aren't funny. You hurt with your teasing. Perley doesn't owe me any money."

His voice is icy. "Little girl thinks I'm funny and she's smarter than the rest of you put together twice."

Logan drinks beer with his supper. He empties his bottle with the dessert and he wants more. Krista is doing the dishes. He shakes the empty toward her. "Would you get me a beer," he says.

"That was the last one, Logan."

"The hell you say!"

She sighs and pulls open the refrigerator door. She holds it wide while he looks at the shelves. "You forgot to put it in there," he says. He looks at the cupboards. "Where'd you put it?"

"It's gone, Logan."

He gets up and starts opening doors. Bending to the cupboard to the right of the sink, he twists his head up to look at her. "You gave it to him, didn't you? My last beer."

"Who? I didn't give it to anyone."

"Perley. The guy who's too good for the navy. You gave it to him."

"No. Perley was drinking a cup of coffee."

He bangs the cupboard door shut.

"Palmer's is open. It's just up the road. You can get some more." Her voice is flat and disinterested.

"Don't you send me on errands!" He lurches at her and grabs her arm and pulls her close.

"Perley drank coffee," Harmony says. She is standing in the doorway. Behind her the TV is playing.

"What did you do with it, Krista?" Logan demands, pushing her.

"It's gone. You drank it."

He keeps pushing until she's backed up against the counter. "I think you gave it to him. I think he drove home with it. To his new home, the one that's good enough for him." He grips her wrist and twists her arm up behind her.

"You're hurting me, Logan!"

"Let go of her. Perley didn't take anything. You saw him leave!" Harmony reaches and touches his arm. "Let go of her!"

"Mind your own business!" Logan snarls, not looking at her. He leans a little harder. He twists Krista's arm higher on her back.

"You're hurting me, Logan!"

Something flies past Harmony and smashes into the back of his head. He sways and his hand goes out and braces against the refrigerator. Pennies are spinning around their feet, tumbling, heavier quarters, some nickels, a few dimes: ricocheting off the baseboards, rolling under the table, turning over flat and gleaming dully, the solid cling and clamor of money. Logan turns, his hand lifting to the back of his head.

Lila, one fist still raised and her doll in the other hand: "Leave my mother alone!" she hollers in a frightened voice. She shakes the fist. "You go back to Toegust and stay there, you!"

His face registers for one moment disbelief, then betrayal, then is overtaken by rage. "I'll kill her! I'll kill her!" he screams, and bringing his foot down hard on the pink china head, crushing the smiling snout, he leaps.

But Lila turns and dashes across the living room, clasps her doll between her knees so both hands are free to open the door. She pulls it half closed behind her and runs.

Screaming, Logan is stumbling over broken china, skidding on money; an egg is already rising on the back of his skull. Without his cane he's precarious. Catching at the wide doorframe between the kitchen and the living room, he looks across and through the picture window and sees her sturdy traitorous figure descending the lawn toward the row of maples. "Who in the fucking hell does she think she is!" he screeches at his wife.

"You frightened her, Logan. She's just a child. Sit down and I'll get you some ice."

"Ice! Screw ice! She attacks *me* and you defend her!" He glares at her as if she's deranged. "I promise you," he says, his voice dropping almost to normal. "She will *never* lift her hand to *me* again." He stands up straighter, still in the doorframe. "Give me my cane," he says.

"What are you going to do?"

"Give me my cane, goddamnit!"

"What are you going to do?"

"You're making me madder!"

Krista gives it to him and he stomps across the living room and goes out the door, leaving it slammed back open behind him. He whacks at the overgrown grass with his cane as he goes down the lawn. At intervals he calls: "You! Little girl!" his voice a short sharp bark.

"He can't catch her, don't worry, Mum." They are both breathing in quick shallow breaths, their fingers are clenched in the same way.

"She hasn't got her jacket," Krista says.

"I'll find her."

"I never thought he'd lose his temper with Lila."

Harmony looks at her, but Krista's studying his descending figure. "I'll find her," Harmony repeats.

Krista turns slowly from the window. "Don't bring her home," she says. "It's not safe yet. I'll call Perley. He can take her to Grandma for the night. Then by tomorrow he'll be cooled off."

"What are you going to tell Grandma?"

"Lila always wants to go there," Krista says quickly. "She loves to stay overnight." She's still watching out the window. The house shadows part of the lawn, but where the setting sun strikes into the maple trees the light is golden. Logan's dark square shape is moving toward them. She can't see Lila anywhere. She hears Harmony withdrawing and then the sound of the back door closing. Logan has reached the trees. He stands there among them, a small and crooked figure in their splendid line.

She hurries to the phone and dials, but Perley and Tripp have gone out and Mrs. Duffy doesn't think they're coming home any time soon. Krista leaves a message for him to call and hangs up. She gets her broom out of the closet and carefully sweeps up the coins, the shattered bits of pink china. She leaves it all in the dustpan and sets it on top of the refrigerator so she can pick through it for Lila's money tomorrow. There's a thumping sound and then Logan comes through the back door. He looks around the kitchen. "Where is she?" he demands.

"She's not back. She didn't come back. It'll be dark soon, Logan, and she's afraid of the dark."

"Good. She'll have to come in and I'll be waiting." He hooks his cane over a chair back and pulls his belt off. He coils it into a tight loop and sets it on the table. Then he lowers himself into a chair and looks at his wife. "My head hurts," he says.

"You're late on your pills. I'll get them for you." She puts them down carefully with a glass of water and listens while he scoops them into his hand and swallows them. Then there are footsteps on the back porch and they both turn toward the door.

But it is Harmony.

"Where the hell have you been?" he says.

Harmony shuts the door carefully. "Out," she says.

"You see her?"

"No."

"She's got lost you scared her so bad," Krista cries.

"She's not lost. She's too damn smart to get lost!" He stands up stiffly and goes out the door again, his cane in one hand, his belt in the other.

Harmony turns to her mother. "Is Perley coming?"

Krista shakes her head. "Mrs. Duffy says they've gone somewhere and won't be back till real late." She snaps on the overhead light, the back porch light; she hurries through to turn on the lights in the living room, the light over the front door.

Harmony follows her. "What are you going to do?"

Krista is again watching out the picture window. "I'll call Freddie," she decides. "I'll call and ask him will he come get her and bring her to Mum's."

Harmony nods. "But tell him to go on by the house and pull over up by Perrault's. I'll bring her there when I find her."

"Oh, good idea, Harmony." Krista follows her to the door. "But put your jacket on," she says.

Logan circles the house. "You! Little girl," he barks. The lump on his head is the shape of a pear and it throbs. He is furious that she thinks she can outsmart *him*. His hands ache that he cannot get a hold of her and settle it. As he hunts, calling and cursing, night begins to settle in the uneven grass like smoke.

Frederick Hewitt is living in a big building on Park Avenue that has been cut up into smaller and smaller units. He worked overtime today, taping Sheetrock in a new building out on Forest Avenue, and he is tired. He passes two brown-skinned young men on his way up to the third floor. They are talking in a foreign language, their voices like a peevish lament. He shifts the bag of groceries onto his hip and puts his key in the lock.

He goes into the kitchen and puts the bag on a broken chair. A white plastic clock on the high windowsill says six-thirty. He puts the groceries away and goes through to the living room with a cold beer, sits on a crate in front of the wide window. Across the street in the park the trees have turned. He lights a cigarette and watches a blind man come tapping down the street. The man wears an old brown coat; his narrow cane searches before him like an insect's antenna. How good the beer tastes—all day long he's been eating Sheetrock dust.

Frederick showers quickly in the windowless bathroom and, wrapping the towel around his waist, goes into the kitchen. He opens another beer, fries bologna, scrambles eggs, heats a can of string beans in a pot. He's pouring them into a bowl when the telephone rings, and it's Krista.

"I'm sorry but can you please come now quick and take Lila to Mum's for the night. I'm sorry, Freddie, but I can't get Perley and there's nobody else. Please." Her voice sounds muffled; she's talking fast.

"That's okay, Krista. But what's wrong?"

He can hear her breathing into the phone. "It's that . . . well, Logan's lost his temper with her and I want him to cool off before he sees her."

"Are you home?"

"Yes. Can you just hurry? I got to hang up. But Freddie, listen: don't come here, just go by the house and park in front of Perrault's. It's the farm on the hill next to us. Park there and Harmony will bring Lila to you."

He drives as fast as he can out of the city and when he gets on the highway he puts his foot down hard. This truck has got a lot of rattles at sixty-five, the motor strives like an old heart. He turns the radio down, starts another cigarette. Traffic is heavy; he passes cars and stays in the outside lane. Not long ago he would have been one of the very few vehicles on the road at seven o'clock in the evening on a Thursday. But everybody's coming to Maine now, all the yuppies, coming to live the "good life" people born here can't afford. He drives up hard behind a maroon BMW until the son of a bitch finally pulls over and the truck pounds by him. What the hell has Logan been doing? Maybe he'll have to take them all in to Viola.

Harmony has gone as far into the pit as she dares. The batteries in her flashlight are weak and the beam it sends is watery. The sand is cold; she can smell the pond down at the bottom, a muddy, reedy odor. She can't believe Lila would go way down there where it's so black. She peers along the thin beam of light into stumpy brush. She calls her name. "It's okay. We're going to take you to Grandma," she whispers loudly. "Lila!"

Krista searches in the garage, calling her name, looking behind old boxes and worn-out tires. "I have your jacket," she coaxes. "It's all right."

During the preceding half hour Logan has been making regular trips around the house, stomping into the kitchen at intervals to curse and complain to his wife. He is sure the cold and the dark will drive Lila home, and he wishes she would come now and end this. He goes out the front door, down the flagstones, and turns up the driveway. There is a small circle of light coming along the path from the pit; he can hear his wife inside the garage. She knocks something over and it clatters on the cement floor. When he shines his flashlight at her Krista doesn't look at him. He goes under the clothesline and stumps up the backyard, is passing the porch steps when he hears Harmony saying something. He turns to listen and, in turning, stubs the toes of his left foot hard against something.

"Jesus!" he cries, and shines his light. It's the large stone he uses to hold down the bulkhead doors. It isn't where it should be. He smiles and turns off his flashlight. He lifts the right-hand bulkhead door and climbs, grunting softly, over the high sill. Placing his cane carefully on each stair, he descends quietly. The door at the bottom is not latched and he pauses to listen, his face pressed against the narrow opening.

The shadows have all gone and it is true night when Frederick reaches the exit. He drives too fast through the village. Main Street is quiet and the golden hands in the clock tower of the Methodist church show seven forty-five. He goes past the gas station and the convenience store and then he has to hit the brakes hard because the gates are falling at the crossing and the long whistle of the train comes screaming toward him.

It goes on and on and on: engines and black tank cars and empty flatbeds rattling: Bangor and Aroostook, Pine Tree State, Engelhard Chemicals; on and on and on, making that *slap-clack, slap-clack* sound, smooth as falling water. Frederick is reared up on the seat, his fingers whitened around the wheel. He tries to make his mind go blank while he must wait, and the train goes on and on and on.

Finally the caboose, red as a child's toy—the man in the last window waves. The gates rise and he guns the truck and bumps over the tracks, the whistle echoing after him as he goes on out Route 110, past houses with their softly lit windows. He wonders what has been happening in the time it took him to get this far; his head aches, his cab is full of cigarette smoke. He climbs over the railroad bridge, and the broad fields of the Burtons' farm are stretching to his right, flat and clean as the sea.

Perched on the bottom bulkhead step, listening at the slightly opened door, Logan hears water flowing, is confused, and then realizes it's the sound of someone pissing. Gleefully he throws open the door and shines his light.

Lila is squatted over an empty paint can. Her eyes meeting his are startled and then frightened. Mary Alice Stanford is lying on the blue sweater Lila has spread out on the cement floor. Around them are the spent matches Lila has been lighting to soothe her fear of the dark. With a sharp cry she stands and pulls up her underwear, her pink corduroy slacks. "Spy, sneak," she cries in a high-pitched voice as he approaches.

He is laughing, pleased to find her and in this vulnerable predicament. She takes her matchbook from her pocket and, lighting her last five, flings them at him. The final one lands on his shoe.

"What in the hell do you think you're doing now!" he shouts, but he's still laughing.

She snatches her doll from the sweater and starts to run with her up the cellar stairs, her hand on the rail to guide her, wailing as she goes for her fear of the dark and of him and of the insult to her dignity.

Logan shines his light on her, to aid her way, but it feels to Lila like a hound at her heels and she climbs faster. When she gains the top she fumbles for the doorknob and then there is light and she turns and looks down at him. "You're bad," she says. "You killed Joseph. You're mean! Burn up! Burn up to stinking ashes!"

"Come back here, you!" He thumps up the stairs after her. How can she, how *dare* she, talk to him like that! Lila screams and turns, running from him, and when he reaches the top she is already out the front door. It stands open. He can see her in the light his wife turned on, running over the lawn his own shoes lately trampled, the whiteness of the doll's porcelain feet. "Come back!" he bellows. But she gets smaller. The dark covers her up.

He hurls himself through the open door and down the steps. He doesn't have his cane. Lurching over the wet and slippery grass, he feels he has to keep going to remain upright. "Stop!" he shouts. "Stop! I ain't going to do anything to you!" He's gaining on her. Lila is tired; she's been maneuvering around him for a long time. "Stop, goddamnit!"

But she keeps going, right between the old trunks of the maples, and it is then Logan becomes aware of the gritty sound of the truck, the flash of its headlights. "Lila!" he yells, and his hand flings out and hits hard against tree bark.

Frederick Hewitt is not thinking about where he is; he is thinking about where he will be in two hundred yards, Perrault's, yes, there on the top of the hill, yes, he sees the lights, such a row of lights front room to ell, and will they be there to meet him like she said?

It's all too quick. He feels the thud, and a small pale face white as a geisha smashes against his windshield, porcelain dust rains down on his hood.

The Perraults, coming along from their church executive meeting, slow their car, puzzling at what they see in its headlights: a slight, bearded man kneeling over something in the road, their neighbor Logan Pembroke, standing above him with his fists raised in the air, and women, running down the Pembroke driveway with their hair streaming out behind them.

KRISTA LEAVING

27 It is white. It is quiet. Just little bells and the squishy noise of nurses' shoes. They are white, pattering around her white bed, squishing on their shoes. Her poor leg is buried in a long white cast; on her hands are white bandages like paws. They do things to her. They feed her and bathe her and push her around in a wheelchair. She rides silently along corridors, down to the basement where the X-ray machine is. They push her past doors and doors and doors behind which lie injured and dying children. She can hear them cough and cry, she can hear them call out and whimper. She doesn't say anything. She watches. She does not remember the accident. She remembers the still-smiling head of her piggy bank sitting there beside his shoe. Her Mum is here when she wakes up, when she leaves the room propelled away in her chair, when she comes back again. Her Mum cries: water, water, washing around in her eyes like rain on a window. Lila watches her. If her Mum goes away and leaves her here she will die.

Frederick Hewitt has not slept much since he hit Lila with his truck. He hasn't eaten much either. He's been smoking cigarettes and drinking beer, not enough to get really drunk, but not much less than that. He feels like a hunted man, but he's barely left his apartment; he's been at home to any retributive force seeking him out. He is not to be charged, however; the police have told him that. But he waits anyway.

At night he sits in his living room and listens, in darkness but for the burning end of his cigarette. He hears people in the building forging up and down stairs, slamming doors, running water, arguing with each other, laughing, until they have all gone to bed. He hears the building then, its vessels and nerves, water and power, the old furnace throbbing below them all in the basement. There are creaks and exhalations, a shutter flaps and bangs like a fractured appendage. The building grows around him: how large it becomes in the darkness, its rackety life more fantastic, the black spaces swelling so that he fears being swallowed and he gets up abruptly and snaps on a light, turns up his radio, moves around until the room regains its daylight proportions.

He has called the hospital every morning but is only marginally comforted by the female voice on the other end: "She is doing well"; "She is going home soon"; "She will be discharged tomorrow." He imagines her injuries more severe than what they will tell him, and what he wants to hear, waits to hear in the next call, or the next, is that she is not there, has never been there. He wants to believe it has all been a terrible nightmare or some other piece of craziness his mind flung out when he wasn't careful. What he does keep hearing, so loud he's ducking and looking over his shoulder, is the train: *slap-clack, slap-clack,* the long whistle. He sees it: Bangor and Aroostook,

Pine Tree State, Engelhard Chemicals. The red caboose with the man in the last window, his lifted arm. If the train had been later . . . If he'd been a minute faster and beaten it at the crossing . . . If it hadn't come down the track just at that moment to intercept him with devilish purpose like a message with his name on the envelope. What Frederick wants is for his life to have ended then.

On the fifth day Lila is in the hospital the circus arrives in her room, without fanfare, like a visitation. First the jugglers. Small dark-haired children in sun-yellow costumes toss balls, bright and intricately painted Easter eggs, red birds that fly from one child to the next. They stand on one another's shoulders, the littlest one on top, and juggle floor to ceiling.

In comes a little dog wearing a green ruff around his neck. The jugglers keep juggling but he jumps up on Lila's bed and delivers a basket full of small round white stones.

A large cat strolls in. He is attached to a green leash held by a very small woman who is carrying a purple parasol and a bunch of grapes for Lila.

Next come two very little boys in blue. They pantomime a seesaw. Up and down they go, up and down, as graceful and balanced as courting birds. A magician makes them disappear. His black cloak swallows the blue boys and beneath its folds they hatch out two black crows and a bunch of flowers. Lila claps her white paws and squeals.

A woman in a butterfly costume lands on Lila's bed. She takes a little paint kit out from under her wing and paints butterfly children up and down Lila's cast. How beautiful her leg looks now, how light it becomes.

A woman and a man clown, their feet like flippers, their noses bright red, grip each other's shoulders and somersault over and over in a human loop. A tall bony man lumbers in bearing a beautiful pony tenderly before him in two hands. The mane and tail are silver, the reins are red. Lila is stroking him with her paw as the last pair comes through the door. She has enormous red hair and the man's eyes are like her father's. Lila stares at them through the clowns and the magician and the sun-yellow jugglers. When the door opens a final time her Mum comes in with a tiny old lady. It is Grandmother Dooley hurrying with her special herbal soup.

* * *

The nurse who arrives with midmorning juice sniffs and sniffs. She could swear she smells the crisp odor of parsley and the murkier fume of terrier. "My goodness!" she says when she gets to the bed and sees Lila's cast. "Beautiful!" she tells her, and, touching the pony, "Who brought you this?" She sets the juice on the bedside table and unwraps the straw. Sniffing and frowning, she plucks two black feathers from the pillow.

"She's going to be fine," Grandmother Dooley declares firmly. "Bones heal. The body is forever remaking itself."

"I'm just so grateful she's alive," Krista says, her eyes brimming with tears. They are in her kitchen, all the Dooleys, Ronnie and Betty Pembroke. "The doctor says what she needs is time."

"Don't we all!" Grandmother Dooley pours more tea. "Every one of us, we're babies learning about life."

"We're just so lucky," Krista tells her.

"You didn't lose your little girl." Grandmother Dooley speaks softly, understanding. She reaches and pats Krista's hand.

"That's how I felt, that's just how I felt. I told Logan I can stand anything so long as we don't lose her." She blows her nose.

Logan is sitting at his table in their midst, his teeth gritted, his back rigid. He'd like to gather the Dooleys up in his fist and throw them out of his house. He'd like to see his brother go up in smoke. He glares at him as Ronnie leans closer to Krista.

"I broke my arm when I was about Lila's age," he tells her, lifting it high and looking at it. "Healed good though."

"You never broke your arm," Logan scoffs.

Ronnie turns to him, his mouth opening, but Betty booms, "That's right, strictly speaking; he didn't, your father did it for him." She catches Ronnie's arm still held into the air and rubs gently.

"What are you talking about?" Logan challenges loudly.

"Don't you remember, Logan." Ronnie's voice is soft. "When he locked Ma out of the house? It was snowing. He broke my arm when I opened the door."

"You're crazy!" Logan looks at him, his face full of hate, and underneath that, fear like a shadow.

"He didn't mean to exactly," Ronnie allows, almost sheepish.

Betty won't take this. "Bullshit," she says, then turns to Krista. "It's a good thing we came now. I told Ronnie, I said, 'We haven't visited your brother since 1979.' I said, 'I don't care if we are late. We're going to stop there 'fore we head south. Florida ain't going anywhere,' I told him." She nods vigorously. "Sent my Midge home in an airplane. She's got her senior year at Florida State."

Krista wipes at her eyes. Her wet face is glowing. "You're the first thing that's made Lila smile since it happened. I just want to thank you all," she tells them, looking around her table.

"Children love magic," Maurice Dooley says. "It helps them believe that what they gave up daring to hope for might come true despite all."

"That's it!" Grandmother Dooley confirms, hugging the smallest girl.

Betty reaches out to take Krista's wrist. "We stayed later than we ever have because of this new fair in Ottawa. I told the fortunes of politicians' wives," she explains, gesturing with her hand so her silver bracelets jingle. "There's reasons for everything. If we hadn't come late like we did we wouldn't have been here now when you need us."

"Betty, you've done so much good, all of you. Lila didn't smile once or even look at anything until today. She just loves that pony," Krista tells Edgar Moss, who's leaning against her refrigerator.

Edgar clears his throat. It's a long, whinnying preparation of his vocal chords. "It's hard to be sad when you got a horse," he says, softly but with feeling.

Betty nods, then turns back to Krista. "Now," she says, leaning her knuckles on the table. "I want you to promise me that you'll bring my niece for a visit just as soon as she can come." She lifts her knuckles and prods the top of Logan's shoulder. "I'm leaving you my phone number, and I'm telling you, nothing will strengthen a leg like running on a beach."

"Ma used to walk the beach," Ronnie remembers. "She said it made her feel almost young again."

"Disney World!" chorus the Dooley children.

"Yes, yes," agree their mothers. "We'll take her there!"

"Busch Gardens!" they gasp.

"J. Fred Muggs!" the two little boys squeak with hilarity.

* * *

When they have gone, departing before the sun is up and as quietly as they did that first spring when they came, Logan rails against their size and their magic and their advice. "Disney World my ass," he says. "Who in the hell do they think they are!"

Krista watches him. He paces the kitchen, thwomping with his cane. "They're your family," she says slowly. "They're your brother and his dear ones. They came and made Lila laugh and be happy. They invited her special. I know it's much too far away for her to go, but they meant it. They meant it and you won't even go visit her."

"I can't stand hospitals!"

"I know you hate 'em. But you shouldn't put yourself ahead of her."

"She's all right! Everyone says so. You say so!" he accuses, raising his cane from the floor and pointing it at her.

"You put yourself first. Always. No matter who it is or who gets hurt." She studies his face. "You never put your children first. Or thought much about me either," she tells him.

He laughs. "You do enough thinking about you for eight people."

"Do I?"

"You bet you do!"

"Logan, I'm looking at you like you're somebody I don't know and only heard about. I'm seeing."

"What the hell are you trying to say now?"

"I'm saying my little girl was chased out of her own home and into the road."

His face twists and gets darker above her. "Don't you—" he cries, raising his cane and bringing it down hard on the table edge so it smashes into two sticks with splintery ends good for nothing but burning.

Krista stands up out of the chair. "And her own mother not facing up to that," she says bitterly, her hands shaking. Then she turns and goes out of the kitchen and down the hall.

On Wednesday evening Frederick leaves his apartment. He goes to the store where, peering in through the window, he can see Viola. She is waiting on two teenage girls. Flynn is sitting on a stool beside her looking at a magazine. Frederick goes on down the sidewalk, then returns. This time he can't see Flynn, but Viola is there, reaching down cigarettes for a customer. When she turns with them in her hand she looks right at where he stands waiting like a zoo creature to endure her scrutiny. She must see him, but her expression shows nothing. He touches his own face, then turns and hurries down the sidewalk.

He waits on Grant Street. It is dark when they come home. His shadowy figure unfolds itself from the stoop and rises before them.

"Dee!" Flynn cries, and hurries to him.

"Hi, Flynn," he says, shaking his hand. Then he looks at her.

Viola has stopped on the sidewalk. The bulb in the entryway sends a greenish kind of light around them all. "I called and they said she was gone home and she was doing good," he says, almost shouts she seems so far away. "Good news!" he cries.

She nods.

He can see her face; the light is shining around him onto her. She is little there below him on the sidewalk while he is up on the stoop with Flynn, but a kind of energy is radiating from her and her face has the overdone and unalterable quality of a mask.

"She's going to be a long time healing yet," Viola says.

He looks down. "A bad break takes a long time," he agrees hoarsely, looking past her toward the buildings on the other side of the street. "But they wouldn't let her come home if she wasn't doing good."

"It's time to go up," she tells Flynn.

"There was no charges, Viola." She is on the stoop now, very near to him.

"Krista's real glad about that," she says, her voice disdainful.

"I just . . . I'm real sorry," he says. He is getting pains in his chest from standing so stiffly before her.

"Well, you must be." She gets a hold of Flynn's elbow.

Frederick climbs down awkwardly from the stoop to make way for them. The door shuts and he turns and goes down the sidewalk, his pace increasing until he's almost running.

He should get the hell out of here, go, escape these cold, tired streets and the landscape of people's backs. Leave for Florida a little earlier than he'd planned, chase out of here before winter comes sliding in on the dawn of frosty mornings, announces itself in windy storms and a yellow moon traveling low and heavy above black trees.

* * *

Perley came home for a while after the accident but he's back living at Duffy's now. He's waiting to hear from the navy and he's anxious to be gone. Krista signed for him; she knows she hasn't protected anybody from anything.

In love with Arliss Foster, who fills up all the space she's been sinking in for the last five years, Harmony is seldom at home. She's either at school, at work, or with Arliss, who is twenty-two and a welder. She knows that if she can make him love her she will never want to do anything else.

Lila goes back to third grade. Fern Wallace gets down out of her bus and she and Krista half lift Lila up the steps so she can sit in the first seat, her crutches and her mother beside her. She's quiet and nervous-acting, "like a different child" her teacher worries. She lets Lila leave ahead of the others for lunch, she gives her extra help at recess for all the work she's missed. Classmates write their names on her cast between the butterflies and the dirt.

"It's good to see you back," Mrs. Bernier tells Krista.

"I'm glad to be back," she says, shredding lettuce. She saves most of the money from her pay and hides it in her drawer, folded inside a box of Tampax. At night she dreams she's in a truck that's surging downhill with no brakes. Around corners it flies, tipping up on two wheels, roaring and clanking while she sits on the edge of the seat with her fingers clamped on the dashboard, her mouth open. When she wakes, thirsty and still half panting with fear, she thinks how her daughter lay in the road in front of their home, her body curled in the primitive shape of a fetus.

Logan feels uneasy, naked, precarious without the focus of their attention. It makes him even quicker to temper, louder in his jokes. He drives around, goes slowly past the school, up to the dump where sometimes he can see Perley pushing garbage into the gully with Mr. Holland's plow. He changes his routine and shops at the supermarket in the late afternoons. Harmony nods to him as he goes by with his cart. She is behind the meat counter in a blood-spattered uniform, the perky white cap set at an angle on her dark head. When she gets home at night he tells her, "You look like a pig-sticker. Those bums at the store too cheap to give you a clean uniform?"

She is confused and she goes in her room, strips off her clothes, wraps up in her bathrobe. She gets in the shower and thinks about Arliss as the hot water pounds down on her skin.

As far as Logan is concerned, Lila is in a kind of quarantine. He doesn't want to be near her. He doesn't want to hear the thumping of her crutches on the floor, her labored uneven gait which is so like his own. She keeps away from him. She is either in her room or where her mother is.

On a grey day in November Krista gets a ride into Portland with Mrs. Bernier. They leave after work, Mrs. Bernier still in her hairnet and her thick white shoes. She is going into Portland to bring her sister some money and she's very angry. She doesn't say anything, but Krista's known Mattie Bernier long enough to know when she's steamed. They ride in silence, except for the heater fan, whirring away like an old sewing machine. Krista settles back against the seat, tired and grateful for the warmth and the fact that she doesn't have to do anything but ride for the next half hour.

"I never did like him," Mrs. Bernier says in a loud, tight voice. "Never!"

Krista looks at her.

"My baby sister married a chiseler. And worse! I never did like him!" she insists, shaking her finger at Krista. "Not that I ever said one word. Though you believe me when I tell you it nearly killed me. She trusted him. I don't know why but she trusted him. Danielle was always like that. She wouldn't believe ill of anyone she'd put her trust in."

"That's real hard," Krista murmurs. "When you've put your trust in someone and you're wrong."

But Mattie Bernier has no patience with that. "Faithful as a dog," she says bitterly. "Blind as a newborn kitten."

"Some people have that kind of nature," Krista argues softly. "It's hard to change."

"Idiocy!" Mrs. Bernier proclaims it, bringing her hand down hard on her wheel and missing so she blows the horn. "Hiding in a women's shelter. Hiding from her husband like she was a criminal and he was the police. I've been saving for our retirement but I can't let that stand, my baby sister in a women's shelter! Roland says they can stay with us. 'We got the room,' he says. My husband has the heart of a giant!"

* * *

Mrs. Bernier leaves her on Park Avenue. "I'm going over my mother's after," Krista explains when she gets out of the car.

"I'll be there a little after five. I'll toot," Mattie Bernier tells her.

Krista hurries up the stairs and knocks on the door. She just catches him; Frederick's on his way out.

"Krista!" he says, stunned to see her in his dark hallway.

"Hi, Freddie, I was hoping you'd be home." She looks him up and down, his boots, his jacket. "Are you leaving?"

"It's all right." He steps back and makes room for her to enter. "Come on in if you want."

She blinks. "I've never been here before," she says. "It's nice."

He shrugs. "How's Lila?" he asks her.

"Real good. That's part of why I'm here, Freddie. To tell you that."

"I'm glad to hear it, Krista."

She looks past him toward the kitchen.

"You want a cup of coffee?" he asks.

He follows her into his kitchen. She seems taller to him, tense in a way he doesn't remember. She takes her coat off and hangs it on the chair back. He turns heat on under his kettle and sits on the broken chair.

"She's doing good. She's back in school, Freddie. Her hands are all healed and her teacher's been real good to Lila. She's catching up on her work and the doctor says her leg is coming along real good." She looks at him. His face is drawn and he looks older around the eyes.

He gets up quickly and takes down two mugs from the cupboard. Krista watches his back. "It's good news," he says. "The best news." He measures coffee into the mugs and stands watching the kettle. Then he turns sharply. "You know how bad I feel about what happened. About what I did," he tells her.

"I do know, Freddie. I know you'd rather do anything than to hurt a child. I know that." She looks tired suddenly. "You wouldn't have come," she says slowly. "You wouldn't have even been there if I didn't call and ask you. I came today to tell you I'm sorry."

He winces and then the kettle behind him rattles and begins to moan. He turns sharply and pours water into the mugs.

"I didn't know what else to do when I couldn't find Perley. I was scared, but I had no right to ask you to get into something you didn't know what it was. I shoulda told him if he didn't stop I was calling up the sheriff. But I was scared. Logan's a bully. He scared Lila. He didn't really mean to. No," she corrects herself, frowning, "he did mean to. He didn't like what she did and he wanted to scare her. But he didn't want her to get hurt."

He awkwardly carries the mugs to the table, pushes a battered tin sugar bowl toward her, reaches into the refrigerator for the milk. They don't quite look at each other.

"Freddie, but I didn't even think of the sheriff. And even if I had I wouldn't have called him. I wouldn't want him to know about my home." She's stirring her coffee and watching the spoon going around and around. "Like I'm shamed telling you even though you're my oldest friend." Her voice is getting higher and tears start flowing but she leaves her hands on the table and lets them fall down her face.

"Krista, it wasn't your fault." He pulls a piece of cloth out of a drawer and thrusts it at her. She doesn't seem to see it and he holds it closer to her face.

"It's all right. I'm all right," she says. "I'm just . . . I'm just too full."

He sits down slowly in the broken chair and repeats, "Krista, it wasn't your fault."

"It was though," she says, wiping at her face with the back of her hand. "Mine and Logan's. The both of us. But I blamed you, Freddie. I did. But just for a little while. But I'm sorry." She drinks the coffee as if she's hungry for it. "I didn't want to see where the blame really went. How things really were. I hope you'll forgive me."

"I do. I did. I was mad though. At you," he says, puzzling. "I didn't like feeling that way, guilty and mad at you too. I was coming to help you, I meant to help you . . ."

"I know you did, Freddie, and I don't blame you for being mad." She takes the cloth up from the table and blows her nose. Then she looks at him and smiles a slow smile. "I'm just grateful I came today. And that you were here. I was so afraid you'd gone to Florida."

"I've been going to. I was leaving a couple of weeks ago. After I knew Lila was out of the hospital. Was home." He makes a gesture. "I just didn't get out of here yet though."

"Well, I should have come sooner. I've just been kind of crazy since it happened. But I knew Mum would tell you."

"Tell me?"

"That Lila was doing good, that she came home."

"I called the hospital. They told me." He starts to get up. "You want more coffee?"

"No. No, thanks. I got to go. I got to go see Mum." She stands up and reaches her coat off the back of the chair. She touches his hand as she passes toward the door. "I'm so happy I came and you were here," she says again. "It's made me feel light." And she touches her chest. "Freddie, I hope you'll tell me when you go and when you come back again."

He watches her hurry down the stairs, the thin pale back of her neck showing now since she got her hair cut. He feels all pulled about inside, loosened and freed from something mortal. He listens until he hears the street door swing shut.

The afternoon is raw, and Krista's face and hands are numb by the time she's climbing the stairs to her mother's apartment.

"What a surprise!" Viola says, gesturing for her to come in. "You alone?"

She nods. "It's turning real cold out!"

"How did you get here?"

"Mrs. Bernier gave me a ride. She's picking me up around five."

"How's Lila? Come and sit, you look cold."

"Lila's good. They're taking the cast off before Christmas."

"That's progress." Viola nods. "I'll make you some tea. Flynn went down the store to buy me milk. But you don't need milk, do you?"

"No." She sits down at the table, still in her coat. "Am I keeping you, Mum? Do you have to go to work or anything?"

Viola waves her hand. "Wednesday's my early day. I get home at one."

"Oh. I . . . I forgot. Mum, I wanted to ask you. I wanted to ask you something serious."

"Oh?" Viola sits down. She folds her arms across her chest and watches Krista. "What is it? Is it Lila? You said she was doing good."

"She is. It's that I'm going to move. I'm going to move to Portland. I want to take training for nurse's aide work. Mrs. Bernier's daughter is a nurse and she told me all about it."

"Nurse's aide? You got a good job. Are you telling me you're going to sell your home?"

Krista shakes her head. "What I wanted to ask is could the girls and me stay here just till I get a job and find us an apartment." Krista fiddles with the tea bag, finally takes it out of the cup.

"You mean you're leaving Logan?"

"I have to, Mum."

"You better think twice before you break up your family."

"It's already broke up. Perley gone in the navy. Harmony never home. I want to make it up to Lila," she adds softly.

"Lila's going to be fine. Kids leave home, Krista."

"Flynn didn't."

"That's different and you know it!" Viola says angrily. "Kids leave home. It's natural. And you're lucky if the navy's the worst thing happens to 'em."

Krista looks at her. Viola puts her cup down hard into the saucer. "Krista, you got a nice home. A nice home like your dad wanted his whole life to give his family." Krista looks down at her cup again, touches the spoon. Her eyes hurt. "You ought to be glad for what you got," Viola tells her. "A woman alone ain't much in the world's regard."

"You're alone, Mum," she says.

"So I should know. Besides, I'm a widow, I'm not someone who left her husband 'cause she wanted to be a nurse's aide, for God's sake."

"Mum, it's not that."

Viola stands up. "It'll work out, Krista, you give it a little time. I know Logan isn't the easiest person in the world to live with. But you got to accept people for what they are. They don't change. You pay attention to what's good and carry the rest."

Krista gets up slowly and buttons her coat.

"I'm glad you're wearing your winter coat, it's cold out," Viola tells her.

Krista looks at herself and then nods. "I better go down to the street and wait. It's almost time." But she hesitates and turns at the door. "Mum, did you tell Freddie Lila was going to be all right?"

"He knew. I didn't have to tell him."

"But didn't you care how worried and upset he was?"

"For God's sake, Krista, he nearly killed your daughter!"

"It was an accident and he's suffering for it. Freddie would never hurt a child. You know he wouldn't."

Viola makes an impatient gesture.

"Mum, don't you care about Freddie?"

"I care about what's mine," Viola says, and opens the door. "If you see Flynn, hurry him up. He always stops and talks to people." She steps out onto the landing. "You work this out in your family, Krista, that's where it belongs. You won't be sorry." They hear the street door open and feet climbing. "At last!" Viola says.

"Star!" he calls, and hurries up the last few stairs, shifting his groceries so he can hug her.

It's cold down in the street. Krista huddles in the doorway until Mattie Bernier arrives.

"I'm late," she says when Krista gets into the car. "I'm sorry. My sister wanted me to stay for the women's meeting. They're trying to help her but she keeps saying, 'He needs us.' " Mattie shakes her head. "I got no patience for that!"

"They've got meetings for women?"

"Yeah. And those women got the right idea but she won't listen."

"Can anyone go to the meetings or do you have to live there?" Krista wonders.

"Well I don't know about that, but I'll ask. How did you make out?"

"I had a real good visit with Freddie," she says slowly. "But now that I've seen my mother I feel like an orphan."

When Krista goes into her room Harmony is lying stretched out on the bed, just home from her job at the supermarket. "Hi, Mum," she says, and sits up a little on the pillow.

"Don't you feel good?" Krista asks, coming in to where she can lean her hand against the bedpost.

"I'm just resting for a minute. I got to have a shower. Arliss is coming to get me at six."

"Oh."

"I won't be eating supper here." Harmony waits but her mother doesn't say anything else, just stands there at the foot of her bed in the path of light coming in from the hall. Harmony starts to think about Arliss again. If he will love her she will never have to need anything else.

". . . I plan on you coming with me," her mother is saying.

Harmony sits up. "What, Mum?"

"I know you won't want to change schools and your job, too, but it's best for all of us."

"Change schools? What do you mean?"

"I told you. I'm moving to Portland and I'm planning on you coming with me."

Harmony goes rigid. "Portland? What do you mean?"

"I think we can have a better life if we move to Portland."

"He won't move to Portland," Harmony says slowly.

"I know that."

"You're leaving him?" She whispers the words, but even whispering she feels like some kind of traitor. "Because of Lila," she says, "because of what happened to Lila."

"That's part of it."

"You got a job in Portland?"

"I'm looking. Mrs. Bernier gives me a ride in. I'm hoping for an interview. She gave me a real good reference."

"Are you going to live with Grandma?"

Krista starts picking clothes up off the floor. "Her place is real small, Harmony. We'll get one for us. A place near them. I want you to have your own room." She sets the clothes on a chair. "I lived there in the city, you know. On my own when Perley was a baby. Before you were born. I got by fine then. I was good then."

"I don't believe you," Harmony says fiercely. "I don't believe you!"

"I did. We had an apartment. There were big windows. The sun came in all day long." She turns and looks at her. "But then your grandpa died."

"I'm saying I don't believe you're going to leave here."

Krista is moving again. She pauses to straighten some little bottles on the bureau top. "I have to," she says. "It's my home and I'm real scared but I have to. I'm telling myself it's like anything else. You got to start, you got to start putting your feet down one in front of the other and you got to not stop."

On an evening a month later Logan is sitting in a bar in Leedsport. It is decorated in green and red crepe paper. Santa Claus and his sleigh fly across the mirror. Logan sees his own face among the reindeer antlers, his hand lifting the mug.

When he came home and found the note Krista had left on the kitchen table—after he became convinced that what she had written was true—he wanted to kill her. If she were dead she couldn't leave him, making him look like a fool, turning his home barren as a husk. He had driven fast into Portland. He had waited outside Viola's apartment, banging up and down the sidewalk on his new cane. He was there every day for a week, but when he finally saw Viola and Flynn come out of the building and start down the sidewalk, he stood watching them and never called out. He didn't want to go chasing after them, humiliate himself by asking Viola where his wife was. He got in the car and went home and he didn't go back. He began to think they had gone somewhere far like Boston, or way down to Virginia to be near Perley.

He checks the mail every day. He keeps the bell on the phone turned up loud. He stays on late at the bar in Leedsport, he sleeps late into the mornings. He gets up and eats, the TVs are playing, he cruises in his car, soon it's night and he can go back to Leedsport and drink beside the other people. But he could still in any next moment begin the long plummet, leap, a naked and terrified child, into the old cellar to wrestle with the snakes, to unmask his father and behold his own face, to grieve his mother who never was.

The apartment Krista found is down the hill off Cumberland Avenue. It is four empty rooms with sloping floors and narrow doorways. Something is so familiar about it, and she puzzles until she realizes it smells like the apartment they lived in on India Street, where her mother hated the fat lady downstairs and her father left them that terrible time and wouldn't come back. It smells too of the building on Cleeves Street, a damp dusty smell it is, the apartment they rented there when they left the little house in West Minot and her father lay on the hot dirty bed, angry and dying.

The wind rattles the glass in the long windows and she buys heavy plastic on a roll. When Mrs. Bernier comes in with her husband they help Krista staple the plastic to the window frames, so now the world looks foggy and slightly distorted but less heat flows out.

"That's going to be so much better," Krista says, climbing off the chair. "Thank you."

"You're more 'n welcome," Mr. Bernier tells her. He is a small sturdy man dressed as neatly as a barber, a die-cutter by trade. He glances at his wife, but Mattie is scowling toward the plastic. She turns sharply and looks at Krista.

"Danielle went back to him again," she reports angrily. "He cried. That's all it took: a little water and she ran back into the flames!"

"It's real hard," Krista says. "Might take her a couple of tries. They say in the group to give encouragement no matter what."

"I told her we had plenty of room," Mr. Bernier says. "Our girls are both gone, but she found it real cruel to think of leaving her home." He looks at his wife. "People need to do things in their own time, Mattie," he says.

"Well, I wash my hands of it!" she insists, her voice breaking. She pulls her coat up around her shoulders. "I got some things in the car for you, Krista. Towels, dishes. Polly Forbes sent you in a rocking chair."

"A rocking chair!" Krista laughs and claps her hands. "I always wanted a rocking chair! And we sure need towels." She hugs Mrs. Bernier, who gets red in the face.

It's snowing out and Mrs. Bernier starts up quickly with the box, her husband right behind her with a lamp he made from an old jug. Krista is easing the chair out of the back of the car, when a taxi pulls up behind it. The door opens and Flynn gets out. He holds Lila's crutches and she gets onto them carefully. Flynn works some money out of his pocket and pays the driver. "Burrs!" he calls, seeing their car.

"Just in time to help with this beautiful chair!" Krista tells him.

EPILOGUE

THE PELICANS

It is late in December and snow is falling. Krista is at the Jewish Home for the Aged, where she works. It is lunchtime and she is helping Mrs. Klein, whose hands are too crippled by arthritis for her to be able to use tools. Krista feeds her carefully. Mrs. Klein is her favorite patient. She is delicate as a bird, with bird-black eyes and hair that is the whitest thing Krista has ever seen. She calls Krista "sweetheart." They talk about Krista's children, Mrs. Klein's children, her grandchildren, her new great-grandchild, whose name is Anna, who weighed eight pounds three ounces at birth, who came to visit Mrs. Klein when she was seven days old and didn't cry once but sat in her bent and bony arms like a queen.

"At sixteen you should never have let," Mrs. Klein tells her.

"I didn't know how to stop her," Krista admits. "I thought she might do it all the more if I tried."

"How much more could she do it?" Mrs. Klein says.

Krista brings the teacup to Mrs. Klein's lips. She knows in what order she likes to eat things, not to give her so much time that she loses interest, not to rush her. "I figure if she wants to change her mind she won't find it so hard to come back home," Krista explains.

Mrs. Klein narrows her eyes over the proffered cup. "You might be shrewder than you look," she says approvingly.

Perley is eating lunch in Virginia, where the winter is easy. He is at a bar in Norfolk with three other sailors. They are all wearing their trim white suits, their shiny shoes. Perley is thinking about submarines. The ashtray on their table is full, their mugs foam with beer; he lifts his and drinks for a long time. Submarines are as far as you can get from this world, metal barks sunk in the sea, removed from the chaos above. Perley is thinking about submarines as he watches Bill go up to the bar to get the next round.

At five that afternoon Logan is sitting at the bar in Leedsport, tall on the metal stool like a baby in a high chair. There are Christmas bells and plastic holly strung along the mirror. He orders a beer and a shot of whiskey. In the glass surrounded by holly, by bells, Logan looks handsome. He's lost some weight, he's got a new green shirt on, his hair is longer, his eyebrows are still as delicate as the bars in a bird's mask. The woman who hops up on the stool next to him is Earlene Campbell. She is about his age, short and sturdy like a Labrador retriever. She has frizzy blond hair and a high complexion. Earlene has been alone for about as long as she can stand it. "Buy you a beer?" she asks him.

On Christmas Day Logan sleeps late. When he gets up he turns on both TVs, tries to find a channel that isn't playing holy music. He eats his breakfast, the movie on the TV so loud that at first he doesn't hear the knocking at his door.

When he opens it his daughter Harmony is standing there, dressed in a man's jacket, bare headed, with a scarf wrapped about her throat. Her hair is loose and heavy around her face. He frowns looking at her.

"I came to wish you a merry Christmas." She has a small wrapped gift in her hand. She nudges herself forward over the threshold.

"How'd you get here?" he asks, looking past her.

"Arliss's mother let me drive her car. I got my permit now."

He doesn't say anything.

"I came to invite you over there for Christmas dinner if you want."

"Over where?"

"Arliss's mother. We're having Christmas dinner with her."

"Who is?"

"Me and Arliss."

"Oh, just you." He nods slowly. He is in his undershirt but the cold air coming in the house doesn't seem to bother him. "What the hell kind of name is Arliss?" he ponders, speaking with exaggerated slowness.

Harmony takes a step backward so she's in the doorway again.

"You ain't eating with your mother and her tribe?" He watches her face. "She is back, ain't she?" he probes, unwillingly to ask outright where Krista is.

"Back? No, I told you, Arliss and me are eating with his mother. Do you want to know how to get there or not?"

"I guess I don't," he says. "I'm having Christmas dinner with my new girlfriend. Name's Earlene. I guess that's a bit more human-sounding than Arliss." He grins at her. "You look surprised. I bet you didn't think I could get a girlfriend, old and ugly as I am."

Harmony reaches to leave the small present. It almost falls and she lunges to push it farther onto the counter before backing out the door.

He stands on the threshold, watching as she crosses the snow and ducks under the clothesline, moving in the hurrying, awkward way of her mother. He steps out onto the porch. The earth and the sky above the thin pines are the palest silvery color. The air burns with cold. Logan leans over the railing to holler after her. "Save your pity, girl!" he calls to his daughter. "You're gonna need it for yourself."

They leave the day after Christmas, an early start. She sits very straight on the seat, her suitcase under her feet, her pony in her lap. He drives carefully; they stay in the right lane almost all the way south. They have mapped out everything and left a copy with her mother. The original rides on the seat between them. It shows red circles where they'll stay each night; a blue flag is pinned in Disney World; their final destination is marked with a D just east of Holopaw, the fifteen-acre compound in the family since 1931 when Great-grandfather Asa Dooley, the pearl diver, bought it. She doesn't talk much, he notices where she's been biting her fingernails, she watches him while his eyes are on the road. When they take a break so they can have their lunch or stop for the bathroom she follows real close but she doesn't say anything. They are in Maryland before she asks, "Are you going to take me home again?"

"You're flying home in an airplane. Your Aunt Betty bought you a ticket. If you want to," he tells her. "Your mother's going to meet that plane in Portland. In eight days," he adds.

She doesn't say anything.

"That okay?"

She looks at him.

"I'll drive you though, if you don't want to fly in an airplane. I'll drive you home if you've changed your mind. We could turn right around."

She shakes her head. "I want to go to Disney World," she tells him, speaking carefully. "I want to see the clowns again. I can fly in an airplane," she decides.

"Okay then," he tells her, "you're going to."

It is the end of the fourth day when they arrive. He takes her straight to the beach before going to the Dooleys. The sun has fallen across the flat width of the state behind them and is burning over the Gulf. They get out of the truck and start to walk. It smells clean. The beach and the ocean and the sky above it are soft shades of grey. Small waves are rocking with a steady shushing sound against the sand. As night falls the horizon draws nearer, and out there the moon is coming up. It is huge, standing on the line that marks the end of this world. It is the luminescent pink that colors the inner corolla of apple blossoms. All the moon's scars and its old damage show clearly as it slowly ascends from the sea. The moon seems massive and yet without weight as it rises, and rises. They stand in the sand and watch; they don't speak. The moon climbs faster, thin blue clouds begin to drift about it, its circumference shortens, its color darkens, its old injuries marble its face. She turns to look at him and a jogger in bright shorts passes by, moving as steadily as a horse in harness. They appear alien with their Portland jackets and boots, their tensed-up ruffled look from the road. She goes on ahead of him, her gait stiff and one leg thin like something that has been starved. She is heading for the pier that runs out into the ocean. The large white-necked birds sitting on the pilings with their long faces tucked down in their chests look like carved wood in these evening shadows. She stares up at them and then turns and hurries back.

"Mr. Hewitt, what are those giant things?" she asks, and raises her arm to point.

"They're called pelicans. They're birds."

She frowns at him.

"Birds that fly out over the sea and dive for fish." He gestures with his hands. "They have big bills to hold them in like baskets."

"Is that true?" she asks, fearful of being mocked.

He nods and leans down closer to her. "That's their name, that's what they're called."

She studies his face for a moment and then says, "Pelicans." She goes half dancing, half hopping along beside him. "Let's go see," she urges. "Let's go see those pelicans."

"They'll fly away if we get too close," he tells her.

"We'll go soft then," she says in a hoarse whisper. "Come on, Mr. Hewitt, and we'll go soft."

ABOUT THE AUTHOR

Elizabeth Jordan Moore was graduated from the University of Massachusetts at Boston in 1970. She has lived in Maine for twenty years and has worked for much of that time in the field of social services. She has published short stories in various journals. This is her first novel.

ABOUT THE AUTHOR

Elizabeth Jordan Moore was graduated from the University of Massachusetts at Boston in 1970. She has lived in Maine for twenty years and has worked for much of that time in the field of social services. She has published short stories in various journals. This is her first novel.